Praise for Michelle Major's

THE MAGNOLIA SISTERS

"A dynamic start to a series with a refreshingly original premise."

—*Kirkus Reviews*

"A sweet start to a promising series, perfect for fans of Debbie Macomber."

—*Publishers Weekly* (starred review)

"*The Magnolia Sisters* is sheer delight, filled with humor, warmth and heart.... I loved everything about it."

—*New York Times* bestselling author RaeAnne Thayne

Also by Michelle Major

The Magnolia Sisters

A Magnolia Reunion
The Magnolia Sisters
The Road to Magnolia

For a full list of titles by Michelle Major,
please visit www.michellemajor.com.

The
Merriest
Magnolia

MICHELLE MAJOR

HQN

ISBN-13: 978-1-335-01500-6

The Merriest Magnolia
Copyright © 2020 by Michelle Major

The Road to Magnolia
Copyright © 2020 by Michelle Major

Recycling programs
for this product may
not exist in your area.

This edition published by arrangement with Harlequin Books S.A.

For questions and comments about the quality of this book, please contact us at CustomerService@Harlequin.com.

HQN
22 Adelaide St. West, 40th Floor
Toronto, Ontario M5H 4E3, Canada
www.Harlequin.com

Printed in Lithuania

MIX
Paper from
responsible sources
FSC® C021394

CONTENTS

THE MERRIEST MAGNOLIA

To Jackson and Jessie.
I love you to the moon and back a million times.

CHAPTER ONE

SHE WAS BEING FOLLOWED.

Although it was nearing midnight, Carrie Reed shouldn't feel nervous walking home on a late November night. She'd lived in the quaint town of Magnolia, North Carolina, her entire life and knew most of its residents by name. The ones she hadn't met likely knew of her thanks to her father, the famous artist Niall Reed, and the drama that had unfolded after his death four months ago.

Pausing before taking the turn onto the street where she lived, Carrie squinted into the darkness, searching for movement outside the branches of a nearby white pine rustling in the cool breeze.

She'd left her downtown art studio without much thought to the late hour. Tonight she'd taught a paint-and-sip class at The Reed Gallery to a boisterous bunco group made up of some of Magnolia's most respected mavens. It had been an eye-opener for Carrie.

A few glasses of sangria and the women had enthusiastically painted the personalized ornament scene she'd created for them. As they'd worked, those "Bunco Babes," as they'd named themselves, had talked about everything from grandkids to menopause to keeping their love lives spicy after decades of marriage or, in several cases, a midlife divorce.

Carrie's relationship with her mother was strained on a

good day and she'd been raised an only child, so she didn't have a lot of experience with that kind of fervid honesty in her relationships with women. Up until her father's will revealed two half sisters from his years of philandering, Carrie hadn't even had close friends. She'd devoted the bulk of her adult life—and a good bit of her childhood if she were totally honest—to taking care of her temperamental father.

Her life transformed, almost completely for the better, thanks to her sisters. But secretly Carrie feared the changes were happening to her and not within her. She was a creature of habit and not the most outgoing person on her best day. The past couple of months had pushed her out of her comfort zone in too many ways to count.

She'd never been paranoid, and with a crime rate bordering on nonexistent, Magnolia could be counted on as a safe place. Yet, one of the most important lessons she'd learned from her father's passing was that looks could be deceiving.

"Who's there?" she called into the night, feeling a little foolish. Part of her wondered if she was talking to the grapevine deer and plastic snowmen that already decorated the lawns of houses on either side of the street, even though they still had a week until Thanksgiving.

Magnolia took the holidays seriously, although there seemed to be some kind of unwritten rule about turning off Christmas lights at eleven o'clock each night. Only a silvery moon high in the sky and one lone streetlight illuminated the darkness now.

A dog barked a few houses down from where she stood. Carrie spun toward the sound but saw nothing out of the ordinary.

When she turned back around, a dark shape had emerged from the shadows on the sidewalk in front of her.

Carrie opened her mouth to scream but no sound came

out. Panic pounded through her until the broad-shouldered man stepped into a sliver of moonlight.

"It's me, Carrie. I didn't mean to scare you."

Pressing a palm to her chest, she silently commanded her heart to stop pounding. "Are you crazy, Dylan?" She held up a hand. "No need to respond. I know the answer already. Why are you following me?"

All six foot three inches of Dylan Scott, with his tousled blond hair, piercing blue eyes and lean, muscled frame, seemed to stiffen at her question. "I'm not following you exactly. I was out for a walk and—"

"A casual stroll at midnight?" She shook her head. "On a Saturday night in Magnolia?"

"I couldn't sleep."

"What are you even doing in town? You don't live here."

"I do now. I moved into a house a couple blocks over."

No. "You don't *belong*," she told him through clenched teeth.

A muscle in his jaw jumped at that comment. "It's my hometown," he reminded her, as if she could ever forget. "I belong just as much as you do."

"I've lived here all my life."

"I'm well aware." One side of his mouth curved, more sneer than smile. "Everyone considers you Magnolia royalty. You've always been the town's shining light."

"Not true," she said on a gasp. Why did people want to fault her because she hadn't been a troublemaker? She'd had to bust through the same preconceived notions with her half sisters, especially the youngest, Meredith, who'd also grown up in Magnolia. It was as if people lived in some alternate reality where being a good girl was a bad thing.

Carrie was darn sick of it.

"The apple of your father's eye. His best girl." Dylan hurled the words at her like an accusation.

Carrie hated the feeling of bitterness they conjured.

"Did you come back just to antagonize me?" She pulled the tote bag she carried tighter to the side of her body, like she could use it as a shield. "Because these past couple months haven't exactly been a shot in the arm as far as my self-esteem. I don't need you to pile any more—"

His eyes widened a fraction before narrowing. "I'm not here for you."

Of course not.

Even though Dylan had been her first boyfriend, her first love, her first in so many ways, he'd also left her behind the first chance he had. In truth, she had her father to thank for that, as well. Niall had never approved of her high school boyfriend, and when Dylan asked her to leave Magnolia with him, Dad had bribed him to leave on his own.

She shouldn't have been surprised that he'd taken the money, but the memory of it burned liked acid in her gut.

"That didn't come out the way I meant," he amended with a shake of his head. "I came back to Magnolia because—"

"I don't care why," Carrie told him, wanting to inflict on him the same kind of hurt she felt then succumbing to guilt when pain flickered across his features. "We're not leasing the space downtown to you." She gentled her tone but not the message. "There's nothing for you here."

Her father's will had brought the sisters together even as it divided his estate into three parts. Niall's paintings, sentimental landscapes depicting idealized scenes of American life, had enjoyed commercial if not critical success for the first half of his career. He'd been Magnolia's most famous resident for decades and had both supported the town and demanded fierce loyalty from its residents.

As his career and health declined, he'd made a series of bad investments and engaged in the type of frivolous spending that left his savings decimated. At the time of his death, he'd owned a farm near the beach outside Magnolia that he'd left to Carrie. In a twist of irony, he'd bequeathed the family home to his youngest daughter, Meredith Ventner, who'd grown up in Magnolia not knowing that the man who raised her wasn't her biological father.

Avery Keller, born in California to a single mother who'd had an affair with Niall, had been left the property he owned in downtown Magnolia. The buildings housed his art gallery, a local dance studio, hardware store and bookshop as well as a couple of vacant storefronts.

Past leaders in the town had relied heavily on Niall's support and generosity without working to modernize the town or attract new businesses and visitors. After a rocky start, Carrie and her sisters were helping to change that.

She couldn't allow Dylan Scott to be a part of it.

He continued to watch her, the intensity of his stare making heat prickle just underneath her skin. He took a small step back, and in the dim light she couldn't read his eyes but knew her words had hit their mark.

"You've changed," he said after a moment.

"It's been ten years."

"I don't mean like that, although you're skinnier than I remember. You always forgot to eat when you were stressed." He rolled his big shoulders. "In high school, you were a people pleaser. Plenty of people took advantage of that, including me. You let me get away with anything."

Her stomach pitched and swooped at the memory of all the things she'd let Dylan get away with in his old Chevy pickup. He'd been three years older than she, dangerous and exciting for a shy girl. She'd felt alive with him and hated the detachment in his gaze as it tracked over her.

Carrie stood in front of him after the end of a long day, in a shapeless quilted jacket over an equally loose tunic sweater with her feet shoved into comfortable work boots and her boring brown hair pulled back into a practical but hardly stylish bun.

She'd harbored plenty of fantasies over the years of how it would go if she ever confronted Dylan. Most of them involved her in some sort of fitted, sparkly dress dancing with a Patrick Swayze doppelgänger and having the time of her life.

No one put Carrie in the corner.

Or got away with breaking her heart.

"I was young and stupid," she said by way of an answer. "I'm not so young anymore."

"You were never stupid," he said, the rough timbre of his voice scratching along her nerve endings like a cat's tongue. "Just too nice for your own good. I don't think you're that kind of pushover now."

He probably didn't mean the words as a compliment, but she'd been working hard to become stronger. "Then you'll understand you have no chance of convincing me or my sisters to lease space to you."

"I have my own space."

Carrie blinked. "What are you talking about?"

"Your dad may have held court in this town, but he didn't own everything. I'm under contract with Bobby Hawthorne."

The breath hissed from between her suddenly dry lips. How had she not heard about that? She and her sisters had been working closely with Magnolia's mayor, Malcolm Grimes, and the rest of the town council as well as local business owners to implement a plan for revitalization. They weren't to blame for Niall's stranglehold on the community, but each of them felt a responsibility to make things better.

"I asked for a confidentiality clause," Dylan said matter-of-factly. "After you derailed my plans to buy one of your father's buildings, I wasn't going to take a chance on you blocking me again."

"Bobby owns the entire block across from the gallery." She shook her head, willing her jumbled thoughts to become ordered. "That's far more square footage than what the space we own would have afforded."

He gave a curt nod. "I'm expanding my initial proposal. We're going to redo the whole block with shops, restaurants and lofts on the second floor above each storefront. Just so we're clear, my company is also buying and developing the old textile factory and the land that borders your dad's farm. By the time I'm finished, no one will even care that Niall Reed once lived here. Magnolia will belong to me."

Carrie's throat tightened, and she glanced around wildly. There had to be another explanation or something she could do to stop him. Dylan had gutted her when he'd accepted the bribe from her father to break up with her. She didn't trust him or his motives. He'd been so intent on leaving Magnolia and making his mark on the world. He'd hated their sleepy town and everything it represented.

He'd sworn to her that he would never come back so his return to Magnolia didn't make any sense.

"You despise this place."

"I despised your father," he clarified. "Now that I'm back, anything he had I want. I'm going to destroy every last shred of his legacy."

Carrie's father had many faults, but she still loved him.

It might be different for Avery and Meredith, but part of the reason she was determined to set Magnolia on a better course was so that her family wouldn't bear responsibility for ruining the town. She'd become more independent, but twenty-eight years as the dutiful daughter wouldn't be undone. Loyalty was ingrained in her.

"I won't let you," she whispered, more to herself than him.

"You can't stop me." He moved closer, using his size to block out her view of the rest of the darkened street. All she could see was the collar of the gray sweater under the wool overcoat he wore. The street was eerily silent, as if even the rustle of the wind had quieted in deference to Dylan's overpowering presence.

Carrie felt her nostrils flare as the scent of him—spice and clean shampoo—enveloped her.

"If you're trying to intimidate me," she said, forcing an even tone, "it won't work. I know you. You might be ruthless and heartless, but you aren't a bully."

"Maybe you aren't the only one who's changed." She could feel his warm breath on her cheek. At five foot nine, Carrie was tall, but he still towered over her. His large body felt like shelter from some nonexistent storm. She'd liked that feeling of being small, of deferring to his size and strength, when they'd been together.

She liked it even now, although she had no intention of surrendering to him no matter how much he blustered.

"Stay away from me, Dylan," she told him, proud that her voice didn't tremble. "From me and my sisters. You have no business in this town, and I'm going to make sure everyone sees that."

Clutching her tote bag to her body, she tipped her chin and elbowed her way past him.

DYLAN MUTTERED A CURSE as he stood on the front lawn of the house he'd rented for the next six months.

An eerie blue light glowed from the window of an upstairs bedroom, which meant Sam was awake and playing video games.

This had been a crap night, and it was about to go even more off the rails. They'd only moved in the prior day, with Sam alternately surly and outright antagonistic.

Dylan didn't blame the kid. Fifteen was a rough time for any teenage boy, let alone one who'd lost the only family he had in a plane crash then been stuck with a guardian who was laughably unequipped to take responsibility for another living being.

Dylan might be a success in business, but his single-minded determination had forced him to sacrifice his personal life. Not that he'd particularly minded. After having his heart shattered once before, he was in no hurry to repeat the venture.

He sure as hell hadn't expected to run into Carrie Reed on a quiet street tonight. In Boston, where he'd lived in a modern loft downtown, his inability to sleep hadn't been a problem. He could always find a party or neighborhood bar for late-night companionship. Or, as he'd taken to more often of late, enjoy the succor of background noise while he silently sipped his preferred whiskey neat on his own.

Magnolia, with its tree-lined streets and festive holiday decorations, didn't offer the same kind of around-the-clock distractions. Instead, he was stuck roaming the neighborhood until the wee hours, needing only a light jacket with the temperatures hovering in the low fifties. That might be cool for this part of North Carolina, but after ten years in Boston, it felt downright balmy.

There hadn't been another soul out so late, but the flash

of a quilted red jacket turning a corner had made the hair on the back of his neck stand on end.

Dylan didn't need to see her bourbon-colored tumble of hair or the delicate line of her jaw to recognize Carrie. It was as if the months they'd dated had imprinted her on his soul. He recognized her deep within his body the way a sailor sensed a storm brewing at the edge of a calm swath of sea.

Scaring her half to death wasn't his plan, but he'd been curious about where she was headed. Although she was a grown woman, he couldn't imagine her living anywhere but her father's ostentatious mansion that sat in the opposite direction from the path she walked.

Her reaction to him hadn't exactly been a surprise. He'd visited Magnolia a month ago, during the time that he was in talks to lease a downtown property that had belonged to Niall. He'd tried to buy the buildings outright but had been willing to settle for renting when his Realtor told him the estate wouldn't sell. When news of Niall's death had reached him almost a year after the plane crash that killed his uncle, his cousin Wiley and Wiley's wife, Kay, Dylan had made the decision to return to Magnolia.

Sam needed a fresh start, and Dylan was determined to honor the promise he'd made to his cousin to take care of the boy. Plus, Dylan wanted a chance to prove wrong all the people in town who'd believed he would never amount to anything. He somehow needed that recompense to demonstrate he could handle raising a surly, grief-stricken teenager. Niall had been at the top of his long list of detractors, but if death stole Dylan's chance for revenge on the man himself, he could at least destroy the famed artist's legacy.

He understood that his mixed desire to raise the boy in a small town but also disguise that more noble pursuit with his personal need for revenge made him ten kinds of a jerk, but it didn't faze him.

He hadn't expected to be so rattled by Carrie. The quiet and shadows had lent an intimacy to their conversation that made his blood run hot. She'd always been out of his league, and not just because of her standing in the community.

Carrie had one of the purest hearts he'd ever known. Just being close to her gave him the feeling of stretching out in a ray of sunshine on a cold winter day. She was everything light and warm, and he had no business wanting her.

Not anymore.

CHAPTER TWO

THE FOLLOWING MORNING Carrie dropped into a booth across from Avery and Meredith at Over Easy, Magnolia's best breakfast diner.

"You need coffee," Avery said immediately.

"Or a mimosa." Meredith lifted a brow as she studied Carrie. "Or twelve."

"Dylan's back," she explained. "I need coffee *and* a dozen mimosas."

Avery's blue eyes widened. "Dylan Scott, the developer who bought your art last month at the showing?"

Meredith nudged the sophisticated blonde. "I think in this situation, the pock-addled Dylan who broke our girl's heart is a more apt description."

Carrie clenched her hands at the thought of her body's reaction to Dylan last night. "I highly doubt there's one pockmark on his entire perfect body." She drew in a slow breath and glanced around, embarrassment filling her cheeks with heat as she took in the curious stares of the other customers. "How loud was that?"

Meredith ran a hand through her chin-length bob, her pert nose scrunching like she'd smelled something funny. "I don't think they heard you across the street, if that helps."

"I wish the floor would open up and swallow me whole."

"I used to wish that for you back in high school," Meredith offered. Although Meredith was a townie like Carrie and only a year younger in school, neither had known they were sisters until their father's death. But Meredith recently revealed that she'd discovered her mother's affair with Niall when she was only five, shortly before her mom left town. She'd grown up with a single dad and two older brothers and had hated Carrie for the elevated status everyone had perceived her to enjoy.

Carrie hadn't known anything but the life she'd had with her eccentric father and overprotective mother. She came to realize shamefully late what a farce their image as a happy family had been. Ever since her father's death, people in town looked at her with a mix of pity and sympathy that made her skin crawl, although being with her sisters made her braver than she could be on her own.

Still, she didn't like to draw attention to herself and kept her gaze on the polished tabletop as the waitress filled their coffee cups.

"Everything okay here, girls?" she asked.

"All good," Avery assured her in a tone that said "mind your own business." Would anyone actually heed a subtle warning in Magnolia when they could smell fresh gossip in the air? Carrie appreciated Avery for trying.

Avery had only come to Magnolia for the reading of their father's will, although she'd ended up finding a home—and falling in love—once she got there.

"Maybe he's home for the holidays," Meredith suggested when the waitress walked away after taking their order of food and a round of mimosas.

"Christmas is five weeks away." Carrie dumped a load of sugar and a generous amount of creamer into her coffee. "He told me he's buying the buildings Bobby Hawthorne owns downtown."

Avery and Meredith didn't look much alike but offered twin expressions of disbelief.

"Why haven't we heard about this?" Avery sipped her coffee. "Mal should have—"

"There's some kind of confidentiality agreement as part of the deal." Carrie shook her head. "I don't understand the details, but he said he didn't want us to derail it like we did when he wanted to buy Niall's property."

"Our property," Avery clarified.

"*Your* property, actually." Carrie had been devastated when she'd first learned that her father had willed his beloved art gallery and the adjacent buildings to the daughter he'd never actually met. It had felt like a slap in the face since Carrie had been the one to devote her life to his career. She'd been his assistant, as well as his daughter, tamping down her own artistic ambitions to fully cater to his.

She'd confused loyalty for love. In the end, her father had viewed her as little more than a poorly paid servant. In return she'd given up everything and been left with nothing to show for it.

"We've already gone through that," Avery said. "It doesn't matter what the will said. Decisions about the estate come from the three of us together."

"I know," Carrie agreed. "I'm tired. Ignore me."

"I tried that most of my life." Meredith chuckled when Carrie stuck out her tongue. "Look where it got me."

Carrie gulped down a swig of coffee, needing the caffeine to work its magic. She'd tossed and turned most of the night after her confrontation with Dylan.

"How am I going to get rid of him?" she asked, her voice little more than a plaintive whine.

Avery reached out and covered Carrie's hand with hers.

"Is it really so bad that he's here? It's been ten years. Maybe you won't see him much."

"He's here to take over the town," she said without emotion, "and destroy whatever he thinks is involved with Dad's legacy."

Before either woman could reply, the waitress reappeared with another server. They placed plates of food and three champagne glasses on the table. By unspoken agreement, all three of them drank deeply from the mimosas when they were alone again.

"I don't understand," Avery said, shaking her head. "He hated our father."

"*Your* father," her sisters replied in unison.

"Stop." Carrie forked up a bite of scrambled egg. "We're not going to have this argument again. What should I call him?" She pointed the utensil between Avery and Meredith. "Our Niall? The jerk who hurt each of our mothers?"

Meredith tapped a finger against her chin as if pondering the questions. "I prefer lowlife scumbag."

A soft laugh escaped Carrie's lips. "I still think 'Dad' sums it up."

"Fine," Avery breathed. "Let's not argue about Niall. Tell us more about why Dylan Scott hates him."

"Dad didn't think Dylan was good enough for me." Carrie placed her fork on the table. Although the classic breakfast of eggs, hash browns and bacon were her favorite and always cooked to perfection at Over Easy, the food held no appeal.

Her stomach churned as she thought about how her father had railed against Dylan once he'd found out about the relationship Carrie had kept secret for almost a year.

Meredith sniffed. "I can't imagine Niall approving of any boy to date his precious girl."

A few months ago that comment would have bothered Carrie. She'd chafed at her reputation as Niall Reed's
spoiled princess. Now she knew better than to believe her
father had ever had her best interests at heart.

"You're probably right, which had more to do with Dad
not wanting to lose his most loyal subject than my worth."

"I'm sorry," Meredith said, her gaze softening. "I know
things weren't as great for you growing up as they seemed
from the outside."

Carrie shrugged. "Dylan wanted to escape Magnolia so
he made plans to work for his uncle in Boston. I applied to
art school at Tufts and got accepted, but when Dad found
out he went crazy."

Avery helped herself to a bite of Carrie's hash browns.
"Of course he did. Tufts is an amazing school. Niall didn't
want you pursuing your art because it would have become
clear to everyone that you were the true talent."

"I don't know about that." Carrie bit down on the inside
of her cheek. She'd loved art in high school but had given up
her aspirations because her dad told her she'd never amount
to anything and she'd just embarrass both him and herself.
As much as she'd loved him and couldn't turn her back on
her loyalty to his memory, he'd been a selfish man—a nar-
cissist in the truest sense of the word.

"Don't make me give you a mantra," Meredith told her.
"Every morning you say to your reflection in the mirror,
'I am beautiful, I am strong, I am enough.'"

Carrie ignored the way her heart seemed to skip a beat
and laughed. "Do you think that would work for my self-
esteem?"

Meredith inclined her head. "I think what you need is
to adopt a pet. Animals can cure anything."

Meredith ran an animal rescue agency on the property

that had belonged to their father. Niall had left Last Acre ranch to Carrie in the will, another convoluted twist in his bizarre estate plan. Although she hadn't known Niall was her biological father, Meredith had come to him a few years earlier when she'd needed a location for her rescue. He'd made her a great deal on renting the property, likely out of guilt—although it was hard to tell with Niall. More likely he'd gotten some sort of twisted satisfaction out of the arrangement.

Either way, until the estate made it through probate, which wasn't due to be finalized for another several months, the three sisters were inexorably linked by their inheritance. At first, Carrie thought that might be the only connection they could ever share, but in the span of a few months they'd become an integral part of each other's lives.

"The last thing I need is a pet," Carrie muttered.

"You might not think a dog is the answer," Avery told her. "But I'm proof that a dog can make everything better. My Spot is an angel." Avery smiled, and Carrie half expected to be shown the latest snapshots of the Chihuahua mix Avery had adopted from the rescue. "She's lost another pound and a half."

"Enough about mantras and chunky pooches." Meredith spread a generous amount of grape jelly on her toast. "You obviously didn't go with Dylan. People break up after high school. That doesn't explain his animosity toward Niall." She lifted a brow. "Or you."

"Dad bribed him to leave."

Avery gasped. "I didn't think that happened in real life."

"Five thousand dollars." Carrie picked up a strip of bacon then set it on the plate again.

Meredith held out a hand. "If you aren't going to eat that…"

Carrie chuckled. "Go for it." She was used to this hijacking of food from the youngest in their trio. Meredith couldn't have been more than five foot three and a hundred pounds soaking wet, but she could eat a teenage boy under the table.

These small patterns in behavior gave Carrie a sense of comfort. No matter how overwhelming life became, she didn't have to deal with it by herself any longer.

"I was furious when I found out," she continued as Meredith chewed the crisp bacon. "Dad was indignant, his usual reaction when someone challenged him. He said that Dylan taking the money proved that he didn't truly love me." She forced herself to take another drink of coffee, needing the caffeine even though her stomach churned at the memory of her broken heart.

"As much as it pains me to admit it," Avery said, "he had a point."

"I told Dylan that when he told me he was leaving." Resentment and pain swirled through Carrie. "He went off on Dad and how he'd manipulated me, and I was his puppet and some other not very flattering assessments I'd prefer not to revisit. Then he stormed off and that was the last I saw or heard from him until he walked into the gallery during the art show last month."

"Now he's back and wants vindication?" Meredith shook her head. "He's the one who screwed up big time. What a jackass."

"Ladies." The three of them turned as Magnolia's popular mayor, Malcolm Grimes, approached the booth.

Carrie moved toward the wall and patted the seat next to her. "We need to talk, Mal."

The sixty-something African American man's dark eyes widened as he slid in next to her. "That sounds serious."

"Did you know about Bobby selling to Dylan Scott?" Avery demanded then drained her mimosa.

Carrie and Meredith followed suit as Malcolm visibly squirmed. "I might have heard something along those lines," he admitted, sounding sheepish.

"Why?" Carrie reached out a hand and squeezed his arm. "Why would you let him have a foothold in the town that way? It won't take long for him to become the most powerful man in Magnolia."

"Power can be defined a lot of ways," Mal answered, exhaling a long breath. "This town needs people willing to invest in it. We've already established that. As much as I'd like to wave my magic mayor wand and make everything better, I don't have that ability." He pointed toward Avery. "You were the one who initiated the plan to attract new resources and fresh ideas into the community."

"Dylan can't be part of it," Carrie grumbled.

"Aw, honey." Malcolm gently nudged her. "I know he was careless with your heart. It speaks poorly of him, or at least who he used to be. You deserve someone who will treat you like the queen you are. But I also know you wouldn't sacrifice the opportunities Scott Development can offer Magnolia because of a decade-old grudge."

After a moment she glanced from Mal toward her sisters. They gazed at her, eyes filled with matching sympathy.

"He wants to destroy my father's legacy," she said quietly, turning toward the mayor. "He admitted as much. Dylan Scott left this town and never looked back. You knew him before. Do you really believe he's returning out of some rediscovered sense of loyalty?"

Malcolm's lips pressed into a thin line. "I'm not sure what I believe at this point. But I know his company has deep pockets and he's committed money we need to make real change around here."

"We should have been told," Meredith said. "I don't care how much money that guy has, if Carrie is convinced he has shady motives, I trust her. Look at how he's starting— with lies and deceit."

The mayor chuckled. "That might be a tad overdramatic."

Meredith leaned forward, eyes narrowed. "Did you just accuse me of being overdramatic?"

Carrie stifled a laugh as Malcolm slowly shook his head.

"Are you sure?" the feisty animal lover demanded. "Is it because I'm a woman? As you mentioned, the three women at this table were integral in developing a plan for this town's revitalization. A plan that's been a success so far."

Meredith elbowed Avery, who immediately sat up straighter. "That's right," she chimed in. "I don't think anyone needs reminding that tourism revenue was up almost thirty percent in recent months. We've already sold out vendor tags for the holiday craft fair, and arrangements for the festival are well under way."

"I know." Malcolm held up his hands, palms out. "Trust me when I assure you, I'm not looking to incite the wrath of the three furies."

Meredith arched a brow. "I prefer goddesses, Mayor."

"Goddesses," Malcolm amended with a nod.

"You don't want to mess with us," Avery added. "If you upset Carrie by keeping pertinent information about town investors from her, you upset all three of us."

Carrie blinked away tears as her two sisters stared down the older man. She understood Malcolm meant well and probably hadn't thought much of omitting the information about Dylan's deal. She also understood that she'd let people, especially her father, underestimate and manipulate her for years because she hadn't believed she had anything to contribute beyond being his underpaid lackey.

"I can't stop you from selling out to Dylan Scott," she told the mayor. "But I won't let him waltz in here and take over without a fight. Our father was a difficult man, but he did a lot of good for Magnolia. I plan not only to continue that but make it better. This is my home."

"It's mine, too," Malcolm reminded her. "I want what's best for the town."

"Even if the investor with the deepest pockets isn't it?" she asked.

Mal sighed. "We won't allow one person to run rough-shod over the rest of us again. Niall proved that doesn't work." He scooted out of the booth. "We're on the same side, ladies. I promise. Scott Development has purchased five buildings downtown and is under contract for the old textile factory off the beach highway. Dylan has submitted an initial set of renovation plans to the town council." He glanced to either side of him then leaned forward. "I'll be sharing them at the next business owners' association meeting on Thursday night. You're welcome to stop by my office to review them before then."

"Thank you," Carrie said, even as her mind whirled. "I appreciate having you on our side."

"I'm on Magnolia's side," Malcolm corrected then nabbed the leftover slice of bacon from her plate. "I recommend you make certain you can say the same before you run that boy out of town."

Carrie gave a shaky nod and watched the mayor make his way through the restaurant, greeting other diners like the old friend he was to most of them.

"Am I being totally self-serving in my wish to see Dylan

go away?" she asked, facing Avery and Meredith. "Maybe I'm more like Dad than I realized."

"Not in any way," Meredith assured her. "It makes perfect sense not to want to deal with the man who broke your heart. Or any guy who does you wrong. Remember when I was supposed to go on a date with that hot guy a few weeks ago? I never want to see him again."

Carrie and Avery both laughed in response.

"It's not funny," Meredith said then stuck out her tongue.

"Uh...you went to meet a blind date and it turned out to be Morris Haegler."

"Who might be older than God," Carrie added.

Meredith rolled her eyes. "It was awkward, not funny. He knew he was meeting me. He copied his profile picture from the internet—total false advertising. But I still don't want to see him, and I'm not going anywhere near the hardware store where he and his buddies hang out."

"Are you equating my animosity for the ex-boyfriend who took money to break up with me with you swiping right on Magnolia's septuagenarian Lothario?"

"I didn't swipe any which way," Meredith said, looking affronted. "It was a reputable dating site."

Avery nudged Meredith's shoulder. "If you're looking for a date, I can ask Gray to set you up with one of his fire station buddies."

Gray Atwell was Avery's fiancé and a longtime friend of Carrie's. He'd grown up in Magnolia and was not only one of the kindest men she knew, but he also loved her sister in a way that made Carrie's ovaries pinch in jealousy.

"Too much testosterone," Meredith said, waving away the suggestion with a flutter of her hand.

Carrie laughed. "That probably wouldn't be an issue with Morris."

"Forget I mentioned my ill-fated date." Meredith clapped a hand to her forehead. "Let's talk more about how we're going to take down Dylan the villain."

"Does everyone need a nickname with you?" Avery shook her head but then a grin split her face. "Never mind. That name actually fits."

Carrie felt that strange tightening of her chest again. It would be simpler if the only thing she felt for Dylan was animosity. The way her body had reacted to him added a complication to the equation she didn't want. "You don't need to be involved. Dylan is my problem, which means—"

"You're stuck with us," Meredith interrupted. "We're with you all the way."

"What she said," Avery added with a gentle smile.

"Thanks." Carrie took a deep breath. She had to believe she could get through anything with her sisters at her side.

CHAPTER THREE

DYLAN WALKED DOWN Magnolia's main street the following morning, trying to stop his heart from hammering out of his chest. Memories rushed at him from every angle. Even the cracks in the sidewalk seemed familiar. Sitting in his office overlooking Boston Harbor, the real estate deal had seemed like a viable option to course correct his and Sam's lives in the wake of so much unexpected tragedy.

Now he wondered if the move back to his hometown had been a mistake. His defenses rallied against the flood of emotions that came with reestablishing himself in such a familiar setting. Memories zinged toward him from every side, like a thousand pinballs pummeling his insides.

"This place sucks," Sam muttered next to him, slouching his shoulders more than seemed possible without actually folding in on himself.

The boy's typical negativity made Dylan's heart ache. He forced a cheerful tone as he asked, "What are you talking about?" He gestured to the festively decorated window of the town's local hardware store. "It's like a holiday decoration tornado touched down right here. Magnolia has more Christmas spirit than the North Pole."

Sam gave him a wicked side-eye. "It's all fake and phony."

"On that we can agree." Dylan wished he could give the boy some pat holiday spirit pep talk, but in his family growing up, this time of year had meant more worries about money, more fights and definitely more drinking on his dad's part. Not exactly the stuff of Christmas fairy tales.

"Christmas sucks," Sam added for good measure.

"Is there anything that doesn't suck?" Dylan asked.

"Fortnite," came the mumbled reply.

"Right." Video games and social media were the only things Sam had shown any enthusiasm for since his parents' deaths. Dylan didn't blame the kid. Dylan's parents, Joelle and Matt Scott, hadn't been Magnolia's answer to June and Ward Cleaver, but he couldn't imagine what would have happened if they'd been killed when he was Sam's age. "Give this place a shot," he urged. "I'm about to blow your mind at the best bakery in the world. I still dream of the nutty sticky buns from Sunnyside."

Sam sniffed. "Sugar and carbs are bad for you."

"You polished off half a box of Lucky Charms last night after dinner," Dylan pointed out as he moved around a mother pushing a double stroller.

"I'm a teenager so I can handle it. You're old. All those extra empty calories will make you fat."

"I'm thirty-one." Dylan patted his flat stomach. "Not exactly in line to apply for my AARP card."

"What's an AARP card?"

"Not important. Sunnyside is worth an extra mile on my morning run. In fact, you should come with me tomorrow."

"Great," Sam agreed, far too readily. "If it means I don't have to go to school."

"You're going to school."

"I hate school."

"You hate everything."

Sam nodded. "Especially you."

Dylan shouldn't let the boy's words affect him, but they cut like the sting of a whip. Sam had been lashing out for weeks, ever since Dylan had announced plans to move to Magnolia. He'd known Sam since he was a toddler and had always thought he had a special bond with him. Sam was the only child of Dylan's cousin, Wiley, who'd been more like a brother. They'd worked together at Wiley's father's real estate development company from the time Dylan had moved to Boston, growing the business into the power-house it was today.

Uncle Russ had stayed involved, even after his retire-ment two years ago, so it had been an especially tragic blow when Russ, Wiley and Wiley's wife, Kay, had died in the plane crash.

Wiley had been his best friend. When he and Kay had asked Dylan to take care of Sam if anything happened to them, of course he'd said yes. He just never expected to be called on for that duty.

Sam had been devastated then angry and resentful be-fore settling into sullen and rebellious. He'd been kicked out of two schools in the past year, with Dylan summoned shortly after this school term started for a meeting with the headmaster at the ridiculously expensive private school in Boston he'd attended. The man had told Dylan that Sam was one detention away from expulsion and slid across his desk several pamphlets for well-respected military schools throughout the country.

Dylan felt like a failure in the one thing he'd been charged with accomplishing to honor his best friend. Mag-nolia had been a distant memory until that moment, but somehow he knew—or at least hoped with all his heart—that a change of scenery would help to heal the boy. It would be nice to think the move might bring Dylan a little peace, as well, but he didn't hold much hope for himself at this point.

"You won't hate Sunnyside," he told Sam now, keeping his tone light. Let Sam lob verbal arrows all day long. Dylan refused to be felled. He could give the kid that much at least.

Sam darted a glance in his direction, clearly surprised that his vitriol hadn't garnered more of a reaction.

That's right, Dylan thought. *Is a little hate all you've got?*

He wanted to believe the boy would eventually realize Dylan's dedication was unwavering and wouldn't be sidelined. Not by the circumstances of life. Not with the glaring anger and resentment Sam harbored. Dylan was in this for the long haul, and he'd do whatever necessary to make things right for the teenager.

Entering the bakery felt like walking back in time. The same bright yellow walls and wrought-iron café tables. The menu, written in loopy scrawl on the chalkboard hanging behind the register, had expanded. It included the now ubiquitous selection of complicated coffee drinks along with something called a "flaxy kale muffin."

"Nasty," Sam said under his breath, his gaze following Dylan's.

"Ignore the healthy items," Dylan instructed. "Check out the display case."

Although the boy tried to hide his reaction, Dylan saw his eyes widen a fraction as he took in the rows of baked goodness inside the lighted case. The shiny pastries and iced cookies looked as delectable as Dylan remembered.

There were a few people in line ahead of them, and Dylan let out a breath he hadn't realized he was holding at the thought that he'd finally found one thing he and Sam could agree on about the move.

"You can get donuts at any gas station convenience store," the boy announced. "What's the big deal?"

A smile curved Dylan's mouth as they moved a few paces toward the counter. "You'll see."

"How many can I get?" he asked, sounding like a normal teenage boy.

"Two for now and another for a snack later."

For once, the kid didn't argue or complain. His gaze roamed over the pastries as they waited. When it was their turn, Sam made his selections—a sticky bun and two iced donuts—with more enthusiasm than he'd seen from the kid in an entire year. Dylan added another sticky bun and a banana nut muffin to the order then handed his credit card to the woman working the register.

"You aren't welcome here," a cool voice said from behind him. He turned to see the bakery's longtime owner, Mary Ellen Winkler, glaring at him from behind the rims of tortoise-shell glasses.

"Hey, Ms. Winkler." He offered a smile, which was definitely not returned. "How've you been?"

"Perhaps you've forgotten the lifetime ban my bakery has against you?" she asked, crossing her arms over a bosom that appeared even more ample than Dylan remembered from his childhood.

He felt Sam go stiff next to him. In his fervor to sell the charms of small-town life, he'd carefully omitted some of the more inauspicious details of his own checkered past in Magnolia. Like the time he'd broken into the bakery and stolen everything from the front case. His wild days were well behind him so he'd figured it was safe to assume people in town would have forgotten the punk he'd been, as well.

Not so much, apparently.

"I'm sorry for the trouble I caused," he told the older

woman, a bead of sweat rolling down between his shoulder blades. "Obviously, I'm not the same person I used to be."

"Tell that to Carrie Reed," the bakery owner countered. "You upset her badly and she's been nothing but a shining light in this town."

At the mention of Carrie's name, shock skittered along his spine. She'd warned him the other night that she wouldn't make it easy for him. He hadn't taken her seriously, but what if she was already turning people in town against him? It wouldn't take much, especially if they remembered his antics as a teenager.

He'd stupidly assumed that his success and money would give him a pass on what had come before. He should have known better. Small towns held on to memories. His past could slither out around any corner, encircling his ankles like the kudzu that had invaded the forests bordering the highways of his home state, determined to take him down.

"What did you do to get banned?" Sam asked, his tone uncharacteristically animated.

"It doesn't matter," Dylan muttered, putting a hand on the boy's shoulder and giving him a gentle push toward the door. "Let's go."

Sam made a sound of protest and glanced over his shoulder toward the bag of pastries sitting on the counter. "What about the food?"

"We'll get something at the gas station on the way to the high school."

"That stuff sucks," Sam argued. "You said it yourself."

Dylan closed his eyes and counted to ten. He'd left off begging for anything on the day he'd grown taller and stronger than his father, who'd believed in teaching lessons with a belt or a closed fist. From that moment on Dylan had vowed he'd use his strength and his will to have his way, never showing weakness.

But for Sam, he'd eschew that vow and get down on his knees to plead for the pastries. Anything not to add one more disappointment to the boy's heaping list.

Ready to grovel, he opened his eyes to see that Carrie had come to stand next to Mary Ellen in what he could only assume was some unwarranted show of solidarity.

No way in hell would he subjugate himself in front of her.

Her moss-green gaze held a mix of defiance and regret, and he knew her determination to run him out of town would take a toll on her inherently kind nature. Understood she'd willingly pay that price to be rid of him again.

"Dylan."

His name on her lips, barely a whisper, had emotions running through him unchecked. He wouldn't allow that. If she was determined to treat him as an enemy, he'd have no choice but to do the same.

Dylan Scott destroyed his enemies.

He half pulled, half dragged Sam out of the bakery, the doughy, sweet scent suddenly making bile rise to his throat.

"Why are you such a jerk?" Sam demanded, yanking free of his grasp once the door slammed shut behind them.

"Born that way," Dylan answered, keeping his gaze on the sidewalk as he started toward where he'd parked his car.

"Seriously." Sam caught up with him in a few steps and matched his fast pace. "What did you do?"

"Dylan?" a voice called from behind them.

Not *a* voice. *Her* voice.

Dylan gave a sharp shake of his head like he was shooing away a gnat and kept walking.

"I have your stuff."

"My donuts." Sam whirled on his heel before Dylan could stop him.

Damn it.

Dylan didn't want to turn around but what choice did he have?

Fist clenched so hard he could feel his knuckles turning white, he faced Carrie, who'd jogged forward to meet them.

"Thanks, lady," Sam mumbled as Carrie handed him the bag. At least the boy still displayed the manners his parents had instilled in him. One positive vestige of the past Dylan hadn't managed to screw up.

"I'm Carrie Reed." Curiosity darkened her gaze. "You're a friend of Dylan's?"

Sam gave a derisive laugh. "Hell, no."

"Language," Dylan warned.

Carrie inclined her head to study the boy, then her gaze darted to Dylan. Questions swirled in their depths and he wanted to answer all of them. He wanted to explain to someone the trials the past year had brought. For a few seconds or minutes or however long she'd let him, he longed to share the burden of the promise he'd made to Wiley.

He knew without a doubt she'd extend her support. She might hate him, but her heart was too kind to hear the story of an orphaned boy and not offer empathy.

"Are you going to ensure the whole town is against me?" he asked instead. It didn't matter what he wanted. He couldn't allow himself to be vulnerable. That path led to pain, and he was full up on that at the moment.

"Mary Ellen's feelings about you have little to do with mine." Her chin hitched, and once again he was reminded that Carrie had changed from the easy mark she'd been back in high school. "Did you think you'd be able to flash your fancy watch and expensive wardrobe in this town and have everyone fawn all over you?"

Sam laughed again. "Dude, I told you those designer clothes you wear make you look like a tool."

"Eat your donut," Dylan commanded.

He tried to ignore the way awareness fluttered along the back of his neck like a summer breeze when Carrie stifled a giggle at the boy's insolence.

But Sam had heard it, and he loved an audience for giving Dylan grief.

"You should see him in Boston," the kid told her, fishing a donut out of the bag. "He wears scarves like they're fashionable."

"I wear scarves when it's freezing and the wind is howling," Dylan clarified then shook his head. "I'm not defending the clothes I wear."

"Because you'd lose." Sam was always ready with a snappy comeback.

Carrie stared between the two of them like she'd seen a ghost.

Dylan took his wallet from his back pocket and handed a five-dollar bill to Sam. "They sell drinks in the hardware store, or at least they used to. Go get one."

"Caffeine, carbonation and sugar to start the morning." Sam nodded. "Breakfast of champions."

Running a hand through his hair, Dylan watched the boy disappear into the nearby storefront before returning his gaze to Carrie.

"Is he yours?" she asked, barely above a whisper. All the color had drained from her face, and he wanted to reach for her. To apologize for shoving back into her life when he had no business being a part of it. To tell her how sorry he was for everything that had gone wrong between them.

"No." He shook his head and tried not to let emotion get the best of him. "Hell, Carrie, he's fifteen. That would have made me—"

"Sixteen. I wasn't your first, Dylan. It's conceivable that—"

"He's my cousin Wiley's son." He cleared his throat and focused on measuring his breathing. The mention of *first* had brought him back to a cold winter night Carrie's senior year of high school. He might have been more experienced but being with her had made everything seem brand-new.

Her forehead furrowed. "Is he visiting?"

"Wiley and his wife, along with my uncle Russ, died in a plane crash last fall. Sam has been with me ever since."

He'd craved it moments earlier but now hated the sympathetic noise she made. It grated along his skin like sandpaper. If Carrie was going to be his enemy, he didn't want any kindness from her. She was too inexperienced at being cutthroat to know, but emotion made her weak. It would have made him the same, so he wouldn't allow himself to be vulnerable. Ever.

He held up his hands. "I'm sure it pains you as much as it does everyone else in Sam's life that he not only lost so much but got stuck with me in the process."

"I'm sorry you lost your family," she said simply. "I remember how much your uncle and cousin meant to you."

The grief he'd buried rose to the surface like some sort of monster waiting to be released from its cage. Carrie could break the chains that held his emotions in check with a few softly uttered words, making her more dangerous to him than any creature that prowled the night.

"You don't get it both ways, sweetheart." He hardened his jaw and made his tone razor sharp. "You can't want to run me out of town one minute then act like you care about the kid I'm saddled with the next. Pick a side, Carrie."

"My side," she said fiercely. "For the first time in my life, I'm taking my side."

He almost laughed but swallowed it back, knowing how much it would anger her. He'd wanted this for Carrie—for her to regain the faith in herself that her father had squashed when she was younger. Ironic as all get out that it seemed to take having him as a target to pry it out of her.

She stepped closer. Although the winter sun peeked through the cloudy morning sky, the connection between them made it feel as intimate as the deserted street at midnight. They were the only two people in the world. That was how it had always been for Dylan. His awareness of her shut out everything else. He'd needed that grounding as a troubled teen, which was why it shocked him how much he still wanted it.

"Life isn't black-and-white." Her eyes were the color of the Atlantic Ocean after a summer storm. "I'm not going to be heartless to get my way. But make no mistake, I'll get it. I'd advise you to stay out of my path."

"And what if I don't?" he asked, reaching out a finger to graze her knuckles. The touch sent electricity spiking along his nerve endings, and she quickly pulled away. "What if I can't?"

She drew in a sharp breath, her warm green eyes turning cold. "Then it will go badly for us both."

CHAPTER FOUR

CARRIE ENTERED THE FAIRVIEW outside Raleigh the following afternoon and immediately felt out of place. The lavish five-star hotel seemed to cater exclusively to guests who were both wealthy and sophisticated by the look of the people milling about the elegant lobby.

She smoothed a hand over her shapeless maxi dress and wished she'd done something more with her hair than pull it back into a messy bun.

It had been years since she'd last seen her mother and now she regretted that she'd agreed to meet Vanessa Reed at the hotel where she worked as general manager. Carrie should have chosen a neutral location where she wouldn't feel so small-town and unsuitable.

The Fairview was already decorated for the holidays, with shining swaths of silk ribbon, beautiful floral arrangements and an array of spectacular floor-to-ceiling trees covered with colorful ornaments and bows. She couldn't imagine how much time and effort it took to coordinate such a lavish display of festivity. It felt as if she'd been working around the clock with the downtown business owners in Magnolia to put together a cohesive theme for their holiday celebration, but their efforts didn't hold a candle to the impressive beauty of the hotel her mother managed.

A woman stood behind the concierge desk, giving Carrie a dismissive once-over when she made eye contact.

Swallowing down the feeling of not belonging, Carrie approached.

"Excuse me?"

The woman, Amy, according to the name tag affixed to her smart uniform, glanced up. "May I help you?" she said in a tone that was anything but helpful.

"I'm looking for Vanessa Reed," Carrie said with a forced smile. "Could you direct me to her office?"

Amy's full lips thinned as she stared at Carrie with a look as if she'd just asked for an audience with the queen. Carrie would guess that she and Amy were around the same age, but the young concierge's condescending attitude made Carrie feel like an annoying child begging for attention.

"The employment office is open by appointment only," Amy announced. "You'll apply online first and then someone will contact you. It won't be Ms. Reed."

Carrie blinked. "I'm not applying for a job." Her chest tightened as she considered how much to share with this rude woman. "I'm here to see my mother."

If she'd expected a shift in the woman's attitude, she would have been disappointed. Amy's big eyes widened just a fraction. "Ms. Reed doesn't have a family."

Carrie took a step back, the casual words a direct hit to her heart. Her mother had worked at The Fairview since she'd left Magnolia. Surely her staff was aware she had a daughter.

"There you are, Carrie. Why are you bothering the staff? I told you to come directly to my office."

The scent of Chanel No. 5 enveloped Carrie as she turned toward her mother, bringing back a flood of memories from childhood. Vanessa might have changed almost everything about herself after leaving Magnolia, but her signature perfume remained the same.

As Carrie had spent time cleaning out her father's house in the weeks after his death, she would have sworn that she'd caught random whiffs of her mom's distinctive scent.

A riot of emotions coursed through Carrie as she looked into familiar green eyes so like her own. Vanessa hadn't seemed to age since Carrie had last seen her. Hard to say if it was good genes or a great plastic surgeon. Her mother's natural brown hair was dyed a few shades lighter than she used to wear it and cut into a stylish layered bob that framed her delicate features.

Carrie desperately wanted a do-over on the morning. She would have taken more time with her appearance before making the drive to Raleigh. Spending her whole life in Magnolia and the last decade as her father's assistant had made her complacent on all levels. She'd once had big dreams for herself, but her existence had become so small that it felt as if it could fit on the tip of a needle.

Her identity in her hometown had seemed set in stone so she'd stopped trying to be something different than what people expected of her. Niall Reed's devoted daughter.

She rolled her shoulders against the bitterness that sat on them like a heavy weight. "Hi, Mom," she said and took a hesitant step forward. What was the appropriate greeting for a parent she had virtually no relationship with at this point in her life?

Vanessa's gaze flicked to Amy, who was watching the interchange with unveiled curiosity.

"You're too thin," her mother said as she leaned in and gave her a quick and awkward peck on the cheek. "I've reserved a table for high tea. You should eat an extra scone."

"Um, okay," Carrie agreed, feeling color rise to her face. First Dylan and now her mother critiquing her weight. Did she really look that bad?

"Thank you, Amy." Vanessa turned to the concierge, bestowing a disarmingly warm smile. "The Ralstons are arriving late tonight instead of tomorrow morning. Please make sure their room is ready."

Amy nodded. "I'll also have the foam pillows Mr. Ralston prefers sent up."

"You're the best." Vanessa reached out and squeezed Amy's hand. "We're so lucky to have you here. *I'm* so lucky." She turned to Carrie, her smile dimming slightly. "Amy is a graduate of the school of hotel administration at Cornell. It's quite prestigious and she's been a wonderful addition to The Fairview family."

Family.

Carrie suppressed a shudder of resentment. This woman had told her Vanessa didn't have any family, but clearly her mother held her employees close to her heart. Meanwhile, Carrie received two obligatory phone calls a year, one on her birthday and the other on Christmas morning.

"It was a pleasure to meet you," Amy said, her tone about a million notches more pleasant than it had been minutes earlier.

"You, too," Carrie lied. For a split second she wished she could be more like Meredith, who said exactly what she thought with no consideration of the consequences. Oh, the things she'd say to Amy the concierge.

But Carrie wasn't like her outspoken, confident sister, and her mommy issues had nothing to do with anyone on the hotel's staff, no matter how much easier it would be to blame them.

If no one knew about Vanessa's life before she came to The Fairview, the responsibility fell on her mother's thin shoulders.

And Vanessa didn't seem to care. In fact, Carrie had to

hurry to catch up to her as she strode across the lobby toward the restaurant at the far end. Her mother walked with purpose, as if she owned the place. Both staff and guests alike looked at her with the kind of deferential respect reserved for VIPs. Carrie knew those looks because she'd seen them on the faces of longtime Magnolia residents back when her father had been the de facto king of the town.

Carrie had always been better at appearing insignificant if someone noticed her at all.

"The hotel looks really pretty with all the Christmas decorations," she said as she followed her mother to a table in front of a window overlooking the manicured grounds.

"Holiday," Vanessa corrected without hesitation. "The Fairview welcomes guests who celebrate a variety of holidays at this time of year."

"Of course," Carrie whispered, duly chastised. Her mother's special skill, laying her low with a few choice words and that sanctimonious tone.

Vanessa glanced up at the waiter who'd followed them to the table. "Two signature tea services, Martin. With a few additional scones."

"Of course, Ms. Reed."

Carrie tried not to gape as the man executed a subtle bow. He actually bowed to her mother. No wonder Vanessa was so happy with her job. Martin didn't bother to glance at Carrie and she resisted the urge to slouch down in her seat like a moody teen.

What had happened to the gutsy woman who'd gone toe-to-toe with Dylan Scott on a public street? He'd told her she changed, and she'd truly thought she had. Her father's death and the revelations that came with it had forced her to take stock of her life in a way she'd avoided for years.

Forging new bonds with her sisters had helped her find an inner strength she hadn't realized she possessed.

A few minutes in her mother's presence had obliterated all of her newfound gains.

"I don't need more food, Mom." Carrie focused on unfolding the napkin and placing it in her lap as she spoke. "The past couple of months have been stressful, but things are getting better. In fact, I've started—"

"Your father was a horrid man," her mother interrupted, tapping one shapely fingernail against the white linen tablecloth. "Surely you can see that."

"He was deeply flawed," Carrie said quietly.

Vanessa let out a soft snort. "An egotistical, narcissistic boar of a human. You must regret staying with him and giving up your life. He wanted you with him because he needed a puppet, and once I wouldn't subject myself to that treatment any longer, that left him you as a stand-in. That town has nothing to offer you now."

Carrie swallowed against the emotion her mother's words conjured within her. "Other than a home and a community."

Vanessa stared at her for a long moment as the waiter set down their tea and the tray of pastries and dainty sandwiches. "We don't need the explanation, Martin. I know the selections. Thank you."

"Of course, Ms. Reed."

Another bow and he disappeared again without making eye contact with Carrie. Truly, she felt invisible in her mother's world.

"I apologize if you're offended by my words," Vanessa told her as she poured the tea. "I thought I'd worked through my anger toward your father. His death opened old wounds for me. I'm sure you understand how hard it was."

Carrie plucked a crustless cucumber sandwich from the silver tray and shoved the whole thing into her mouth, earning a disapproving frown from her mom. At least it gave her an excuse not to respond.

On the surface, her parents had always seemed like the epitome of opposites attract. Niall, the eccentric and nonconformist artist and her polished mother, who'd enjoyed being the wife of someone famous but hadn't wanted to stick it out once the spotlight faded along with the sales of her husband's mawkish paintings.

She'd come to realize they were more alike than she'd understood, both self-centered and emotionally immature. She'd lost her father and discovered that he'd kept the secret of her two sisters from her. A revelation that, coupled with the financial mess he'd left behind, had rocked her world to its core. Her mother, who'd been divorced from him for a decade, felt justified in lamenting how difficult his death had been on her.

"It's good to see you," her mother said, inclining her head.

Carrie took a big bite from one of the scones and nodded.

"You should try the jam and Devonshire cream." Vanessa nodded. "Your appetite seems to have returned."

As Carrie swallowed the pastry, it seemed to turn to ash in her throat. There wasn't enough clotted cream in all of England to make the questions she had for her mother any easier to ask.

She placed the uneaten half of scone on the bone china plate. "Did you know about Avery and Meredith?"

Her mother's lips pursed. "We've been through this already, Carrie."

"I've asked you the question," Carrie countered softly. "Over the phone after I learned about them from the attorney. But you didn't answer me."

"Have you come to see me after years of estrangement out of some bizarre need to understand how much I knew about the levels of your father's betrayal?"

"I wouldn't call it bizarre."

Her mother breathed out a laugh, and something that might have been respect flashed in her eyes. How strange. Carrie had spent most of her life trying to make everyone around her happy and now that she was growing a proverbial pair, people seemed to like her more.

"Your father cheated on me many times during our marriage." Vanessa's fingers tightened on the cup. "Probably more often than I even knew. There were things I overlooked in order to make the marriage work or maybe because I didn't want to see that part of him." She shrugged. "I wanted the fairy tale and was enamored by his larger-than-life personality."

"And the fame," Carrie added softly. She expected her mother to argue but she only looked into her half-empty cup as if reading the tea leaves.

"We were a good match, or at least that's what I told myself. He needed me because of who he wanted to be in the community. I could host parties and talk to wealthy clients and make him…" She waved her fingers as if searching for a word to pluck from the air.

"Respectable," Carrie supplied.

Vanessa sighed. "We were a team for a time. But it became clear that the compromise needed to make a marriage work wasn't what either of us wanted, especially as his ego took hits when the criticism of his talent began to outweigh his sales. That's a long-winded non-answer to your question. I knew about the other women, but I never had a clue he'd fathered more children."

"So you knew about Meredith's mother?"

"Yes, although not when the affair happened. I found out later. Niall and I had a huge fight shortly before I left him."

Left us both, Carrie thought but didn't say the words out loud. She wanted to understand what had happened between her parents, and putting her mom on the defensive wouldn't help that goal.

"I pushed him to admit how many times he'd cheated over the years," Vanessa continued. "Specifically, I wanted to know about the women from Magnolia. Despite what you might believe, it wasn't easy for me to walk away, and that was before I realized you weren't going to come with me. The understanding that if I stayed, I would have to continue to make nice with women who'd slept with my husband spurred me on."

Carrie sucked in a breath. She hadn't considered that part of the situation. "That's a terrible position to be in."

"I shouldn't have let him get away with it for so long." Vanessa nibbled on the edge of a sandwich. "More than that, I shouldn't have let the choice you made impact our relationship the way it did."

"He needed me," Carrie said simply, then shook her head. "At least that's how it felt. He was larger than life to me at that point. I wasn't trying to sever ties with you, but leaving Magnolia seemed impossible at the time."

"You don't have to explain his allure to me. It's part of why I walked away without looking back. There was too much chance of being sucked into his orbit again. He was like a black hole, Carrie, pulling in and warping everything and everyone that got too close. There was no escape. I still don't understand why he revealed everything to you in the will. Such a cowardly thing to do."

"Yes," Carrie murmured, her chest constricting with the memory of that revelation and how it had felt like a bomb exploding the life she'd known, pieces of her heart raining down like shrapnel around her. So much good had come from learning about her sisters, but the betrayal had changed everything about her feelings toward her father. He'd been her hero, and the disillusionment made her fearful of trusting her instincts on anything.

"There's nothing keeping you there now," her mother said. "You could travel or move anywhere and start over." She paused then added, "Raleigh is a lovely place to live and there's always room on my staff."

Carrie glanced around the stylish restaurant to the well-dressed patrons and formal waitstaff. "I don't think I'd fit in here."

"In Magnolia, you'll always be Niall's daughter."

"I'll always be his daughter no matter where I am." Carrie shrugged. "I don't want to run away from that because he's part of me. Maybe I let him eclipse me too long but pretending he didn't matter isn't the answer."

"What kind of answers are you looking for?" Vanessa asked, taking a dainty pastry from the tray.

"I'm still working on figuring out the questions I need to ask," Carrie admitted. "I appreciate you making time for me today. I know you don't like revisiting the past or talking about Dad."

"Your father and I both made mistakes." Her mother's tone gentled in a way Carrie barely recognized. "Just know that one of my few regrets is that leaving Magnolia affected my relationship with you. You don't deserve everything that's happened, although I guess it's good that you like these other women."

"They're my sisters," Carrie said, some of the tension knotted inside her loosening as she spoke the words. She cleared her throat, knowing it was too soon to share with her mother how much Avery and Meredith had come to mean to her. Things were still too fragile with Vanessa. "I've started painting again."

Her mother sucked in a quick breath. "Because it gives you the feeling of still being connected to your dad?"

Carrie shook her head. "We both know he didn't want me to be an artist."

"I hope you know why," Vanessa said. "Petty, jealous man."

Back in high school, when her father had derided her talent, Dylan had been the first one to accuse Niall of jealousy. She hadn't believed him, of course, and her mother had stayed silent on the subject before she'd left. It still pained her to think that her father, whom she'd loved with all her heart, would have undermined her in that way.

"It doesn't have anything to do with Dad." She picked up her teacup and hoped her mother didn't notice that Carrie's fingers trembled. "I feel like myself when I'm painting."

"You could move to New York City," Vanessa suggested. "I have friends there who'd help you get settled. The art community there is far more vibrant than anything you'll find in some piddling coastal town."

Carrie opened her mouth to protest then shut it again. She'd never been to New York—or anywhere, really. It shamed her to admit, even to her own mother, how small her life had been. Her father had traveled but he'd always claimed he needed Carrie "holding down the fort" in Magnolia. She hadn't even had the guts to put up a fight. Niall had never been abusive, but his emotional manipulations had taken their toll on her over the years.

If she ever challenged him, he'd go straight into the silent treatment, freezing her out of his life until she'd felt like she was living in Antarctica instead of the Carolinas.

She'd learned to assess his moods and not push him too far in a way that would anger him. Only now after months of being truly on her own did she see how twisted their relationship had become.

"I'll think about it," Carrie told her mother, slathering jelly on another scone. "Dad left a mountain of debt behind so Avery, Meredith and I have been working on increasing tourism in town and cleaning up the house so that we don't lose everything to the bank."

"I did love that house," Vanessa murmured. "I don't suppose Niall kept up with the maintenance on it?"

Carrie shook her head but didn't share how far into disrepair the stately mansion had fallen. She'd moved out on her own several years ago and her father had quickly deteriorated into a secret hoarder. She'd been unaware of how bad it had gotten until after he was gone but suspected her mother would place some of the blame on Carrie. Her one job had been taking care of her dad, and his house and his finances were a mess. She had enough guilt all on her own, thank you very much.

They finished tea with talk of the hotel and plans for the holidays. Carrie had never done much to celebrate Christmas. Although her father's paintings showcased an idealistic version of American life, he hadn't actually liked traditional holidays. But Vanessa's long list of festivities gave Carrie an idea or two she could suggest at the Magnolia business owners' meeting later that evening. If they continued the uptick in revenue, their properties might actually make money by the following summer.

If Dylan Scott didn't mess everything up with his scheme to take over the town. She sighed as she followed her mother back toward the front of the hotel.

Worry over today had chased away thoughts of Dylan

for a few hours, but as she said goodbye to her mom and began the drive home, he invaded her mind again.

Would he show up tonight at the meeting? She certainly hoped not. Dylan was a distraction she didn't want or need in her life at the moment. And if her heart seemed to thump a crazy rhythm at the thought of him, contradicting her determination to keep him at arm's length…

Well, what did her heart know anyway?

CHAPTER FIVE

DYLAN ENTERED THE meeting room in the basement of the town hall building that night trying not to appear nervous. Or bitter. Or angry. Or anything like the punk teen he'd been back in the day.

He paused just outside the doorway and took a breath. There was no need to pretend those things. Dylan Scott had come a long way in the decade since he'd left this small town fading in his rearview mirror.

And he was thinking about himself in the third person? Bad sign.

Damn.

What was it about Magnolia that made him doubt everything? He thought about pulling up his bio on the company website, just to assure himself he had the credentials to back what he wanted to do in this town.

"Idiot," he muttered, running a hand through his hair.

"Exactly what we were thinking," an unfamiliar voice said from behind him.

He turned to see Carrie staring at him, color high on her cheeks. She was flanked by two other women. The tall blonde gave him a cool once-over then narrowed her eyes to glare.

The petite woman on Carrie's other side wrinkled her nose as if she'd just smelled a wicked dog fart. "Since we're all in agreement that you're an idiot, it would be the perfect time for you to leave."

He'd seen these women with Carrie at her art show when he'd come to Magnolia a month ago and made an unannounced stop at The Reed Gallery. Niall's three daughters. Carrie and her sisters.

Even though there was a decent chance none of them would care if he stepped off the curb and got struck by a random garbage truck, his heart warmed at the thought of Carrie finally having people in her life who truly cared for her. Niall had been one of the most selfish, self-centered men Dylan had ever met. Carrie's mom wasn't much better, leaving her only child to take care of that egotistical jerk.

The way her half sisters leaned in, as if ready to pounce on him if he so much as raised a brow in Carrie's direction, told him she'd found her tribe.

A sharp ache darted along his spine as his mind immediately went to his uncle and cousin. They'd been his only true family and now he was left with no one.

Not true. He had Sam, who hated him with the burning heat of a thousand suns. Dylan was basically hosed all the way around.

Except that he had money and power and planned to use those to carve out a place for himself and for Sam. He wouldn't fail his cousin on that count.

Even if that meant taking down the Reed sisters in the process.

"I'm just getting started here," he said, offering the trio a wide smile. "I'd recommend you stay out of my way, ladies. It will make things easy on all of us."

The little one stomped a booted foot. "That sounds like a threat. We don't take kindly to threats, you big bully."

Dylan half expected to see a dusty tumbleweed roll by

like he'd been cast in some old Western movie. This mini standoff with the Reed sisters definitely made him the villain, but he didn't mind. The role seemed suited to him and gave him an excuse to ignore his unwelcome feelings for Carrie.

"I'm not known for kindness, Meredith," he told the spitfire and saw her eyes widen slightly, shock that he knew her name making her frown deepen. "Your older brothers can attest to that."

"The meeting's about to get started," someone announced from the doorway.

Malcolm Grimes stepped forward and placed a hand on Dylan's shoulder. "Let's try to remember that we all want what's best for the town."

Dylan gave a tight nod even as he saw Carrie's mouth thin. He knew his plans for the properties in downtown would make her even angrier but told himself it wasn't personal. He'd never let his emotions get in the way of a good business deal and didn't plan to start now.

He entered the meeting room and felt the weight of a dozen distrustful stares upon him. No one greeted him or even offered the hint of a smile as he took a seat near the back of the rows of chairs.

In contrast, as Carrie and her sisters entered, almost every person in the room smiled and waved or called out a greeting. A not so subtle reminder that Dylan was the outsider, an interloper in their tight-knit community.

"I've saved seats for you," an older woman said from the front of the room. Dylan recognized Josie Trumbell, whose dance studio had been around even when he was a kid. The sisters moved forward and he could almost feel Carrie's effort to not look at him as she walked past.

He had a sudden urge to reach out to her, to ground himself in the feel of her softness the way he used to. Of course, he kept his hands at his side. He had no right to touch her and there was a better than average chance her sisters would relish the opportunity to claw out his eyes if he dared.

Once the women had taken their seats, Malcolm stepped behind the podium and smiled at his audience. "It's great to see so many of you here tonight. This is an exciting time for our town." His dark gaze tracked to Dylan. "I'd like to formally welcome back to Magnolia one of our own, Dylan Scott."

Dylan cringed inwardly at the pathetic, halfhearted round of applause that greeted the mayor's words.

Mal frowned. "Come on, people. Don't forget we're all on the same team now. Dylan's company has a strong track record of developing real estate in Boston, and he's going to use that expertise to inject some new life—" one thick brow rose "—and hopefully revenue into Magnolia."

"Have you looked at his track record?" Dylan blinked as Carrie stood and faced the crowd. "He destroys the integrity of established neighborhoods with his high-rises and dense urban revivals."

She'd researched him? Oh, hell. It appeared Carrie was taking seriously her promise to make things difficult for him in Magnolia.

"I renovate dilapidated buildings and give communities a second chance at prosperity," he countered, rising to his feet.

"Renovate with a bulldozer," she shot back. "You decimate the character and change neighborhoods to the point where the people who love them don't even recognize their homes anymore."

Dylan felt a muscle in his jaw clench. She'd read the editorial from the Boston paper accusing him of pushing an agenda of new urban blight. "We only go the route of a tear-down if a building isn't structurally sound."

"What are your plans for the properties you've purchased in Magnolia?" Malcolm asked, his tone a bit cooler than it had been moments earlier.

"We're in the initial stages," Dylan said, "so no final decisions have been made."

"But you aren't going to tear down any buildings?" The question came from Stuart Moore, whose family had owned the bookstore across the street from Dylan's properties for as long as anyone could remember. "I just started turning a profit again thanks to the new wave of visitors in town this fall. A big mess of construction will impact that."

"For a time," Dylan conceded, trying not to show his impatience. Normally, he focused on the big financial and marketing aspect of the deal. Wiley had been the one to work with the established businesses around their properties. He'd had a way with people that Dylan obviously didn't. "But if we convert the properties to mixed-use spaces with condos as well as upscale commercial properties, that will bring in a brand-new customer base."

"How much will the condos sell for?" Carrie demanded, her chin lifted in challenge.

She'd done her homework.

Dylan cleared his throat. "Typically, our properties start at a base price in the mid-six figures."

He fought back a groan at the round of gasps and disbelieving murmurs that greeted those figures.

"Magnolia locals can't afford that," the woman sitting next to Carrie exclaimed.

"We're hoping to attract new residents to the town," Dylan explained, hoping he sounded enthusiastic.

"And chase out everyone else," Carrie accused, pointing a finger at him.

"I'm sure Dylan doesn't have some grand scheme to return to Magnolia and take over the town," Mal interjected before Dylan could respond.

Carrie let out a delicate snort. That was pretty much what he'd told her he planned to do that dark night when seeing her again had weakened his defenses and loosened his tongue all at once.

"I want to make things better," he said. That much wasn't a lie. Not for himself. His life was fine. Great. Maybe lonely. Perhaps lacking much substance outside of the relentless pursuit of success. Dylan wouldn't complain.

But Sam needed something more. A home. A community. A chance to heal from the tragedy that had robbed him of his family.

It might be a long shot to think they could find that in Magnolia, but Dylan had to try. He'd run out of options.

"That's the spirit," Mal shouted with what sounded like forced enthusiasm.

No one else in the room looked convinced.

"Speaking of spirit," the mayor continued. "Another item on the agenda for this meeting is to discuss the upcoming holiday festival. It kicks off Thanksgiving weekend. Most of the plans are well underway, but maybe you have any ideas to share, Dylan?"

Dylan struggled to keep up with Malcolm's rambling train of thought. "About what?"

"Christmas?" the mayor prompted.

"Ho, ho, ho," Dylan mumbled, throwing a narrow-eyed glance at Carrie and her sisters.

To his surprise, Carrie's lips twitched as if she were fighting a smile.

"I'm serious," Malcolm said, leaning forward on the podium. "We want to continue the success of the fall tourism campaign to attract visitors to Magnolia for the holidays. You're from the big city. Surely you have some creative suggestions for making our town more festive."

Dylan pressed a finger to his right eye, which had begun to twitch. The entire room seemed to be waiting for him to offer up some brilliant idea.

"I don't do Christmas," he said finally.

Another round of gasps and disapproving murmurs.

"Hanukkah?" Mal asked tentatively. "I guess I never realized you were—"

"No." Dylan shook his head. "The holidays. Thanksgiving, Christmas, Hanukkah, Kwanza, New Year. All of them. None of them, actually. Celebrating fake holidays isn't my deal."

"Those holidays aren't fake," Carrie said to a universal chorus of nodding heads and a few amens.

"Not as phony as Valentine's Day," Dylan agreed. "But they're all about materialism. Which means that you should reconsider obstructing my proposal when your plan for the festival is about pushing people into spending money."

"It's about celebrating the most wonderful time of the year," Carrie argued. "We're going to have Santa, craft booths, light shows, games for kids and all the holiday fun anyone could want."

"That's right, Dylan McScrooge," Meredith added. "Your heart must be at least two sizes too small."

"That's the Grinch," Carrie told her.

"He's like Scrooge and the Grinch rolled into one annoying package," Meredith said.

"No name calling," Malcolm warned the feisty brunette. "I run a civilized meeting."

Dylan wanted to slouch down in his seat again, or better yet stalk out of the stuffy basement room and head for the nearest bar, which in Magnolia would probably mean Murphy's Pub, his dad's old favorite.

"Is Sean Murphy still around?" he asked the man sitting next to him. Thomas Mayfield owned the gas station on the edge of town.

"Yep," Thomas confirmed. "Serving the same watered-down beer for over two decades. You should try the new microbrewery that opened out on the highway toward the beach. It's a big improvement."

"I'll check it out," Dylan answered then glanced up again when Mal called his name.

"What do you think of Carrie's plan?" the mayor asked. He'd missed whatever ideas she'd proposed during his side conversation about finding a drink. He shrugged and switched his gaze to Carrie, who was staring at him with an expression that dared him to challenge her.

Suddenly, Dylan didn't have the heart for it. He was tired of pushing, tired of fighting. It felt as though he spent most every day engaged in a battle of wills with Sam; ironic when the move to Magnolia had been to make things easier for both of them.

"Her dad ran the town the way he wanted for decades," he pointed out to the assembled business owners. "You all know where that got you. But if the same old Reed family monarchy is what you want—"

"That isn't what *I* want," Carrie interrupted. "I'm trying to fix the problems my father caused." She gestured to Avery and Meredith. "We all want that."

"Dylan has a point," someone called from the side of the room, and he watched as the color drained from Carrie's face. Damn. He might not want a fight, but it seemed he couldn't help but pick one with her. "This town needs fresh suggestions."

"The Merry Magnolia Festival is a good idea," Avery said, rising from her chair to stand next to Carrie. "It's new and exciting. He doesn't have anything better to offer, and all of you know how much Carrie cares about Magnolia. You can't punish her because of what Niall did."

"And don't forget he wants to price us all out of our own town," Meredith added, continuing to glare at Dylan.

"Calm down, everyone," Malcolm said when people erupted into buzzing grumbles. "I have a solution that will work for all of us." He pointed toward the Reed sisters. "Carrie's festival will bring people to town for the holidays, and Dylan assures us he wants the best for Magnolia. I propose we make them the co-directors of this year's event. The first annual Merry Magnolia Festival."

Dylan pressed two fingers to his chest. What the hell was going on inside him? It felt like a million butterflies had just taken flight. Of course, the mayor's proposal was monumentally stupid on several levels.

Most important, Carrie hated him. Even now, she gaped at Malcolm as if he'd suggested she bed down with a venomous snake. Dylan wanted to destroy the last vestiges of her father's reputation in the town, simply to prove that he could. That put them on opposite sides of everything. Enemies.

Yet, his heart hammered in a crazy rhythm at the thought of spending time with her. Even if that time needed to be focused on the nonsense of celebrating crass commercialization and sham holiday spirit.

"No way," Carrie told Malcolm, rising to her feet again. "He doesn't care about this town or about Christmas. We don't need him." She looked around the crowd as if entreating them to take her side. "I don't want him."

Well, that pretty much summed it up.

But Mal only shook his head. "We're on a roll with re-invigorating things around here, but Dylan's company is going to be part of Magnolia's future whether you like it or not." He paused then added, "Whether any of us want it that way. This is what's best for the town, and that's my priority."

The murmurs of assent surprised Dylan. Maybe the town was willing to give him a chance even if Carrie wasn't. He cleared his throat. "I'd be honored to help with the festival," he lied. "It will give me a chance to get to know the community and determine how I can make the biggest impact to benefit everyone."

Carrie's gaze narrowed on him, but she nodded. "Fine. Dylan and I will work together," she muttered. "Can we adjourn now?"

The mayor gave her a wide smile. "We look forward to hearing about all of your exciting suggestions that will make this holiday season the best Magnolia has ever seen." He drew in a deep breath. "Meeting adjourned."

CHAPTER SIX

CARRIE FORCED HERSELF to smile and nod as her friends surrounded her, offering words of encouragement and pledging to help with whatever she needed to make her plan a success. The Merry Magnolia Festival would be spread across the weekends leading up to Christmas, with each weekend building on the others as far as activities and themes.

They wanted to encourage residents and visitors to visit downtown Magnolia multiple times throughout the holiday season. The events would kick off with a tree lighting on the Saturday after Thanksgiving. Shops and restaurants were scheduled to stay open late to accommodate the crowds they hoped would materialize. From there, the activities and events got bigger each weekend, from visits with Santa to concerts and a craft fair. She continued to rent lights and inflatables and create background sets for the town square. By the time Christmas rolled around, downtown Magnolia would give the North Pole a run for its money.

"Are you okay?" Avery whispered as the crowd started to disperse.

"Fine," Carrie grumbled. "This is actually the best possible outcome."

"How do you figure?" Meredith demanded, glancing over her shoulder. "Seems to me the best outcome would be if I kidnapped Dylan Scott and shoved him into an abandoned shed somewhere."

"You scare me sometimes," Avery told their younger sister.

Meredith grinned. "I scare myself, too, but that's how I like it."

Carrie shook her head. "Dylan hates Christmas," she told the other two women. "He always has. I'm going to make sure that becomes clear in the next month while I figure out how to prove his proposal for the town needs to be stopped. I don't trust him, and the best way to derail whatever scheme he has planned is to get close to him."

"Can you handle that?" Avery asked.

"He did a number on you back in the day," Meredith added as if Carrie didn't remember the heartbreak he'd caused her.

"That's all in the past," she assured her sisters with more confidence than she felt.

After saying goodbye to Malcolm, they walked out into the late-November night together.

"You know you aren't in this alone," Avery said as they paused at her car parked along the curb. "We'll help with whatever you need. Gray will, too. He can rally some of the guys from the station."

"Firefighters under the mistletoe," Meredith murmured, rubbing her hands together. "Yes, please."

Carrie laughed, grateful as ever that she had her sisters in her life. "You both are busy with your own lives. I've got this."

Avery's brow furrowed as she studied Carrie. "Just a reminder that you aren't responsible for the mistakes your father made."

"*Our* father," Carrie made the habitual change without an iota of hesitation. Carrie might be the only one who'd truly known Niall Reed as her dad while he was alive, but she liked the feeling of connection it gave her to share him with these women.

"More like sperm donor," Meredith said with an eye roll. "But no use arguing about that fact once again."

"Do you want a ride home?" Avery asked Carrie as she took out her key fob. The hulking truck Meredith drove was parked behind Avery's Lexus.

"Thanks, but I'll walk." Carrie hugged each of her sisters. "I could use the fresh air."

"Smells like rain." Meredith tipped her head up to look at the sky, dark and cloudy without any moon or stars visible.

"I'm good with rain now as long as it's clear when we get closer to the festival weekend." She leaned in closer. "I'm thinking of renting a snowmaking machine."

"Even you can't control the weather and you do realize this is the South," Meredith said, laughing. "We rarely get snow. I can't remember ever having a white Christmas."

"Exactly," Carrie agreed. "Think of how special it will be if we can manufacture it."

Neither of her sisters seemed convinced, but there was time for that. Carrie said goodbye and then started down the sidewalk. She waved as both Avery and Meredith drove past.

"Manufacturing Christmas," a deep voice called from the shadowy alley between two buildings. "You really are a chip off the old block."

"Do you have some sinister plan to give me a heart attack?" she demanded as Dylan appeared from the darkness. "Or have you just taken up stalking in your spare time?"

"Stalking for sure," he agreed easily, falling into step beside her.

She gave him her nastiest side-eye. "What are you doing?"

"Walking you home. It's late."

"Unnecessary," she muttered, even as a thrill passed through her. She'd gotten used to taking care of herself so the idea of Dylan waiting for her in the darkness sent a shiver of pleasure running along her spine. Of course, Avery had just offered her a ride, but this felt different.

Things always had with Dylan, and that was dangerous.

"I want to make fake snow, but the holiday spirit is genuine." She crossed her arms over her chest when their hands accidentally brushed. "Magnolia is going to become a premier winter destination. We managed it in the fall and if the town has a strong holiday season, we can keep the momentum going into spring and summer..." She blew out a breath, excitement skittering across her skin. "I'm going to turn things around."

"*I'm* going to turn things around," he corrected, and she couldn't tell if he was teasing or goading her into lashing out at him. "In the meeting it sounded like you'd done your share of online stalking. You know how I run my business."

"Like you have no soul. You plow forward with no consideration for the history or essence of the community."

"That's not true," he protested. "We make things better."

"Let's agree to disagree that different isn't always better," she said, and they fell into a silence that should have been awkward but felt almost companionable.

"You're taking this whole holiday festival thing really seriously," he told her as they reached the corner of the block where she would turn off for her house.

Carrie couldn't help grinning at him. "Yeah, I am. It's going to be the best ever."

Dylan smiled. "Who are you and what have you done with the shy girl I used to know?"

"A lot has changed since you left."

He leaned closer, just an inch, but her body went on high alert. "Including you."

If only she'd outgrown her reaction to this man. She didn't want this, the tightening in her belly and the way her breath caught as his gaze fell to her lips. Especially not if they were going to work together. The last thing she needed was to let down her guard with Dylan.

It would be like inviting the big, bad wolf to tea.

"I have a boyfriend," she blurted.

Dylan blinked. "Oh."

"It's kind of new," she continued, ignoring the fact that in this case *new* was another word for nonexistent. "I don't even know why I'm telling you this…"

One thick brow rose. "Because you were looking at me like you wanted me to kiss you."

She sniffed and took a step back. "I was not. Maybe you're confused because you were staring at my mouth like you were going to maul it."

"Maul?" He rolled his eyes. "Your memory must be going bad because I don't maul women. I have it on good authority that I'm a damn fine kisser."

Her limbs went heavy as she thought about the blissful hours she'd spent kissing Dylan. Damn fine didn't begin to cover his skill in that area. But she had no intention of admitting that to him.

"Average," she said with a shrug.

His mouth dropped open. "In your dreams."

"I have vivid dreams. You couldn't possibly compete." His pupils darkened and she wondered what the heck she was thinking goading him on in this way. It was like waving a red flag in front of an irritated bull.

Suddenly, he stepped in front of her, turning to face her so quickly that she almost ran into him. "I'd bet my last dollar that I can outperform your wildest dreams. And we'd both enjoy every moment of it."

He stepped even closer and she resisted the urge to back up. Stand her ground. That was the only choice with Dylan. "We'll never know because you chose a check over me."

The words spilled from her mouth before she could stop them, but she regretted it almost immediately. She didn't want Dylan to think she still cared about how he'd broken her heart. No way. Not ever.

His gaze hardened and he moved away from her. "We never would have lasted anyway," he said and as much as she wanted to argue, she nodded.

"Right."

"And you have a boyfriend."

"Um... I do."

"Who's a better kisser than me?"

"He is."

Dylan studied her for a long moment, his mouth curving into an almost-smile that did funny things to her insides.

"Will he be helping with your little winter carnival plan, too?" His big shoulders rolled as if adjusting the tension they held.

"It's not little," she argued automatically. "And he lives in Charleston."

"A long-distance love affair? How long have the two of you been dating?"

Carrie narrowed her eyes because it felt like Dylan was asking questions even though he didn't believe a word she said to him. "Six months," she told him. "He's very kind. And refined. Gentle. A true gentleman."

"Sounds boring as hell. What's his name?"

"Randall," she blurted.

"You're dating a guy named Randall?" Dylan sniffed. "Is he eighty years old?"

"Stop." She held up a hand and pushed her palm against his chest.

Big mistake. The instant she felt the hard muscles of his body and the heat coming from him, need pooled low in her belly. She drew back her hand and glanced up to find him staring down at her again, nostrils flared and color high on his cheeks.

"I have to go," she murmured, desperately searching for control. Purchase over her desire. A cold shower. Anything to stem the tide of yearning she felt for this man. "And call Randall."

His lips quirked. "Tell him I said hi."

"Su-sure," she stammered. "I'll talk to Malcolm, too. He couldn't have been serious about us working together."

"Your mayor seems like he's always serious when it comes to this town."

Yeah. "We'll figure it out anyway," she insisted. "You can't want to work with me any more than I do with you."

She expected an immediate agreement, but Dylan only quirked a brow. "Sweet dreams, Carrie," he said, his voice thick and rich like warm honey. "You be sure not to think of me while you're asleep. But if you do, know that real life would be even better."

She bit down on the inside of her cheek to suppress a groan. "Never," she told him and stomped past, knowing her dreams would be nothing but that irritating man.

THE FOLLOWING AFTERNOON Dylan pulled into the Magnolia High parking lot with a knot of anger balling in his stomach.

He'd gotten the call from Principal Johnson twenty minutes earlier. Sam had been caught vandalizing the building during fifth period, when he should have been in algebra.

Was the kid trying to get kicked out of yet another school?

After turning off the ignition, Dylan rubbed two fingers against his temples, which had started to throb in a familiar way when it came to dealing with Sam's defiance. He wanted to be a patient, understanding guardian. Sam had been through something no child of any age should have to deal with.

But his need to act out, while normal according to the therapist they'd gone to during the months after his parents' deaths, was going to impact the boy's future if it didn't stop.

The therapist had agreed that a fresh start might help Sam recover. He seemed to want to pull away from everything that reminded him of his family or who he'd been before their accident.

It had been less than a week that he'd been enrolled at Magnolia High. Dylan had tried to remain upbeat about the close-knit school, listing off the clubs and activities he'd read on the website. He hoped like hell Sam didn't get any of the teachers he'd had during his time there. It wouldn't be good for the kid if they remembered him.

Now it seemed like Sam was hell-bent on not only living up to but also surpassing Dylan's dreadful reputation at school.

Taking several deep breaths, Dylan climbed the stairs to the school. He checked in with security, trying not to cringe as the burly officer behind the glass gave him a cool once-over. After the guy buzzed him into the locked front entrance, Dylan entered the administrative office.

He'd been naive to think that Sam would have a smooth transition but refused to give up hope that the boy would take life's lemons and make something drinkable with them. "Mr. Johnson is waiting for you in his office," the secretary told him, her tone clipped.

Two days and Sam had already been pegged as a troublemaker. Dylan hated that. He wanted to show these judgmental educators Sam's baby photos and all the videos Kay had taken to document the precious milestones in her son's life.

Sam had always been a shy kid, quiet and introspective but with a sweet smile and easygoing temperament that had made everyone in his life love him. His parents and grandpa had doted on him, and Dylan was embarrassed to admit he'd been jealous of the boy on occasion, unable to fathom what it would have been like to grow up surrounded by so much love and affection.

Only to have it stolen by a tragic accident.

He opened the door to Tim Johnson's office and the wiry-thin man, who looked to be in his late fifties, gestured him forward. Dylan's gaze tracked to Sam, who sat hunched in one of the upholstered chairs in front of the desk. The boy didn't bother to turn around, but Dylan saw his shoulders stiffen as if he knew who entered the room without looking.

"Thank you for joining us, Mr. Scott," the principal said. "Please have a seat. I'm Tim Johnson, and I apologize that we're meeting under these circumstances."

"Call me Dylan." He placed a hand on Sam's back. "You okay, bud?"

"Never better," the kid muttered, although his body language told a different story. Sam never showed weakness to the world. It was something Dylan appreciated in the boy because, for better or worse, he had the same tendency.

The principal cleared his throat. "I hope that isn't the case. Sam has committed a serious infraction, and despite the extenuating circumstances with which he comes to us, we need to ensure that nothing like this occurs again."

He adjusted his glasses as he looked at Dylan. "The other option is that Sam isn't a fit for Magnolia High."

Extenuating circumstances. Angry heat rushed through Dylan. Surely the principal could come up with a better way to describe being orphaned.

"Tell me what happened," Dylan told Sam.

"Nothing."

"I wouldn't call defacing school property *nothing*," Tim said tightly.

"Defacing in what way?" Dylan asked the principal.

"Our security system caught it on camera. Instead of going to class, Sam chose to spend fifth period spray-painting school property."

"The stupid, ugly modular classroom." Sam shook his head. "It's not even a big deal."

"Vandalism," the principal said. "Skipping class is a big deal. I'm certain your..." He cleared his throat. "I'm certain Mr. Scott agrees."

Dylan pressed his lips together. In theory he agreed with the principal, but the truth was he'd done much worse during his time in high school. Still, he couldn't let Sam start off in this way.

"What's the punishment?" he demanded, figuring it was easiest to cut to the chase.

Tim Johnson raised a brow. "Do you think we should talk about why this happened?"

"Math is boring," Sam grumbled. "The modular is ugly. Everyone thinks it looks way better now."

"That isn't the point," Tim said, shaking his head.

It surprised Dylan that the principal didn't argue. He

hadn't checked out the building where the graffiti had taken place when he'd arrived, and now he regretted that decision.

"I think more than worrying about why it happened," Dylan told the principal, "the major concern should be ensuring it doesn't happen again. Which it won't."

"My recommendation is a one-day school suspension," Tim said with a nod. "That will take us into the Thanksgiving holiday."

"What holiday?" Dylan asked, panic grazing along his spine.

"The school district is closed Wednesday, Thursday and Friday due to the holiday." The principal looked at him like he was a total idiot.

"Right," he agreed. "I forgot about Thanksgiving."

"Because you always came to our house." Sam suddenly turned to him, his tone filled with accusation. "You never had to remember it because my mom took care of everything."

"It's not like I forgot the holiday," Dylan protested, the words sounding weak even to his own ears. "I've been busy, Sam. I just didn't remember that it was this week." He massaged a hand over the back of his neck. "Or that you'd be off school."

"Stuck with me, again."

Dylan blew out a long breath. "We can discuss Thanksgiving plans and whether you want pecan or pumpkin pie later. Right now we're talking about you vandalizing the school." He looked at the principal. "Do you have photos so I can see the damage? Sam will take care of cleanup and any costs involved."

Tim nodded, flipping open the laptop that sat on his desk and turning it so the screen faced Dylan.

"As far as the suspension goes, we do have another option," the principal offered, almost reluctantly.

Instead of hearing him out, Dylan held up a hand, unable to focus on anything but the images on the screen.

"How long is a class period?" he whispered.

When Sam didn't answer, the principal cleared his throat. "Forty minutes."

Dylan felt his mouth drop open and quickly shut it again. "You did this in less than an hour?" he demanded of Sam, who gave a tight nod.

"It's just some spray paint," the boy mumbled. "I don't know why everyone is making such a big deal about it. I can paint over it with no problem."

"Young man, this is a big deal as you call it because you vandalized district property and disrupted the school day for everyone involved."

"This isn't graffiti." Dylan used the arrow key to scroll through the close-ups of what Sam had done. "It's art."

He wasn't simply saying it to get Sam out of trouble. Dylan had expected foul words or inappropriate scribbles, the kind of stuff he and his friends would have done for a stupid prank as teens. Sam had drawn—or sprayed—a boy standing on the top of a jagged mountain. It was a black-and-white design, simple in some ways, but the emotion of the piece practically took his breath away.

"You're talented," he told Sam. "Why didn't I ever hear about this from your dad?"

The boy seemed to sink lower in the chair. "He wanted me to focus on real classes and playing hockey. Dad didn't care that I wanted to draw. He said art was for pansies."

Dylan sighed. That sounded like something his cousin would have told his son. Wiley was a great guy and a loving father, but he was old-school in a lot of his thinking.

Boys played sports and learned to hunt and work on old cars. He and Kay had a traditional marriage, with him as the breadwinner and head of the household.

It had worked for them, and they seemed happy, so Dylan hadn't even thought to question it.

"You didn't enroll in any art classes here."

Sam shrugged. "It would have pissed him off."

Hell. The boy was trying to please his father even now. In one instant, the situation turned more complicated than Dylan could have guessed it might. And it was a mess of monumental proportions in the first place.

He wanted to argue, to tell Sam to follow his bliss or give some kind of insightful advice, but he had no idea what to say. Why couldn't this moment be like something out of a coming-of-age movie where the adults offered sound-bite words of wisdom? Where was Mr. Miyagi when a guy needed him?

"You said there was another option." Dylan looked helplessly at the principal, grasping for anything to turn things around.

He sat forward in his chair as Tim Johnson nodded. "One of our extracurricular art club instructors is looking for volunteers to help with a project. It would be after school and Sam needs to interview with her then log his hours and have her sign off on his work and attitude. I texted her photos of what he did here…" The man laughed softly. "She's interested in speaking to him. If he agrees to this, it would be an alternative to the infraction going on his permanent record."

"He'll take it," Dylan said.

Sam let out a snort of disbelief. "I'm not volunteering. Just punish me and have it over. Kick me out if you want. I don't care."

"You do." Dylan stood and paced to the edge of the office then back again, frustration pounding through him. "You're running out of options, buddy. I don't know what we're going to do if you get expelled from another school."

"Don't worry about it," the boy muttered. "I'll figure things out."

Who was this kid trying to fool? Half the time he could barely remember to brush his teeth.

"The suspension will be enforced either way," the principal told Dylan, his tone bordering on sympathetic. He pushed a slip of paper across the top of his desk. "Consider the option and let me know by the start of Thanksgiving break. Here's Ms. Reed's number if you want to call her and talk about where she needs help."

Ms. Reed? With numb fingers, Dylan picked up the paper and read the name and phone number scrawled there. Blood roared through his head. The woman who could get Sam out of hot water if she took him on was the woman who had every reason to want Dylan out of town.

Just when life couldn't get any more complicated, it did.

CHAPTER SEVEN

LATE THURSDAY MORNING, Thanksgiving Day, Dylan stalked toward The Reed Gallery. A pale sun shone down on him from a cloudless sky, but the mild weather did little to curb his mood.

He'd actually woken feeling hopeful, a rare occasion of late. The house had been quiet and because of the holiday his phone and email had been, as well.

He and Sam had gone to the grocery the previous day and bought a random assortment of food to make their Thanksgiving feast. Despite his company's financial backing of several trendy restaurants around Boston, Dylan couldn't cook worth a damn. But instant potatoes weren't exactly high on the culinary challenge scale.

When Sam hadn't made an appearance by ten, he'd started to get concerned. Much to the teen's irritation, Dylan had implemented a policy of electronic devices charging in the kitchen. If not for that, Sam probably would have spent all his time behind a closed bedroom door.

But the kid always came down as soon as he woke to check in on social media. The constant worry over monitoring Sam's online activities and the negotiations around screen time made Dylan feel old. And like a real parent, which terrified both him and Sam.

He'd checked the charging station in the corner of the

counter and realized Sam's phone was missing, which had sent him rushing up the stairs to bang on the kid's door.

Sam hadn't answered and when Dylan finally opened the door, he found the room empty. Panic had pounded through him. He didn't think the boy would run away, but it was an ever-present fear in the back of Dylan's mind given how often he'd considered the option when he'd been a teenager.

When he checked the app that tracked the location of Sam's phone, he'd been shocked to see it show up at Niall Reed's gallery downtown. Sam hadn't seemed the least bit interested in a community service project and despite what he'd told the principal, Dylan hadn't pushed the idea. He could handle working with Carrie on the silly winter festival. He figured it would be a way to showcase how his larger vision for the town would benefit everyone more than relying on small-scale tourism events.

Sam made Dylan vulnerable, and he had no intention of showing that side of himself to Carrie. Hell, he hated to admit he even had a vulnerable side.

But now he approached the local landmark with a strange mix of anticipation and dread. Although much of downtown Magnolia remained the same from when he was a kid, Carrie and her sisters had transformed the gallery from a tacky shrine celebrating Niall's ego to a warm and welcoming studio, complete with bright colors, plush rugs and lots of crafty-looking signs with quotes about following your bliss and being grateful for a variety of things, including coffee and wine o'clock. Whatever that was.

He still couldn't understand why she was wasting her time teaching frivolous sip-and-paint classes in the evening or working at the high school instead of focusing on her art.

He'd bought most of her paintings when he'd come to Magnolia in the fall and seen them through the window of the gallery. He'd recognized the work she'd done during their time together a decade ago. He hadn't been able to resist them, but he'd made sure to have his assistant arrange payment so that Carrie hadn't realized he was the buyer until he'd shown up at her show.

Was she making new art now?

Although the rest of the block appeared dark with the stores closed for Thanksgiving, the gallery windows glowed warmly with light.

Both Sam and Carrie looked up from the drafting table where they sat next to each other as he stormed in. Neither spoke as they stared at him. How was it that he once again felt like the outsider?

"You scared the crap out of me," he told the boy. "What the hell were you thinking leaving without telling me?"

The boy rolled his eyes like he had a master's degree in the gesture. "You were in the shower, so I wasn't going to risk seeing your saggy butt. I like my corneas just how they are, man."

That earned a burst of laughter from Carrie, but what irritated Dylan was the way his heart seemed to loosen and sigh in response, even though she was laughing at *him*.

"You could have left a note." He crossed his arms over his chest and did his best to look intimidating. He also tried his best not to worry whether his butt was actually sagging. Of course it wasn't true. Dylan was in the best shape of his life and knew the kid teased him just to get a reaction. "Or texted me."

Sam shrugged. "I thought I'd be back before you noticed I was gone."

"You weren't," Dylan said through clenched teeth.

"Please don't be angry." Carrie pushed back from the

table and stood, tucking a long strand of hair behind one ear, and Dylan's nerve endings buzzed with awareness.

His reaction to her made him feel ridiculous. She wore a chunky sweater and faded jeans with a rip over the knee. The sliver of skin that showed was enough to make his mouth water. "Principal Johnson told me he didn't think Sam was interested in volunteering for Merry Magnolia. When he texted this morning I asked if he could meet me here right away. He's got so much talent."

"For trouble," Dylan muttered, earning another eye roll. He took a step forward. "We'd agreed you weren't going to get involved."

"Why do you care?" Sam demanded. "You were so upset that I got busted so what's your problem with me doing this?" The boy's face flushed. "You probably think the same way my dad did. That art is for pansies."

"Art isn't for pansies," Carrie said, sounding both shocked and affronted as she leveled a glare at Dylan.

"I never said that," he explained.

"But you believe it," Sam accused him.

"Not true."

"Then why discourage him from helping me?" Carrie shook her head. "He has some great ideas for backdrops and with his talent…" She broke off, mouth dropping open in shock. "That's the reason. You don't want the festival to be a success."

Dylan squeezed shut his eyes for a moment, wondering how every interaction he had with this woman spun out of control so quickly.

"Cold, man." Sam faked a shiver. "Dad always said ice ran through your veins when you were making a deal, but that's arctic levels of frozen."

It was more complicated than either of them knew, but how could he explain it without sounding like an ass?

"I don't have a personal stake in whether or not your fake cheer is successful in conveying the right amount of frivolous support for Magnolia as a tourist destination. But I still maintain that a Podunk town known for kitschy holiday decorations and folksy charm isn't what we want to be known for."

Carrie gaped at him. "My ideas aren't kitschy. They're homey and festive."

"Also unnecessary. I want Magnolia to become for this region of the Carolinas what Aspen or Park City are to the mountains. A premier destination for vacationers with deep pockets, people looking to get away from the rigors and stress of daily life to unwind at the soothing beach for the holidays."

"That sounds boring AF," Sam muttered.

Before Dylan could reprimand him, Carrie pointed a finger in the boy's direction. "Watch your mouth, young man. My sister can get away with talking like a sailor, but she's the only one."

Sam's gaze swung from Carrie to Dylan, who grinned at him. "Yeah, young man," Dylan agreed. "What she said."

"What I say—" Carrie stepped around the table and toward Dylan "—is stop trying to turn this town into some generic, yuppie playground."

"I don't think yuppies are a thing anymore," Dylan told her, captivated by the spark in her eyes.

"Do you mean guppies?" Sam asked. "Like the fish?"

The finger that had just put the teen in his place poked at Dylan's chest. "You know exactly what I mean. Magnolia isn't Aspen or Park City or any other trendy enclave for the rich and entitled."

"Why not?" Dylan wrapped his hand around her finger, marveling at the softness of her skin.

She drew back like he'd scalded her. "Because that's not who we are. We're a real town filled with real people."

"Who could use a real influx of revenue," Dylan countered.

"We're getting there."

Dylan leaned in closer. "I could get you there faster."

He hadn't meant the words to sound suggestive. Not with the way they couldn't seem to agree on anything and the fact that Sam was sitting a few feet behind Carrie.

But she sucked in a shallow breath and her pupils dilated, causing his body to race into overdrive. Yes, he could get her there. Fast, slow…however she liked it.

In fact, the urge to find out what turned her on now and if she'd changed from when he knew her had consumed his thoughts more often than he'd care to admit since returning to Magnolia.

"Let him volunteer for me," she said softly, pink tongue darting out to wet her lips.

Dylan's limbs felt heavy with need, and he completely lost the thread of the conversation.

"I think it will help him adjust."

Adjust.

He shook his head. Damn it. She was talking about Sam, and Dylan was caught up in a daydream of his own lascivious imagination.

"Your plans don't align with what I want to do in town," he said, trying to keep his emotions out of the conversation. Hard to do when everything involving this town and this woman made him feel things he hadn't in years.

Her gorgeous mouth turned down at the corners. "You're wrong."

"I'm never wrong."

"Dylan," she whispered, and his name on her lips took him back to another time and place. "Please."

And didn't that just about slay him?

"What do you expect from me, Carrie?"

"You committed to working on the holiday festival with me," she reminded him gently.

"So I could prove what a stupid idea it was."

"Always offering up the positivity," Sam called out sarcastically. "Gonna give Tony Robbins a run for his money."

Dylan blew out a laugh. He'd given the boy a book by the famed life coach but never dreamed the kid would read it. The fact that he had made Dylan's heart clench.

"Just give it a chance," Carrie urged. "You'll see how amazing Magnolia can be without all your plans for changing it."

"The festival plan is actually kind of cool," Sam added.

As much as Dylan wanted to say no, he couldn't deny either of them. This silly holiday event was the first thing other than his phone or video games that Sam had shown interest in since Dylan became his guardian.

Of course, Dylan still believed his plan for the town was a better choice, but not much happened in real estate and construction over the holiday season. It wouldn't hurt to postpone the start of what he wanted to do. He could line up a crew and all of the subcontractors in order to hit the ground running in January.

"Well?" Carrie prompted in that soft voice that drove him crazy.

"Fine," he told her, ignoring his body's reaction to the huge grin she gave him. "But it doesn't change my feelings about what's best for the town."

"Or the fact that you're the bad guy in this scenario," she agreed a little too readily. "Every good story needs one."

"So that they can get their butt kicked," Sam said, smoothing a hand over the paper in front of him.

"The only person who's going to do the butt kicking is me if you sneak out again." Dylan turned toward the drafting table where Sam sat. The scent of vanilla and lemon lingered in the air, as if Carrie infused every inch of this space. Of course Sam would be happier spending time with her. How could anyone resist her sweet spirit?

Tamping down that thought, Dylan leveled a hopefully parental stare at Sam. "No more leaving without a note or some communication."

"I thought you'd be happy to be rid of me for a while," the boy grumbled.

Dylan hated that the kid still saw himself as a burden, although he understood it. According to the therapist, it was normal for Sam to test Dylan's commitment. "How can I enjoy my free time if I have to worry about you?" he asked casually.

Carrie elbowed him in the ribs then seemed to relax when Dylan winked at her, and Sam only gave another eye roll.

"Just so I'm clear on the situation," the boy said, his gaze darting between the two of them. He pointed toward Carrie. "You want the festival to help put Magnolia on the map as some kind of picture-postcard getaway."

Carrie nodded. "Yes."

"Like the creepy paintings your dad did," Sam continued.

"Seriously?" Dylan asked, shaking his head.

Carrie only laughed. "I don't think *creepy* is the word I'd choose to describe them."

"Creepy for sure," Sam told her. "Like demented Norman Rockwell."

"Do you have any semblance of a filter?" Dylan demanded of the boy, even though in his heart he might agree. At first glance Niall Reed's paintings were sappy and sentimental but knowing what Dylan did about the man and the choices he made in his own life, the depiction of an idyllic outlook on American culture definitely bordered on perverse.

"I saw some of your old stuff," Sam told Carrie, ignoring Dylan. "I didn't put it together the other day when we met that you were the artist. Dylan hung it all over his properties in Boston. You were way better than your dad."

Dylan could have hugged the boy. And Carrie for that matter. She needed to hear that she had talent. He imagined he'd made her angry by buying her paintings but hadn't been able to resist.

Not only was she an amazing artist, she was also one of the best people he'd ever met. One morning spent with Carrie had prompted Sam to string more words together than he had in the past six months. Not to mention the monumental victory of the kid taking an interest in something other than video games or social media.

"Thank you," Carrie said, amusement lacing her tone. "I'm glad you don't think they're creepy."

"No ick factor," Sam confirmed then looked toward Dylan. "You don't like the cutesy vibe and want Magnolia to become some kind of snobby second coming of the Hamptons or wherever rich people want to hang out."

"Filter," Dylan repeated.

"You should talk," Carrie said with a laugh.

"Right?" Sam threw up his hands. "He's the worst. You

should hear him on the phone. My sheltered ears can barely understand half the words he says."

"Too much even for me to believe." Carrie grinned at Sam.

Dylan sighed. It was like herding cats getting these two to stay on topic. "My vision for the town is going to make it a premier destination on the East Coast."

"While sucking all the personality and charm out of it."

"Struggling to make ends meet is only charming in fairy tales," Dylan told her. "You might not realize that because you breathed such rarified air growing up."

"I did not," Carrie said through clenched teeth.

Dylan wasn't sure how he always managed to step in it with her but had to believe it was for the best. They both needed to remember they were on different sides in this situation.

Sam laughed. "Who needs the filter now?"

"If you're done stirring the pot," Dylan told him, "let's go home. You'll work with Carrie as a community service effort, and the two of you can plot to save this town from the nefarious mastermind." He pointed a finger at his chest. "Me, in this case."

"Mastermind," Carrie repeated with a laugh. "No lack of ego on this one."

Sam grinned and flipped his notebook closed. "Fine. I'm so excited for deli turkey and instant potatoes."

"I got a pie, too," Dylan said when Carrie turned to him with a grimace. "And green beans. Give me a break. The grocery was cleaned out by the time we got there."

"It doesn't matter." Sam rose from the drafting table. "You'll feel guilty and then we can watch TV while we eat."

"You could come to my sister's," Carrie said suddenly, then placed a hand over her mouth like she was as shocked to hear herself make the offer as Dylan. "No pressure but there will be plenty of food and all of it will be better than what you have."

He shook his head. "I don't think—"

"Okay," Sam agreed.

"You don't like being social," Dylan reminded the kid.

"I like eating Thanksgiving dinner." He glanced at Carrie. "Homemade mashed potatoes?"

She nodded. "That's the plan, along with a roast turkey, gravy, dressing and all the trimmings. I'm bringing the pies so I can vouch for dessert."

"If Dylan is too scared to go, I'm still in."

"I'm your family," Dylan told the boy. "We stick together on holidays."

Sam's smile vanished and Dylan realized his mistake. Way to remind the kid that he was saddled with a second-rate guardian instead of the parents and grandpa who'd loved him so well.

"Wait." Carrie held up a hand as she turned fully to Dylan. "Why would you be scared to come to Thanksgiving at Meredith's?"

"I'm not," he said automatically.

He leveled a "don't you dare" look at Sam, who offered Carrie a smile so sweet it made Dylan's teeth ache.

"I heard him on a conference call yesterday talking about the Magnolia project. He said the three harpies fighting him on the plan were terrifying in a horror movie sort of way. I don't know why he'd compare you to some oversize musical instrument."

"Great attention to detail," Dylan said under his breath as Carrie gave an incredulous gasp. "Also..." He glared at Sam. "You shouldn't have been home yesterday. If you hadn't gotten suspended, you wouldn't have been able to eavesdrop on my private conversation."

"Thank heavens he did," Carrie announced.

Dylan blinked. "You're glad he got in trouble for vandalizing the school?"

She shook her head. "I'm glad we discovered what an amazing artist Sam is and that he's willing to volunteer to help with the winter carnival." She smiled at the boy. "I'm also happy you're coming to dinner tonight." She narrowed her eyes at Dylan. "Both of you. Maybe my sisters and I will pull out our harps and do an impromptu concert."

Sam seemed to consider this. "Weird but kind of cool," he agreed finally. "Especially if the music will aggravate Dylan."

"Thanks, buddy." Dylan touched Carrie's wrist when she started to turn away. "This week was frustrating on a lot of different levels," he explained. "Maybe you could refrain from mentioning my dumbass comment to your sisters?"

"Bring a bottle of wine and be out at Last Acre for dinner at four," she said by way of an answer. "Leave the instant potatoes and store-bought pie at home. Along with the attitude."

She and Sam walked toward the front door, setting up a time to meet again the following day. Emotion welled in Dylan's throat as the surly teen smiled when she gave him a quick hug.

Dylan would hang up his attitude and just about anything else if it meant seeing Sam smile more often.

Well, anything but altering his plan for the town. That could wait. He didn't imagine that the teenager's obvious infatuation with Carrie could last indefinitely. Once Sam decided she was just like every other adult in his life—

annoying and superfluous, Dylan could return to business as usual.

He moved past her with a quiet thank-you, shock ricocheting through him when Carrie reached out and squeezed his hand.

"He's going to be okay," she said softly.

Damn if Dylan didn't want to believe her.

CHAPTER EIGHT

"ARE THERE ANY other people we hate who you invited for dinner?" Meredith asked as she opened the oven door to check the temperature sensor on the turkey later that afternoon.

Carrie took a generous sip of the white wine Avery had just poured for the three of them. "You two don't hate Dylan. I do."

"We hate him on behalf of you," Avery explained. "Hate by proxy."

"His company made an inordinately large donation to the Firefighters' Relief Fund," Gray said as he walked into the kitchen. "The chief announced it last night."

"You didn't mention that," Avery told her fiancé.

"It would have made you grumpy," Gray said with a shrug.

Avery let out a disbelieving sniff. "Heck yes, that news would have put me in a bad mood. We don't need that jerk greasing hands all over town, so people support his crappy plan."

Carrie's heart pinched as Gray wrapped his arms around Avery and kissed the side of her neck. "I had my own plans last night that hinged on you being in a good mood."

Meredith picked up a dinner roll from the baking sheet cooling on the stove and lobbed it at the couple. Gray caught it then bit off a chunk.

"This is a PG-rated event," she told him. "Enough with the sexy times talk."

"You're just jealous," Avery said playfully.

"Duh," Meredith answered, earning laughs from all of them.

Carrie took another drink of wine. She wasn't exactly jealous of Avery and Gray. They were an adorable—if unlikely—couple. She simply wanted someone to love and adore her the way Gray did her sister. Was that really too much to ask?

"Do you think he'll convince people to back him because of his deep pockets?" she asked the room in general. "What if they don't get that what he wants to do in town will change it and not in a good way? Money can have a big influence on opinions. Dad is a great example of that. He didn't always have Magnolia's best interests in mind, but everyone ignored it because of how much money he'd put into the town over the years."

"Things are different now," Meredith said as she stirred the gravy.

"I think the response from the guys at the station was more shock than anything else," Gray said as he bent down to scoop up the little dog who sat whining at his feet.

"Don't feed her," Avery warned.

"It's Thanksgiving," Gray protested. "Spot wants to celebrate."

"She can have some gravy on her kibble later," Avery conceded reluctantly. "Nothing more."

Carrie smiled as her sophisticated sister leaned in to drop a kiss on the top of the Chihuahua mix's furry head. The mutt had been one of the dogs Meredith had taken in as part of the animal rescue she coordinated from the expansive beach property she'd rented from Niall.

It baffled Carrie that he'd given Meredith an incredible deal on the property, but still never owned up to his true identity in her life. Each of the sisters had different thoughts on what they should do with the estate, although they were slowly coming to agreement on each of the separate holdings.

The land near the beach was valuable, but the farm meant the world to Meredith. Her tough and sometimes crusty exterior protected a tender heart. Carrie was committed to holding on to the buildings downtown, feeling both loyal to and a responsibility for the business owners that had depended on her dad for so many years.

The question was could she really help to turn this town into a small-town tourist mecca?

"Why do *you* think Dylan made the donation to the fire station?" Avery asked Gray, pulling Carrie from her wandering musings.

He shrugged. "I think he was making a statement about who he'd become in his time away from Magnolia. He wants to be seen as a major player, someone we should respect because he can use the resources at his disposal to our benefit. A lot of the guys remember him from when we were younger. He was a hell-raiser whose mission in life seemed to be causing chaos wherever he went. None of us thought he would amount to anything." He shot Carrie a sheepish glance. "No offense to you."

"None taken," she assured him. She was well aware of Dylan's reputation back in the day. He hadn't been like that with her, and in the naive way of teenage girls, she'd believed that made her special.

In the end, not as special as her father's bank account.

The sound of the doorbell ringing followed by a chorus of dog barks interrupted the conversation.

"They're here," she whispered, glancing first to Avery and then Meredith.

"It's nice that you invited them," Avery said.

"Yeah," Meredith agreed, coming forward and giving Carrie a quick hug. "The kid shouldn't have to eat deli turkey on Thanksgiving."

Carrie swallowed back her tumbling emotions and then moved through the house, Meredith's three dogs plus Spot circling her legs like the official welcoming committee they were.

She opened the front door, Dylan and Sam standing on the other side looking as uncomfortable as she felt. The pack of dogs tumbled out despite her best efforts to block them.

"What the hell," Dylan muttered as he stumbled back a step. Gracie, the massive German shepherd with only one ear, placed her paws on his chest and licked his chin.

"Gracie, off," Carrie commanded, secretly amused at seeing Dylan so obviously flummoxed. "Sorry," she said, even though it was a lie. "I should have warned you that Meredith's crew of animals is a little too friendly."

"Is this a zoo?" Sam asked, bending down to pet Spot as well as Marlin, the young bulldog.

Buster, the three-legged lab hopped down the steps, lifted his leg on the tire of Dylan's Porsche SUV then hobbled back toward the house.

"Epic," Sam said with a laugh at the same time Dylan groaned.

"Meredith runs an animal rescue," Carrie explained. "The three bigger dogs are the ones she's adopted permanently and the little Chihuahua belongs to Avery."

"You could have mentioned that," Dylan said tightly, and Carrie suddenly remembered that he'd never liked dogs after being bit by a neighborhood stray as a kid.

"Sorry," she said, and this time she meant it. She grabbed Gracie's collar and herded her back into the house. "Don't worry, though. They all have great temperaments and are well trained."

Dylan dusted the paw prints off the front of his navy sweater. "Clearly."

"I want a dog," Sam said as he straightened.

"You should talk to Meredith."

Dylan made a strangled sound.

"Or don't," Carrie amended. The boy rolled his eyes. He did that a lot. She supposed most teenagers were experts at eye rolling. She hadn't been, of course. She hadn't done anything to rebel or talk back, always her father's perfect daughter. What a waste of effort.

"Come on in," she said, moving back from the doorway into the foyer of the old beach house. "I'll introduce you to everyone."

Sam followed her, but Dylan hesitated. "I forgot the wine in the car," he said when she gave him a questioning look. "Sam can go with you. I'll be there in a minute."

She led the boy to the kitchen where her sisters and Gray welcomed him as if he was the honored guest. Gray's five-year-old daughter, Violet, came in through the back door with Shae Delich, the high schooler who worked at the rescue for Meredith. Shae's parents were on shift at the local hospital, so she was having Thanksgiving dinner with them before joining her mom and dad later.

"Do you like goats?" Violet asked Sam, tugging on one of her braids.

"Doesn't everyone?" he responded without hesitation, and Carrie wanted to hug the boy. Violet didn't have much of a filter and her big personality was sometimes a little much for people.

Sam glanced at Shae, and Carrie noticed a blush stain his cheeks. The girl was in tenth grade and absolutely adorable. Sam might have a penchant for trouble, but he also had good taste in girls.

"We still have some time before dinner is served," Meredith said, patting Violet's head. "You and Shae can take Sam out to the barn and introduce him to the animals."

"Sam is also interested in adopting a dog," Carrie told her sister.

"Dylan says no," the boy muttered.

"Leave that to me," Meredith assured him. "The girls can show you the dogs we have here now, and we'll talk later about what you're looking for."

"I don't think I can get one without his permission," Sam said, almost apologetically.

"I'll help convince him," Meredith promised. "Or we can have Carrie run interference for you."

The boy looked toward Carrie, who nodded despite her better judgment. "Dylan's already irritated with me. I might as well make the most of it."

Sam grinned then followed Violet and Shae out the back door.

"Irritated," Avery said with a laugh. "You basically told the guy you want to run him out of town. I'm not sure *irritated* is going to cover it if you now go to bat for Sam getting a dog."

"And yet you invited them to Thanksgiving," Meredith pointed out. "Are you sure you don't still have a thing for him?"

"That's ridiculous." Carrie glanced over her shoulder to make sure Dylan hadn't walked into the room.

"Where is he anyway?" Gray asked.

Carrie shook her head. "I'm not sure. I'll go check on him."

"Maybe hold off on mentioning the dog until after he's blissed out in a Thanksgiving food stupor," Avery suggested.

Carrie made her way to the front of the house again, a chorus line of butterflies dancing across her stomach. But Dylan was nowhere to be found.

She looked out the window of the sidelight and then opened the front door.

"Everything okay?" she asked as she stepped onto the porch.

Dylan sat on the wooden steps, a bottle of red wine at his side.

"Why did you invite me here?"

"Because Sam needed a real Thanksgiving meal and the two of you are a package deal."

He chuckled and looked up at her. "I appreciate the honesty. I wondered if you and your sisters had some plan to lock me in the basement so I can't move forward with my plan for the town."

"Or we might feed you to the rescue pigs," she suggested as she dropped down onto the step next to him.

Dylan blinked. "There are rescue pigs?"

"Meredith can't turn away an animal in need."

"Big hearts must run in the family despite your father. You couldn't help but reach out to Sam."

"That was purely selfish on my part. He's got talent and I need help with the backdrops for the carnival."

"Either way, thank you," he said softly, and the rough timbre of his voice set sparks alighting across her skin. "Sam needed this."

She nodded, understanding at some bone-deep level all the things he wasn't saying about how difficult the past year must have been for both him and the teen. "Are you coming in or should we bring out a plate of food for you to the porch?"

"I hate the holidays." He turned to her and his denim-

clad knee grazed her leg. She'd worn one of her usual comfortable dresses with ankle boots, and the thin fabric felt
like not nearly enough of a barrier between them.

"I remember," she said softly. "I hated that your mom
and dad didn't make more of an effort."

He shrugged. "Sam's parents always hosted Thanksgiving and Christmas. They did big events with people from
the office and their extended circle of friends. I'd stop by
for a drink or some food and then duck out when no one
was looking. Because you know what?"

She inclined her head.

"The holidays can bring out the worst in people. All the
crap from childhood comes up and everyone is pretending
to be happy even if they're miserable on the inside. Society has put overblown expectations on this time of year
and when no one can live up to the ideal people are pissed
about it. So now I've got this kid who's already sad—and
with good reason. I'm supposed to come up with fake cheer
and hope that's going to make things all better for him."

"What about the part that isn't fake?" she asked, shifting
closer and placing a hand on his thigh. It was a conscious
move but somehow Carrie had to get through to him, to
make him understand that there was more to Christmas
spirit than the materialistic side of things. "This time of
year is a reminder for people to do better, to care more."

He snorted.

"I'm serious," she insisted. "As corny as it sounds, sometimes we need the holidays to pull us from our normal routine. To motivate people to focus on what's good in their
lives. They can remember what they loved about this time
of year in the first place."

"News flash, Carrie. There is no ghost of Christmas past
to reminisce about the halcyon days of yore."

"Maybe not for you," she admitted. "But Sam has great memories and lots of other people do, as well. It's time you made some, for both of you. What we want to offer isn't just about getting people to shop in Magnolia, although yes, the financial aspect is part of it. We want to give them a true Christmas experience."

"You really believe that?" he said with a laugh.

"With my whole heart."

"You amaze me." He reached out to trace a finger along her jaw. "With everything you've been through you should be cynical and bitter. Your dad built his reputation of manipulating emotions and selling the promise of an ideal life that had nothing to do with his own actions."

"Don't put me on some kind of perfect pedestal," she warned. "I hate that."

He didn't smile but his eyes crinkled at the corners in a way that made her think he was amused. "*Hate* is a strong word."

"Strongly dislike," she amended.

"I don't want or expect you to be perfect. But I'm still amazed by you."

The words sent shivers cascading through her. As if he could read her unspoken response, his eyes darkened, and he leaned in so close she could feel the warmth of his breath against her mouth. She'd never admit how much she wanted him to press his lips to hers. That would be such a mistake.

Carrie had never in her life wanted to make a mistake more.

Dylan wanted to kiss Carrie so damn much it made his body ache with need. He could tell he wasn't alone in his desire because her lips parted, and her breath hitched as if in anticipation.

It would be easy to give in to the need.

Easy and stupid as hell.

He pulled back and stood, grabbing the bottle of wine with one hand and offering the other to her. "We should go in before your sisters think I'm trying to kidnap you and come out like the cavalry."

She pressed a hand to her chest as if he'd startled her.

He'd certainly shocked himself with his restraint. It wasn't something Dylan was known for in his life. He did what he wanted and said what he thought with little concern for the consequences. Being responsible for Sam had changed more than just his propensity to bring home women to his condo.

Dylan had never aspired to be anyone's role model but remained committed to doing his best for the boy. Sam liked Carrie, and for whatever reason, the kid was excited about helping with her holiday festival. It probably had something to do with thinking that making Carrie's plan a success would screw with Dylan in the end, but the reason didn't matter. Sam's happiness did.

The last thing Dylan needed was to give in to his physical longing for Carrie. He couldn't risk making her even angrier with him and shutting Sam out of the opportunity to volunteer. Not that she would take her feelings for him out on the kid. Carrie could argue until she lost her breath about not being perfect. He knew her heart and it would always be pure.

Still, he wouldn't take the chance on making things awkward. And he sure wasn't planning to examine why all of his internal rationalizing felt more like a flimsy excuse to keep his own heart safe.

After a moment, Carrie rose without his assistance. "Okay, then," she said, her tone light. "I hope you're hungry."

"You have no idea," he answered and followed her inside.

CHAPTER NINE

"WE'RE NOT taking home a dog."

Carrie hid her smile as Dylan squared off with Meredith later that evening in the barn behind the house.

Thanksgiving dinner had been filled with not only good food but also tons of laughter. Even Dylan had relaxed, recounting some of his more colorful childhood antics for the group. Sam's eyes had gone wide at hearing about the class clown side of his often-recalcitrant guardian.

At one point Carrie had laughed so hard she thought she might pee her pants. The celebration had been so different from the past few years for Carrie, when it had been just her and her father. As Niall's fame and fortune dwindled, he became more of a recluse and had insisted on Thanksgiving dinner eaten with just the two of them at the carriage house Carrie had rented from Gray.

She hadn't ever thought to question her dad's choice or suggest that they expand their holiday social circle. Only in retrospect could she see how her father had systematically cut her off from potential friends or even boyfriends with his demands and fits of temper.

If she was honest, Dylan had been the last person to make an effort to be close to her, despite her father's objections. She still questioned whether he'd initially gotten closer to her hoping for a payout from her dad or if that had come later. But she put thoughts of the old pain aside to focus on the present.

"What about a goat?" Meredith asked.

"It's a rental," Dylan countered. "They aren't going to allow goats."

"Barry Knox owns the house, right?" Carrie offered him an innocent smile. "I could give him a call if you want."

"Please," Sam begged. He sat on a low bench in the barn's center aisle. Meredith had opened the doors to several of the stalls, which had been converted into pens for her menagerie of rescued mutts.

Shae, Avery, Gray and Violet had left about thirty minutes earlier. She could tell Dylan was ready to head home, too, but Sam had insisted he visit the barn first.

An entire gang of dogs milled about, with two adorable blue heeler puppies doing their best to climb onto Sam's lap. "They're so cute," the boy said with an infectious laugh.

She watched Dylan pinch the bridge of his nose between two fingers and knew he was a lost cause. It was difficult to resist Meredith when she set her mind to coaxing a person into opening their home to one of her animals.

Carrie didn't even like animals and in the past two months she'd fostered a litter of kittens and three guinea pigs.

Meredith took a step closer to Dylan. "Dogs are good for teenagers. They teach responsibility and can help with stress."

"I'm under a ton of stress," Sam confirmed.

Dylan shook his head. "Not as much as you'll be when a puppy poops on the carpet."

Just then there was a noise from one of the closed stalls. "What's going on in there?" Dylan asked as Sam continued to pet the puppies and the other dogs played in the open space of the barn.

Meredith sighed. "I take in special cases as well and try to work with the animals to rehabilitate them enough to be adopted. You met Avery's dog, Spot. She was one of those because of her extra weight when she came in. Sometimes it's more behavioral than physical or a mix."

Carrie and Dylan moved across the barn at the same time and looked over the half door. The stall had gone quiet, and Carrie's breath caught at the sight of the scruffy dog cowering in a corner. The animal had medium-length brown fur. When the dog lowered its head, the fur hung over its eyes like the animal was trying to hide behind a curtain.

"What happened to this one?" Dylan's voice was tight with an emotion Carrie couldn't name.

Meredith joined them. "Someone found her on a property outside of Wilmington. She was severely underweight, so we have the opposite issue from Spot. I think they were tormenting her with food. It's obvious she's hungry but is often scared to eat." Meredith indicated the untouched bowl of kibble in the corner. "Eventually, she'll take a few bites, and it's getting better. But she's too nervous to be with the other dogs. The social part is going to take a lot of work and training. I'm hoping to find an experienced pet owner willing to take a chance on her."

"Do you ever think a dog is a lost cause?" Dylan's gaze never left the trembling animal as he asked the question. Her pointy ears flicked forward as if she were interested in Meredith's answer, as well.

"No," Meredith said emphatically. "It's a matter of finding the right fit for each animal."

"Sam, come over here." Dylan gestured the boy forward. "This is the dog," he said when Sam had joined them.

Meredith shook her head. "You heard me say that Daisy needs an experienced owner, right?"

"Daisy," Dylan murmured. "I like it."

"I want a puppy," Sam complained. "I'll clean up poop."

As if she could tell she was the topic of conversation, Daisy stood up and slowly moved toward the food bowl. She sniffed at it then lowered her head to take a bite.

"The puppies are adorable," Dylan agreed then glanced at Meredith. "How long will it take before they're adopted?"

"With the holidays coming up, they'll be gone as soon as I post them on the website. People love puppies."

"Of course they do," Dylan agreed. "Puppies are easy to love." He glanced back into the stall. "We'll take a chance on Daisy. Do you offer dog training?"

Meredith nodded dumbly, and it was strange for Carrie to see her confident, outspoken sister at an apparent loss for words. That was the thing about Dylan Scott. He gave one impression on the surface but then could turn around and surprise a person with his depth. It didn't shock Carrie that he wanted to take on the challenging rescue. Other than the moment when he'd accepted the bribe from her father, she'd never known him to take the easy way out of anything. He seemed to thrive on making things harder for himself than they needed to be.

Sam seemed as dumbfounded as Meredith. "You can't deal with a puppy, but you'll take some sort of reject mutt who no one else wants?"

As the boy's glare sharpened, Carrie's breath hitched. Was that how Sam saw himself? Losing his parents had made him an orphan that no one wanted and Dylan was stuck with him? It broke her heart that any child could believe that about themselves.

Although hadn't she known herself to be expendable on some level? Her parents had loved her in their own way, but their affection was so conditional and their personalities so inherently narcissistic that she'd made sure she was indispensable in all the ways she could. It sickened her to think about how much of her childhood had been spent with her stomach in knots hoping she could please her mom and dad.

"She's not a reject," Dylan said, his gentle tone somehow easing the tightness in Carrie's chest. Sam still didn't look convinced. "She's a creature who got dealt a crappy hand in life," Dylan continued. "But she still deserves love and a good home. Hell, I don't even like dogs, and I can see her potential."

The boy's lips twitched at that.

"Let's try it, Sam. We might not know what we're doing or be experts or have all the answers, but I bet with some help we can figure out how to love her."

Carrie swallowed back tears as Meredith reached out and gripped her wrist.

Sam turned away, swiping his sleeve across his cheeks then looked back at Dylan. "Okay," he whispered. "But you're scooping the poop."

"We'll thumb wrestle for poop duty," Dylan offered then reached out and ruffled the boy's shaggy hair. "What do you think?" he asked, turning to face Meredith. "Can you trust us with her?"

Meredith took so long to answer, Carrie thought she might actually deny them the chance to adopt Daisy. Finally, she nodded and pointed at Dylan. "I'm still not convinced you're a good bet. But Sam has a way with dogs. I have a feeling Daisy will thrive with him."

Carrie knew that Meredith valued the lives of her rescues more than anything, so she wouldn't agree if she didn't truly believe they could handle it.

"Then it looks like we've got a dog," Dylan said.

"I'll gather the adoption papers and a starter pack of

supplies." Meredith gestured to Sam. "Why don't you help, and we can go over some of the transition instructions for a shy pup?"

A slow smile spread across Sam's face and he glanced at Dylan. "You're serious?"

"Crazy," Dylan answered with a smile. "But serious."

"Yes." The boy pumped his fist and then looked over into the stall again. "Don't you worry, Daisy. You've got a home now and you'll never have to be alone again."

Carrie let out a small noise and looked at Meredith, who was blinking rapidly as if she was trying to not cry. "Happy Thanksgiving, indeed," her sister murmured then led the boy down the aisle toward the office at the far end of the barn.

"I blame you for all of this," Dylan said with a laugh as Carrie joined him in front of the stall. The dog had eaten a few bites of food and then lay down next to the bowl, chin resting on her front paws.

"How did you decide it's my fault?" Carrie asked.

"You invited us to Thanksgiving dinner. If we'd stuck with the instant potatoes Sam never would have gotten the opportunity to finagle me into a dog."

"Don't forget I know you, Dylan. You can make everyone else believe you're the classic villain with a troubled past and an ax to grind now that you're back. It would be easier if I could believe that's all there is to it. But I know you have a heart under your hard exterior." Unable to help herself, Carrie rose on tiptoes and kissed his cheek. Her heart was just so full. "You did a good thing for Sam tonight."

Before she had a chance to step away, Dylan turned to her, cupping her cheeks between his palms. "It doesn't mean anything," he said and pressed his mouth to hers.

The kiss was like a homecoming. It felt as if she was

finding her way back to the one place she'd always belonged. Not true, of course. She wasn't a naive teenager anymore who would read into a physical connection to believe it meant more.

But she could still enjoy the moment. His lips soft on hers and the lingering taste of sugar and vanilla from dessert. He held her face as if she was the most precious thing in the world to him. God help her, she wanted that to be true.

The sound of a soft whine had her pulling away. A glance into the stall showed Daisy sitting up straight, head cocked to one side like she was trying to figure out what she was witnessing. Maybe the dog could help Carrie understand, as well.

"That can't happen again." She pressed two fingers to her lips. It felt as if Dylan had branded her, her skin marked by his touch. She hoped her heart wasn't, as well.

"Agreed," he said, and she noticed that his chest rose and fell in uneven breaths.

At least she wasn't the only one affected by the kiss.

"I don't even like you." Whether she was reminding him or herself remained unclear.

"With good reason," he confirmed. Her heart sank. Of course he wasn't going to fight her opinion of him. He seemed to revel in their opposing goals and allowing her to think the worst of him.

"I'm going to go back to the house," she said. "You and Sam will be here awhile with Meredith."

He opened his mouth and for a second she thought he might argue with her. He might ask her to stay. She'd never admit to either of them how much she wanted to be here.

But he gave a sharp nod and turned his attention back to the dog. A clear message if Carrie'd ever received one.

She walked back to the house, crossing her arms over

her chest and rubbing her arms as if to ward off a chill. The temperature outside had only dropped a few degrees but she felt cold all the way to her soul.

DYLAN TURNED THE corner onto his street Sunday morning to see a now familiar red jacket on the front porch of his rental house.

His heart seemed to skip a beat and Daisy let out a soft whine next to him. "My thoughts exactly," he told the dog only to have her plop her butt onto the sidewalk at the sound of his voice.

He tugged on the leash, but the animal didn't budge. She'd made it farther on the walk this morning than on any of her other outings on the leash. Per Meredith's instructions, they were going the slow and steady route on Daisy's training, using treats and positive reinforcement as their main techniques. Pulling a treat from his pocket, Dylan tried to lure the dog forward. Daisy sniffed at the small biscuit but didn't move.

"You win again," he muttered and bent down to scoop the dog into his arms. Daisy didn't think much of the leash and had trouble settling in the house, but they'd quickly found that she was forty pounds of lap dog. As bizarre as it sounded, she actually seemed to like being carried around and would climb into Sam's lap whenever he sat on the floor or sneak her way onto a couch or bed at every opportunity. The dog relaxed against him, her snout resting on his shoulder.

"Is that an official training method?" Carrie asked with a laugh as he approached the house.

"Yeah. The dog is training me to be her Sherpa."

"I'm not sure Meredith would approve."

"Then let's not mention it to her," he answered with an exaggerated wink.

Daisy lifted her head to take in Carrie then settled against Dylan more snugly. He cringed when Carrie pulled out her phone and snapped a picture.

"I couldn't resist," she said. "That's pretty darn adorable."

"Pathetic is more like it. I don't think anyone's ever called me *adorable*."

"Well, you are when you're holding Daisy like a baby." She held up a bag. "I brought a new dog gift."

He raised a brow, gratified when color flooded her cheeks.

"I also want to talk to you about plans for the festival," she added quickly. "You and Sam weren't at any of the holiday kick-off events this weekend."

"Busy with the dog," he muttered, the lightness in his chest deflating like an old balloon. He opened the front door to the house and gestured Carrie inside. It was strange to be back in a town where he didn't worry about locking his door. In Boston his downtown condo had been in a secure building with a doorman and a state-of-the-art alarm system.

In Magnolia his biggest concern was curious neighbors taking too much interest in his life. Even now, he saw the curtains flutter in Mrs. Grady's bay window across the street. He could imagine the gossip train firing up that Carrie Reed had stopped by for a visit.

He followed her into the house and walked over to deposit Daisy on the dog bed he'd placed next to the sofa in the living room. The animal licked his hand like she was saying thank you and his heart melted a little. Dogs had always seemed like a nuisance.

So had kids and now he had one of each.

"How is she settling in?" Carrie asked, glancing around the house.

"The dog is fine. And it came fully furnished," he told her when her eyes went wide.

The interior was a mix of traditional antique wood pieces and overstuffed sofas and chairs.

"Trust me, I'm not here to judge." She ran a finger along the edge of a porcelain basin that held a bouquet of dusty dried flowers. "It's taken me months to clean out my father's house and I still can't figure out how he managed to accumulate so much. This place is old, but at least you can walk through it without tripping over piles of old magazines."

"Your dad became a hoarder?" He led her down the hall and into the small galley kitchen. After washing his hands, Dylan pulled two glasses out of an upper cabinet for water.

"I don't like to use that word," she admitted, "but yes."

"Are you selling the house?"

She shrugged. "Not until the estate is out of probate, but none of us feel emotionally tied to the property."

As he handed her the water, she gave him the gift bag. He set it on the counter. "I don't believe you aren't attached to that house. It's the place where you grew up."

"And now represents everything that was a lie about my childhood. I'd moved out a few years ago when I needed my own space."

"Niall couldn't have liked that."

She smiled but pain shadowed her gaze. "He understood."

Dylan wanted to call bull on her words but what was the point? He didn't need to point out what a jerk her dad had been. She had plenty of examples of that. In the weeks and months after he'd left Magnolia, nursing his broken heart, he'd told himself it was for the best. That Carrie had been a spoiled princess who would never give up her privileged life.

Even in his angriest moments, he'd known he was just trying to rationalize his decision to walk away.

"Thanks for the dog-warming gift," he said, digging through the tissue paper to pull out a chew toy, a Frisbee and a box of gourmet treats.

"Meredith told me what to buy."

"Then thanks to you both."

She took a small step closer. "Why didn't you come this weekend? Don't tell me it was about the dog. She doesn't seem that high maintenance."

"Looks can be deceiving." He busied himself with examining the plastic disk but could feel Carrie's gaze on him. "It's not a big deal. You know I don't like the holidays. What would have been the point of me being at a tree lighting or sipping hot cocoa in the town square? I don't need more people trying to convince me to change the plans for my properties."

"But you agreed to help with the festival. This weekend would have shown you its potential. The crowds at the tree lighting were the biggest ever. Everyone had a great time."

"I don't care."

"Why? Il Rigatone served over two hundred cheesy breadsticks. It's a great restaurant, Dylan. You need to understand that Magnolia doesn't need to be burned to the ground and rebuilt from scratch. Yes, the town relied on my father's reputation and kowtowed to his whims for too long. But we're changing that."

"I'm going to change things," he argued, forcing himself not to react to the disappointment in her eyes. "We're going to put this place on the map."

"For all the wrong reasons."

"As an upscale destination. How is that wrong?"

"Because it's already a great place to live and visit."

"How would you know whether it is or not?" he demanded, running a hand through his hair. "You haven't lived anywhere else. Remember when we had dreams to see the world together? You've been stuck here for too long to have any perspective beyond your provincial life."

He swallowed back a groan when her breath caught. "I'm not provincial," she said quietly.

"I didn't mean to hurt your feelings."

Her shoulders stiffened. "You no longer have the power to hurt me," she told him and, once again, his body reacted to her show of strength. He just wished when she took a stand it didn't have to be against him.

"Christmas is all about fake community spirit. I'm not interested in selling tourists a false sense of joy. That was Niall's domain. I deliver real-life dreams."

He could almost feel the tension bristling from her. "Then why agree to help with the festival?"

"The mayor volunteered me."

"You know even rich people like Christmas?" She threw up her hands. "It's not as if you can abolish the season from town."

"But I don't have to buy into all the phony fa-la-la-ing."

"It isn't phony," she insisted. "The holiday spirit is real, especially in Magnolia. Even Sam can see that."

"Don't bring him into it." Dylan glanced up at the ceiling. The boy's bedroom was directly above the kitchen.

"Sam has agreed to help me," Carrie reminded him through clenched teeth. "We're all supposed to work together. It could be good for the two of you. Bring you closer."

"I got a dog. I've scooped all the poop so far. Isn't that enough?"

A chuckle burst from her mouth, surprising them both, and he smiled in response. He loved hearing her laughter, even if it was at his expense.

"I'll be at the high school tomorrow afternoon," she said after a moment. "There are a few other kids from the art department helping with backdrops for the festival. I hope Sam will join us. You should come, too."

"You're really dedicated to this idea of a perfect holiday town."

"I'm dedicated to helping Magnolia succeed."

"What about your own success?" He heard water running from upstairs and knew Sam would join them shortly. But he needed to press Carrie on this.

"I get a lot of satisfaction from working for the greater good."

"Maybe you haven't changed as much as I thought," he said casually.

"What's that supposed to mean?" Her sea-green eyes narrowed.

"Sam told you the paintings I bought now hang in the buildings I own in Boston. They're good, Carrie. Better than good. But they're also from a decade ago. What are you painting now?"

"I'm kind of busy trying to save the town and all that," she muttered. "I'm still painting. The work is just…"

"Don't talk to me about the frivolous art you do during the painting parties. Those are fine for regular people who just want to dabble in art or feel like they've created something fun with friends. You have actual talent."

She stared at him for a long moment then glanced away, her breath hitching. He knew he'd struck a nerve. She'd always been sensitive about her ability. Another strike against Niall Reed in Dylan's opinion. What kind of father dismissed his daughter's talent because he knew it would eclipse his own?

Parents were supposed to build their kids up, not tear them down. Although he knew there were plenty of parents who did just the opposite. His mom and dad fell into that category. Although they hadn't so much torn him down as they'd made it clear from the start, he had little to offer and it wasn't worth trying. When the expectations on a kid were so low as to almost scrape the ground, he got used to clawing his way from the bottom of the pack.

But Dylan wasn't the same as Carrie. Yes, he'd gotten out of Magnolia and made a success of himself, thanks in large part to the chance his uncle had given him and the support of his cousin. Anyone could figure out a way to make money. Carrie made the world more beautiful with her paintings. Hell, just with her presence.

He didn't care about her holiday festival, but he couldn't stand to see her continuously putting herself on the back burner in life to take care of others. She'd done it for years with her dad and now this town she loved so much seemed to be her new excuse for not pursuing her dreams.

"I didn't come here to discuss my life," she said, twin spots of color flaming on her cheeks. Yep, he'd struck a nerve.

"Where's Daisy?" Sam asked as he padded into the kitchen. "Hey, Carrie."

A low bark sounded from the living room.

"Hi, Sam." Dylan watched Carrie work to settle her emotions. He had a real talent for bothering her, but part of him didn't feel bad. Someone needed to push her out of her comfort zone.

He shook his head, thinking of all the ways he wanted to force Carrie to go after what she truly wanted. Obviously, no chance of that happening since her teeth seemed to be perpetually grinding every time they were together.

The dog appeared at the doorway to the kitchen. She glanced at Sam with a whine but didn't move farther into the room.

"Hey, girl."

Dylan's breath hitched at the love in the boy's tone. Sam moved forward then dropped to the ground next to her. One weekend with the quirky pup and Sam was smitten.

"I don't think she likes me infringing on her territory," Carrie said quietly. "Sam, I'm looking forward to seeing you after school tomorrow to begin work on the festival backdrops."

"Okay," the boy answered without hesitation. "I've been looking online for ideas, so I'll bring my sketchbook with me."

Carrie's grin seemed to light up the room. Plus, between the dog and his excitement over being involved in Carrie's silly holiday project, Sam seemed happier than Dylan had seen him since the accident. It was almost too much for Dylan's stony heart to handle.

"You don't have to leave," Dylan told her, not wanting the moment to end. "Daisy will get used to you. I'm going to make some breakfast and—"

"I need to go," she interrupted, her smile fading.

"Can I take Daisy in the backyard?" Sam asked.

"Sure," Dylan murmured absently, studying Carrie, whose gaze had lowered to the floor.

"Come on, Daisy," Sam coaxed, beckoning the dog to him. "Your ball is on the patio."

The dog flicked a glance toward Carrie and, deeming her not a threat, followed Sam through the kitchen to the door that led to the backyard.

As soon as the duo had disappeared, Carrie started for the front of the house like she had an urgent need to put some distance between herself and Dylan.

No doubt she had a lot of smart reasons, but he wasn't having them. He caught up to her in the hall, whispering her name but forcing himself not to reach for her. The choice to stay had to be hers.

Suddenly, she whirled and stepped toward him, wrapping her arms around his neck like he was a lifeline.

A million questions swam through his mind, but he didn't ask a single one. Instead, he fused his mouth to hers, savoring the taste of her and the heat radiating between them. She kissed him like she was trying to make up for years apart, and although he didn't understand the reason for it, Dylan was smart enough to go with the moment.

He hated the weakness it showed in him, but he knew deep in his soul that he'd take whatever this woman was willing to give him.

But as abruptly as the kiss had started, she pulled away.

"Sorry," she said, her breath coming out in tiny gasps. "I shouldn't have—"

"Never apologize for that," he told her, tracing his thumb across the seam of her lips.

Her eyes drifted closed for a moment as if she was rebuilding her defenses. "I need to go," she repeated, then turned and walked out of his house.

As the door clicked shut behind her, Dylan knew that nothing about returning to Magnolia was going to be as straightforward as he'd imagined.

CHAPTER TEN

WEDNESDAY MORNING DYLAN walked by Sunnyside Bakery on his way to the makeshift office he'd set up in one of the empty storefronts he owned in downtown.

The scent of cinnamon and sugary dough wafted from the cheery shop. He considered taking a risk and walking in for a sticky bun and a coffee. Maybe he'd get lucky and Mary Ellen Winkler wouldn't be around, and he could sneak in an order and be gone before she had a chance to kick him out again.

How sad that he was willing to risk his pride for a pastry, but damn did she make the best.

"Don't bother," a voice said behind him.

He turned to find Carrie's sister Avery standing on the sidewalk holding a brown bag he could only imagine was filled with the bakery's delicacies. "Mary Ellen is behind the counter this morning. She'll boot you to the curb without a second thought."

"I wasn't planning on going in," he lied. "Her quality has gone way down so it's not worth it."

Avery studied him for a moment then reached in the bag and pulled out a scone. "I'm bringing breakfast to a meeting at the mayor's office," she reported. "I ordered extra if you want one."

His fingers flexed at his sides as she moved closer. "I mostly eat low-carb anyway," he told her.

"It's blueberry." Her lips twitched as if she could see his inner turmoil. "Just take the stupid pastry. Not everything has to be a battle."

He wished that were true, but life had taught him a different lesson. Still, he took the scone from her with a heartfelt thank-you and bit into it. "How does she make everything so damn good?"

Avery grinned, her blond hair almost shimmering in the morning sunshine. "I think she uses unicorn tears in all the recipes."

He paused in his chewing then huffed out a laugh. "Tell me you didn't spit on this one or poison it before handing it over."

"Tempting," she admitted, "but no. Aren't you attending the meeting? The agenda is mostly about Santa at the Shore."

He shook his head but fell in step next to her. His office was on the corner across from the town hall, so they were going in the same direction. "I have real work to do. My architect sent the initial plans for the restaurants and shops on my side of the street. If we're going to open by—"

"You have a restaurant on your side of the street."

"A mom and pop Italian joint isn't the look I'm going for."

"It fits with Magnolia. I don't understand. You grew up here. How can you not see how special this town is? You need to honor the character we have here, not scorch-earth it in order to build the ubiquitous yuppie playground other towns already have."

"No one but you and your sister use the word *yuppie* anymore," he pointed out and then popped the last bite of scone into his mouth.

"Not the point." She let out a frustrated growl.

"Why do you even care? You're new to this town. With what I'm doing, the property you own will increase in value. You, Meredith and Carrie will be able to actually make some money if you sell. And the land out at the beach is going to be worth a fortune by the time I'm done."

"This is my home," Avery argued. "I may not have been here a long time, but Magnolia is important to me. And the town means everything to Carrie. You cared about her once. How can you destroy something so important to her?"

They'd come to the corner where his building sat. Magnolia's town hall was across the street, a stately brick two-story that had been built in the middle of the last century. He knew the first floor of the building had been turned into a makeshift community center and wondered if he could convince the town council to sell the property if he built them a state-of-the-art facility in another part of town. The town hall's location would make it a perfect second phase of his plan to rebrand downtown.

"I don't believe it's important to her," he told Avery, still thinking of options for the historic building in front of him. He snapped to attention when Avery swatted him on the arm. Hard. "Hey," he complained. "What was that for?"

"Not important to her?" she demanded. "Are you joking? Carrie has dedicated most of her life to this town."

"She's hiding behind her reputation as a do-gooder."

Avery scoffed. "That's rude. No wonder you get under her skin so badly."

"I'm not being rude. You're underestimating her or at least allowing her to do that to herself."

"What do you mean?" She turned to fully face him. "I love Carrie. She's one of the kindest people I've ever met, and kind isn't usually a big draw for me. But she's different."

"And also hugely talented," Dylan pointed out.

"You bought her paintings from the gallery show out of spite."

"I don't spend thousands of dollars on art because of a grudge. I purchased those paintings because they're good. The way she uses light and shadow to elicit emotion is special."

Avery stared at him for a long moment. "You're right," she said finally.

"I know." He blew out a breath. "She shouldn't be wasting her time heading up small-town festivals or giving painting lessons to book clubs or bunco groups or whatever other foolish customers she has in the studio."

"Paying the mortgage isn't wasting time," Avery countered.

"Then sell your property to me. I offered to lease the empty building, but I'll buy the whole damn block."

"And tear everything down?"

"And make it better."

Avery's blue eyes narrowed.

"Did you just growl at me?" Dylan asked with a laugh.

"I thought Gray was irritating as all get out when we first met, but you have him beat by a mile."

Dylan winked. "I like Gray, so I'll take that as a compliment."

She rolled her eyes then her gaze turned thoughtful. "Carrie has a deep commitment to seeing the town get back on its feet."

"She's not responsible for the damage Niall did."

"I know," Avery agreed. "But good luck convincing her. You aren't going to stop her from working on Merry Magnolia. But Meredith and I will try to get her to focus on her own art. There was a gallery owner from New York City who contacted her after the paper in Raleigh did a write-up on her. I doubt she followed up with him."

"That would be a good start." Dylan nodded. "I wish she could see herself the way the rest of us do." He startled when Avery smacked him on the arm again. "Seriously, you have a problem with physical violence. What was that for?"

"Now I'm annoyed because you've got her best interests at heart. I want to loathe you outright but that makes it difficult."

"Carrie can tell you I'm a difficult person to hate even when you should."

"Are you sure I can't convince you to come to the meeting?" She lifted the brown bag higher. "I might have a donut with your name on it."

"I do like a decent bribe," he said with a smile then immediately shook his head when Avery's gaze darkened. He knew Carrie must have shared with her sisters the fact that Niall had given him a check to break up with her. She still didn't know the truth of why he'd really left town, and he couldn't share it. "I didn't mean it like that."

"I should go," she said quickly. "Thanks for the reminder to make sure Carrie takes care of herself as well as everyone else."

"She's got too big of a heart for her own good."

"But now she has sisters to help protect it."

"I'm glad for that." He nodded and turned away, walking into his cold and drafty building. The temperature outside hovered near sixty with the sun shining overhead. But in this dank and dreary space, unused for years, it felt like perpetual winter. It suited Dylan's mood just fine.

LATER THAT AFTERNOON Carrie stepped back to admire the mural Sam had just finished that would hang at the entrance of the roller rink. They'd gone with a winter wonderland theme, and Sam had painted a backdrop that gave the impression of entering a Bavarian ski village, complete with a sledding hill, skiers on a gondola and groups of snowboarders carving tracks down a mountain.

"It's so cool," she told the boy, marveling at what he was able to do in such a short amount of time. They were in the main art room at the high school, which had been transformed into a kind of Santa's workshop of festival decorations. Holiday music played from the speaker she'd connected to her phone, and it felt like a scene out of some classic Christmas movie.

The other students had gone home, but Sam continued to work even when she'd assured him they were ahead of where they needed to be to have everything ready for the central weekends of the festival. Although much of the town was already decorated in holiday finery, Carrie planned to kick up the Christmas cheer at least a dozen notches. Every day she added more lights to the displays around town and continued to receive orders of life-size decorations from online stores around the country. The town was nearly overflowing with cheer.

Avery had done an amazing job with the marketing campaign, building on the momentum they had from the fall season. Carrie had checked in with the hotel owners and all of them were near or at capacity over the next two weekends. It seemed that the Merry Magnolia activities resonated with folks from up and down the Atlantic coast. They had the chance to create something really special and make Magnolia a premier boutique vacation destination.

She couldn't help but wonder what her dad would have thought about all of this. Much of the spirit of what she wanted for the town emulated the images of American culture he'd portrayed in his paintings. Niall had always wanted the main focus in town to be him and not his work. He liked the fame, craved the recognition and people pandering to his whims.

Carrie wanted to create an event that would stand on its own within the town. Tourists who visited for the holiday would come back again throughout the year to experience the small-town charm with its homey shops, comfortable hotels and unique restaurants. Once the initial framework was solid, anyone could run the tourism campaigns and activities for each year.

She had detailed timelines and steps in a folder on her computer and had kept copious notes in the binder she carried almost everywhere. Her efficiency might make her presence obsolete in coming years. She gasped as she realized she was organizing herself out of her role in town.

Was that the plan? Get Magnolia back on track from some of the damage her father had done and then finally go live a little herself? Not that she didn't love her life here. But ever since Dylan had mentioned that she needed to pay attention to her own work, the thought had niggled in the back of her mind. What had she been missing? What new adventures might await her if she was willing to grasp them?

"Does it ever snow in Magnolia?" Sam asked, breaking into her thoughts.

"Very rarely," Dylan said.

Carrie turned as he walked into the room. He wore dark pants and an olive-colored shirt, looking both professional and a little rugged. "Not true," she argued. "It snows sometimes. Plus, don't you remember that one winter when we had the blizzard?"

"Four inches of snow isn't a blizzard."

"I like snow," Sam said, dotting flakes onto the night sky

of the backdrop. "My dad used to complain about shoveling all the time."

"Boston gets a lot of snow," she murmured, giving Dylan a look when his expression turned stony. She understood it might be difficult to hear reminders of the boy's parents but believed it was good for both Dylan and Sam to be able to talk freely about the loved ones they lost. "I bet you built a lot of snowmen."

"Yeah," the teenager agreed, his focus still on the mural. "One time we got close to two feet and school was called off for three days. Me and my friends made a whole snowman army."

"That's awesome." She shot a pointed smile at Dylan. "What do you think of Sam's work?"

"It's great. Very festive and all that. We need to get going."

She could almost see Sam's eyes rolling, but he continued to add details to the scene.

"Have you been to the beach, Sam?" she asked as she began to put away the art supplies. "Not really an opportunity for building snowmen around here, but sandcastles are a year-round activity." She held out a caddy of paint supplies. "These go in the cupboard on the far wall."

Sam turned to face her. "Are we close to the ocean here?"

"Of course," she said. "That's why the festival is called Santa at the Shore. The beach is really close when you're out at Meredith's farm. I'm surprised you couldn't smell it in the air. You can walk from Last Acre, but there's plenty of parking right at the public beach, too. No crowds at this time of year." She glanced at Dylan. "You haven't taken him to Magnolia Beach?"

"It's the first week of December," Dylan answered with a shrug. "Why would we go out there?"

"Because it's still beautiful and fun to walk along the shore."

"It's windy and the water's cold," he countered.

"I'd like to go," Sam offered.

Dylan's mouth opened then shut again. "Okay, sure. Let's go to the beach this weekend before the festival. Carrie will come with us, so I don't miss all the beauty."

Nerves zinged along her spine at the teasing quality in his tone. She wanted to refuse because spending time with Sam was one thing but adding Dylan into the mix changed the whole equation. "Sure," she answered instead, mimicking Dylan's answer.

Sam nodded like it was no big deal that she'd been invited and agreed to join them. He took his brushes to the sink.

"I like the way you varied the brush strokes," Dylan said suddenly, stepping forward. "It really makes the stars in the sky pop and the Christmas trees look real."

Sam went stock-still for a moment. Carrie could see the boy digesting Dylan's words, trying to decide if there was a veiled criticism somewhere in them that he was missing. "Thanks," he muttered, sounding almost breathless. "It's sort of decent."

"I called the school counselor today," Dylan told him, "to see about adding an art class to your schedule for the second semester. She said Intro to Drawing is available the period you have study hall if you're interested."

Carrie squeezed together her hands, resisting the urge to clap. Happiness flooded her chest at the thought of Dylan helping Sam pursue his art.

"That'd be fine, I guess," Sam said with a shrug. His tone might be casual but the twin splotches of color on his cheeks showed how moved he was by Dylan's gesture.

She hadn't talked to him about the comment he'd made that his dad hadn't supported his art but understood what it meant. She knew it could destroy his confidence or push him away from something that could help him in the process of healing.

"You can leave your brushes soaking," she said. "I'll take care of them. I appreciate the extra help today, Sam."

"It was fun." The boy glanced around the studio. "I must have left my backpack in my locker."

"The hallway with the freshmen lockers should still be open because of basketball practice. You can go through the door by the gym."

"I'll meet you out front at the car," Dylan told Sam.

The boy nodded and disappeared out of the room, the door clicking shut behind him.

"He really does have talent," Carrie said, hugging her arms around her waist. "Have Yourself a Merry Little Christmas" played softly in the background. With the murals and the twinkling lights she'd strung around the perimeter, it felt as though she and Dylan were in a curious holiday escape.

"I can't believe I haven't taken him to the beach." Dylan ran a hand through his hair. "I don't ask him about memories from his childhood because it's too difficult. I still barely know how to interact with him." He laughed without humor. "A few hours working with you after school and he already seems happier than he has since I can remember. It just shows how ill equipped I am for taking care of him."

"Don't compare the two." She stepped closer, unable to resist comforting him when he was so obviously trying to hide his distress over the situation. "What I'm doing with him is an easy diversion. You've got all the hard stuff.

You're trying, Dylan, and not taking the easy way out. Give yourself a break."

"I can't," he whispered, sounding miserable. "I'm so damn afraid of failing him."

She pressed her palm to his cheek, the rough stubble along his jaw tickling her skin. She heard his sigh and felt the gentle easing of some of his tension as he relaxed into her touch.

When he reached for her, gripping her waist and pulling her closer, she went without hesitation. Every cell in her body seemed to awaken at his touch.

It was difficult to know whether he kissed her or she initiated it. Their mouths joined as if pulled by the same invisible force.

The kiss started slowly but quickly ramped up in need and intensity. She'd never not wanted more with Dylan. More heat and closeness.

He lifted her into his arms, his strength enveloping her. He moved forward until her bottom hit the edge of the worktable. Markers and pencils skittered to the floor as he lifted her onto the hard surface. She threaded her fingers through his hair. Her body buzzed with need.

She'd been completely inexperienced when she and Dylan had first dated, a sheltered high school senior overwhelmed by what he made her feel. She'd dated since then, nothing serious and nothing that came anywhere near the level of her feelings for him.

But she at least understood how special it had been. She was suddenly grateful for the table because her knees might have given way under the force of her desire. His mouth trailed along her jaw, down her neck to the sensitive nook at the base of her throat.

She tried to hold back a whimper, tried not to think about

ripping off his clothes right there. Anyone could walk in and he needed to get to the car for Sam.

But still she shifted, pressing her palms to the table-top for support so she wouldn't melt into a puddle of lust. And then—

"Tell me that's not your idea of mood music."

Carrie realized the sound of Judy Garland's crooning about making the yuletide bright had gotten progressively louder until she could barely hear Dylan over the song.

Moving her hip, she realized she'd put her weight on her phone, inadvertently adjusting the volume to its highest setting. The Bluetooth speaker at the edge of the table practically vibrated with the chorus.

Stifling a laugh, she quickly turned down the sound. Silence filled the space, and heat colored her cheeks.

When she glanced up, Dylan was staring at her with an unreadable expression.

"Oops," she whispered and they both gave in to the temptation to laugh.

"I hated holiday music before this moment," he told her. "Now I'm worried that for the rest of my life the sound is going to turn me hot and bothered."

Her grin widened. "You're hot and bothered?"

"In all the best ways," he confirmed, leaning in for another quick kiss.

That was both gratifying and dangerous, just like everything seemed to be with this man. She couldn't deny that she wanted him to want her, but her own desire made her feel too exposed. After her dad died, Carrie promised herself she'd never let any man derail her life in favor of their own goals. She'd wasted too much time subjugating herself for her father and his needs and his art.

She wanted to believe she could be strong, but what

would happen if she allowed herself to fall for Dylan again? What if he asked her to put aside her plans for the town in order to support his?

Would she be strong enough to say no if her heart told her to give in?

"You're thinking too hard right now." Dylan traced his finger along the worry line between her eyes.

"Why did you invite me to go to the beach with you?" she asked, pushing him away. She bent to pick up the discarded supplies that had fallen to the floor.

Dylan drew back his hand and shrugged. "I thought you'd have fun."

"Dylan."

"You're good with Sam. It's rough for him sometimes with just me. I'm not the best at making things fun. He relaxes around you."

"He'd relax if you did," she said quietly.

"Probably," he agreed, surprising her.

This new Dylan was just full of surprises.

"I'm still not sorry I kissed you," he said suddenly. "I don't care if you consider me an enemy. I like kissing you, Carrie."

She straightened, holding a wad of pencils in her fist in front of her body like a sword. "The kissing's okay," she muttered.

He threw back his head and laughed. "If I didn't have to meet Sam, I'd take great pleasure in wiping that lie from your lips."

"He's going to beat you to the car if you don't go now."

"Then I'll take a rain check." He leaned in closer. "Keep that in mind, sweetheart."

A quiver raced through Carrie as he turned and walked away. She would have liked to toss off some great comeback but wasn't sure she had enough control of her mouth to even form words at that point.

Instead, she hit Play on her phone and continued to clean up the art room to the sounds of her favorite Christmas songs. The most wonderful time of the year indeed.

CHAPTER ELEVEN

"SHE'S GOING TO kick you out," Dylan said as he pulled his Porsche into an angled parking space in front of Sunnyside Bakery Saturday morning. "The donuts at the gas station near the water tower aren't horrible."

"Are you nuts?" Sam smoothed a hand over his hair. "Those taste like a dog turd in comparison to Mrs. Winkler's."

Daisy perked up from the backseat at the word *dog*. Dylan couldn't believe he'd allowed the shedding, drooling animal on his premium leather. Daisy lifted a paw and scratched it against the console, silently asking to be invited into one of their laps.

"You know I paid extra for the interior upgrade," he told Sam.

"Daisy likes it," the boy answered with a grin. "I'll get you a biscuit, girl."

"Don't say I didn't warn you," Dylan called to the boy as he exited the car.

They were meeting Carrie at the beach, and Sam had insisted they stop by Sunnyside for pastries to bring with them.

Secretly, Dylan hoped that Mary Ellen Winkler either wasn't at the shop that morning or didn't realize his connection to Sam. He really could use a sticky bun.

The dog whined as Sam disappeared into the shop. "He'll be back," Dylan told her, then placed his arm as a barrier between the seats to prevent Daisy from hopping into the front.

The dog remained skittish with random noises and new people when they went on walks, but she'd bonded with Sam like she'd imprinted on him.

Every night Daisy curled up at the end of Sam's bed, and Dylan had to admit it tugged on heartstrings he hadn't even realized he possessed to see how happy the dog made Sam. So much that he hadn't even minded Meredith's gleeful gloating when she'd come by to check on Daisy's adjustment. Of course, that hadn't made him take on the stray cat she'd tried to convince him to foster. Not yet anyway.

A knock on the window and Daisy's ensuing clamor had him jumping in his seat.

He rolled down the window to glare at the old man grinning at him. "Damn, Skeeter. Why would you sneak up on me like that?"

Skeeter McIntire adjusted his ever-present wad of chew from one cheek to the other, spit out a disgusting stream of brown liquid then leaned in. "You gotta be on your toes, Scott. I thought yer daddy taught you that lesson."

"We both know he did," Dylan muttered. His father hadn't exactly been what Dylan would have considered abusive, but he also hadn't been shy about pulling off his belt for a teachable moment. He and Skeeter had worked together at the textile factory throughout most of Dylan's childhood until the layoffs started. After that they'd spent a lot of time airing their grievances about the unfairness of life over cans of cheap beer. "But he's not here anymore."

"God rest his soul." Skeeter touched his gnarled fingers to his chest. "How's your mama doing?"

"Fine, I guess." Dylan hadn't heard from or reached out to his mother in months. He'd send her a fruit basket and a hefty check for Christmas, and she'd call from Florida to chide him for not visiting then they'd go about their separate lives until the following year. It was a relationship dynamic that seemed to work for them both.

"I've been lookin' for you at Murphy's. Tommy and the boys are ready to buy the first round."

"I'm taking care of my cousin's boy right now," Dylan answered noncommittally. "Doesn't leave a lot of time for a social life."

"Kid don't sleep?" Skeeter asked with a laugh. "Bar stays open till one most nights."

"I'll remember that."

Skeeter's gaze sharpened. "I heard you bought the factory."

Dylan's mouth went dry, but he kept his expression steady. "Yeah."

"That place was a thorn in the side to me and your dad."

"I know."

"It's also a big part of this town's history." Skeeter ran a hand through his thinning hair. "Someone told me that Reed girl wants to turn the place into a community center."

"Is that so?" Dylan's heart began to hammer in his chest.

The old man shrugged. "Article said it would make a big difference for people. Kind of a new lease sort of thing. Way better than ritzy condos."

It shouldn't surprise Dylan that everyday folks like Skeeter had heard about his initial plan for the factory. News traveled in a small town. "Since when have you become an avid reader?" he asked with a laugh, doing his best to keep his voice neutral. He wasn't going to engage in a conversation with some old-timer about the factory, although it surprised him that Skeeter didn't see the merit of razing the building and starting over. He'd hated that place as much as Dylan's father had.

"I got the Google," Skeeter replied with a nod. "Tommy got me one of them smarty pants phones for my birthday. Reckon it makes me as smarty pants as the next guy."

Daisy yipped from the backseat, and Sam climbed into the truck, glancing warily at Skeeter. Dylan couldn't blame the kid. Skeeter looked half-crazed on a good day.

"That the boy?" Skeeter asked, bushy brows raised.

"Skeeter, this is Sam Scott." He gave Sam a reassuring smile. "Sam, this is Skeeter. He and my dad were friends."

"Besties," Skeeter reported. "That's what my grand-daughters call it these days."

"Nice to meet you," Sam said then busied himself with petting Daisy around the headrest of his seat.

"How old's the kid?" Skeeter asked.

"Fifteen."

"And you can't leave him to grab a beer? He like to start fires or something?"

Dylan ignored Sam's indignant snort. "No fires. I'll stop by Murphy's one night next week."

"Alrighty, then. I'll print off that article for you. Tommy got me a laser jet, too."

"Good to see you, Skeeter."

"Nice to have you back where you belong, Scott. I miss your old man."

"Can't say the same," Dylan said under his breath then rolled up the window.

Jaw clenched tight, he backed out and then started toward the road that led to the beach.

"Was Grandpa friends with that guy, too?" Sam asked after a few quiet moments.

"No." Dylan shook his head, wishing he could also shake

off the black mood that had descended over him in large part due to the conversation with Skeeter. "Your grandpa left Magnolia for college and never came back. I'm sure he knew Skeeter, but they weren't friends."

"Grandpa used to tell me stories about the trouble he and his brother got into growing up. Did you know one time they hid a dozen chickens in the high school and the teachers had to chase them all around?"

Dylan smiled despite his mood. "The Scotts have a long history of causing trouble in this town."

"A little risky bringing me back here," Sam said with a cheeky grin. "You know I like trouble."

"There's trouble and then there's being a reckless idiot," Dylan clarified. "Just make sure you know the difference. It took me way too long to learn that lesson."

"I'm smarter than you." Sam reached into the brown bag. The scent of sugar and fresh dough filled the truck's interior. The boy tore off a piece of a cookie and handed it to Daisy.

"No people food for the dog," Dylan reminded him.

"It's a dog treat," Sam clarified. "Mrs. Winkler gave it to me for Daisy. Carrie's sister told her I adopted the dog."

"*We* adopted," Dylan reminded him.

"Yeah, man, I don't think she mentioned you." Sam tried and failed to mask his laughter with a cough. "Ms. Winkler really doesn't like you."

"I know. Did you get me a sticky bun?"

"In fact," Sam continued as if Dylan hadn't spoken, "she gave me an extra chocolate donut and told me everything was free if I promised not to share it with you."

Dylan felt his eyes narrow. "She did not."

"She said it cost over six hundred dollars to fix the damage you did when you broke into the store."

"I know," Dylan repeated, "and my dad not only tanned my hide for it, but I had to work at the bakery for an entire summer for free to pay it back. Let my mistakes serve as a lesson for what not to do."

"Would you tan my hide?" Sam asked, sounding genuinely curious.

"Hell, ye—" Dylan shook his head. What was he saying? He'd never lay a hand on the boy. "I'd make you pay it back *with* interest. I can't believe she's held a grudge against me for this long. She's worse than an elephant with that memory."

"Bro, I don't know a lot about women, but not even Mrs. Winkler would want to be compared to an elephant."

"Don't say a word, then." Dylan turned onto the beach road. The sky looked more expansive out here and he rolled down the windows a bit to breathe in the first scent of salty air. "You can wait until you get out of the car to eat. My stomach is already rumbling. If you pull out one of your special free pastries, I might lose it."

Sam fed Daisy another piece of biscuit and Dylan cringed as crumbs scattered to the seat. So much for the damn leather.

"I wonder if Mrs. Winkler would give me the biscuit recipe?" Sam asked absently. "Daisy likes those way better than her kibble."

"They're probably not as nutritious." Even to his own ears, Dylan sounded like a petulant schoolboy, but he didn't care. He hated being punished a decade later for the stupid things he'd done as an angry teen. And he wanted a sticky bun.

He parked the car a few spaces down from Carrie's ancient station wagon. He knew it was hers because she'd driven the same car in high school. How had their lives gone in such different directions?

As he turned off the ignition, Sam held out a pastry wrapped in butcher paper.

"I told you to eat it outside the car," he snapped at the boy.

"This is yours." Sam shrugged. "I got you a glazed donut, too."

Dylan stared at the kid. "I thought you said Mary Ellen gave you everything with the condition that you didn't share with me."

"She offered, but I turned her down."

Dylan's lungs constricted and he had trouble drawing in air. He didn't exactly recognize the emotion squeezing his chest, but it overwhelmed him just the same.

Sam wiggled his eyebrows. "I was going to pay for it. Then I told her my parents would have been happy we'd moved to Magnolia where I could be surrounded by a community of good role models on how to treat people. The extra donut was actually her idea."

"A combination of guilt and sweet talk," Dylan murmured, taking the pastry from the boy. "Do you know how proud your dad would have been at this moment?"

"Mom used to say he could charm a cobra."

"Clearly, you inherited the gift."

Dylan held his breath as he waited for the boy's reaction. He didn't usually bring up reminders of Wiley and Kay. It wasn't as if either he or Sam ever forgot, but he didn't want to make the kid sad by constantly reminding him of the loss he'd suffered.

Sam seemed to take it in stride, a grin playing around the corners of his mouth. Dylan immediately discovered another reason to judge himself. In truth, his reluctance to discuss Sam's parents had more to do with how uncomfortable it made him than in upsetting Sam.

"Let's go, Daisy." Sam got out of the car with the bakery bag and opened the door to the backseat.

The dog paced and whined, obviously anxious at the thought of leaving the safety of the truck but also not willing to be separated from her favorite person if she could help it.

"You're going to like the beach," the boy assured her. "Come on. It will be fun. I promise."

"She can stay in the truck if she's going to freak out too much," Dylan said, opening his door.

As if she understood his words, Daisy daintily hopped out of the backseat.

"She's coming with us. Daisy's going to the beach." Sam's voice held a level of enthusiasm Dylan hadn't heard before. He understood the sullen, grieving teen he'd come to know like the back of his hand could return at any time, so he had to get over his shock and simply enjoy this moment.

With a scruffy dog, a few sweet pastries and Carrie, maybe there was hope after all.

CARRIE WASN'T SURE she'd done the right thing for today. Then she saw the look in Sam's eyes as he crested the path that led to the beach and noticed the canopy she'd set up in the sand.

"This is awesome," the boy said, taking in the battery-operated lights strung across the tent and the garland she'd wrapped around each of the four poles anchoring the structure. "Is there some kind of party out here today?"

"Just us," she said with a shrug. "I know it's not the same as a huge snowfall that gets you off school, but I wanted you to see that winter at the beach could be fun, too."

The boy tried to hide his smile, but she could tell he liked the effort she'd made. "The lights are shaped like seashells."

"I bought molds, buckets and shovels for sandcastle making at the hardware store. Don't feel pressure to build a sandcastle. I get that you're a teenager and this isn't your first time at the beach. You don't have to feel pressure to do anything."

"It's cool," he said finally, and it seemed like they both felt relief she could stop talking. "Daisy can help me."

The dog stood behind his legs, peeking out at Carrie around one knee. Normally, Meredith's rescue pets instantly liked Carrie. The fact that Daisy didn't made her want to win over the dog, just like she wanted to persuade Sam to give her a chance and...

She broke off as Dylan approached. He wore faded jeans, a dark T-shirt under a gray flannel and a bewildered expression.

"Here." Sam shoved a bag toward Carrie. "We got food from the bakery. Mrs. Winkler helped me order your favorites."

"Thanks," she said but before the word was out of her mouth, the boy had moved past her, grabbed the tub of beach toys and headed closer to the shore where the wet sand would be better for packing.

"Is there a party we didn't know about?" Dylan gestured toward the hanging lights and decorations.

Carrie felt suddenly embarrassed by the effort she'd made. It was stupid to try so hard when she should want to run Dylan out of town, not make him and Sam feel more welcome. But it went against her nature to be cruel. Unfortunately, more times than she cared to count, that had left her in the unenviable position of doormat to the people in her life.

"Sam asked the same thing, but no." She crossed her arms over her chest. "I thought it would be fun to have a festive day at the beach."

Dylan whistled under his breath. "You went to a lot of work."

"Not really."

He bent his knees until they were at eye level. "I appreciate it," he said with what looked like a genuine smile.

"Oh."

His eyes flicked to a place over her shoulder and then he leaned in and brushed a quick kiss across her lips. "Thank you for coming today. Sam doesn't hate me quite as much when you're around."

She shook her head. "He doesn't hate you at all."

Dylan didn't answer and she wouldn't push him to agree with her. That would come in time.

"Are you going to have something to eat?" he asked, tapping a finger on the bag.

"Sam got a cinnamon roll for me," she murmured. "He didn't have to do that."

"You don't like to let people do anything nice for you."

"Not true," she protested.

"You take care of everyone else," he continued, his voice gentle like a summer breeze.

"Is that a bad thing?" Frustration moved through her. She hated that she sounded defensive but couldn't help it.

"No, but sometimes it's okay to let someone else be the hero."

"Just not you," she snapped.

He grinned as if she'd given him a compliment. "Definitely not me."

She stared at him for a long moment then burst out laughing. "You're the worst, Dylan."

"I know. Stop eyeing my sticky bun."

She reached into the bag. "I thought Mary Ellen cut you off. Don't tell me you made Sam go in there and lie."

"I didn't need to. The kid did better than I ever could have imagined. He played to her decency."

"That's impressive. Let's take the chairs closer to Sam and Daisy. You can help him with the sandcastle after you finish your sticky bun."

"What about you?"

"I don't like touching sand."

His grin widened as he reached out to touch the red sweater she wore. "I forgot about that. A girl grows up at the beach but doesn't like sand. Yet, you suggested it for Sam."

"I'm weird."

"You're amazing," he said quietly.

She ducked her head and placed the bakery bag on the folding table she'd set up. She didn't want to hear Dylan call her amazing. Her heart couldn't handle it.

She pulled out the pastry, took a big bite and then reached for a beach chair.

"I've got it," he told her, popping the last morsel into his mouth. He picked up both chairs, and they walked toward the ocean.

Carrie couldn't remember the last time she'd been to the beach and wasn't sure when she'd first developed an aversion to it. It was strange, living in a coastal town, and not liking the ocean. Her father had used the setting for some of his most iconic paintings, even one that ostensibly showed Carrie and her mother frolicking in the surf.

A scene that never happened in real life.

In high school her peers went to the beach for sunbathing and after-dark bonfires, but she never joined. She didn't do much socially as a teenager, at least until Dylan came into her life. Even then she didn't think she liked the ocean.

But he'd invited her today, and it had been obvious that he hadn't remembered her aversion. The past couple of months had been an overhaul of the life she'd known. A trip to the beach represented something, overcoming her fear and stepping out of her comfort zone.

Now she wished she hadn't waited so long. The empty expanse of shore made her feel like she was in some sort of private paradise. Although she wore shoes, she could feel the texture of the cool sand under her feet. It didn't bother her the way she'd expected it to. The sound of the crashing waves made her feel at once small in the grand scheme of the world and yet somehow connected with the rhythm of the tides.

Dylan and Sam were busy scooping sand into the molds and digging a moat around the structure. They laughed as Daisy dug a hole nearby, sending clumps of wet sand flying in all directions.

She sat in a chair and watched the two of them working in companionable silence. With the sound of the ocean and the cool breeze whistling along the shore, there didn't seem to be much need for words. The serenity of the moment gave her a sense of calm even with the turmoil still swirling through her life.

"Is the old pier still there?" Dylan asked as he glanced down the beach.

"I think so." She shrugged. "Although I remember hearing something about damage to it during hurricane season a couple of years ago."

He straightened, dusting sand from the front of his jeans. "Want to check it out?"

"Sure."

"Sam, you need a break?" he asked the boy.

"I'll stay here and finish," Sam answered. "I've got an idea for another tower."

"Just you and me, then," Dylan told Carrie, sending her heartbeat racing.

She glanced down at her feet then toed off her espadrilles.

"Sand in your toes. How brave," Dylan said.

He was teasing, but she felt oddly brave.

They started down the beach toward the pier. Daisy trotted after them but when the dog realized Sam was staying behind, she deserted the adults for the teenager.

"I'm glad you chose her and not a puppy," Carrie said. Her arm brushed again Dylan's, and to her surprise, he took her hand, linking their fingers together. It was natural and right for the moment. They were here on this empty stretch of beach like it was their own private oasis.

It was dangerous to crave this connection to him, but Carrie couldn't seem to stop herself. They could go back to being enemies in town after the holiday festival. But for now she wanted to remember how easy it was to be close to him.

"I can't believe Sam is building a sandcastle," Dylan said with a grin.

"I was a little worried about suggesting it," Carrie admitted. "But from what I see teaching classes at the high school, teenagers are forced to grow up too fast. They give up art because they're athletes or too busy with core classes and they let go of play because it's not cool to be a kid."

"Losing both of your parents at one time definitely makes you grow up fast."

"I can't imagine," Carrie whispered.

"Me neither." Dylan shook his head. "I've been with him

every day since it happened, and I still can't imagine how he deals with it. Or me. I'm impatient and short-tempered. I have no idea the right things to say, and I sure as hell can't go from personal experience. My parents messed things up left and right." He stopped, turned to her. "What if I screw that kid up beyond repair?"

"You won't," she told him. "Your mom and dad were like mine, totally unaware of their own flaws. You're trying, Dylan. Sam might not appreciate it now, but somewhere deep inside he realizes it. That counts."

His gaze softened. "This is why everyone relies on you so much. You can make a hopeless situation seem hopeful."

She had a feeling he was going to say more and knew that one additional kind word would push her over the edge of her ability to resist her attraction for him. She glanced over her shoulder but a bend in the shoreline obstructed her view of Sam.

Nothing to stop her from jumping his bones. Nothing but her own good sense, which was fast disappearing.

"There's the pier," he said suddenly. "It's still here. I want Sam to see it. His dad came to visit one summer when we were kids and we spent hours under that pier building homemade rafts."

Right. The whole reason they'd walked down the beach was not for a private moment so they could make out like a couple of teens, but because Dylan wanted to revisit a place from his past that had meaning. A needed reminder that they might share a past but not the future.

"Let's bring him down," she suggested brightly, immediately turning on her heel and heading back toward the chairs and umbrella she'd set up.

"How's your painting going?" Dylan asked as they walked. He reached for her hand again, but she moved away.

"I'm busy with the festival and the holiday painting parties scheduled at the studio. My work isn't going anywhere."

"Especially not if you don't do anything with it."

"What's that supposed to mean?"

"You're avoiding your art. Even Avery agreed. I'm sure Meredith would, as well."

"You talked to my sister about me?" It was difficult to believe that minutes earlier Carrie had found Dylan almost irresistible when right now she wanted to punch him in the face.

"Only that we both think you're ignoring your talent and keeping yourself busy as a way not to put yourself out there with your art. You're too talented for that, Carrie."

She lifted a hand to shade her eyes from the glare of the winter sun. "Where's Sam?"

"Don't change the…" Dylan's gaze followed hers to the patch of beach where they'd left Sam and Daisy. "He probably had to go to the bathroom," he said but picked up the pace.

They were both jogging by the time they got to the canopy she'd set up earlier.

While the structure still stood, lights twinkling above them, the chairs had been knocked over and the sandcastle destroyed.

Carrie scanned the area for the boy and his dog. She called his name, but the only answer was the breeze whistling off the crashing waves.

"Do you hear that?" Dylan cupped a hand over one ear. "It's Daisy."

He took off toward the parking lot, and Carrie followed. The muffled sound of the dog's frantic barking grew louder and as they crested the rise, she could see Daisy pacing in the backseat of Dylan's Porsche.

"Sam," Dylan shouted, but only the dog answered with a series of almost manic yips and howls. "Sam, do you hear me?"

A piece of paper tucked under the windshield wiper fluttered, drawing Carrie's attention.

She reached for it as Dylan opened the back door. His muttered curse had her glancing up from the note.

"Daisy chewed up half the backseat."

"Sam went somewhere with friends."

"Where? What friends?" Dylan grabbed the paper from her hand. "He doesn't have friends."

Carrie couldn't answer either question. The boy's scrawled sentences didn't give any details or make sense. When they'd left him, Sam had seemed so content. Now he was just...gone.

CHAPTER TWELVE

TWO HOURS LATER Dylan pulled to the side of the two-lane highway that led out of town. He parked behind a police car, its lights flashing, and stalked down the road's gravel shoulder while his heart raced.

As he passed the hulking red fire truck, Gray Atwell stepped out. He wore a firefighter's uniform and appeared both calm and commanding. "Slow down, Scott. You're not going to make anything better when you look like you're ready to murder someone."

Dylan swallowed back the urge to drive his fist into Gray's jaw. He owed the other man a debt of thanks. Gray had been the one to alert Carrie that Sam was in the backseat of the car that had run off the road and into a ditch on the edge of town.

Dylan would have been notified eventually, but he appreciated being able to get to Sam as soon as possible. So he could kill the kid himself.

With that in mind, he met Gray's measured gaze. "How would you feel if it was your kid in that car?"

Gray sighed. "Point taken, but they're already shaken. You might want to start with being grateful no one was hurt and then move into the butt chewing."

"Right." Dylan closed his eyes for a moment and relived the panic that had gripped him when he'd received Carrie's call. How the hell did parents manage to raise children without going absolutely insane? "Thanks for letting Carrie know about the accident."

"You bet." Gray reached out and squeezed Dylan's shoulder. "Give yourself and Sam a break. He seems like a decent kid. I have a pretty good instinct on people thanks to my line of work. He's just floundering a bit, but he'll straighten out."

"There's floundering," Dylan said, "and then there's making monumentally stupid decisions. The kind that could get you killed." He held up a hand when Gray would have said more. "And I don't need to be reminded of my own stupidity back in the day. Why do you think I'm freaking out so badly?"

Gray offered a sympathetic smile. "Sam's on the other side of the truck. We separated all the kids so the cops could get a straight story. Everyone seems to agree that Sam was just along for the ride."

"Got it." Dylan moved past Gray, wishing he could believe that. In reality, he didn't know how to deal with any part of this situation, from his conflicting emotions to understanding why Sam had made the choice he did today.

All of that seemed to fall by the wayside when he caught sight of the boy sitting alone on the bottom step of the fire truck, a blanket draped over his hunched shoulders.

He must have whispered the kid's name because Sam glanced up, his expression a mix of defiance, fear and apology.

"I'm fine," he said, rising to his feet as Dylan approached.

"Good for you," Dylan answered. "I'm not." He pulled the boy toward him, wrapping Sam in a tight hug. "Don't ever scare me like that again."

Sam stayed stiff for a long moment then sagged against Dylan. "Sorry," he whispered.

"I know." Dylan pulled back. He placed his hands on

Sam's thin shoulders. "You're also grounded for the rest of your life."

"Why aren't you yelling?" Sam asked, forehead wrinkling.

"That will come," Dylan promised. "But right now I'm still basking in the fact that you're okay. Don't push your luck."

A stricken look flitted across Sam's features. "The noise was terrible. The brakes and the car skidded and hit the guard rail." He sniffed and looked away. "Can you imagine how much worse it was in a plane?"

"Don't go there right now. You're here and you're fine, Sam. We need to keep it that way."

The boy nodded as he swiped the sleeve of his jacket across his cheeks.

"I'm going to go talk to the police for a minute and then we'll head home."

"Yeah." Sam nodded. "I don't want to see anyone right now. The other guys..."

"The car is unlocked." Dylan gave Sam another hug. "I'll be there shortly."

Sam handed Dylan the blanket then started down the shoulder toward the Porsche. It was strangely difficult to watch him walk away. The hours Sam had been gone were the most terrified Dylan had felt in a long time. How was he supposed to keep the boy safe if he couldn't even keep track of him?

He found the police chief talking to another man near the wrecked vehicle. A wave of nausea spun through Dylan as he took in the mangled front of the SUV. From what he understood, there'd been five kids in the car, so they were extremely lucky no one had been seriously injured.

The officer turned slightly as Dylan approached. "I'm

Sam Scott's guardian." Dylan reached out a hand. He ignored the other man, who appeared to be the owner of the wrecked car, which meant his kid had been the one drinking and driving. Dylan knew if he engaged with the guy, it would go badly. He needed to focus on Sam. "If there's nothing else you need from him we're going to head home."

The chief, whose name badge read Drew Garrison, nodded. "There was a lot of stupidity today, but the other boys were quick to tell me that Sam hadn't been drinking with them. He made a bad decision getting in that car, though, when the driver had been."

"Khale doesn't drink," the other man interjected. "Your test must be screwed up."

The officer held up a hand to silence the angry father. "In a minute, Mr. Morris." He returned his attention to Dylan. "I hope Sam understands how serious this is."

"His parents died in a plane crash a year and a half ago," Dylan said tightly. "He gets it."

Chief Garrison blew out a breath. "No wonder he seemed especially shaken. If you need anything, reach out. He's new to the high school, right?"

Dylan nodded.

"He's the student who vandalized the school before Thanksgiving," the dad offered. "My son has never been in trouble and suddenly this juvenile delinquent shows up and I've got a totaled car. Coincidence? I don't—"

Dylan spun on the man and grabbed his shirtfront, pulling him close. "Not another word about my kid."

"He's not even yours," the dad muttered.

"Hey, Kevin," Garrison said, "don't be more of an ass than you already are. Khale was drinking and driving. That's on him and it's for the two of you to deal with, no one else."

"Sam is my responsibility," Dylan said, enunciating every syllable. The rage coursing through him made his voice tremble. "He's a good kid who's made some bad choices. We're working on it." He forced himself to calm down and released Kevin. "I'd advise you to do the same with your son. Because if I hear one more word about how today was Sam's fault, you and I are going to have issues. I guarantee you don't want that."

"Are you threatening me?" Kevin demanded, flicking an imploring glance toward the officer. "Did you hear that?"

"Nope," the chief said. "Not a word."

Kevin threw up his hands then turned and stalked toward the tow truck that had just pulled up to the scene.

"Thanks," Dylan said to the lawman.

"Take care of your kid," Garrison answered. "Gray Atwell told me about how he came to be in your care. I'm new to Magnolia, but a few guys at the station have been talking about your return."

Dylan blew out a soft laugh. "That can't be good, but just know Sam isn't like me back in the day. Hell, I'm not the same person, either."

"We all grow up eventually. People like Kevin grow up to be jerks. Hopefully, he'll take this as a wake-up call and do the right thing with his son. Gray vouched for you, and that means a lot."

"Thanks." Dylan looked to where a cluster of firefighters stood next to the red truck. It had been a long time since he'd wanted or needed someone to vouch for him. His uncle and his cousin had been the people closest to him, so since the accident he'd felt as much like an orphan as Sam.

Magnolia might be his hometown, but he hadn't exactly received a warm welcome back. It did funny, uncomfortable things to his insides to know that Gray had spoken up for him.

"Thanks again," he told the officer then headed toward the car. He waved to Gray as he passed and received an understanding nod in response.

Processing the events of today was going to take some time. Dylan wasn't big into being insightful. His success in life had come from taking action and never slowing down.

But that attitude obviously wasn't going to work with Sam and nothing else was as important as the boy.

"Pizza's here," Carrie said when Dylan opened the door to his house later that night.

He stared at her. "Is pizza delivery your side hustle?"

She shook her head. "I got here at the same time as the kid delivering your order so since I was coming up the walk anyway, I tipped him and sorry I didn't call first. I was just so worried and…" She gulped in a breath, embarrassment heating her cheeks. "I'm babbling. Take the pizza. You probably want privacy. I can go. I'm glad Sam's okay and if you need—"

She broke off as Dylan leaned in and kissed her, taking the cardboard box from her hands in the same movement.

"What was that for?" she asked, pressing her fingertips to her lips.

"Thanks for calling me about the accident. And for the pizza delivery." Dylan offered a slow half smile that had warmth spreading through her. "Come on in."

She followed him through the house to the kitchen, where Sam sat at the table, a sketch pad in front of him.

"Hey, buddy," she said quietly.

He glanced up, his gaze both wary and remorseful. "Do you hate me, too?"

"No one hates you," Dylan muttered, placing the pizza box on the table. "Hell, I gave you a hug."

Sam rolled his eyes with an enthusiasm only teenagers could manage. "Then you grounded me forever and told me I have to pay for the damage to your stupid, fancy car." The boy reached down to pet Daisy, who sat at his feet. "It wasn't me who chewed up the seats."

"I grounded you until the New Year," Dylan clarified, "which is not the same thing as forever. And the reason the dog went berserk is because she was crazy with worry about you."

"We were all worried." Carrie started to reach out and muss the boy's hair then stopped herself. He wasn't a kid and he didn't belong to her. Maybe she couldn't help it if she'd quickly come to care about him, but she had to remember that her role in both Dylan and Sam's lives was on the periphery. "I don't hate you. Dylan doesn't, either. His go-to emotion is anger, so if he's angry it means he cares."

"That's messed up," Sam mumbled.

"Not as messed up as going joyriding with a bunch of loser kids who'd been drinking."

"I thought you were done with the lecturing." Sam flipped the page on his sketchbook when Carrie tried to take a closer look.

"He also seems hungry." Carrie slid into a chair across from Sam. "He's always grumpy when he's hungry."

"Tell me again why you stopped over," Dylan said, deadpan, as he grabbed a stack of paper plates from the counter.

"Because I care," Carrie answered without thinking.

Sam looked up at her, his eyes narrowed in concentration. Dylan paused, drawing in a sharp breath.

She'd shocked both of them. Herself as well, but she didn't mind at the moment.

They needed someone or something to shock them out of their dispirited rut.

Dylan cleared his throat. "I hope you like pepperoni."

"My favorite."

"Can I get you something to drink?"

"I'll have a Monster," Sam said.

"You'll have water," Dylan corrected.

"I'm fifteen. I can choose for myself."

"I'll have water, too," Carrie announced.

"Three waters it is," Dylan said with a nod.

Sam rolled his eyes again, but Carrie could see his small smile.

"I'm sorry I ruined the time at the beach," he said softly.

"You could have told me you didn't want to build the sandcastle." She reached out and patted his hand. "I'm sorry if I encouraged you to do something you didn't want to."

"I was having fun." The boy shrugged, suddenly looking a lot more like a kid and less like a surly teen. "The beach is cool. Those guys showed up and I just felt... I don't know."

"You felt peer pressure. It's normal."

"You have to be strong enough to say no." Dylan placed three glasses of water on the table and took the seat next to Carrie. "You have to not care what people think. At least be choosy about whose opinions matter."

Sam opened up the box and grabbed two slices of pizza. "Says the guy who drives a Porsche and wears a five-thousand-dollar watch."

Carrie gasped and grabbed Dylan's wrist. "Is he serious?" She tugged up his sleeve and studied the oversize silver watch that encircled his wrist. It was classy and shiny and cost enough to pay the mortgage on the studio for two months.

"It's a vintage Rolex. I bought the car and the watch because of the quality. I don't care what other people think."

Sam covered his mouth and coughed, making Carrie laugh because of the obvious swear word he muttered.

"You're not helping by encouraging him." Dylan placed a slice of pizza on her plate when she released his arm.

"She's helping a lot." Sam grinned. "I feel much better giving you grief than I did being on the receiving end of it. Can we talk more about how much you care what people think of you?"

"Eat your pizza," Dylan said through clenched teeth.

"It's a nice watch." Carrie tried to sound supportive.

Dylan gave her an annoyed look that made her dissolve into a fit of giggles.

As they ate, she told Sam about the snowmaking machine she'd rented and the LED light projectors that would beam multicolored effects on the town hall and other buildings along Main Street as part of a stunning light display during the festival's final weekend.

"I've got a to-do list for you, too," she said to Dylan after swallowing her last bite of pizza.

"No way." He shook his head. "I'm anti-Christmas ridiculousness."

"You volunteered to help."

"I was told to volunteer."

"Oh." Carrie worked to keep her features neutral. She knew that, of course. So why did she keep forgetting that he wasn't her ally?

"The festival's gonna be awesome," Sam said, wiping a sleeve across his mouth. "I think we need a gingerbread town backdrop around the Santa Claus display." He reached for the sketchbook that he'd set to one side of the table. "I'm not sure what it would take to build it, but I drew some initial plans."

"That's a good idea, Sam." Carrie reached under the table and poked Dylan's leg. "It seems like it wouldn't be too complex. I wonder who could help build something like that."

She could almost hear Dylan's teeth grinding. "I'll help."

"But you don't even want to be involved," Sam reminded him.

"I do want to help you." Dylan got up from the table and picked up the empty pizza box. "If you promise to stay out of trouble, I'll make an effort with the festival."

"A real effort," Carrie clarified. "Not one that includes snarky comments."

Dylan scoffed. "I don't do snark."

"He says in a tone full of snark," Sam said as he shared a grin with Carrie.

"I'm going to separate the two of you," Dylan threatened.

Carrie gave Sam a high five. "He's bothered. Mission accomplished."

She got up to help clear the glasses and plates. "I almost forgot that I brought cookies." The bag she'd brought in sat on the edge of the counter.

"We can have dessert while we finalize Sam's plans for the gingerbread town," Dylan said, pointing to the boy. "We'll need to come up with a list of what we need from the hardware store. If I'm going to build this thing, you're going to be my trusty assistant."

"Meredith asked if Sam would be willing to come out to the rescue and paint a new sign for her booth. She's going to make a big adoption push with some of her animals during the festival. The timing is perfect just before Christmas."

"Sure," Sam agreed. "Dylan can help." The boy swallowed and hunched his shoulders, obviously embarrassed that he'd volunteered Dylan for additional work without asking, the way kids often did with their parents.

"I'll help," Dylan said casually, even though Carrie understood by the look in his eyes that the moment was anything but casual for him.

Her heart melted at his willingness to be there for Sam. Once again, she tried to focus on the reality of the situation. She and Dylan wanted different things in life and for Magnolia. But when the three of them were together, it felt like they had more in common than what separated them.

Carrie was still learning what it felt like to have things in life that belonged to her, outside of her identity as Niall Reed's daughter. Her sisters had been a blessing in helping her to achieve that goal, but their lives still seemed to have more than hers.

Avery had only been in town for a couple of months, but already she'd found love with Gray and was making her mark as a small-town marketing whiz. Meredith had always marched to the beat of her own drum, and Carrie couldn't imagine anything taking precedence over her devotion to the animals she rescued and rehomed.

It had been a decade since Carrie'd had something to call her own. Dylan had been the one thing that felt like hers. Their relationship had made her feel special and seen in a way that still resonated. Obviously, since she couldn't seem to keep her boundaries in place with him.

They spent almost an hour working on plans for Sam's planned structure and the timeline for building it. After Sam couldn't control his yawning any longer, Dylan suggested the boy go to bed and rest after the day he'd had.

To Carrie's surprise, Sam had given her a quick hug on

his way upstairs. He smelled like sweat and soap, and she couldn't help but grieve for the mother he'd lost.

"He really likes you," Dylan said when they were alone again in the kitchen. "I haven't seen him open up to many people the way he does with you."

"Being nonthreatening is my superpower," she said, trying not to sound bitter. "I make everyone more comfortable that way." She laughed softly as Daisy padded over and nudged her knee. "I've even won over your dog."

When Dylan didn't respond, she glanced up at him. "You can't be serious," he told her.

Carrie shrugged and looked away, suddenly self-conscious under the weight of his stare. Daisy trotted out of the kitchen when Sam called her name, her nails clicking on the hardwood stairs.

"I shouldn't have said that. I'm glad Sam likes me. He's a great kid with so much potential. If he could only—"

"We're not talking about Sam." Dylan took her hand, tugging her closer to him. "For your information, you are a huge threat to me."

She tried to laugh but it came out sounding like a croak. How was she supposed to think rationally when being near Dylan did this to her? She had a sudden empathy for the tiny moth, drawn to a flame without any hope for survival. That was who she was around this man but couldn't find the strength to walk away. She craved the nearness of him, the way he added a spark to her life that hadn't been there before.

"Because I want something different for Magnolia than your grand plan?" She took a cue from Sam and rolled her eyes. "I wouldn't exactly call that a threat."

"This has nothing to do with the town," he said, his voice pitch low, humming across her skin like a warm breeze.

"You threaten my self-control at every turn. I don't even know who I am when I'm with you. All I know is I want to be the man you need me to. We both know there's a strong chance of me failing in that regard." His gaze intensified on hers until she felt as if she were catching on fire from the inside out. "I don't like to fail, Carrie, and that makes you my greatest threat."

She started to answer, having no idea how to respond to that kind of a declaration, when her phone suddenly chirped with a frantic series of text notifications.

Dylan raised a thick brow. "Could it be Randall?"

"I...need to check that," she said on a rush of breath, trying to ignore the flash of amusement in his gaze.

The texts came from Meredith, to both Carrie and Avery. A puppy mill had been discovered about thirty minutes outside town and her sister needed a recon team.

"I've got to go." She shook her head as she looked at Dylan. "It's an emergency with Meredith. With the rescue."

To his credit, he nodded instead of arguing. "We're not through here. Come back when you're finished."

"It might be late."

"I don't care. Please come back."

The soft note of pleading in the words undid her. "Okay," she whispered and leaned in to kiss him. "I'll text you when I know more about the time."

CHAPTER THIRTEEN

"YOU CAME BACK."

Dylan spoke the three simple words with a mix of what sounded like shock and relief.

Carrie frowned as she stepped through the front door of his house. "You told me to," she reminded him.

"Yes, but I thought you agreed just to shut me up."

"That might be true. Also, I lied about having a boyfriend," she blurted.

"I suspected as much. I'm glad to be rid of Randall."

She laughed softly. "You might regret me coming over." She pulled at the front of her cable-knit sweater. "I'm covered in dog hair and who knows what else. I stink and I'm so tired I can barely keep my eyes open. Not exactly great company for—" what were they supposed to be doing here? "—anything."

"I have plenty of regrets in life," he told her. "You here tonight could never be one of them." He smoothed a piece of hair away from her face. "But you do smell a little gamey."

"Oh, no." She started to turn toward the door. "My sisters told me to go home. Why didn't I listen to—"

Dylan wrapped his arms around her from behind and pulled her close. "I want you here in whatever shape you show up."

She resisted the urge to sag against him. Truly, she was exhausted. "I need a shower. The dogs were in filthy conditions. We bathed them when we got back to the rescue, but now I'm the one who's a mess."

"A shower is easy enough to manage."

He took her hand and led her through the quiet house toward the master bedroom, which was on the main floor. He'd told her the house had come furnished, but the bedroom looked just as she'd imagined it would if he'd picked out the decor. The furniture was dark and solid, a pale gray comforter spread over the bed. Dylan's bed.

This was the part where Carrie's lack of dating experience made her feel like a bumbling idiot. She stood silently in the doorway to the connected bathroom and watched. Was she supposed to start undressing while he turned on the water of the walk-in shower and gathered towels? Invite him to join her?

The thought of showering with Dylan had nerves zipping along her skin. At the same time, her muscles ached from the work she'd done, and she could actually smell herself. Not quite a recipe for sexy times.

"You look like you could fall asleep standing up," he said, his tone laced with amusement and sympathy. "Tonight couldn't have been easy."

She shook her head. "I've only gone on one other rescue with Meredith. It's heartbreaking to see the conditions those animals live in before they get to her."

"She does remarkable work."

Carrie dashed away a tear when it tracked down her cheek. Great. Now she was crying. "I'm sorry," she said automatically. "I'm just tired. This can't be what you had in mind. I should go—"

"Don't apologize." Steam began to rise in the air, heating the small space. "The water's hot so take as much time as you need. I want you here, Carrie. In any condition."

She nodded, afraid to speak around the emotions clogging her throat. The door clicked shut as Dylan exited the bathroom. She undressed and climbed into the shower. The water felt amazing and her tears mixed with the hot spray as she let herself succumb to the emotions from the night.

She washed her hair and body quickly, planning to make her time in the shower efficient. But her limbs grew heavy as another round of tears bubbled up inside her. It wasn't just about the animals. Every emotion she'd been running from caught up to her in one moment. She hadn't broken down like this since her father's death and the aftermath of learning his secrets. She'd kept moving, always moving. Her role had been helper, righting the wrongs Niall had inflicted on the town with his selfishness.

She'd never allowed herself to stop and consider what she'd lost or what she'd never truly had in the first place. Why now? Why did it all have to come crashing down around her in Dylan's shower?

She should be having this breakdown in the privacy of her own home, preferably with a carton of ice cream in one hand and a glass of wine in the other.

Instead, she stood under the slowly cooling stream of water, trying to pull herself together. Carrie had no idea how long she remained there, but she startled when the glass door slid open a few inches and Dylan flipped off the water then pushed a towel toward her.

"I think you're ready," he said from the other side of the shower door, his voice a gravelly rumble.

She dried off and wrapped the fluffy towel around her, sliding the door fully open.

His blue gaze met hers, searching her face in a way that made her know he'd heard her crying, even though she'd tried to muffle the sound of it.

"I'm leaving a T-shirt and gym shorts on the sink for you," he said. "Your clothes are in the wash."

"You didn't have to do that." She clutched the towel more tightly to herself. Goose bumps rose on her skin under his scrutiny. "This is… I'm not sure what to do next."

"Get dressed," he commanded then took a step away from her.

A yawn escaped her as she glanced at the pile of clothes. "I'm not sure I have the energy for that. Apparently, bawling your eyes out is exhausting. I guess that's why I've avoided it for so long."

He chuckled. "In general, I find feelings overrated and taxing." He picked up the shirt and pulled it over her head. A part of her wanted to protest. She was a grown woman and obviously capable of dressing herself. But she allowed him to help, grateful for a few minutes of not having to take care of herself, even for such a simple task.

He didn't break eye contact with her as she put one arm and then the other into the shirt, allowing the towel to drop to the floor as the T-shirt grazed her thighs.

"Shorts next," he said as a parent might to a child.

Heat flooded her cheeks as he knelt in front of her and she stepped into the soft cotton. "I can manage," she whispered but didn't shrug away his touch. The truth was she felt too damn tired to move a muscle. Even if she wanted to make an escape at this point, she didn't think she had the energy to make it out the door.

As if sensing that she was on the verge of collapse, Dylan scooped her into his arms as he straightened, one arm supporting her back and the other behind her knees.

"I'm making a fool of myself," she said miserably. "I was supposed to come back for a booty call."

"Is that all you were interested in?" Dylan asked, sounding entertained as he moved into the bedroom.

"My only interest at the moment is sleeping."

"I can help with that." He bent and pulled back the comforter and top sheet on his big bed.

Carrie sighed as she sank against the soft mattress.

"Sleep as long as you want," he told her, tucking the covers around her. "I'll take the couch."

"No."

He gave her a funny look. "I know you aren't up for anything but sleep, and I want you to feel safe with me. I promise I don't care why you're here, Carrie. I'm glad you are. No pressure."

"It's a huge bed." She yawned again. "Just get in, Dylan. I'm too tired to argue right now."

One corner of his mouth kicked up. "Bossy," he murmured then turned off the bedside lamp.

A moment later she felt the mattress sag on the opposite side of the bed.

She was still embarrassed and more than a little disappointed at how this night had turned out. Then Dylan moved closer, tucking his body behind her and draping an arm around her waist. "Is this okay?" he asked.

"More than okay." Enveloped in his heat, she drifted off to sleep.

THREE-ELEVEN IN the morning according to the clock on the unfamiliar nightstand. Carrie blinked several times to clear her head. This wasn't her bedroom.

A rumbling breath from behind her had her alert in an instant. Memories from earlier flooded her mind. Her mental and physical exhaustion, the tender way Dylan had taken care of her. She turned carefully on the mattress, trying not to disturb him.

Not that she had much to worry about. Dylan lay on his back, one arm bent above his head. In the soft moonlight she could see his chest rise and fall in rhythmic breaths. It had been over a decade since she'd seen his body. He was both familiar and not. In the ensuing years since he'd left Magnolia, Dylan Scott had become a man.

His shoulders had broadened, and lean muscles defined his arms, even in sleep. It seemed almost unfair for someone to have that golden tone of skin in winter, like he'd come back to town after years of living in the tropics instead of the big city. A fine sprinkling of wiry hair covered his chest.

"Hey."

Her gaze flicked to his face, where a small smile curved his full lips and his eyes danced with amusement in the soft glow of the light that remained on in the nearby bathroom.

"I was checking you out," she admitted with a grimace.

"I noticed." He turned onto his side, propping himself on one elbow. "How are you feeling?"

"Better. Embarrassed at how I was earlier. I should have gone home."

"No." He reached out and traced one finger along her cheek and jaw. "I'm glad you were with me." His smile widened a touch. "Although you snore."

She sniffed. "I don't snore."

"It's cute."

"No wonder you're single." She grabbed his wrist and shoved his hand away from her. "Your moves are awful." But the moment she started to flip off the covers, he moved toward her. More quickly than she would have thought for a guy who'd just been woken from a deep sleep. She was suddenly pinned to the bed with Dylan over her, his warm body pressed against hers in a way that had every inch of her coming fully awake.

"Awful?" he asked with a deep chuckle. "That sounds like a challenge."

Carrie licked her suddenly dry lips. "And are you up for the challenge?" she asked, barely recognizing her own voice.

"You decide," he whispered and then claimed her mouth. His tongue melded with hers as the kiss became hot and demanding. His hand pushed up under her shirt, and she gasped as his fingers grazed the underside of her breast, sending quivers spiraling through her.

He urged her to lift her back and pulled the shirt over her head. Gazing up at him, she forgot about being self-conscious.

All thoughts other than Dylan disappeared from her mind. There was no worry over the estate or the town or what was left of her family's birthright. Dylan might not be her forever, but right now she wanted anything he could give.

She wanted to take her pleasure and dismiss all the stress of real life for a while. In this bed Carrie didn't have to be dutiful or helpful or anything but a woman with needs.

Needs she had no doubt this man could more than fulfill, despite her teasing.

She wanted to feel alive.

Without another thought, she hitched up her hips and shimmied out of his boxers.

Dylan swore under his breath as he took in her naked body, his gaze filled with appreciation. She'd never felt more beautiful.

Then he lowered his mouth to one breast and then the

other, licking and sucking until she moaned and arched under him. Her fingers grazed along the tight muscles of his back. It felt as though all of her nerve endings were standing upright and singing his praises, and not just because it had been far too long since a man had touched Carrie in this way.

No one had ever made her feel the way Dylan did.

She tugged on the waistband on his boxer briefs, and he growled low in his throat when she pushed them down over his hips. The evidence of his desire for her was like its own form of foreplay.

Lifting away from her for a moment, he took his boxers the rest of the way off then grabbed a condom wrapper from the nightstand drawer.

"Expecting company in your new house?" she asked as he tore open the packet.

"Hoping," he said with a sexy half smile, "that you might stop by for—" he kissed her like he'd been saving up his need for a decade "—anything."

Her breath hitched at the vulnerability in his tone. This wasn't exactly the Dylan she remembered. That boy had been at once cocky and sweet, patient with her inexperience but sure of his own control.

The man who covered her body with his felt different. Not just grown-up or world-weary, although she knew he was both of those things. This Dylan had experienced loss and tragedy; he'd made himself into a success, but she somehow understood it had come with a price.

The same way the choices she'd made had changed her from an innocent girl into the woman she'd become. So even if they returned to being enemies again tomorrow or at the end of the holiday season, for now she wasn't ready to let him go.

"Are we good?" he asked, poised at her body's entrance. "I only want this if it's what you want, too."

"More than anything," she told him honestly and the way his face lit with relief and gratitude made her heart hurt just the tiniest bit.

Then he pushed into her, filling her body and her senses until their current reality vanished. All that was left was need and desire. They moved together like their bodies were made for each other, pressure building within her and around her until she wasn't sure where she ended and Dylan began. Carrie rode the blissful wave until she couldn't hold out any longer and her release crested over her.

She held on to Dylan, whispering his name and taking him over the edge with her.

It was everything she'd remembered and more. So much more, which she knew could only mean one thing. It would hurt so much worse when it ended.

CHAPTER FOURTEEN

"Carrie!"

Carrie stepped away from where she stood in front of the easel, pulling the earbud from her ear and pausing the music. "What's wrong?" She looked between Meredith and Avery, who were staring at her from the doorway of the studio. "What's going on?"

Meredith thumped the heel of her palm against her forehead. "You haven't been kidnapped and held captive in some crazy basement bunker."

"Are you disappointed?" Carrie asked with a surprised laugh.

Avery stepped forward. "We've been calling and texting for the past hour. You never showed up for dinner."

Carrie blinked then glanced at her watch. "Oh, shoot. I lost track of the time." She'd made plans to meet her sisters, along with two members of the town council to discuss next steps for Magnolia's tourism plan after the first of the year.

"Tonight was important." Avery's soft admonishment made the hair on the back of Carrie's neck stand on end. "Everyone was expecting you. We need to capitalize on the success of the festival activities if we're going to stop Dylan."

"I realize that." She put down the paintbrush gripped tightly between her fingers and wiped her hands on a towel. Letting people down was not something in Carrie's usual repertoire. Normally her life was based on a solid under-pinning of how she could help, what she could do better and her need to go above and beyond with the way she contributed to the community. She should feel guiltier about forgetting tonight and worrying her sisters and her friends.

She glanced toward the canvas that engulfed her attention and pride swelled inside her chest, despite knowing she'd disappointed the people who mattered to her. Tonight she'd also taken care of herself, and that mattered.

She mattered.

"Does this have something to do with Dylan Scott?" Meredith demanded.

"Excuse me?"

Her petite younger sister put her hands on her slim hips. "Has he gotten to you? Convinced you that the festival and what comes next in Magnolia isn't as important as his plan? You know if we fail at this, it sets him up to prove our vision for the future as a legitimate tourist destination is just a pipe dream. He'll gather support and momentum to turn this place into the North Carolina coast's version of Monte Carlo or some other snobby playground for the wealthy. He's using you to ruin everything we've worked for."

"He's using me?" Heat crept up Carrie's spine. Since the previous weekend, she'd spent every night in Dylan's bed, drawn by their connection and the way she seemed to come alive in his arms. He'd invited her for dinner tomorrow night, a real date, he'd called it. At the time the gesture had seemed sweet. He wanted her to know she meant more than just a secret tryst. Which was exactly the reason she'd only visited under the cover of darkness, once Sam and most of the rest of the town had drifted off to sleep.

The invitation flattered her, but she had her priorities straight. The physical pleasure of being with him didn't change the fact that they were on opposite sides of Magnolia's future. She almost never lost sight of her goal.

"You know what I mean," Meredith added, her tone softer, as if she realized she'd overstepped some invisible line.

"We don't want you to forget what's important." Avery smiled. "This town is everything to you."

"Not everything." Carrie shook her head. "For too long it's been everything. I'm dedicated to Magnolia's success, but maybe I want something for myself, as well." She pointed a finger at Avery. "Isn't that what you and Dylan discussed? That I need to focus on myself."

Avery sucked in a breath. "He told you that?"

Meredith nudged Avery's arm. "You talked about Carebear with that jerk face?"

"In a moment of weakness."

"No." Carrie took another step forward. "You were right. You and Dylan both. For too long I've tamped down my own desires. It doesn't change my commitment to Magnolia, but I need to consider myself, as well." She blew out a long breath. "I'm sorry I missed dinner and the meeting tonight, but I had an idea for a new painting and..." She gestured the two of them forward. "Would you like to see?"

Nerves ratcheted through her as the two of them approached. Carrie backed up, and her sisters joined her and then turned to view the canvas, a landscape scene of Magnolia Beach. Carrie had returned there early in the morning yesterday to see the sunrise, inspired by the promise of a new day dawning on the horizon.

"Wow," Meredith murmured.

"The colors of the sky are amazing." Avery reached out and squeezed Carrie's fingers. "I'm blown away."

Carrie couldn't describe her style based on the techniques she'd learned from formal classes and watching her father through the years, but dipping the paintbrush in the vibrant palette of acrylic paint she'd chosen unleashed something inside her. All the emotions she'd tamped down for so many years had burst forth onto the canvas.

"This is different than the way you normally paint," Avery said, her tone filled with astonishment.

"I wasn't trying for a huge departure." Carrie laughed softly. "Honestly, so much of what I've painted lately has been owls and flowers and holiday scenes from the classes. Not to mention the festival backdrops. I'm not even sure what my own style is at this point."

Meredith raised her delicate brows. "I think you can safely call it 'lots of mind-blowing sex.'"

Carrie felt her mouth drop open. "What are you talking about?" she demanded, narrowing her eyes at her sister before turning her attention back to the canvas. "There's nothing sexual in that painting."

"Maybe not overtly," Avery murmured. "But it's definitely sensual."

"It's a landscape." Carrie stepped forward and then turned, using her body to block the canvas. It felt suddenly personal for the other women to view it. "Not even a Georgia O'Keeffe type flower."

Meredith and Avery shared a look and then grinned at Carrie. "You didn't deny the great sex," Meredith pointed out.

Carrie closed her eyes for a moment and tried not to groan out loud. She hadn't talked to anyone about the change in her relationship with Dylan. If she could even call it a relationship. More like a mutual scratching of an itch.

Whatever she called the arrangement, it worked for her on a lot of levels. Her body felt satiated in a manner that made her want to purr with pleasure at the thought of all the ways Dylan had touched her. She continued to ignore the faint warning bells going off in the vicinity of her heart that told her she was in too deep with him. She knew better than to trust her heart.

Carrie had been a dutiful daughter, a faithful friend and a devoted member of the Magnolia community. She was everyone's go-to for help, known far and wide as dependable, practical and boring as all get out.

Being with Dylan was freeing, her own little act of rebellion from what was expected of her. That didn't mean she was ready to share the details of her personal life with anyone, even her sisters. Somehow speaking about it would make things more real and prevent her from keeping her emotions and hopes in perspective.

"It's not a big deal," she told them, trying and probably failing in the attempt not to sound defensive.

"Taking up with Dylan again is a huge deal," Meredith countered. "The biggest."

Avery put a hand on Meredith's shoulder. "She looks happy."

Meredith sniffed. "Delirious from great sex and happy aren't the same thing."

"Is it more than sex?" Avery asked gently. "Do you have feelings for him?"

"It's been a few days. He and I want different things from life." Carrie shook her head. "I haven't lost sight of the goal," she repeated. "I know his plan isn't right for Magnolia."

"Are you sleeping with him to butter him up in order to win?" Meredith tapped a finger on her chin. "I wouldn't have expected it of you, but it's not a bad idea."

"Of course that's not what I'm doing."

"You're painting," Avery remarked.

Meredith turned to the polished blonde. "Does Dylan get credit for that?"

"No, but it's a good thing if he's helping her realize she has to take care of herself in addition to everyone else."

"You're talking about me like I'm not standing here."

"True," Meredith said with a nod. Carrie wasn't sure who she was talking to. "Maybe he's not all bad other than the business about wanting to change the very fabric of the town we love."

"Enough." Carrie put her brushes in the Mason jars of mineral spirits, and then stalked to the doorway before looking over her shoulder. "I missed dinner, and talking to the two of you is giving me a headache."

"She's hangry," Avery said to Meredith.

"Happens to the best of us," Meredith agreed.

Carrie wanted to shout in frustration, but a laugh bubbled up inside her instead. It was crazy to think that she'd spent most of her life as an only child. At this point she couldn't imagine not having her sisters to frustrate, annoy, entertain and support her.

"There's food in the office fridge," she told them. "You two can fill me in on what I missed from the meeting while I'm eating."

Meredith winked. "And you can fill us in on your new and vastly improved love life."

"It's not love," Carrie whispered.

Avery gave her a funny look but didn't argue.

"I just realized something tragic." Meredith made a face. "I'm now the only one of the three of us who's all shriveled up and lonely in the lady parts department."

Carrie grimaced. "Shriveled up? Too much information, sis."

"You know what I mean."

"Then we need to find a boyfriend for you, too," Avery offered.

"Dylan isn't my boyfriend," Carrie reminded them as she walked toward the small office at the back of the studio. She grabbed the half sandwich leftover from lunch and joined her sisters at the small cluster of chairs they'd set up for sip and paint customers.

"Boyfriend. Netflix and chillin'. Friends with benefits." Meredith let out an exaggerated sigh. "I don't care what name you use. I'm jealous."

"We'll find you a man," Avery assured her.

"Dylan isn't *my* man," Carrie argued. "It's a…"

"Fling?" Avery suggested.

"Mistake?" Meredith offered at almost the same time.

"Diversion," Carrie supplied after a moment.

"Nothing wrong with a diversion that makes your toes curl." Meredith chuckled.

Carrie folded her arms across her chest. "I didn't say that."

Avery leaned closer. "You didn't have to, sweetie. It's written all over your face."

"And painted all over that canvas."

"You two need to mind your own business."

Avery threw back her head and laughed. "I remember thinking the exact same thing after Gray and I got serious."

"It's not serious," Carrie insisted then held up a hand. "I'm done talking about this. Tell me about the meeting."

She took a bite of sandwich and waited, wondering if the two of them would let the subject go.

"Your vision is coming to life all around Magnolia," Avery said finally, grinning widely. "You're like a flippin' holiday festival genius. The town council is so excited, they want me to come up with a tourism plan for the first quarter of the New Year. I think they might actually give us a decent budget. Tourism revenue is strong again with local businesses, and they've even had interest from several mid-size companies that are looking to build new headquarters in an up-and-coming East Coast town."

Carrie listened as they spoke, pride filling her at the same time that guilt made her stomach twist. She really should have been at tonight's meeting. Dylan was a fun distraction, but she had to keep her eye on the prize. There'd be plenty of time to focus on herself, her art and even her love life if that was what she wanted.

Now she had to get through the next few weeks of the holiday season and make sure Magnolia was positioned for the future she and her sisters planned.

"This is so dumb," Sam muttered as he and Dylan walked across the parking lot of the old textile factory building Friday afternoon. "Why do I have to be here?"

"Natural consequences," Dylan replied.

"You can trust me," Sam insisted. "I learned my stupid lesson. At least let me sit in the car."

Dylan turned on his heel, placing his hands on the boy's shoulders when Sam almost plowed into him. He paused for a moment, noticing that Sam seemed taller than he had even a week ago and would soon catch up to Dylan in height. A kid in a man's body.

It shouldn't be a surprise. Wiley and Uncle Russ had both been over six feet. Height ran in the family. But the reminder of time passing whether he wanted it to or not still made his chest pinch.

"The last time I left you alone, we ended up out on the county highway surrounded by cops and firefighters. I almost pissed my pants with worry, Sam. Not going there again."

"You mean anger," the boy corrected. "You were angry not scared for me."

Dylan huffed out a small laugh and bent his knees—only a little now—so he was at eye level with the boy. "Scared to pieces," he clarified. "The anger came after I knew you were okay."

"Oh." He registered Sam's sharp intake of breath. It killed him that Sam could still believe Dylan didn't want him. Carrie would say that trust took time to build. Sam had lost everything, his entire life, so it made sense that he was going to test Dylan's devotion. According to her, Dylan just had to stay the course and the boy would come to see that Dylan would never abandon him.

Carrie.

After three blissful nights with her in his bed, she'd seemed to drop off the face of the earth. Or at least out of his life. He'd seen glimpses of her as she worked on the festival, which was ramping up to have a hugely successful weekend. He'd been doing his part with the gingerbread village and other tasks vendors needed, but somehow Carrie had managed to keep her distance.

Had he simply been an itch she'd wanted to scratch? Or worse, had she been trying to soften him so that he'd change his plans for the real estate he owned in town? Several people had mentioned to him the names of companies that might be interested in leasing or buying the factory and surrounding land if he wanted to go in a different direction with his plans for it.

He straightened and rubbed a hand over his face and tried to put thoughts of Carrie out of his mind. Hell if he wouldn't have done just about anything to entice her back to him.

"This place is creepy," Sam said as he fell in step next to Dylan with slightly less attitude.

Dylan had to admit that Sam's assessment of the factory was spot on. The building was not only dilapidated. An air of sadness surrounded it, as if the structure knew the role its closing had played in Magnolia's downturn.

"The town suffered a big hit when Tremaine Industries pulled out," Dylan explained. "My dad had worked here half his life. A lot of the machinists were at a huge loss once the factory closed."

"Is that why your mom and dad moved?"

Dylan nodded. "It was a forced retirement."

"And now you're going to demolish the whole thing to build rich-people condos?"

"Luxury housing."

"Same thing," Sam said with a knowing snort.

"You know that your father came up with the current Scott Development business model. I'm trying to bring his vision to life in Magnolia."

Sam kicked an old, rusted beer can away from the entrance. "I thought that Dad was all about making poor neighborhoods nice again. At least that's what he'd talk about over dinner. How the communities he revitalized should appreciate all the good he did for them. He thought you guys were like construction rainmakers or something."

"That's exactly why the company chooses the projects it does, to make a difference. We're going to make a difference in Magnolia with the added bonus of this being a great place for you to live."

"But Magnolia isn't failing in that way. Things are kind of dated, but it's basically a cool town. Carrie has plans to make it better and you want to gut everything and start over."

"Not true." Heat crept along the back of Dylan's neck.

Sam sounded exactly like Carrie but somehow it felt more difficult to argue with the teen, who didn't actually have skin in the game of this town's next steps. It had been simple to convince himself he wasn't the bad guy when his motivations were building a future for Sam's benefit.

The kid had three and a half years of high school to manage. It would take a couple of years to really get everything off the ground the way Dylan wanted. It hadn't seemed like a big deal to leave the running of the operations in Boston to his very capable right-hand woman and spearhead the project in Magnolia.

Besides, everyone knew that Sam was his primary consideration in life. He hoped they did anyway. But what if his decisions were motivated by the fear of failing both his late cousin and Sam? If he stayed busy he could often ignore the panic that always seemed to swirl under the surface, doubt in his ability to take care of Sam, run the company his uncle and cousin had built and generally live up to expectations he'd never asked for or wanted.

What if both Carrie and Sam were right and he was making things worse instead of better? He'd always prided himself on keeping emotions out of business. He truly believed that the moment he let them rule was the moment he'd lose control of everything.

Maybe he'd never had that much control in the first place.

"You concentrate on keeping your head in the game at school and let me focus on the company." He sighed. "This would have made your dad happy."

"Whatever," Sam mumbled. "Very little made that guy happy, especially not me."

"How can you say that? Your dad loved you more than anything on the planet."

"But he didn't like me much."

Dylan's heart lurched at the resignation in the teen's tone. As if that was simply an indisputable fact.

He wanted to argue but the truth was he didn't know much about the inner workings of his cousin's family. Wiley had been a no-nonsense hard-nosed businessman. He and Kay doted on Sam and had seemed like the picture of a perfect family. Maybe that had simply been what Dylan wanted to see and not the full reality.

What did he do with that information now? Pretend like Sam had it wrong? Make excuses or defend the boy's dead father against an accusation he knew nothing about?

"I never got that impression from your dad," he said honestly, "but it sucks you felt that way. I had a crappy relationship with both my parents growing up. No one benefits in those situations."

"It doesn't matter."

He put a hand on the boy's shoulder and squeezed. "You matter. You're a great kid, Sam. I may screw up a thousand things in your life but never doubt that I like you. I do."

"Okay," the boy agreed.

Thankfully, Dylan was saved from saying more by a sleek black Mercedes pulling into the empty lot. A man and a woman climbed out, both looking out of place with expensive clothes and the air of the big city coming off them in waves. Steven Ross and Elizabeth Christiansen were the investors Scott Development had partnered with on the last several large projects the company undertook.

"What a dump," Steven said, his lip curled in distaste as they approached. "Are you sure we're not going to be tripping over dirty needles or passed-out hookers in this place?"

"The building is empty," Dylan said, taking a step forward as if to block Sam from the crassness of the words and the implied judgment in them.

Steven gave a mock shudder. "I can't believe you came back to this place. I see the potential to take over but it's way too quiet for your lifestyle."

"It's fine," Dylan said through clenched teeth. He felt Sam stiffen next to him. The last thing he wanted or needed was for the boy to think that Dylan had sacrificed his own happiness.

"Don't be a jerk." Elizabeth nudged Steven's arm. "Magnolia is charming," she said with a smile. "It's got to be a nice change from the bustle of Boston. If I get stuck in traffic on I-90 one more time, I might move here myself."

"Never gonna happen, babe," Steven told her. "You're too much of a pampered princess to leave the comforts of the city for small-town life. Are you going to trade out kale for collard greens or Manolo heels for Muck boots? I don't think so."

"Why don't we check out the inside," Dylan suggested, needing to defuse the tension between the couple. Steven and Elizabeth had been a couple as long as he'd known them, although he couldn't understand how they made it work. For all of Steven's brilliance as a powerhouse in real estate ventures, the guy was a womanizing jerk. But Elizabeth, who was a visionary architect in her own right, sported a nearly golf ball-size diamond on her left hand. Something kept them together as a couple. Another example of looks being deceiving.

He gestured to Sam, whom he could feel still sulking next to him. "You both remember my cousin's son, Sam. I picked him up from school right before this so he's going to join us on the tour."

"How do you feel about rats and the smell of stale

urine?" Steven asked with a mock shudder. The guy was a complete tool.

Sam glanced up at Dylan. "Nasty."

"The building is clean," Dylan assured him, leveling a glare at Steven. In the past Wiley had been the one to work with Steven's firm. The two men had even been friends. Dylan could hardly believe it. Five minutes of dealing with the guy and he wanted to punch him in the face.

Elizabeth looked like she felt about the same despite the fact that she was engaged to the oaf. "Don't listen to him." She gave Sam a genuine grin. "You look like your dad."

Sam's shoulders hunched even more. "Thanks, I guess."

This had been another mistake of epic proportions, Dylan realized as he led the small, disjointed group into the building. Sam didn't need reminders of his father or the past or to act as Dylan's wingman on a deal that had so much personal meaning for him.

He ushered them through the space, trying not to let memories overtake him. The cool interior of the building smelled musty, yet the scent of oil from the machines still lingered in the space even though operations had been closed down for years.

The local real estate agent he'd worked with to broker the sale had sent him photos of the building, both inside and out, but this was Dylan's first visit since he'd returned to Magnolia.

With Steven making disparaging comments every few feet, Dylan's head was pounding by the time they returned to the entrance. They stood inside the building to finish talking as the sky outside had gone from partly cloudy to fully gray with a spitting rain coming down.

The gloomy weather only added to his melancholy. Sam

looked like he felt about the same. The kid had been quiet and dour during the tour, not even cracking the hint of a smile at any of Steven's lame attempts at humor.

Elizabeth saved the day, rattling off a list of tasks for each of them to push the project forward. She was efficient and upbeat, which Dylan appreciated. Although that didn't make him want to accept when Steven invited him to dinner before they headed back to Boston.

Instead, Dylan sent the couple on their way and headed to the car with Sam after locking the factory's heavy front door.

"Sorry about that," he said as the defrost air blew from the vents. "I forgot what a tool Steven could be."

Sam gave him a look that could only be described as withering. "I thought you'd be thrilled because spending time with him was a true punishment."

"Good point." Dylan slowly pulled out of the parking lot, glancing up through the front windshield. "It looks like the rain is going to pass. I have some work to do this afternoon. Is there anywhere you want to go first?"

"Back home to Boston and my friends," Sam answered automatically.

"Christmas tree shopping it is," Dylan replied, ignoring the boy's request.

Sam gaped at him. "You said we could only have that stupid little fake tree I found in the basement."

"I changed my mind. Maybe all the holiday spirit around here is finally wearing me down."

"Maybe," Sam agreed, almost reluctantly.

If the kid suspected that Dylan made the offer about a tree out of guilt, he didn't let on. Dylan was happy to pretend if it meant a chance at changing both of their moods.

As he turned onto the road that led to downtown, he flipped on a holiday channel on the vehicle's satellite radio system. Anything to drown out the doubt that seemed to fill his mind and heart.

CHAPTER FIFTEEN

CARRIE FELT COLD all the way to her bones. She'd been helping at the Wainright's Christmas Tree Lot, situated on the far side of the town square, for the past several hours.

Phil Wainright, who owned the hardware store a few doors down from The Reed Gallery, had been running his tree operation every year for as long as Carrie could remember.

In addition to the rows of fragrant trees brought in from farms in the Great Smoky Mountains on the western side of the state, they had strands of twinkling lights, holiday-themed inflatables, garland and gorgeous wreaths. The festive operation attracted more people into downtown and ramped up the holiday vibe. With additional tourists coming through for the festival, the Wainrights were having a banner year in sales, both of Christmas trees and decorations and accessories sold from the hardware store.

So when Lily Wainright, Phil's youngest daughter who'd recently moved back to Magnolia to help with the family business, burst into the gallery earlier and told Carrie that her dad was having chest pains, of course Carrie had offered to help with ringing up customers at the tree stand so Lucy could take Phil to the hospital.

She wasn't alone. A couple teenagers who worked part-time at the hardware store had also been recruited. The boys did most of the heavy lifting, leaving Carrie to help customers select the perfect tree and then take payment for the purchases.

Unfortunately, the weather hadn't cooperated most of the afternoon. After almost an hour of drizzle, it was finally starting to clear up. Despite the rain they'd had a steady stream of customers thanks to a new shipment of trees and the impending countdown to the holiday.

Now Carrie understood why she'd seen Lily in heavy jackets, leather work gloves and layers of warmth since the lot opened. The temperature was only in the low fifties, but standing outside in the dampness had chilled Carrie right through her puffer coat. She smelled like sap, and her hands were covered in scratches from helping people move trees around.

She lifted her chapped hands to her mouth and blew on them in a feeble attempt to warm herself.

"Another side hustle?" a deep voice asked from behind her.

The butterflies in her stomach took flight once again as she turned to find Dylan staring at her, one corner of his mouth curved up in amusement.

Carrie resisted the urge to groan out loud. Of course, he looked like the picture of alpha male hotness with the black sweater and leather jacket that covered his broad shoulders. His blue eyes looked even more magnetic against the dark green of the pine tree background.

On the other hand, she felt like a drowned rat. She'd pulled her hair into a low ponytail that she'd tucked into the back of her jacket. One of the boys had given her a hardware-store baseball cap to shield her face from the drizzle. She was cold, tired and slightly mortified at her current situation. Dylan's belief that she did too much for the town was unflagging, and schlepping Christmas trees on a dreary afternoon confirmed exactly what he thought about her. All things considered, this wasn't her best moment.

"I'm helping a friend." She adjusted the brim of her cap. "Don't judge."

"No judgment," he assured her then leaned in closer. "Although I'm wondering why you're nice to everyone in town except me."

"I'm nice to you."

"You've been ghosting me all week." His tone teased, but she had to look away when a sliver of vulnerability flashed in his gaze.

She sniffed. "How do you even know the word *ghosting*?"

"Sam explained it. Even he felt bad for me."

Guilt stabbed at her chest. "I'm not trying to blow you off. Things are busy and being with you is…" She broke off, searching for the right word.

"Amazing?" Dylan suggested.

"Complicated."

"I'm guessing you're going to tell me your life is already complicated enough."

"In so many ways."

His eyes clouded over in a way that matched the sky above them. He opened his mouth, but Carrie was left wondering whether he'd planned to argue with her or say farewell because Sam appeared through a gap in the aisle of trees.

"I found one," he announced before his gaze tracked to Carrie. "Oh, hey, Carrie. I didn't know you worked here, too. You have more jobs than anyone I know."

She pasted on a bright smile and turned to the boy. "I'm helping a friend."

Sam nodded. "You're a solid friend to stand out in the wet and cold."

"The best," Dylan murmured under his breath so only she could hear him.

"You've found the perfect tree?" she asked the teenager. "I thought you guys didn't want to deal with shedding pine needles."

"We're getting into the Christmas spirit," Dylan said, moving nearer to her to let another couple pass. She almost swayed into him just to be enveloped in his heat but forced herself to remain still.

Sam gave Dylan a funny look then grinned at Carrie. "He made me go tour the old textile mill with some tool architect my dad used to work with, and now he feels bad because the guy was such a total butt head."

"Can you ever give me a break?" Dylan asked Sam with a sigh.

"Doubtful. Come and see the tree before someone else picks it. Carrie can give her opinion, too. I know she'll side with me."

"I'm sure," Dylan agreed, placing a hand on Carrie's back to guide her forward. "There's nothing the two of you seem to love more than banding together to annoy me."

"You deserve it." Carrie threw him a sharp glare over her shoulder. "I thought we agreed you were putting plans for Camp Beverly Hills Magnolia on hold until the New Year. There are companies interested in developing the factory location into something more than fancy housing if you'll give them a chance. We're going to prove to you that the town is great just the way it is."

"We both know that's not true," he countered. "If it was you wouldn't be constantly scrambling to make sure everyone is taken care of around here. Before you find another excuse to vilify me, today's meeting has been set up since I signed the contract on that property. I'm not denying that I make a perfect villain, but I'm not violating anything."

It was strange how much Carrie wanted—or maybe needed—Dylan to be the bad guy. She clearly needed some outer force to help her keep up her resolve to stay away from him.

She'd managed it, barely, for a few days, but running into him this way made her long to return to those precious nights in his arms and his bed—any part of his life she could have or when the intimacy they shared took away all that stood between them. Also, her heart ached at the thought of the role in which they'd both so willingly cast him.

"You're not the bad guy," she said softly as they stopped in front of a clump of trees. Unable to resist, she covered his hand with hers, squeezing gently, her body flushing from the innocent touch. He had every reason to be frustrated. There was no denying she'd been avoiding him, like she'd used him for the great sex and then walked away without looking back.

As if it was possible to get enough of Dylan.

"What do you think?" Sam asked as he hefted a giant Douglas fir to its full height.

God love teenagers for being so blissfully self-centered. Sam didn't give any indication that he'd picked up on the sparks flying between her and Dylan.

Dylan laughed and shifted closer to Carrie. "I think we're going to have a Griswold family Christmas trying to wrestle that thing into the rental house."

Sam's brows furrowed. "Are the Griswolds friends of yours from Boston? Tell me they aren't like that Steven dude."

Carrie smothered a smile as Dylan gaped at the kid. *National Lampoon's Christmas Vacation*. It's a movie. The best Christmas movie ever."

"I thought you hated everything about Christmas because it's a holiday engineered to elicit fake emotions," Sam said in a perfect imitation of Dylan's rumbly tone.

"I'm not sure *hate* is the right word." Dylan massaged a hand along the back of his neck and Carrie noticed color rising to his cheeks. "That might have been too strong."

She'd fallen for the tough bad boy a decade earlier, but this version of Dylan—the "somewhat uncertain father figure willing to try anything for Sam" guy—was almost irresistible.

"So this Griswold movie is the best?" Sam asked.

"Yes," Dylan said at the same time Carrie shook her head. They both turned to look at her.

"*Elf* is the clear winner. Or maybe *Miracle on 34th Street*. There are so many classics."

"I've seen *Elf*," Sam told her. "Will Ferrell is hilarious."

"Nothing compares to Chevy Chase," Dylan argued. "We need to watch *Christmas Vacation*." He nudged Carrie. "You should join us so you'll be convinced."

"We can watch after we decorate the tree," Sam said with a hopeful smile. "I found a box of ornaments in the basement along with the fake tree we're not using."

Dylan shook his head. "You know that tree actually fits? This one is way too big."

"The bigger, the better." Sam's smile turned cheeky. "Let's take the big one home."

Carrie glanced over at Dylan's sharp intake of breath. He opened his mouth, closed it again and then shrugged. "Fine. The Rockefeller Center-size Christmas tree it is."

As if on cue, Zak, one of the high school helpers,

rounded the corner. "You buying the Sasquatch tree?" he asked with a nod, looking between Sam and the adults standing a few feet away.

Carrie held up her hands. "I'm just going to ring them up."

"Y'all must have one of those great rooms with the vaulted ceiling," Zak said, lifting his chin to take in the top of the tree.

Sam grinned but didn't answer.

"Something like that," Dylan said.

"I'm gonna need extra rope and another set of hands to get this monster out."

"I can help," Sam offered, leaning the tree back against the others. Carrie had a feeling he didn't want to give Dylan a chance to change his mind.

"Let's head over to the register and I'll ring you up," she told him.

"I'm probably going to lose my security deposit because of that tree."

Carrie laughed and headed toward the makeshift counter where the register was situated. "I never thought you'd agree to Sasquatch."

"Sam called our house *home*," he said, and she could hear the emotion threading through his words.

Her heart seemed to skip a beat in response. Who knew vulnerability could be so damn sexy?

"You'll make it work," she told him.

They were silent as she processed his credit card, an AmEx Black. Her father had tried and failed for years to qualify for that level of plastic but had always been denied. It should have been a warning to Carrie that his finances weren't nearly as flush as he pretended. Dylan didn't seem to even register that his card was something special.

"What time are you finished here?" he asked as he took

the credit card from her, his finger brushing against hers and sending electricity dancing along her skin.

She glanced at her watch and then to the sky. Anywhere except Dylan's blue eyes. "The tree stand closes at six. I'll be finished shortly after that unless Lily comes back sooner."

"Then you can join us for dinner as well as tree trimming and movie viewing."

"I don't know." She wrapped her arms around her waist, the cold that had disappeared standing next to Dylan seeping into her bones again. "It's been a long day. I need a shower and to check on the litter of foster kittens I have at the moment."

"Dinner at seven?" Dylan asked as if she hadn't offered up the lamest, spinsterish excuses known to man. Washing her hair and taking care of cats? Could she *be* any more of a cliché?

She should decline the invitation. Spending time with Dylan made her feel too much. It made her want too much.

"Okay," she answered after a moment, both because she liked spending time with him, and she didn't want to be alone. "But only so that I can make sure you don't convince Sam that *Christmas Vacation* is better than *Elf.*"

Dylan's eyes crinkled at the corners. Would he call her out on the lie? Was it totally obvious that she couldn't resist him?

"Whatever you say, sweetheart," he answered and then leaned in and brushed a quick kiss over her lips.

"You can't kiss me in public," she whispered.

He flashed a cheeky grin. "I just did."

It was pointless to argue with him, so she simply made a face then went to greet another family approaching the tree stand.

She congratulated herself for not turning back to look at Dylan again. As if that made her any less aware of him or his effect on her.

As if anything could.

DYLAN GLANCED AT the clock for what felt like the millionth time in the past ten—now eleven—minutes. Seven-eleven.

Carrie was eleven minutes late. Did that mean she wasn't coming? His phone remained dark and silent on the kitchen counter. A direct contrast to the light parade of disappointment flashing inside him.

Had he pushed her too hard about coming over? Given her no choice but to ghost him once again?

Why did it matter anyway? He didn't need her, or any woman, in his life. His hands were more than full with running the business and worrying over Sam.

Since the accident, he'd taken over the bulk of responsibilities in the company that had previously been split between his uncle and cousin.

In addition to his own duties and remotely, since he and Sam had moved to Magnolia.

There was no time for distraction, and Carrie sidetracked him on every level.

He watched the clock as another minute passed.

The doorbell rang a moment later. Before Dylan had gotten to his feet, the sound of teenage footsteps thundered down the stairs and Sam ran past him.

"We need to eat fast," the kid called over his shoulder, "so we can start decorating."

Worth it, Dylan thought to himself as he followed Sam to the front door. Even if their enormous, ill-fitting tree shed every one of its needles before the New Year, it would be worth it for Sam's excitement tonight.

Dylan still didn't believe in Christmas magic or any of that garbage, but he couldn't deny the impact the holidays were having on Sam.

Just like he couldn't deny Carrie's effect on him.

He felt his heart settle as she stepped into the house, as if she were some kind of weighted blanket or special lovey that could help ease any anxiety.

Then he noticed the oversize cardboard box in her arms and heard the tiny mewling sound coming from inside the plastic carrier balanced on top.

"Is that a kitten?" Sam asked, his eyes going wide. Daisy, who'd trotted to the door at Sam's heels, gave a low growl then sniffed at the box.

"I'm not trying to foist him off on you," she told Dylan with an apologetic smile even as she gestured for Sam to lift the carrier from her. "Barnaby is why I'm late. He got stuck behind the radiator and it took forever to coax him out. He was limping a little. I called Meredith, but she said just to keep an eye on him."

"Do we get to keep him?"

Dylan felt his eyes go wide. If Carrie wanted to get back at him for pressuring her to come over tonight, she'd found the perfect way.

"He's going home with me after the movie. I promise."

"Unless he's happier here," Sam told her. "He might be better with us. We have vents not radiators."

Dylan snorted as he saw her try to hide her smile. "You're pretty convincing when you want something," she told the teenager.

"No doubt," Dylan agreed. He took the box from Carrie's hands. "Let's get the wee beastie set up in the laundry room for now. I'm not sure the dog is going to like sharing her space."

"Daisy will love Barnaby," Sam said emphatically, and Dylan shook his head.

It truly was amazing how quickly the boy could turn on the charm when it served him.

The dog yipped as the tiny animal hissed inside its container.

"I'm sorry," Carrie said quietly as they followed Sam to the back of the house. "I should have just canceled."

"Oh, no. I wouldn't have let you out of tree trimming that easy. I can handle a kitten more easily than I can deal with tinsel."

They set up the kitten with the litter box Carrie had brought, a few towels and a water and food dish.

Sam was reluctant to leave the baby, but finally joined them in the kitchen.

"I need to Google how to introduce a cat and dog to each other," he said around a bite of the Chinese food Dylan had ordered.

"Slowly is the most important part," Carrie told him. "I'm sure Meredith would be thrilled if you guys wanted to foster either a litter of kittens or even an adult cat. That way you could see how Daisy does with a new animal."

"That's a great idea," Sam said.

"You got the gigantic Christmas tree," Dylan said. "Don't push your luck, kid." He pointed his chopsticks at Carrie. "And no encouragement from the peanut gallery."

"None at all," she answered immediately, holding up her hands.

He narrowed his eyes as he realized her fingers were crossed. Then she flashed him a teasing smile and winked and he felt happiness skitter along his spine.

Sam took one more small bite of Szechuan beef then pushed back from the table.

"You hardly ate a thing," Dylan complained, stunned at how naturally the words tumbled from his mouth. Damn. He sounded like a parent.

If Sam thought the comment strange coming from Dylan, he didn't let on. Instead, he shrugged. "I'm sick of Chinese. It's that or carryout burgers all the time. This town needs more options."

"Have you tried Il Rigatone?" Carrie asked with a sweet smile for Dylan.

"The place he's closing down?" Sam shook his head. "It's supposed to be gross and dirty."

Dylan cringed as Carrie's eyes narrowed. He was going to pay for that offhand remark. "You're getting Italian tomorrow night," Carrie told the teenager. "It's the best restaurant in Magnolia, and they deliver."

"Seriously?"

"Not the best," Dylan argued.

"Without a doubt," Carrie told him.

"Can I go see Barnaby now?"

Just as Sam asked the question, there was a commotion from the back of the house. A door banging against the wall followed by a series of high-pitched barks.

"Crap," Dylan muttered, jumping up from his seat to race after Sam, Carrie on his heels.

He skidded to a stop at the doorway of the laundry room when Sam blocked him from entering. He hoped the boy wouldn't be traumatized for life by whatever they found in the room.

"Good girl," Sam murmured.

Dylan peered over Sam's shoulder at the crazy scene in front of them.

"This is what you call a Christmas miracle," Carrie whispered.

Daisy was sprawled on her belly, chin resting on the tile floor, staring at the kitten, who swiped at her nose with a tiny paw.

Dylan held his breath as Barnaby got bolder, nipping at Daisy's snout, then head butting the dog and rubbing his fuzzy head against hers.

"Should we be terrified?" he asked Carrie under his breath.

"Daisy loves him," Sam said. "I knew she would."

The dog whined softly as if confirming the boy's words.

Suddenly, Dylan felt the gentle touch of Carrie's fingers brushing the side of his hand.

He pressed two fingers to his chest as some of the walls he'd spent so much time building around his heart began to crumble. Not that this had anything to do with Christmas. Or miracles. Or falling in love for a second time with Carrie Reed.

Definitely not the last.

"Let's bring him out while we trim the tree," Carrie suggested. "We can watch the two of them together."

"They're bonding," Sam said. He scooped up the small kitten, and Daisy scrambled to her feet. He walked out with the two animals. "Dylan, will you bring the litter box?"

"We've got the supplies," Carrie assured the teen. "Just keep a watch on them."

"You're going to pay for this," Dylan told Carrie when they were alone in the room. But there was no heat in the words, and obviously she knew it. And he forgot all about being angry when she drew him closer and pressed her mouth to his.

"You're not quite as Scroogey as you want everyone to believe," she said against his lips. "I like that about you."

Damn if that didn't feel like an accomplishment.

CHAPTER SIXTEEN

"Your sister should put you on retainer."

Carrie smiled at Dylan over the rim of her wineglass later that night. Sam, Daisy and the kitten had gone to bed an hour earlier after Sam had convinced Dylan to let the tiny animal sleep with him for the night. "You're kind of an easy sell."

The only illumination in the family room came from the glow of the strands of lights on the Christmas tree, so she could sense rather than see his eyes darken as he approached the sofa where she sat.

"I'm not keeping the kitten."

"Maybe not." She took another sip of wine then placed her glass on the end table. "But Sam and Daisy are planning on it."

He sighed. "Why do all the things that make Sam happy end up being a pain in my ass?"

"I'm not an expert on kids, but rumor has it that's fairly typical."

"Why don't you have any forever animals?" he asked, settling back against the soft cushions. "It seems like Meredith should have found your perfect pet match by now."

She felt her shoulders tense but tried to hide it. "I like fostering," she answered, which wasn't a lie, just not the whole truth. "I don't want the responsibility of permanent pet ownership."

"You're the most responsible person I know," Dylan told her with a laugh. He reached out and traced one finger along her jawline as if to smooth away the tension she held there. "I bet half the town has you on speed dial to call in case of emergency."

"I hate it sometimes." She whispered the words like she was imparting a great secret. Or as if lightning might strike her down for the admission. But that didn't stop it from being the truth.

She'd been responsible and practical and dependable and all the other boring adjectives for as long as she could remember. Not adopting an animal from Meredith's rescue was a tiny thing but Carrie couldn't take on one more level of obligation in her life.

She had a feeling Meredith understood because although she was constantly asking for fostering favors, she never pressured Carrie to keep any of the fur babies she took on. Not the way Meredith had pushed Avery to adopt the adorably overweight mutt, Spot, a few months ago. Or how she subtly strong-armed Dylan into opening his house to a dog at Thanksgiving. In fact, Meredith had tried to make forever family matches with almost everyone Carrie knew. Except her.

She wasn't sure whether to be shocked or grateful that her sister could read her so well. Not that the animals didn't tempt her. She could have been content to keep any number of them. But she couldn't. Wouldn't.

"You don't owe them anything." Dylan cupped her chin in his warm hand, and she wanted to curl into him the same way Barnaby had with Daisy. To trust him to keep her safe because he was the one person who'd always liked her just the way she was.

She didn't have to be perfect or compliant or dependable with Dylan. It was a wholly liberating sensation.

Even if he was wrong for her in the end.

But this wasn't the end.

This was now.

She moved closer to him, wrapping her arms around his neck. "The tree is beautiful," she said, turning her gaze when the intensity in his eyes became too much to handle. It felt like being under the scope of some sort of lust-filled laser beam or what.

They'd decorated the tree with the lights and ornaments Sam had found, along with a few extras Carrie'd brought over. She'd cajoled Dylan into turning on holiday music, and she and Sam had sung at the top of their lungs while Dylan grimaced and tried to hide his enjoyment.

Was there anything more festive than trimming a Christmas tree?

Carrie realized that she'd been so focused on making the holidays magical for the entire town she'd forgotten to enjoy the simple moments of the season herself.

In fact, she feared she'd been going through the motions for longer than she cared to admit, checking off the appropriate Christmas spirit boxes without truly appreciating the meaning of the season.

The evening with Dylan and Sam made her long for a family of her own. For the chance to create her own traditions that didn't revolve around expectations from anyone else. Her father had always had very specific ideas about how the holidays should be handled. When she was a kid, he'd relished playing the role of benevolent Santa for the people in town even if it meant they didn't have time to celebrate privately as a family.

Once her mother left, Carrie had spent most Decembers

trying to keep Niall out of the spiral of holiday depression that regularly overtook him.

She hadn't given much thought to the emotional cost of setting aside her own wishes for Christmas in order to cater to her father's needs. To the needs of the Magnolia community. To everyone except herself.

"Should I take it personally?" Dylan asked, jolting her back to reality.

She tried to move away from him, but his arms stayed steady on her waist. "Take what?"

His mouth quirked into that almost-smile. "One moment I thought you were going to kiss me and the next you're wearing a scowl like someone pulled off Santa's fake beard."

"Sorry," she said automatically. "I was just thinking about past Christmases and how much I missed because my focus had to be on my dad."

"Or the town?"

"That, too," she admitted. "The evening was great, even if the tree is way too big for your house."

He followed her gaze to the tree, which filled the room with the scent of pine. It looked both massive shoved into the corner of the room and oddly perfect.

"I have to admit I had fun. It's been years since I've decorated a tree."

"You didn't put one up in your condo in Boston?"

He shrugged. "The building had a tree in the lobby. That seemed close enough."

Carrie reached out to stroke his arm. "Did Sam's parents go all out for the holidays?"

"I guess. To be honest, I didn't pay much attention. Normally, I scheduled a vacation over the holidays."

"You left town for Christmas?"

"Don't knock it. I'd ski Aspen if the snow was good out west or head to the Caribbean for some beach time."

She blew out a soft laugh. "Actually, I might be jealous."

"Are you admitting the foolishness of the holidays isn't all it's cracked up to be?"

"Not one bit. But I will say there were a few holidays in the past couple of years I could have skipped." She stuck out her tongue. "This isn't one of those."

As a slow grin spread across his face, he glanced toward the tree and then back to Carrie again. "This one is not that bad."

"Big praise," she murmured as hope blossomed in her chest. If she could make Dylan see the importance of the holiday spirit in Magnolia, surely she could convince him that the town needed to remain quaint and quirky.

There were plenty of places to build luxury townhomes and upscale retail centers.

Magnolia didn't need that kind of an overhaul to be reinvigorated. It only needed people willing to capitalize on the things that already made it special.

Maybe she and Magnolia had that in common.

Maybe Dylan could see it in her and the town.

Thoughts for her continuing campaign evaporated like a water droplet on a hot radiator when he kissed her.

"We keep getting distracted," he said as he shifted her closer.

Her pulse fluttered as he trailed kisses down her throat, nipping at the sensitive place in the crook of her collarbone. "From what?"

"From us."

Us. She liked the sound of that word on his lips.

"What about Sam?" She managed the words despite her body commanding her to be quiet and enjoy the moment.

"He's the soundest sleeper I've ever met," Dylan said. "We have the main floor all to ourselves."

Reassured, she smiled as he tugged the sweater over her head and then did the same with the thick Henley he wore.

He claimed her mouth again as he maneuvered them so that he was lying on the sofa with Carrie straddling his lean hips.

She lifted her head to look down at his broad chest. The glow from the Christmas tree bathing them in gentle light, she ran her palms across the corded muscles there and along his shoulders. Unable to resist, she lowered again and licked one tight nipple, the hiss of breath that escaped his lips both gratifying and exhilarating.

Their mouths came together, more insistent in the need that sparked between them. She felt his hands moving along her back, deft fingers making quick work of her bra clasp. The straps fell from her shoulders and she tossed aside the delicate fabric without a second thought, wanting to feel his skin against hers.

A moan broke from her lips as he cupped her breasts in his hands, flicking a thumb across the sensitive tips.

"So beautiful," he said, urging her higher until he could close his mouth around one nipple.

Heat pooled low in her as her hips moved against him, sensation spiraling through her as he sucked harder then blew cool air against her heated skin.

"Naked," she said, pressing her hands on his chest for balance.

"Is that a request or a command?"

"Command," she said without hesitation, earning a sexy grin from Dylan.

"I like you in control."

So did she, although she never would have guessed it.

She climbed off him, and he led her to his bedroom before peeling the black yoga pants she wore down over her hips and legs. It didn't take long until they were a tangle of limbs and kisses and whispered murmurs between the sheets of his big bed.

When he entered her and they moved together, it felt so right that Carrie had to blink away the tears that sprung to her eyes.

What kind of silly fool cried during sex?

She fused her mouth to his instead, kissing him deeply even as emotion clogged her throat.

As the pressure built inside her it was like being on a roller coaster making its way up that first big hill. Sensation spiraled through her along with anticipation of the pleasure she knew was imminent.

And when her release broke over her, careening through her and plunging her over the edge, Carrie was helpless to do anything but hold on to Dylan's broad shoulders for the wild ride.

He groaned into her mouth and she felt his body tense for several languorous moments, and then he relaxed against her.

She held him, or they held each other, in the minutes after, the soft whirl of the wind outside the bedroom window the only sound in the quiet house.

"It only gets better between us," he said when he finally lifted his head.

"Too much better and you're going to kill me with the satisfaction of it," she told him with a forced laugh. Concentrate on the physical part of it, she counseled herself. Not the emotional. Keep that separate. Keep her heart safe. Although somewhere deep inside she knew it was too late for that.

"What a way to go," he said, unaware of the struggle going on inside her. He placed a gentle kiss on her forehead and then dropped beside her, keeping one arm draped across her stomach. Like she belonged to him.

Oh, how she wanted to belong to him.

But Carrie was smart enough not to let herself give in to that wish. Dylan scratched an itch she'd had for too long. It had been years since she'd dated, an embarrassingly long time to be without a man's touch.

That was why this felt like more. She was a plant soaking up water and sunshine after being ignored in a dry, dark place. Of course it would mean something to her. But she couldn't let it.

As much as she wanted to snuggle into him and let sleep find her safe within the comfort of his arms, she moved away, throwing back the sheet and allowing the cool air of the room to bring her to her senses.

"I need to go home," she said back to him. She felt him shift and moved before he could reach for her. It was like pulling herself away from a magnet. Her clothes were strewn across the floor, and she quickly gathered them and padded to the bathroom.

In the bright light of the small space, Carrie dressed and then studied herself in the mirror over the sink. Her face was flushed, but she couldn't quite keep the panic from showing in her eyes. Her chest rose and fell as she struggled to curb the panic that threatened to rise up inside her. She blinked several times, telling herself that she had things under control.

She understood that the physical connection could be amazing with Dylan, but it wouldn't translate to anything more.

Allowing her heart to lead would only end in him breaking it all over again.

She straightened her sweater, finger-combed her hair
and then exited the bathroom with what she hoped was a
serene expression on her face.

"Is everything okay?" Dylan asked. He stood next to the
bed wearing a faded T-shirt and athletic shorts and looking
as invitingly rumpled as the sheets and comforter.

"I have to check on the other kittens," she told him, once
again using them as an excuse like some sort of throwback
spinster.

"Are you going to come back?"

She shook her head. "Not a good idea." Before he could
argue, she took a step toward the door. "Are you okay with
Barnaby staying here? It really wasn't my intention to add
another animal to your household. You can sneak in and
grab him from Sam's room now or I could pick him up in
the morning if…"

"He's fine." Dylan's tone was laced with frustration. "I
don't want to talk about the kitten, Carrie."

Funny, she didn't want to talk about anything at all. Not
with the effort she was making to control her feelings, to
prevent them from overruling her good sense. "Okay," she
answered. "I'll see you later."

He ran a hand through his hair, tugging on the ends
until it stood out in a half dozen spiky peaks. God, how
she wanted to smooth them down. To smooth over all of
both of their rough edges. "That's it?"

"It's better this way," she told him, clenching her hands
into fists at her sides. "We have fun together, but both of
us know there's nothing more to it."

"We do," he murmured without sounding the least bit
convinced.

"Don't forget the meeting tomorrow and the final run-
through of the weekend schedule. We're also going to talk

about the new businesses interested in coming to Magnolia. They might be a good fit for the buildings you own."

"I've got plans for those buildings and we both know they don't involve whatever mom and pop shops might want a deal on a lease. That was Niall's territory and look where it got him."

A sharp ache cut across her chest. His callous reminder should make her happy. This was exactly the reason they couldn't be together long-term.

"We're not repeating the mistakes my father made in town."

He walked toward her, and she instinctively backed away. Between the emotions of what had just happened between them and the overwhelming anger and frustration at his hardheadedness, she didn't trust herself to allow him to touch her. Not when she felt like she might shatter from the inside out due to the riot of feelings pulsing through her.

Dylan immediately stopped. "Do you really want to do this now?"

"No," she admitted. "I want to go home."

His mouth thinned but he nodded. "Like I said, the kitten is fine here. What's a little more poop to scoop in the grand scheme of things? At this point I'm up to my eyeballs in crap as it is."

She knew he didn't mean that as a personal attack, but the words still stung.

"Thanks for tonight," she said, the manners her mother had insisted upon hard to relinquish.

"For the orgasm?" He gave a tight laugh. "Anytime, Carrie."

Her cheeks flushed hot, but she didn't respond. What in the world could she say to that?

Instead, she turned on her heel and fled the room, detouring to the kitchen to grab her purse and then heading out into the cool December night. She didn't pause as she hurried to her car, driving the few blocks to her house on autopilot.

There was far too much to process about this night. Things she couldn't deal with in her current state.

Things she wasn't sure she'd ever be ready to handle.

"I ALREADY OWN one of your dogs," Dylan complained the following morning as he filled out paperwork at Meredith's rescue. "I'm not sure why I need more forms for an animal that weighs less than three pounds."

"It's policy," Meredith told him from where she sat behind a desk crowded with paper, trial-size bags of dog and cat food and various animal toys.

A movement in the corner caught his eye, and he glanced down to see a lop-eared bunny nibbling on the corner of a cardboard box.

Meredith cocked a brow. "You like rabbits?"

"Don't even think about it," he warned.

"I think you're placing the blame on the wrong sister. Carrie invited you here for Thanksgiving and brought Barnaby to your house. She's the reason you've opened your house."

And your heart, a little voice inside him said. He mentally choked that voice until it was silent. She didn't have his heart. Hell, no. He was a grown-ass man, more than capable of understanding the difference between love and sex.

He sure wasn't interested in setting himself up for a good kick in the heart again.

"She's sneaky," he said instead, "but we're full up now. No more rescues or lost causes."

Meredith didn't answer but her eyes narrowed slightly

as she studied him, like he was some kind of puzzle she was trying to solve.

"I didn't peg you for an unsung hero sort of guy," she said, rising and handing him a manila envelope.

He shrugged. "You were too busy casting me as the villain."

"Not exactly a villain, but maybe a second-rate bad guy," she admitted. "Remember I have two older brothers. I heard plenty of stories about you."

"All of them true, I'm sure." He took the envelope from her hand as heat prickled along the back of his neck. He hadn't thought much about the stupid choices and monumental mistakes he'd made as a teenager until he'd taken responsibility for Sam. Then all the ways he had no business caring for another human came rushing back to him. "By the way, I'm not a hero of any kind. I could give a damn if every single person in this town considers me the bad guy."

"Even Carrie?" Meredith asked. He hated the way her gaze gentled when she looked at him, like he was some kind of wounded animal who needed rescuing.

Which was absurd.

"We both know how she feels about me," he said instead of answering the question. Because never in a million years would he admit that he wanted Carrie to look at him the way she used to, as if he hung the moon and the stars. Not when he could walk outside on a sleepless night and count his faults like a million spots of light across a clear sky.

"Do we?" Meredith walked around the desk, bending to scoop up a hulking black cat. "I heard that you told Carrie to focus more on her art."

"Yeah. You might not remember her from high school, but her paintings were everything to her. At least until her parents divorced and her dad…" He cleared his throat. "Your dad," he amended but Meredith held up a hand.

"The man who raised me is my father. Niall Reed is the jerk who screwed around with my mom."

There were so many levels of anger and betrayal in those words, Dylan didn't even know how to formulate an answer. He nodded, hoping Meredith didn't expect more than that.

"Niall put the three of you in a horrible situation. He also did a number on Carrie's confidence. She's had too many excuses over the years to put her talent aside."

"Excuses like bailing out the town from the financial mess he caused?" Meredith asked with a humorless laugh.

"Among others." He gave a pointed look to the fluffy feline in her arms. "She helps you out quite a bit with fostering, right?"

"Are you blaming me?"

"I'm not blaming anyone," he corrected. "But if the people in her life continue to give her a pass for not pursuing her art because it's scary or hard, that isn't going to help her. She needs to be painting."

Meredith's mouth thinned and he thought she was going to physically kick him out of her office. But she closed her eyes for several moments—maybe even to the count of ten—and when she opened them again, she nodded.

"Avery and I will talk to her." She dropped the fluffy cat onto her desk where the animal immediately stretched out like some kind of feline centerfold showing off its private bits. "Again."

He pointed to the cat. "Is that what I have to look forward to with Barnaby?"

Meredith flashed a cheeky grin. "He's a kitten so you have tons of fun ahead of you. Unwound toilet paper rolls… shredded curtains…being climbed like a jungle gym."

"Fantastic," Dylan muttered. "Can't wait. I'll see you at his next vet appointment."

He turned to go but Meredith stopped him with a hand on his arm. He looked down at her fingers, noticing that they were the same elegant shape as Carrie's. Did Avery have the same hands as her two sisters? Was this a trait they shared from their father's DNA?

She quickly pulled away her hand. "I'm joking about the bad behavior. Get a scratching post and some interactive cat toys. Call if you run into an issue. I just want you to know you're doing a good thing with the animals. Not just for them but for Sam, too. Studies have shown that pet ownership is good for a person's emotional and physical health. Daisy and Barnaby will give him something to think about other than himself and what he's been through. And unconditional love. Everyone needs love."

"I don't," Dylan answered automatically. He'd learned too many hard lessons about how love led to pain. "But I get what you're saying about the kid. Just no more animals."

"Fish are easy," Meredith said, tapping one finger against her chin.

"No more," he repeated with an eye roll and she laughed.

He left the rescue with a feeling of lightness in his chest that he didn't understand or appreciate. He had no desire to make friends with people in Magnolia, and certainly not Carrie's sister. He might not consider himself the enemy, but it was better if other people did. Then there would be no surprises if and when he hurt them.

CHAPTER SEVENTEEN

CARRIE RUSHED DOWN the stairs into the conference room of the town hall building, where the business owners' meeting was already underway.

First, she'd totally blown off last week's dinner with her sisters and the two town council members, and tonight she was twenty minutes late. As a rule, Carrie was never late but she'd been painting for hours and lost track of the time. Again.

Returning from Dylan's house, she'd only managed a few fitful hours of sleep before giving up. In the second bedroom of her rental, she'd picked up a paintbrush and put it to the canvas set up on her easel without much conscious thought. Years ago art had been both her escape and a path to emotional freedom. It was strange that it played the same role for her now, like slipping back into a comfortable pair of shoes.

She'd continued to paint as the light from the window went from shades of gray and pink to the bright morning sunshine and throughout the day. She hadn't stopped for food or to go to the bathroom, propelled by some force she barely understood.

"I'm here," she announced as if her arrival wasn't obvious.

"Nice to see you, Carrie," the mayor announced from where he stood at the podium in the front of the room. "We were about to adjourn to the square to test the lights before things really get rolling tomorrow."

Tomorrow. The biggest weekend of the festival—her festival—kicked off in earnest tomorrow with the elaborate LED and twinkle light displays she'd installed to be synchronized with a soundtrack of holiday carols, along with a twenty-minute snow show. And she'd blown off her entire to-do list in order to spend the day working on a new canvas. What was wrong with her?

She smiled and kept her head held high as the members of the committee filed past her on their way out the door, ignoring the strange looks she got from almost every person, including her sisters. She hadn't seen Dylan yet but the way the little hairs on the back of her neck stood on end told her he was in the room.

"Is everything all right, dear?" Josie Trumbell seemed genuinely worried as she looked Carrie over from head to toe.

"I'm fine," Carrie answered and tried not to cringe as she glanced down at herself. The faded sweatshirt she wore was wrinkled and splattered with paint specks and the bulky boots she'd shoved her feet into were a glaring contrast to the patterned leggings she wore. She smiled at Josie and swiped a hand at the front of her shirt.

"Don't bother," Avery said, coming to stand next to her. "Your cheeks are streaked, as well. Embrace the eccentric artist mantle, sis. It looks good on you."

"I've been painting, but I'm not what anyone would consider an artist," Carrie protested automatically. "Eccentric or otherwise."

"Then you do a great impersonation of one," a deep voice said from behind her. She turned to find Dylan smiling at her, and not the smug grin she would have expected.

He looked genuinely happy to see her and somehow satisfied that she was in such a state of disarray. "People who paint are generally known as artists," he said, his voice pitched low.

"Captain Obvious strikes again," Meredith said with a laugh as she joined them.

"I'm sorry," Carrie murmured. "I lost track of time today and—"

"Don't apologize," Meredith interrupted. "We've got things under control for the festival."

"Your sisters have your back," Malcolm added as he approached.

"Carrie's done the heavy lifting," Avery said, and Carrie wasn't sure whether to be grateful for the loyalty or embarrassed how clear it must be to everyone that she was shirking her responsibilities.

Maybe she had more in common with her father than she wanted to admit. He'd always professed his good intentions with regard to the town. At least he'd talked a good game about his commitment. But when push came to shove, Niall had been in it for himself. Carrie didn't think of herself that way, but she couldn't deny the tinge of resentment that had colored her mood as she'd finally put away her paint supplies in order to rush to this meeting.

No one had forced her to devote herself to making the holidays in Magnolia the biggest and best the region had ever seen. But how else would she prove that she wasn't like her dad? That she hadn't allowed herself to ignore how bad things had gotten, just as he had, because it was easier that way.

Dylan's warm hand on her back snapped her out of her meandering thoughts. She darted a glance at him and then to the cluster of family and friends surrounding them. Her sisters and Malcolm watched her with the same curious expressions. Like they were questioning whether she'd lost her mind.

"Let's go see the lights," she said with a purposefully bright smile. "It's going to be amazing."

The mayor let out a relieved breath. "It sure is," he agreed and led the way toward the staircase.

Avery and Meredith shared a look that Carrie didn't bother to try to interpret.

"I'm fine," she insisted, stepping away from Dylan's touch even though her first instinct was to move closer to him. There was no reason why he should feel like her ally at the moment. For all she knew, his insistence that she needed to devote more time to her art was a ploy to distract her from her duties on the festival committee. The number of visitors in town for the holiday events had been impressive so far, but they needed even bigger crowds to show up the next two weekends for the down-home holiday celebration she'd planned. A lack of visitors would help prove Dylan's point that Magnolia needed an image overhaul instead of a simple enhancement.

"You should have kept painting," Avery said over her shoulder. "Meredith and I could have handled this."

"You both have enough going on in your own lives," Carrie argued. "The town is my responsibility."

"No, it's not," Dylan said, leaning closer.

"I hate to agree with him," Meredith said, "but he's right. Your dreams and goals are just as important as the ones that involve the town."

Annoyance pricked along Carrie's spine. "My goal is to see Magnolia thrive again."

"But you're *painting*." Avery held the door open as

Carrie walked through. "And not just silly sip-and-paint-themed canvases. That should be your priority."

"Those silly parties were your idea," Carrie reminded her half sister, not bothering to hide her annoyance.

"You should stage another show with your new works," Meredith suggested. "Bring in some other artists and do a showcase of local talent."

Carrie crossed her hands over her chest. "I'm not selling my new paintings."

"We could put it on the town calendar for late January." Malcolm tapped a finger on his chin, gazing at Carrie with those too knowing chocolate-brown eyes. "You'd be a great midwinter draw."

"I'll make fliers to hand out at the festival this weekend and next," Josie offered. "My granddaughter is teaching me how to use templates on my computer. I'm very high-tech now."

"I'm not a draw." Carrie tried to keep the panic out of her voice when she realized every member of the festival committee—people she'd known her entire life—stared at her like she was some kind of second coming. "I doubt anyone wants to see my current art."

"Yes, they do," Avery argued. "Especially if we market the event the right way."

"Your dad might have been a critical hack most of his career," Phil Wainright from the hardware store said, "but he's still famous. People will be curious to know whether you're going to carry on the family tradition. Think of the publicity you got from the show of your old stuff, and we hardly did anything to market that but announce it on the town Facebook page." His words earned nods of agreement from the group, making Carrie unsure of whether to laugh or cry.

Without thinking about it, she shifted nearer to Dylan. She should be angry with him. His encouragement had inspired her to begin painting for real again. She hadn't even realized she missed it before he came back into her life. She hadn't realized she missed a lot of things before his return.

"We need to keep our attention focused on the task in front of us," he told the group as he stepped in front of her like some kind of buffer against a storm. "Let's get these lights going and show the crowds who attend the festival a great time and then we'll focus on what comes next."

Carrie appreciated the reprieve from being the center of attention, even if something about the way he spoke about the future made her hackles rise. She ignored the clang of warning bells sounding in her brain. Dylan was here. True to his word, it felt like he was giving her and the other volunteers a chance to prove they had Magnolia on the right track.

If they stayed the course, things would keep moving forward with tourism and, hopefully, they'd forget about the idea of her doing a show. She should want to embrace the opportunity, but as much as painting filled her heart, the thought of putting her work out for public consumption remained a terrifying prospect. Her old high school paintings had been easy enough to display, especially when the sales had helped raise the money to pay off a few overdue bills and buy supplies for the paint-and-sip business.

But her new work felt different, more personal. In truth, it terrified her to think of sharing it publicly. There would be no way to prevent comparisons to her father, and Carrie had watched him struggle for years dealing with his career. The constant pressure to do more, sell more, be more to everyone. It was one thing to give her all to help Magnolia succeed. She imagined putting that much effort into a career as an artist might feel like constantly walking around with no clothes on.

Tamping down the panic that threatened to overtake her, she followed as Malcolm led the group across the street toward the center of the town square. She'd deal with the harsh reality of what it meant to truly embrace her art after the holidays. Carrie held her breath as he placed a hand on the control panel the electricians had set up behind the main bandstand.

He flipped the switch and for a moment the entire square was flooded with light. Thousands of light strands twinkled from where they'd been strung across the wide expanse of park, around the trunks of trees and along the perimeter of the square. Every building that bordered the park was lit in festive colors. Overhead there was a canopy of light in the shape of Santa in his sleigh, complete with reindeer and a giant bag of toys.

Tears sprang to Carrie's eyes as the lights danced like stars overhead and all around them. She heard the rumble of the snowmaking machine and seconds later flurries gathered in the air around them. The effect was everything she'd imagined and more.

A collective gasp went up from their group. It was like a holiday fairy tale for a few seconds. Then it all went dark.

"THE LIGHTS WERE overkill anyway," Stuart Moore, the crotchety owner of the bookstore, told Carrie as he awkwardly patted her shoulder. "People don't want to be wearing sunglasses at night."

She gave a halfhearted laugh at his attempt to make her feel better. Even to her own ears it sounded just this side of hysterical.

"We'll fix this," Avery assured her.

"It's a disaster," Carrie murmured, pressing two fingers to her pounding heart. "I shouldn't have gone so crazy with the lights."

Her plan for the biggest light display on the coast seemed to have overloaded the main circuit, plunging the entire town into darkness, or maybe it was the whole county. Shae had called Meredith from the rescue to report they'd lost power and ask about any possible electrical storms.

No storm on the horizon other than the tornado blowing apart Carrie's confidence.

Even now all she could seem to do was stand in place as people moved around her, putting in calls to the utility company and unplugging cords to ease the pressure on the system.

"I saw this on an episode of that Christmas light fight show," Josie reported. "But they only knocked out the block."

"It was beautiful while it worked," Mary Ellen offered. "At least we tried it before the entire festival was ruined."

"It was too much anyway," Stuart said, shaking his head. "Should have listened to Dylan in the first place. Who would have thought he'd be the rational one in all of this?" He gave a long look at Carrie, Avery and Meredith. "I guess we should have expected it with you three."

"Expected what?" Meredith demanded. "That we would have turned things around in this town in the course of a few short months. Between Avery's marketing and the work that Carrie has put in to make the holiday events special, we're still going to have the best holiday celebration this town has ever seen. Which will mean sales for you."

"Back in the day we didn't have to work so hard. People flocked to this town just because..." Stuart shrugged, as if realizing he'd gone too far. "Anyway, I'm going home.

We should post something to the town's Facebook page that everyone needs to bring flashlights tomorrow night in case the power goes out."

"No one is posting about flashlights," Avery said then turned to Mary Ellen. "Would you check in with Malcolm and see if there's a time frame on getting things back to normal?"

"Sure thing."

"Ruined," Carrie whispered when she was alone with her sisters. "What if I ruined everything with my stupid need to go overboard?"

"Nothing you do is stupid," Avery assured her.

"The same can't be said for Stuart. That guy is inbred for sure."

"Maybe he was right." Despite the cool temperature as night fell, a bead of sweat trickled down Carrie's back, and her stomach ached from her embarrassment at the scene she'd caused. "I'm creating a lot of work for myself and everyone else with no guarantee it will pay off."

"It's going to pay off." Avery gave her a quick hug. "I talked to Miriam at The Magnolia Inn. She's at full occupancy this weekend and almost half of her guests are visitors returning to spend a second weekend in town. According to her, the local bed-and-breakfasts are experiencing the same thing. That never happens this time of year."

"I can't remember the last weekend of no vacancy in Magnolia." Malcolm gave her an approving nod as he approached. "You've done good here and we appreciate it."

"I'm sorry about the power."

At that moment the lights flicked back on, and Carrie breathed a sigh of relief. Relief tinged with a smidge of disappointment. Power had been restored to the buildings she could see from where they stood, but the town square remained dark.

"We had to unplug," the mayor explained. "At least until someone from the utility company can figure out how to light the whole thing without other disturbances. They're sending a crew out first thing tomorrow morning."

"We'll find a way to turn on at least some of the lights," Avery promised. "I'm sure Gray will think of a solution."

"He's a firefighter," Carrie reminded her sister, "not an electrician."

Avery's expression took on that dreamy look Carrie had come to expect when Gray was the topic of conversation. "He can do anything."

"Her own personal superhero," Meredith added, deadpan.

"I'll call Gray in the morning," Malcolm promised. "Any ideas are good ones at this point. Right now the three of you should head home. It's all hands on deck first thing tomorrow."

"We'll make sure the weekend is great no matter what." Avery gave Carrie another hug and even Meredith joined in. Carrie knew things must be bad if her normally flippant sister was offering solace.

"Want to grab dinner?" Meredith asked. "I've got to get back to check on Shae and the animals, but if we got something quick…"

"I told Violet I'd help with her costume for the Christmas pageant," Avery said.

Carrie stared at her sophisticated, former city-girl sister. "You can sew?"

"No, but I bought a glue gun." Avery grinned. "You can make anything with a glue gun."

"Just don't glue your fingertips together," Meredith

warned. "My dad did that once when he was trying to fix my favorite piggy bank after Theo broke into it."

Carrie felt her chest pinch at the sadness in Meredith's voice. Discovering their connection and the secrets Niall had left behind affected each of them in a different way. She knew Meredith had struggled with her new identity and what that meant for the father she'd grown up with and who'd raised her on his own for so many years.

"How is your dad?" she asked gently, feeling Avery go still next to her. Meredith rarely opened up to either of them.

"Still staying with Erik down in Wilmington," she said casually. "He might be back for Christmas."

Avery tsked under her breath. "Will you go there for the holiday if not?"

"Hard to find animal sitters at that time. We'll see." Meredith made a show of checking her watch. "If we're not getting dinner, I'm going to grab some carryout and head home. I'll see you both bright and early tomorrow."

Carrie said goodbye to Avery, as well, and headed across the darkened town square on her own. This wasn't how things were supposed to go—any of it.

The warring emotions of guilt and resentment crept along her spine like dueling spiders making her skin itch with discomfort.

She'd planned to test the lights on her own before tonight to ensure everything worked the way they should. How many other details had she overlooked? Between the time she spent with Dylan and the hours in front of a canvas, she hadn't given nearly as much to the festival as she'd planned.

Now it felt like the whole thing was in jeopardy. But the piece of her that had spent the past decade catering to her father's every whim and need rose up inside her like some kind of stubborn weed. What would happen if she really changed her mind about dedicating all of her energy toward the town?

Avery and Meredith worked hard, too, but they were doing it to help make sure the properties they'd inherited would be worth something. They didn't seem to have the same driving compulsion to right the wrongs of their father in the same way Carrie did.

She paused as she caught sight of Dylan near the entrance to his building. He'd disappeared after the town went dark, and she'd figured he'd headed home to celebrate the fact that her plan seemed to be falling apart just when it counted the most.

His back was to her and she could see the cell phone against his ear. She thought about backtracking through the park and taking the long way home around the far side of downtown.

But that would just prolong the inevitable gloating. Why not pull up her big-girl panties and deal with it while her mood was already in the toilet?

She wasn't sure whether he heard the heels of her boots clicking on the sidewalk or simply sensed her approach. Either way, he turned and held up a finger then pointed to the phone at his ear.

"Just get down here with the generator first thing tomorrow," he said, a muscle ticking in his jaw. "I don't care about the overtime, Cody. Make it happen."

He ended the call and shoved the phone into the pocket of his dark jeans. Once again Dylan proved he could look good in any situation. He wore a nondescript gray sweater and his worn leather jacket. Somehow, he managed to appear like he'd just stepped off the pages of a magazine spread featuring men of alpha style.

Carrie bit down on the inside of her cheek, hoping the pain would keep her focused on what she needed to say to him and not how he made her feel. Yet, she couldn't help but remember how he'd come to her defense with the committee members earlier. "Do you want to start with the 'I told you so'?" she asked, proud that her voice didn't waver. "Or should I go first?"

His thick brows drew together as he stared at her. "What are you talking about?"

She hitched a thumb at the town square behind her. "The mess I've made of the light ceremony. I went too big, too far, too bright. Just like you probably knew I would."

"It's not a mess. We just need a backup power source. I'm having my company's master electrician drive down with a portable generator tomorrow. I've already contacted the local utility company, so they know it's on the way. We're meeting here first thing in the morning and it will be ready by the time the ceremony is scheduled to start. Magnolia is going to be the brightest town on the eastern seaboard for your Merry Magnolia Festival."

Carrie felt her mouth drop open. She could barely contain her shock. Dylan told her the plan like it was nothing. As if they were really on the same team.

"I don't understand," she said when she regained enough control to speak. "Why? Why would you go out of your way to make it work instead of using the issue against me?"

He moved closer, cupped her cheeks in his large hands. "I'm not the bad guy," he said simply. "I gave my word that I'd help with the festival and that's what I'm going to do. It's important to you, which makes it important to me. We might have different ideas for the future of the town, but we can deal with that later."

Her mind whirled. Not only was he not the bad guy. At

this moment Dylan Scott was *her* personal hero. She didn't say that, knowing it would make him uncomfortable. Instead, she leaned forward and kissed him.

"Thank you."

He smiled against her mouth. "If you let it slip that I'm not the villain everyone wants me to be, I'll deny it."

"I don't understand." She pulled back and looked into his eyes, trying to figure out why he wouldn't admit that he cared about things.

"I've gotten used to people around here having low expectations of me." He flashed a self-deprecating grin. "I kind of like it that way."

"You don't mean that," she argued. "Especially because I know you love the bakery's sticky buns. Wouldn't it be nice if Mary Ellen let you in the front door? That way you wouldn't have to bribe people to smuggle baked goods out to you."

"How do you know I pay for pastries?"

"I know a lot of things."

"Not everything," he said, and the low timbre of his voice made sparks dance along her skin.

She wanted to know more. At this moment she wanted Dylan to open up and admit that his feelings for the town and for her had changed.

His willingness to pitch in when she needed him the most made her believe in her vision for her home in a deeper way than she had before. Magnolia was a place of community, not some generic wealthy vacation destination. Dylan might not want to concede yet, but she knew he saw how special it was here. Otherwise he wouldn't work to help.

"You look good covered in paint smudges," he told her.

"I feel bad that I lost track of time," she admitted, tucking her arm into the crook of his elbow as they walked down the quiet street.

"You can't take care of other people if you aren't taking care of yourself."

Carrie laughed. "Are you a closet Oprah Winfrey fan?"

"Not exactly," he said, giving her a playful nudge. "Sam and I went to a therapist together for about six months after the accident. I did a couple of solo sessions at her suggestion, and that was one of the main pearls of wisdom she dropped."

"Dylan," she breathed, feeling like a jerk for making light of his advice.

"Trust me, the lesson didn't exactly stick. But I think it applies as much to you as it did to me."

"You're right."

"Say that again," he urged, amusement lacing his tone. "I like the sound of it."

She laughed again, amazed at how easy it was to relax and let down her guard with this man who should raise her hackles instead. They came to the corner where her Volvo was parked.

"I walked," he told her, "so I guess I'll see you tomorrow morning."

He seemed as reluctant to leave her as she was to let him go. Neither of them spoke about the way last night had ended. She didn't want to go there, not after he'd just stepped up to help save her vision for the festival. Most of her life was complicated, but at the moment her feelings for Dylan were the most straightforward thing she could imagine.

She wouldn't ruin this, too.

"Do you want a ride home?"

"Sure. Sam's at a movie so he won't be back for another hour or so."

An hour. Imagine all the things that could happen in one hour. Carrie's body hummed with the possibility of it. They climbed into the station wagon and she pulled away from the curb.

"Would you like to see what I'm working on?" she asked, her awareness immediately replaced by nervous energy. She had an opportunity for sexy time and instead had offered to show him something that revealed every hidden shred of her vulnerability.

"More than anything," he answered before she had a chance to take it back.

She swallowed down the anxiety rising up in her throat.

"Great," she whispered. "Let's go."

CHAPTER EIGHTEEN

DYLAN COULD FEEL anxiety radiating from Carrie as she led him through the front door of the bungalow a few blocks from his house.

He didn't understand it. She knew he believed in her talent, possibly more than she did. He also understood her willingness to share this portion of herself was a gift, one he wouldn't take for granted.

She flipped on the light, revealing a charming space filled with neutral-toned furnishings interspersed with colorful pillows, rugs and accents that lent the room an eclectic yet inviting feel. The homey living room connected to a small but functional kitchen with white cabinets, stainless-steel appliances and a small maple dining room set on one side.

"This place looks like you," he told her with a smile.

"I used to rent Gray's carriage house, but it felt a little too cozy once he and Avery got together. This house works for what I need just as well, although I dream of owning a place of my own one day."

"What's going on with your dad's house?"

She shrugged as she placed her purse and keys on the table behind the sofa. "We've got to get through probate before we can sell it. I'm not sure who would buy the place at this point. It's kind of oversize for Magnolia. Maybe a family new to town or someone who'd want to convert it to a bed-and-breakfast."

"I still can't believe none of you want it." Living in that big house overlooking the rest of the neighborhood had seemed part and parcel to who Carrie was. Her father's princess. Dylan knew the old antebellum structure had been as much a prison as a castle, but he still associated it with her.

"Not at all," she answered without hesitation. "It's strange but after we cleaned it out, I wanted nothing more to do with that house. In fact, I haven't been over there in almost a month. Avery says we can deal with it once the estate is settled, but I'm not sure how involved I'll be. It represents a time in my life that I'd prefer not to revisit."

"Then don't ever go back," he told her, understanding the need to leave the past in the past. He never went near the part of town where he'd lived as a kid. There was nothing for him there but bad memories.

He turned as a cacophony of tiny meows and cries sounded from the back of the house.

"My fosters," Carrie explained, her eyes darting to the hallway and then to him. "I need to check on them for a minute. You can wait here or else I'm using the spare bedroom—second door on the right—as my studio."

"Okay," he said as she walked away. He wasn't sure which she wanted him to do but curiosity left him unable to resist heading down the hall.

He passed her bedroom and tried not to notice the intimacy of the sliver of bed he could see from the partially open door. Instead, he opened the door she'd indicated as her studio space. The room smelled of turpentine and acrylic paint, a mix of scents he'd always associated with Carrie.

She might have stopped painting for years, but she'd

never quit being an artist. It was a part of her, much like her identity as Niall's daughter.

His breath caught in his throat as he flipped on the light, and he heard her soft footsteps approach behind him as he walked into the room.

"You've been busy," he said, taking in the rows of a half dozen canvases. "Do you sleep?"

"Not a lot," she answered, her voice tight with anticipation.

"They're stunning."

"You don't have to say that," she told him, almost defensively.

"It's true. The style is different than what you used to do."

"I don't even know what to call it. Something between intense impressionism and fluid realism. It's certainly a change from the paintings I do at the store. This is just what comes out when I let myself feel. Back in high school I was so concerned with getting all the technical bits right. I thought I needed to be deliberate and methodical because that's how my father taught me to paint. Now it's like the brush has a mind of its own. I get totally engrossed and lose track of the time. I love the unpredictability of it, which kind of feels like a joke given how much the chaos of the past few months has been a burden to me."

"You feel it," Dylan said, drawn forward by the emotion he could see in the work. The color and bold brush strokes, along with the unique compositions of the pieces. "They're sensual," he murmured then chuckled at the incredulous look she gave him.

"My sisters said the same thing, but I don't paint like that on purpose. I'm not trying to be provocative."

"Doesn't change that they are. It's not a criticism, Carrie. These paintings express who you are. I can't believe how many canvases you have with how busy the rest of your life has been lately."

She moved to stand next to him, ran a finger along the edge of one canvas. "It's like a dam broke inside me. All those years of not painting. I told myself I didn't miss it, that I was happy taking care of my dad. But…"

"You weren't happy," he said, hating himself for leaving her with Niall. Maybe if she would have gone with Dylan, things could have been different for them.

"I wasn't unhappy." She turned to him, her eyes flashing as if daring him to argue. "My dedication to this town isn't fabricated. I love it here. I always have. Yes, I had moments that I wished my life could have gone in another direction. You were a part of one of those moments."

"I wish we'd both made different choices back then," he murmured.

"I understand that everyone wants to think badly of Niall for how he handled his life. I'm not denying that my father was a deeply flawed man who made innumerable mistakes, but in most of those he wasn't alone. Take the money he gave you." She laughed without humor. "I mean, you took money to break up with me. Yes, it was awful that he bribed you, but you had a choice. We all make choices."

Dylan did his best not to wince. He hated the reminder of how much he'd messed up. But not for the reasons Carrie thought.

"I didn't deserve you," he said softly, remembering that time in his life. The anger that had overwhelmed him to the point where he didn't know if he could control the darkness inside him. "You were so filled with light and—"

"No." She held up a hand. "Don't do that. Don't act like breaking my heart was some kind of altruistic gesture. I might have been young, but I wasn't totally naive. I wanted you and would have done anything to make it work. You were the only reason I would have found the nerve to leave. But you gave up on us. More than that. You threw me aside for a check. Just be honest. Tell me I wasn't enough. I could deal with the truth easier than I can manage your placating lies."

Her words gutted him. Without thinking he reached into his back pocket and yanked out his wallet. "You want the truth?" He opened it and took out the worn slip of paper, thrusting it toward her before he could think better of it.

Her delicate brows furrowing, she opened the folded check. "What's this?"

"What does it look like?" he demanded, then forced himself to take a breath as her eyes filled with tears. "God, Carrie, don't cry. The last thing I wanted to do by giving you that was to make you cry."

"Why?" she asked, her jaw set in a tight line. "Why didn't you cash it? How come you let me believe you took his money?"

"I did take it," Dylan said. "Not because I wanted your father's money but when he gave me the check, he told me that I wasn't good enough for you. He knew my dad and his temper. He knew the trouble I'd been in and the path I seemed set to go down. Hell, the whole town knew you could do better than me."

"I didn't," she whispered.

"That was the problem. You saw something in me that wasn't there. I had to prove to you I couldn't be the man you wanted—needed—me to be."

She flipped the check around and held it up to him as if he hadn't looked at it a thousand times in the past ten years. "By lying?"

His name across the "pay to the order of" line in Niall's

loopy scrawl. The date of it—twenty-four hours before Niall told Carrie about the bribe. Two days before she tracked him down and confronted Dylan, nursing the worst hangover of his life. Three days before Dylan packed up his meager belongings and left behind Magnolia and the girl who'd captured his heart.

For good he'd thought at the time.

"I didn't lie. I took the check."

"Dylan." The way she said his name, like an exasperated teacher trying to rein in a recalcitrant student made his lips quirk. He continued to be shocked at how much he liked her displays of inner resolve. He'd always known she had that strength inside her. "You never cashed it."

"I planned to," he lied and the way her eyes narrowed told him he wasn't fooling her for a minute. "I would have if I'd ever needed the money."

"You needed the money."

Yeah. He had. He'd made it to Boston and his uncle's doorstep with literally pennies to his name. "It wasn't about the money," he said honestly.

"No," she agreed. "It was about finding a way to break it off with me."

"Because you deserved better."

"Enough with that tired line." She ripped the check in half and then ripped it again and again and tossed the tiny scraps of paper toward him. "Do you think this makes it better? You let me believe for all these years that you'd been bribed by my father. At least I could take solace in knowing the money he gave you would have set you up in a new life."

Dylan muttered a curse. "I can't believe you made that statement. I allowed myself to be bought off by your dirtbag father and you rationalize things by telling yourself that I needed the money?"

Her eyes blazed. "It's an easier pill to swallow than knowing you were so hell-bent on getting away from me that the check was just a lousy excuse."

He shook his head, wishing he could shake her until she understood what it had done to him to walk away from her. She'd been the only good thing in his life, and he'd crushed his own heart in order to save her from him.

"I would have let you go. If you didn't love me, I wouldn't have wanted to hold on to you." Her voice cracked and she drew in a shuddery breath. "You didn't have to lie."

"I loved you more than anyone or anything I'd ever known." He stepped closer to her, studied the freckles sprinkled across the bridge of her nose. So many aspects of both of them—who they were and who they'd become— had changed in the intervening years. Somehow, the small physical reminder of the girl she'd been gave him a huge measure of comfort.

"You shouldn't have left me that way," she said, her tone firm.

"You're right."

She sucked in a breath as if his agreement defused her anger in a way that surprised her. He wished he could explain it or promise her that he wouldn't hurt her again.

If he believed that about himself, he'd take her in his arms right now and never let her go.

Instead, he forced himself to look away from her. Her paintings surrounded them—the passion she'd put into each one evident. What if he ruined things again? What if he found a way to hurt them both?

"This is who you are," he told her. "An artist. You deserve to explore your gifts, to figure out what you want from your life away from your father's shadow."

"Possibly away from Magnolia." She gave voice to the truth he didn't want to hear.

"Yes." He traced one finger along the curve of her cheek. "I know you had dreams that didn't involve this town, Carrie. I remember everything, each little detail you shared. You wanted to travel. To go to Europe and see the Eiffel Tower, to walk along the Seine and spend the afternoon at a small café."

Her eyes drifted closed as she pressed into him. "It seems ridiculous now that I stayed. I was such a coward."

"Don't say that."

"Why not? It's true. My mom left. You left. I can tell myself and everyone else that I stayed because Dad needed me, but I needed him just as much. I wanted an excuse not to face the world and risk failing." She swallowed, looked away. "To risk knowing whether my father was right about my lack of talent."

"You're talented." Unable to help himself, Dylan reached for her, pulled her close.

For a weighted breath she remained stiff in his arms. Then she sagged against him and he held her, hoping that his embrace, the beat of his heart, would tell her all the things he couldn't say out loud.

He didn't want to be her enemy but wasn't sure he knew how to accept the thought of being her friend enough to satisfy him.

"Thank you for sharing your art with me." He might not be sure of anything, but he knew this was a special gift.

She inclined her head, gave him a crooked smile. "Thanks for not letting my dad bribe you."

"I'm sorry I took the check at all."

"Me, too." She brushed a kiss across his lips. He appreciated her honesty even if he wanted more. The kiss was filled with apology and acceptance. It was as if they'd come to an understanding and moved beyond their damaged past.

At least that was his hope.

"I should go," he said before he lost himself in her. With the truth in the open between them, the last bit of the wall guarding his heart also came down. If he let himself, he could fall for her again.

Who was he kidding? Dylan was tumbling down the hill full speed at this point. But he knew that meant nothing but trouble for both of them.

She looked like she wanted to argue. Damn if he didn't want her to.

She stepped away instead. "Thank you again for rescuing my lights."

"My pleasure," he said, realizing it truly was. He might not believe in all the Christmas fanfare, but even he could see that Carrie embracing her identity as an artist was a true miracle.

He walked out of her house into the cool evening, feeling a level of contentment he hadn't known in ages.

Just as he got to his car, a text message flashed on his phone. It was from Steven Ross.

Signed the deal. Let's do this.

Dylan's stomach tumbled then went into a free fall like a boulder dislodged from the side of a mountain and pitched over a cliff. He had the funding he needed to turn the old textile factory into luxury housing. No more possibility of a new company taking over that space, the way Carrie and Malcolm seemed to hope.

As he drove through the festive streets, bright with colorful lights and cheery holiday inflatables, he tried to convince himself that wouldn't change anything. Carrie had always known his plans.

Nothing had changed.

Nothing except his heart.

"What are you doing?"

Carrie whirled around at the sound of her sister's voice early the next morning. Avery stood in the entrance to the gallery, eyes wide as she took in the newly transformed space.

"I'm sorry," Carrie offered without preamble. "I know we'd talked about a few pop-up sip-and-paint events throughout the weekend to encourage more business for the studio."

Nerves fluttered across Carrie's spine and she forced her voice to stay even. She didn't like disappointing people and understood her painting classes brought in much-needed revenue. "But this is The Reed Gallery. I want it to continue as an art gallery. I mean, technically you own it so you can tell me to shut the heck up and teach book clubs and bunco groups how to draw cutesy scenes all day long."

"You're really painting," Avery murmured as she moved forward into the space.

"You knew that." Carrie shrugged. "I showed you one of my canvases."

"Yes," Avery agreed, "but it was only one. I didn't know you were doing this much."

Carrie followed her sister's gaze. She'd gone to bed after Dylan left last night, somehow physically exhausted from the emotional release of knowing the truth behind his leaving years ago. Not that his reasons changed anything. He'd taken the check, let her believe he'd cashed it. He still left.

But knowing he hadn't been bribed by her father... mattered.

She'd slept better than she had in weeks but woken in the wee hours, suddenly consumed with the thought of truly revealing herself. Not just to Dylan but to the town, to the world, to herself. She wanted to be more than Niall Reed's daughter. More than everyone's most reliable helper.

She wanted to finally claim her place in the town.

She'd stacked the canvases in the back of the station wagon and headed for the gallery while the winter sky was still inky dark.

After carrying her work into the gallery, she'd pushed the paint party supplies to the back wall, stripped the posters and canvases they'd hung and started positioning her works throughout the main gallery. It was like putting a bit of her soul on display.

Her palms sweat and her heart pounded like she'd just sprinted down Main Street stark naked.

These paintings weren't just color and brush strokes. They were a part of her—who she was and what it had taken for her to get there. Maybe other people wouldn't be able to see how much of herself she'd put onto each canvas, but Carrie knew.

The expression on Avery's face conveyed that she understood, as well.

"It's time," Carrie said simply.

Avery didn't answer. Instead, she enveloped Carrie in a tight hug then picked up the hammer that sat on a nearby chair. "Let's get the rest of them up. If you don't put Magnolia on the map with the festival, then certainly the art will do it."

Carrie released a breath she hadn't realized she was

holding. "You aren't upset about me changing the plan for today? I do understand the gallery legally belongs to—"

"This space is yours as much as it is mine," Avery said, squeezing Carrie's shoulder. "Your art belongs here."

Carrie turned on her favorite holiday music playlist and they worked in companionable silence until the bells chimed over the door to the entrance sometime later.

"What the hell is going on in here? You're hijacking the festival," Meredith announced.

They'd gotten all of the paintings hung over the course of the past hour. For the first time in years, the gallery felt alive. Yes, she'd kept it open even after her dad had stopped painting—or at least stopped selling his art. She'd had enough of his old works to space out on the walls. But they'd felt tired and haphazard, a desperate attempt to stay relevant instead of a true expression of his talent.

Now, with the vibrant colors and bold lines of her own compositions under the professional light Niall had installed when money was flush, it all felt real.

Right.

"We're just finishing," she said, turning to her younger sister. Carrie gasped as she realized Meredith wasn't alone.

She'd entered the gallery, but a row of people stood on the other side of the big picture window, their gazes moving between Carrie and the art that surrounded her.

"Is this all yours?" Meredith asked.

"Yes," Carrie breathed, feeling like a deer caught in headlights. "They've been pouring out of me. It feels like ten years' worth of emotion dumped onto the canvases." She gave a strangled laugh. "And now I'm wondering why I picked this morning to hang them."

Avery came out of the office at that moment. "What's everyone doing?"

"I just got to town and this is how I found them." Meredith glanced over her shoulder. "No one is working on setup for the festival because they're all too busy gawking at our soon-to-be famous artist sister."

"I doubt that," Carrie answered.

Meredith whistled as she approached one of the larger canvases. "Now I get why Niall made you believe you had no talent. His ego never would have been able to handle how much better you were than him."

"We had different styles." Carrie crossed her arms over her chest, suddenly self-conscious. "Seriously, I need them to stop staring in at me like I'm some kind of zoo animal."

"Get used to it," Meredith advised. "I have a feeling this is only the start. Wave to your adoring public, Care-bear. It's good practice."

Cheeks burning, Carrie forced herself to meet the gazes of the people watching, most of whom she'd known since childhood.

As if on cue, all of them broke into applause. Even with the door closed, she could hear the cheering.

Her eyes filled with tears that she blinked away. "Now I know how Sally Field felt at the Oscars," she told her sisters, trying to keep a hold on her emotions.

"That's right." Meredith patted her shoulder. "They like you and your immense talent. Now let's go get ready for the festival."

"Okay." Carrie nodded and swiped at her eyes.

She grabbed a jacket and followed Avery and Meredith out onto the sidewalk.

"We know she's amazing," Meredith announced, "but we need to focus, people. You can come to the gallery later tonight and fawn over Carrie." She pointed a finger at the group. "No talking about the art. Not yet. Carrie will get all verklempt and we need her on her 'A' game today."

"'A' game," Carrie repeated then huffed out a laugh. "Good to know."

Avery patted her back. "There's no point in arguing when she's like this."

"I understand."

So did everyone else, apparently. Even Mayor Mal nodded and started across the street to the town square where most of the activities would be centered for the weekend.

"It's her dog trainer tone," Avery said.

"I like it."

Carrie followed the crowd. Josie opened her mouth to speak then snapped it shut again when Meredith threw her a warning look. Instead, the older woman gave an enthusiastic thumbs-up and hurried along with the rest of the business owners.

Carrie couldn't help the glow of pride radiating through her chest.

But now she needed to focus on the festival.

She glanced at her watch and then up at the sky. Streaks of pink and purple trailed above her. It was going to be a good day. A great day.

Everything was finally working out right.

CHAPTER NINETEEN

THE NEXT FEW HOURS went by in a flash. By the time the booths were ready and the skating rink open, cars were already lining up on the street around the town square.

Carrie continued to pitch in wherever people needed help. She fitted families for roller skates and mixed hot chocolate for visitors to the town's information table. The central weekend of Merry Magnolia was a huge success.

It was as if every one of her dreams of a perfect holiday had come true. Everyone from longtime locals to tourists in for the weekend milled about the square, sampling cookies from Sunnyside. Children took part in the craft activities while their parents watched the groups of carolers from the high school choir or shopped at the vendor booths selling festive ornaments and nativity sets, one-of-a-kind gifts and vintage toys. She could hardly wait for the light show and the snowmaking machine to add to the fun.

"I've never seen it so busy." Malcolm joined her as she stacked another sleeve of cups for cocoa. "Not even when your dad was in his heyday."

"Magnolia is more than my father's former domain," she reminded him. "For too many years the people around here forgot that."

"I think he wanted us to forget," Mal said.

"That doesn't excuse it."

"True enough." He waved to a family walking past and

then turned to her. "Have the three of you decided what to do with the house?"

"My sisters and I can only manage one all-encompassing project at a time, Mr. Mayor," Carrie said with a sigh. Since she'd discussed her childhood home with Dylan, thoughts of the house no longer seemed to bother her in the way they had before. "But the house belongs to Meredith. She's in charge of its fate."

"Come on now. Are you telling me that because he left you the farm property that you're going to do what you want with no thought to her rescue?"

She sighed. "Of course not. Although the taxes on that property are going to be rough. Maybe if we can make some money on his house, that will offset it. But there's so much debt."

"I have a feeling you'll be fine," he assured her. "Remember, I saw your paintings. We all did." He glanced toward the gallery. A steady stream of people walked in and out of the building.

"So what?" She shrugged. "That was cathartic."

"You're going to be a big deal."

"I'm going to be a local artist in a small coastal town. When all the fanfare of this weekend dies down, I'll put the sip-and-paint supplies back out and return to running my little business that pays the bills. I'll paint in my spare time, and nothing will really change."

"You haven't been in there yet?"

"Um… I've been busy with other things."

"Are we going to need to discuss excuses again?" the mayor asked with a deep chuckle. "Everyone's talking about Niall Reed's talented daughter."

Satisfaction glimmered inside her like a newly polished diamond but was quickly sullied by the dark smoke of anxiety that rose inside her at the realization of how much of herself she'd exposed by displaying her new work in the gallery. She blinked back tears, not wanting Malcolm to see how his words affected her. "I need to check on Santa's supply of candy canes," she said brightly.

"Save me a dance tonight," he told her. When the sun went down, they'd close the roller rink and turn it into a dance floor for a few hours. "This is truly an incredible feat you've pulled off. I know he wasn't always the most gracious man, but your dad would have been proud."

Carrie nodded even though she knew that wasn't true. Her father would have hated this festival because it didn't revolve around him.

She walked away from Malcolm but instead of heading toward the gingerbread workshop Dylan and Sam had built, she veered off down a path that led to a quiet corner of the square.

Her lungs expanded and contracted as she gulped in air, trying to stem the rising tide of panic inside her.

"Why is the star of the show not center stage?"

Dylan approached with a smile that faded when he took in her expression. "What's wrong?"

"Have you been to the gallery?" she demanded.

"Yeah," he answered slowly. "You're the talk of the festival."

"It was a mistake," she whispered. "A horrible mistake."

"What do you mean?" He reached out a hand, but she shrugged away from him. She already felt ready to explode out of her skin. The heat of Dylan's touch might push her over the edge.

"I'm a novelty, a curiosity. Niall Reed's wannabe artist daughter." She threw up her hands, the residual paint stains around her fingertips making her want to cry with frustration. "Just like he always told me."

"Stop. You know that's not true, Carrie. You have talent. More than your father ever did. He knew it, too."

"It doesn't matter." She gestured to the crowded park. "In Magnolia I'm always going to be dwarfed by both the good and bad of his reputation. Everything I do will be measured against him. I don't want that." Why couldn't she move beyond the doubts and fears of her past and stop letting Niall Reed define her and her worth?

"Then change it." A muscle ticked in his jaw. "Trust me, I know all about living down the past. You're way tougher than me and people around here love you."

This was her home. It had always been home to her, even when she'd thought of leaving. But how could she claim her life when the ghost of her father seemed to haunt her at every turn? She could no longer even make herself drive by the house where she'd grown up. It was one thing to be trying to fix her mistakes, but would she truly be able to build a life where her own light could shine?

"I don't know if I can." She hated to admit it, even to herself. But somehow with Dylan she couldn't deny the truth.

"You won't know until you try," he said softly and laced his fingers with hers, not letting her pull away this time. "Neither of us will. What do you say we try together?"

"Together?"

"Go roller skating with me."

She laughed. "Seriously? You just invited me roller skating?"

"I did." He tugged her closer, his eyes clear and kind. "I'm going to request the cheesiest love song they have, and I want to hold your hand as we skate around that rink with all of Magnolia watching." His lips grazed across the sensitive flesh of her earlobe. "I might even steal a kiss."

"Oh." Roller skating might seem like a trivial thing, but Carrie understood the magnitude of it. They'd be outing themselves as a couple.

Were they a couple?

She should deny it. No matter how he made her body feel and what her heart craved, she and Dylan wanted different things from life and for Magnolia. That hadn't changed.

Being together in the quiet of night or in private moments was one thing. Allowing herself to be claimed by him publicly and claiming him in return would set tongues wagging even more than the response to hanging her paintings in the gallery.

She hadn't even admitted the truth of her feelings for Dylan to her sisters.

His blue eyes went from confident to cautious as he watched her. She guessed the vulnerability in his gaze was also reflected in hers. What was the point of denying her feelings?

She'd fallen for Dylan again. Or maybe she'd never really let their love die in the first place. She might not be ready to say the words out loud, but she was willing to take a risk.

"You won't let me fall?" she asked, squeezing his hand.

His breath released in a shallow whoosh, like he'd been holding it waiting for her answer. Like her response really mattered.

She wanted to matter to this man, the way he did to her.

He grinned, the way he used to when he was dragging her into some crazy adventure. "I haven't been on roller skates since before I hit puberty." His lips brushed against hers gently, both an expression of gratitude and a promise of things to come. "No promises I won't be the one to fall. But I'll catch you if we go down."

"It's a deal," she told him, understanding the truth of those words. She'd spent far too long avoiding uncertainty because of her fear. So what if she landed on her face? The important part was a willingness to get back up.

Her heart pounded as she laced on the skates Dylan rented. The rink was perfect with the plywood sides, a colorful backdrop of cheery holiday scenes painted by her students at the high school. They might not have real snow in Magnolia, but she'd put her town's holiday spirit up against any winter wonderland.

She waved to Sam, who skated around the rink with a group of teens, several of whom she recognized from her art club.

They were good kids, and it made her happy to see the boy finding his way in Magnolia. The whole scene in front of her made her happy. She'd done this. She and her sisters had brought this town together in a way that seemed impossible a few months earlier.

Her breath caught in her throat as she watched Dylan talking to the man deejaying inside the rink's ticket booth. Was it possible her life in Magnolia felt complete because of his return?

She hadn't been pining for the past decade, but now that she'd opened her heart to the possibility of happiness with Dylan again, it was difficult to imagine her life without him in it.

The fact that he'd pitched in to help make the festival a success despite his reservations meant something. He'd brought Sam here when he needed the boy to have a sense of home. That meant something, too.

Dylan might think he needed to change everything about

this town, but he was the one changing, which would give them a chance together. If she admitted the truth to herself, she wanted that more than anything.

He winked as he turned back to her, and she felt a blush rise to her cheeks. He'd been handsome as a young man, all attitude and swagger with movie-star looks that made girls of all ages swoon.

When he'd picked Carrie, she hadn't been able to believe it. Dylan had a reputation that was the polar opposite of hers. She'd been the consummate good girl while he was known by everyone and either revered or vilified depending on whether a person appreciated or hated his brand of rebellion. Now it seemed almost comical that their lives had gone in such different directions.

He'd made his mark on the world, become a success despite his troubled youth. His face and body had matured into strong planes and angles, the fine lines fanning from his eyes only making him more attractive. It was unfair how men so often got better-looking with age.

She'd stayed at home, her life small in many ways. But despite the resentment she had for her father, she still loved this town. Now Dylan did, too. He might not admit it yet, but she could tell. This place was important. Otherwise, he wouldn't have brought Sam here.

That boy meant the world to him.

Both of them meant something to Carrie.

They were coming to another crossroads, and this time she had to believe they'd end up on the same side.

"They're playing our song," he said as he skated back to her.

"It's wrong that you look hot in roller skates." She stood up, wobbling a bit as she tried to balance.

"I need a comb for my back pocket," he told her with a laugh.

She let out a yelp as her legs almost went out from under her.

Before she could fall, Dylan wrapped an arm around her waist. "Got you."

"This is a terrible idea." She did her best to stand. "I have no balance."

"But you skated as a kid. It will come back to you."

"I didn't." She shook her head. "Not once."

"Everyone in town skated at the old rink before they tore it down."

"Not me. Mom didn't think it was dignified."

"Do you have some tie to the royal family you've forgotten to mention?"

"She was a snob."

"I remember that."

Carrie tried to push away from him. "I'll watch from the side."

"This is the sweetheart skate." He gripped her arms at the elbows and began to skate backward toward the rink's entrance. "I need a partner."

"Dylan, I can't." She locked her knees to keep them from shaking. Why was the thought of falling in front of an audience almost as scary as hanging her paintings in the gallery for everyone to see? "I thought I could, but it won't work. It just—"

"I've got you," he repeated against her ear. "Remember, we stay upright or go down together."

She swallowed back her nerves and followed him out. Truly, when the man looked at her with that stupid, sexy twinkle in his eyes, he could get her to do just about anything.

Sam called out a few words of encouragement as he sped past. "Is ice skating this scary?" she whispered.

"Worse," Dylan confirmed. "Because when you fall, it's cold on your ass."

"Tell me again why I thought this was a good idea." She gripped his arm like it was the last lifeboat on the Titanic and tried to concentrate on his warmth, the way the strength of his body supported her still-wobbly legs.

"Look around, Carrie. You've created a winter wonderland in Magnolia."

"It's pretty cool," she admitted. "But it wasn't all me. Everyone pitched in to help. Even you. That's how it works in this community. You understand that now, right? Magnolia is special just the way it is."

"One lap already," he told her instead of answering.

She looked around and realized they'd made it around the rink, and she hadn't fallen. In fact, she was slowly getting the hang of skating. No way would she let go of Dylan's arm, and he continued to hold her close. But she started to relax and enjoy the feeling of the cool breeze across her skin as they skated.

"This song," she murmured as the music changed to another ballad, this one a sweet track by Norah Jones. "I love it."

"I remember," he said, his voice tickling her ear. "That's why I requested it."

They'd danced to this song at her senior prom. Carrie hadn't brought Dylan although they'd been dating several months at that point. Her parents had forbidden it, and she hadn't been strong enough to defy them.

Instead, she'd gone with a group of friends, telling herself she didn't care about not having anyone to slow dance with when the time came.

But Dylan had surprised her, sneaking into the dance in his rented tux. She'd been shocked because the weeks leading up to the prom, he'd done nothing but make fun of school functions.

He'd come because it was important to her. If she hadn't been in love with him before then, that night had sealed the deal.

Here she was a decade later, her heart undeniably his again despite her best efforts to keep it guarded.

"Are you ready to go it alone?" he asked and the panic that gripped her was mortifying. He was talking about skating, she realized, not life in general.

Even so, she wanted to protest as he loosened his arm from her grasp. The rink was crowded with skaters and even more people watched from the square. She understood that many of them were watching her and Dylan.

But she put aside her worries about what other people thought as she focused all her concentration on an attempt not to fall on her face.

"I've got this," she answered because she wasn't going to let fear—even a silly fear about roller skating—dictate her life any longer.

Dylan released her and for a moment her legs stiffened, and she thought she was going down.

"Relax," he reminded her. "I'm right here."

She forced herself to take a breath and concentrated on the music and the rhythm of moving her feet. She had no delusion about looking graceful, but she managed an entire loop around the perimeter of the rink without tripping or falling or in any way making a spectacle of herself.

The longer she skated, the more confident she became. How many other trivial things could she master if she tried?

"I can't ride a bike, either," she announced when Dylan skated close again.

His eyes widened but he didn't make fun of her. "Do you want to learn?"

"Yes," she breathed. "I want to try everything."

He reached for her hand, the hold gentle but still supportive. "I like the sound of that."

Just then a trio of prepubescent kids whizzed by, skating far too fast and darting in and out of other skaters.

"Slow down," a father holding hands with his young daughter called.

The last speedster immediately slowed, his left foot kicking back and catching the edge of Carrie's skate.

She wobbled and Dylan moved to pull her close, but it was too late. The toe of her skate caught, and she pitched forward. She closed her eyes and instinctively held out her hands so she didn't actually land on her face. Instead of hitting the hard floor, she was yanked to one side and ended up sprawled across Dylan.

The fall had knocked the air from her lungs, and she worked to make her breathing normal again. People continued to skate around them, giving the pair a wide berth.

"You okay?" he asked, smoothing a hand across her face.

"You dove under me," she said, stunned.

He smiled, almost shyly. "I wasn't joking when I said we were falling together."

"I love you," she whispered, unable to stop the words. Then she kissed him, not willing to give him a chance to respond.

At this moment she didn't need to know how he felt. He'd told her everything in the simple gesture of catching her.

The kiss quickly turned heated and only the echo of cheering and wolf whistles forced her to end it. She scrambled to her feet, unwilling to let go of Dylan's hand. They made their way to the edge of the rink, where Avery and Gray stood with his daughter, Violet.

"That was subtle," Avery said with a grin.

"I was being spontaneous," Carrie answered as Dylan draped an arm over her shoulders.

Her sister nodded. "As everyone in town will soon hear."

"Nice work on the additional generators," Gray told Dylan. "They made a big difference when we tested the lights again."

"No problem." Dylan looked uncomfortable with the praise. "I bet you're an expert skater," he told Violet. If Avery or Gray noticed the quick subject change, they didn't point it out.

The little girl lifted up one foot to show off her pink glittery roller skates. "I got my own pair that go super-fast."

"Not too fast," Gray cautioned, ruffling her hair. "You saw what just happened to Carrie out there."

"Yeah," Violet agreed, "but she's not very good." She hitched a thumb at Avery. "She's not, either, so don't feel bad."

Avery gave a mock gasp of horror. "Just for that comment I'm not going to let you win when we race."

The girl did a hair toss worthy of a Hollywood starlet. "I'll bet you a week of garbage duty that I win."

Avery stuck out her hand to shake. "And when I win, you owe me a weekend of watching Hannah Montana reruns."

Violet giggled and shook Avery's hand. "I'd do that anyway, although it's weird how much you like Hannah Montana."

"Excuse me," Avery said with mock formality to Carrie and Dylan. "I have some five-year-old butt to kick."

The two of them headed for the rink's entrance and the

look of pure adoration on Gray's face as he watched made Carrie's heart squeeze.

"The bets are their newest thing," he said with a shake of his head. "I can't tell which one of them loves the competition more."

"Does it worry you?" Dylan said. "I know Avery isn't... I mean...that doesn't seem like traditional motherly behavior."

"Tradition is overrated," Gray said. "And in my mind, anything that works is fair game in parenting these days. The rules keep changing, you know? We're making our own as we go along." He grinned. "I need to get out there. It's not going to be pretty when Violet beats her. My kid is a powerhouse skater."

He moved away, and Dylan hopped over the guardrail, but Carrie shook her head as he reached for her. Instead, she skated on her own to the exit.

"Just so you know," she told him as they unlaced their skates, "Avery wouldn't change a thing about Violet's spunky personality. She loves that girl to the moon and back and has every intention of raising her to be a complete badass."

"What about the mom?"

"They're navigating that, although she isn't as involved as Gray would like." She shrugged. "Like he said, they're making their own rules."

"You and your sisters are the same way. Did you think that when you first learned about them that you'd become as close as you are?"

"Good Lord, no." She shoved her feet into the boots she'd chosen for the day and stood, grateful for the feeling of balance on solid ground. "Avery was one thing but a stranger was almost easier to deal with than Meredith. She hated me in high school and didn't exactly hide that fact."

"Talk about spunky." He took her hand again, waving at Sam as they walked toward the booths that lined the far end of the town square. The air had just enough chill to make her feel like Christmas was really right around the corner. "I hung out with Meredith's brothers, although neither one of them liked trouble the way I did. Meredith was always trying to tag along." He sighed. "She turned out okay."

Carrie laughed. "More than okay," she said and stepped in front of him, turning so her body just grazed the front of his. "So did you, by the way."

His eyes rolled toward the blue sky. "I have money. That doesn't mean I turned out okay."

"Dylan, stop." She reached up and placed her hand against his cheek. "I know this is about Sam. You're doing a good job with him."

"How do you know?" He covered her hand with his as if afraid she'd pull away.

She smiled and said simply, "He looks happy."

"Looks can be deceiving, especially in this crazy age of social media perfection. I read an article last night on the potential negative effect of too much social media on a developing brain."

Her grin widened. "What made you read something like that?"

"I want to make sure Sam doesn't overdo it. He has online accounts and plays video games with his friends. There's no way in hell I'm letting that stuff impact his mental health."

"You just proved my point." She leaned in and kissed him. "You're trying. Like Gray said, there are no hard and fast rules anymore, but you keep trying."

"He lost his parents," Dylan whispered. "How can I ever make up for that?"

"You don't have to. All you have to do is be there for him."

"That feels insufficient."

"It's more than enough," she promised.

"I spent way too much on Christmas presents," he said as they began walking again. "I might not care about the holiday, but I want it to be good for him."

"Christmas isn't about material gifts."

"Tell that to your vendors today."

"You know what I mean."

"Have you been to the gallery?" he asked, starting to turn down a path that led to that corner of downtown.

"I need to check on the hot chocolate supply," she lied.

He tugged her forward. "If you could handle roller skating, you can make an appearance to see how people are responding to your paintings."

She fought against the rise of her raging imposter syndrome. "It might be easier to flay my skin off with a rusty knife."

"I'll be with you the whole time. You've got this, Carrie."

His words and steady presence eased some of her anxiety. She could tell herself all day that the people this morning were just being nice about supporting her art.

"Mal said that my dad would have been proud." She kept her steps in time with Dylan's even though she wanted to slow down as they approached the crowded sidewalk. "But I know he would have hated it."

"He's not here," Dylan reminded her. "And this isn't about him. Don't let the past be a road map for your present."

"Right," she agreed. "This is about me. Finally."

They entered the gallery and immediately all eyes turned toward Carrie. Lindy Walker, the retired librarian whom she'd hired to look after the gallery for the day, rushed forward.

"They can't stop talking about you," she said, grabbing Carrie's hand in hers.

Carrie blinked. "Who?"

"Everyone." The older woman shook her head. "But you don't have prices on the paintings. I tried calling you, but it went straight to voice mail and you didn't respond to my texts."

"My phone was on silent," Carrie answered. "I didn't realize… I put them up to share because it felt important for me, not because I wanted to make money."

"But are they for sale?" a man asked.

He was someone Carrie didn't recognize, holding several bulky shopping bags. "My wife and I drove down from Virginia for the weekend. She's into Christmas crafts of every sort. I thought I was going to spend my day following her like an unpaid lackey. But your exhibit makes the trip worth it."

"Thank you. Yes, the paintings are for sale. Or they will be as soon as I figure out that part."

She spent the next hour talking to potential customers who were all so excited about her art that it made her throat nearly clog with emotion. At some point Dylan slipped away after dropping a kiss on top of her head and promising he'd see her later.

A wild tangle of hope and fear bloomed inside Carrie. She'd put her work out into the world, like sending a child off to the first day of school, wondering if her precious baby would make friends or sit alone in the corner. If the response from the people in the gallery now was any indication, her future and the possibility of making a success of her art, had never looked brighter.

CHAPTER TWENTY

CARRIE WALKED INTO Sunnyside Bakery on the morning of Christmas Eve, humming "All I Want For Christmas" under her breath. She was hosting her sisters along with Dylan and Sam, the Wainrights—Phil, Lily and her fiancé, Garrett, as well as Shae Delich and her parents for dinner later that night after the Christmas Eve service. It would be cozy in her small rental, but she loved the idea of filling her home with friends and family.

The five days since the festival had been the happiest she could remember. The event had, by all accounts, been a huge success. According to the mayor, local businesses brought in more revenue in one weekend than in the previous holiday season in its entirety. Everyone Carrie'd spoken to had enjoyed the events she'd worked so hard to plan, and the renewed energy she felt within the town made all the hours of effort worth it.

Meredith had adopted out every animal she'd brought to the festival, which was amazing although Carrie's house felt a bit too quiet without any fosters in residence at the moment.

Maybe it was time for her to think of adopting a pet of her own, one that got along with Daisy and Barnaby, of course. Her relationship with Dylan had shifted and deepened once again.

She'd been afraid that her proclamation of love would

push him away. Although they hadn't discussed those three little words and he hadn't said them back to her, the way he held her close at night, like he never wanted to let her go, made her heart sing.

"I've got your pies ready," Mary Ellen said when she caught sight of Carrie. The pastry counter was crowded with a long line of customers picking up last-minute treats for the holiday. Sunnyside had remained popular even when the town's future seemed bleak, but there was a new energy within the cozy walls.

"Are you sure I can't convince you to join us?" she asked as she took the brown paper sack from the woman. "It's casual and I made an extra lasagna. There's plenty to go around."

Mary Ellen smiled. "Thank you, but I'm heading to Charlotte after the bakery closes to spend the night with my daughter and her family. My grand babies are two and four now. I want to be there for Christmas morning."

"It must be hard not seeing them all the time."

"Yes, but I was telling Danielle about all the new potential in Magnolia. And if it works out with one of the companies looking at the town for its headquarters, things will really change around here. She said they might even consider moving when the kids start school. She wants a real community feel for raising the girls."

Carrie gave Mary Ellen a quick hug, joy rushing through her. This was exactly what she wanted for Magnolia, rebuilding the town in a thoughtful way that attracted young families and economic momentum.

She turned to leave then spotted Sam sitting at a table on his own, slouched over his phone with a scowl on his face.

"Hey, buddy," she said as she approached.

He glanced up from the screen, and then his gaze darted away from hers, almost guiltily. "Dylan's not here."

"I see that. Merry Christmas Eve." She took the seat across from him without waiting to be invited, doubting he would ask her to join him.

"Yeah," he mumbled. "You, too."

"I'm just picking up dessert for tonight. We're going to have quite a feast."

"Cool."

He sounded about as enthused as he would be to a forced march through a hurricane. Carrie tried not to take offense.

"Shae will be there with her parents."

"I heard. She messaged me."

Carrie reached out and placed two fingers on the edge of his phone, moving it down to the top of the table. "Is everything okay, Sam?"

"Yeah, why?" He chewed on his bottom lip.

"Does Dylan know you're here? He mentioned that you two were going to the beach today."

"Yeah, but later." His shoulders hunched up toward his ears. "If he has time after his stupid meeting."

Curiosity pricked along Carrie's spine. "What meeting?"

"He probably doesn't want me to talk about his plans because he knows they make him look like a butt head."

"Harsh," she whispered, an unsettled feeling overtaking her curiosity. "It seems like whatever the meeting's about is upsetting you. Does it have something to do with your parents?"

Sam shook his head emphatically, then pushed back a lock of too-long hair that flopped across his forehead. "It doesn't matter what Dylan says. My dad would have never let this happen. He could be a jerk, but he cared about things other than the company."

"Dylan cares about more than business," she assured the boy. "He loves you and…" She stopped short of claiming he loved her. He cared about her and she thought he might actually be falling for her again, but it felt like bad luck to give voice to that delicate hope.

"Everyone is going to hate him and probably me when he tears down the old factory along with half of downtown."

Carrie's breath caught in her throat, but she forced her expression to remain neutral. "That's not going to happen. The festival was a success and we all see that the town is on the right track. I'm sure you've heard about the company that wants to buy the old factory. I think we're going to have more businesses moving to downtown, as well. We have a meeting scheduled after the holidays. Dylan will see that he has options besides his plans for a luxury renovation."

"It will be too late," Sam said. "He's out at the factory now and he's going to sign a partnership agreement with some other creepy developer. I saw the contract on the kitchen table this morning."

"You must have been mistaken," she told the teenager even as panic snaked across her skin.

"I hated it here at the start and did some stupid stuff, but I've found better friends. Two of them have families who have lived here since the town was founded. They don't have a ton of money and if everything gets all jacked up expensive, I don't know what's going to happen to them. Other than people are going to turn on me."

"No one will turn on you." She reached out to pat the boy's hand, but he yanked it away.

"Dylan told me about your dad. How he was a big shot in town because of his art, and then when he didn't have money, he only pretended to be a big shot."

"Yes," she said slowly.

"Were your friends still your friends when everything changed for you?"

Carrie pressed two fingers to her chest as memories from her childhood assailed her. "I didn't have many friends to begin with," she admitted.

"Why not?" Sam asked, inclining his head.

"I didn't fit in."

"Because…" he prompted, and she realized she hadn't given the boy enough credit. He understood way too much about her past and the potential parallels to his own life.

"Because my family had money. It set us apart from most people in Magnolia. And when my dad lost it all, things got even worse."

"That's what's going to happen to me." Sam didn't sound angry, just resigned. She hated that acceptance because it reminded her of herself at his age. "In my other schools in Boston, almost all of the kids had rich parents or at least they pretended to have these fabulous lives. When my parents died and my life wasn't perfect, I was like a leper or something. Like if they hung out with me some of my crappy life might rub off on them. Here no one cares."

"People care," Carrie insisted.

"Not in a bad way," he clarified. "But they'll care if the guy who's my stupid guardian changes everything."

"I don't understand."

"He made a promise to my dad about the company and how it's my legacy. Now he thinks he needs to make it huge, so I have all kinds of money or security or whatever. I don't even want the dumb company. I'm going to study art, like you."

"I wish I'd had the courage to do that in college," she told him even as her mind raced with what he'd revealed about

Dylan's plans. "I was a business major and took a few art classes without my dad knowing about it."

"That's what Dylan said when he was lecturing me this morning. Art is fine for a hobby but I'm going to need to get serious about my future."

Another dagger to Carrie's heart. Not only had Dylan broken his promise to give her vision for Magnolia a chance, apparently, all his talk about her making a career of her art was just lies, as well. He might think it was good enough for her living in Magnolia, but he wanted more for Sam.

More than the town. More than she could offer.

Just as she'd always known.

"I THOUGHT WE were done with changes to the contract," Steven Ross told Dylan as they stood in the factory parking lot. To Dylan's shock, his potential partner had driven down to Magnolia after receiving Dylan's response that Scott Development had a few additional line items to revise in their agreement. "But whatever it takes at this point. I'll have my lawyers review your updates, and then we can both sign and move on from negotiations to making money in this godforsaken town. It's going to be huge."

"Call me after the New Year," Dylan said automatically. "Give your people the holidays without bending over backward."

Steven let out a disbelieving laugh. "Who are you and what have you done with Dylan Scott?"

Dylan didn't bother to answer, only rolled his eyes.

"I'm serious," the other man insisted, adjusting his mirrored Ray-Ban sunglasses. "I know this is our first deal together, but I expected more from what Wiley had said about you. You'll barely return one of my calls let alone push through his contract."

"You're getting in on the bottom floor of a redevelopment that's going to be a model for introducing premier housing and retail space to a small-town demographic. This could lead to opportunities around the country. How can you want more?"

"I want the guy your cousin told me about, the baller who worked with single-minded determination. Why should either of us give a rat's ass about our people working over the holidays? That's why we pay them, and money is the bottom line."

Aggravation burned in Dylan like the brand from a hot poker. Steven's development company was one of the most successful in the Boston area. The fact that he wanted to partner with Dylan in Magnolia was a huge achievement. Wiley had been the one to work this end of the company, and Dylan knew he had big shoes to fill.

He didn't like being compared to his cousin, not that he had any doubt that he'd come up short. But he'd lost his passion for this potential partnership. Just as Carrie'd predicted, this town and its damn holiday spirt had gotten to him.

Corrupted him. Ruined his focus.

Ruined him for anything but the satisfaction he got from making her smile.

She definitely wouldn't be happy when she found out about this deal and what it meant for the factory and his downtown plans.

That was part of the reason he wanted to wait until the New Year to finalize everything. It would give him more time to explain it to her in a way she'd understand.

He had no choice but to go forward with his original plan, despite how things had gone with the festival. Despite their agreement.

He'd made a promise to his cousin to take care of Sam, and that meant growing the business that would eventually belong to him.

Wiley would have loved this deal in the same way Dylan had when he'd first conceived it. Surely his enthusiasm would return once he could put Christmas and all of the cloying small-town spirit behind him.

The New Year would bring a fresh start and a clean slate. This was his, no matter what anyone thought of it.

"Nothing's going to happen down here until January," he said, ignoring the other man's frown. "Go home and enjoy the holiday."

"My ex-wife has the kids for Christmas," Steven said. "Elizabeth flew to Chicago to see her family. I'm going to be swiping right on a couple of my fave dating apps. You wouldn't believe how many lonely chicks are out there on a major holiday."

Dylan's stomach rolled. "Probably not. Sounds, um... interesting. You do realize you're engaged?"

"No ring on my finger yet," Steven said with a deep chuckle. "I know having a teenager in the house might be cramping your style. Wiley had mentioned sending Sam to boarding school at one point. My son went to a prep academy in upstate New York. Best thing we ever did for him."

"Wiley never said anything to me about boarding school."

"I think he wanted more freedom for him and Kay. Kids are a time suck."

The guy was truly a jackass. "Speaking of time," Dylan said, backing away. "I need to get back to town."

"We'll talk soon." Steven headed for his sleek Mercedes.

Dylan opened the door of his SUV then paused as a car came barreling down the gravel driveway that led to the factory, and Carrie's silver Volvo station wagon came into view.

He took a few steps forward then stopped when she didn't slow down as she approached. What the hell was going on?

"You okay?" Steven asked as he pulled up beside Dylan.

"Fine. It's my girlfriend. Probably needs me to pick up something for dinner tonight before the grocery store closes."

"She takes dinner seriously," the other man said with a laugh then drove out of the parking lot.

The Volvo lurched to a stop. "Who was that?" Carrie demanded as she got out and stalked toward him.

"Just a business associate," he said, ignoring the guilt that roared through his gut. "I needed some advice and he was in the area. Is everything okay?"

"I saw Sam in town just now."

"Oh, hell. What did he get into now?" Dylan pulled his phone from his back pocket, ready to punch in the boy's number. "If he's causing trouble on—"

"Sam isn't the problem." Carrie stepped forward, jabbed a finger into Dylan's chest. "You are."

"I told you I'd take care of wine for tonight." Dylan checked the time on his phone. He remembered the holidays being stressful for Kay when she hosted big gatherings. Wiley would joke about needing to stay clear of her path, so Dylan wanted to believe this was part of the territory and it was a coincidence that she'd sought him out at the textile mill. Once everyone showed up and she saw how happy they were, things would get better. "I still have an hour before the liquor store closes. Plenty of time. I won't let you down."

"You already have," she said, her hand dropping to her

side. "Why did you have a business meeting at the factory on Christmas Eve, Dylan?"

"I told you he was driving through town. I know I should be with Sam today, but—"

"I know about the partnership deal."

He closed his eyes for a moment as he tried to process her words. This wasn't how he'd wanted her to find out. The timing couldn't have been worse. He shook his head. "Sam wasn't supposed to say anything yet."

"Did you expect him to lie for you?" she asked, her tone ice-cold as if they were in the Arctic tundra and not the temperate Carolina coast.

"Don't make this a bigger deal than it is," he insisted. "You know my plan."

"I thought you'd stay true to your word." She crossed her arms over her chest. "The festival was a success. We proved to you that Magnolia can be revitalized without changing the fabric of the town. There are options, Dylan. Companies have taken notice. Young families are excited about living here."

"I'm not denying things went well. You did a great job, Carrie."

"Don't patronize me."

"I'm not trying to," he assured her, an uncomfortable sensation he didn't quite understand fluttering through his belly. This was no different than any other economically stagnated community that Scott Development had redeveloped. He hadn't helped build his uncle's company into a multimillion-dollar venture by allowing emotions to rule the day. "But my plan will take this town so much further than you can even imagine. I made a promise to Sam's father."

"You made promises to me, too."

He hated the hitch in her voice, the accusation that told

him he'd screwed things up simply by being himself and doing what he needed to. He didn't want to hurt her. It was why he'd tried to put off signing the contract until after the New Year. Get through the holidays and then he could make her understand.

Now he had less than twenty-four hours until Christmas and the whole thing was blowing up in his face.

"It will be fine," he said, reaching for her. "Probably better for you in the long run."

She shrugged away his touch as her green eyes widened, a storm swirling in their depths. "Excuse me?"

The ground shifted underneath him. Not literally of course, but some seismic movement he couldn't describe. It rocked him to his core. He knew this moment was important, but all he could think to do was bluster through and hope Carrie would prove herself to be the generous soul he knew and let him off the hook. Even if he didn't deserve it.

"Yes," he continued, swallowing back the idea that he was feeding her a complete line of bull. "This will benefit you, as well." He'd learned in negotiations that conviction was half the battle. Maybe more.

If he could convince her, he could win the day. Win everything. He could keep his promise to both his cousin and Carrie without changing the man he'd become. He didn't even know how to begin the thought of transforming.

"I just spent the better part of the past several months working on a specific vision for this town. You're going to undo most of that with one signature. How is that good for me?"

"You need customers for your art. People who have money and are willing to spend it. You need to cultivate a devoted following the way your dad did in his heyday. I'm going to be bringing that to Magnolia. Money. Exclusivity."

"At the expense of the community," she reminded him. "We want people who will make Magnolia their home and visitors who can appreciate the charm and serenity a small town has to offer."

Guilt spiked again but he clamped an invisible muzzle over it. Emotions had no place in business. His way of doing business had worked for so long now. It was the model his uncle and cousin had created within the company that gave Dylan his first taste of belonging. What good did all that small-town charm do if it didn't pay the bills? Allowing emotions means vulnerability and that meant pain. He'd learned to live without emotions since he left Magnolia.

He could finally prove he wasn't the troubled, worthless kid he'd been by changing this town into something better.

"The community will adapt on its own or be forced to change."

"This place is special. I don't care about rich patrons. That's not why I paint."

"Or maybe you want to take over your dad's position in the town?" he suggested, grasping at anything to make her stop this gentle assault that stung like the bite of a whip. "You have talent, Carrie. Everyone knows that now. If things are managed right, you're going to be a huge success, bigger than Niall ever was."

"That's not why I paint," she repeated, her tone steely.

"It's a good perk and will get you and your sisters out of the financial mess he put you in. This change in the town will only help with that. You and I can work together. You'll see. This will be even better than your vision. I know I'm right."

"It's funny that you bring up my father, because you sound like him."

"I do not," he protested.

"Oh, yes." She held her arms wide. "Niall Reed was the original 'Father Knows Best.' For his career. For Magnolia. For me." She shook her head. "Even when his vision sent his life and everything around it spiraling down the toilet, he never wavered. He never let other people's needs get in the way of his own desires." She sniffed. "I shouldn't be surprised things went this way. I was bound to have daddy issues. I guess since we didn't get to play them out ten years ago, it had to end like this."

"Nothing is ending. It's a beginning. For both of us. You said yourself that you don't want the responsibility that people around here have put on you. Yes, your dad made big mistakes. But they're his. I'm doing this for both of us."

"Lying to me and this community?"

"It isn't that."

"Sam had a different opinion when I talked to him."

"This is for Sam most of all. He can have the best of both worlds. The benefit of small-town life and making sure the company will be as strong as I can make it."

"He wants to pursue art," she said like they were discussing what to have for dinner.

Except it felt like this might be his last supper. "Fine," he agreed. "I don't care if he takes art classes. But his future is the business. His family's company."

"And if that isn't what he wants?"

"He's a kid. He doesn't know what he wants. His father had a plan, and it's my job to execute it."

"Nothing about these weeks in Magnolia changed anything for you."

"Are you joking? I've shown more holiday spirit in the past month than I have in years. I'm fully invested in all this Christmas crap. I stayed up last night wrapping Sam's gifts until almost midnight. I even found the new video game he wanted on a bootleg website and paid more money than I care to admit on shipping. I'm like the second coming of Kris Kringle."

"Christmas isn't about spending money. You've missed the whole point."

"Spoken like someone who was never poor," he spat, then hated himself when her eyes flashed with pain. "The best thing I can do for Sam is to make sure his future's secure. This isn't personal, Carrie. It's business."

"Bad business," she murmured.

"What do you want me to do?"

She smiled, and he had a sudden flash of memory. She'd given him that same sad smile when she'd walked away from him ten years ago. He couldn't believe it. He refused to believe this was ending. Not when he was trying to do the right thing. If only she'd open her eyes and see it.

"If you have to ask, there's nothing to be done."

"Carrie."

"I'll see you tonight."

"Is it better if I don't come to dinner?"

"You're not getting off the hook that easily, Dylan." Her smile suddenly vanished, replaced by the fierceness he'd seen in her when he'd seen her walking that first night. When he couldn't have imagined all that had transpired over the past several weeks. "You and Sam will have your time at the beach. Join us for Christmas Eve service and then dinner at my house. You won't say a word to him or to anyone about this deal for the factory."

"Is that really—"

"It's necessary," she interrupted. "I haven't worked this hard to make Christmas in Magnolia perfect only to have it wrecked now."

"I'm not trying to wreck anything."

"Then I hope you're a better actor than you are a friend," she said.

The words felt like a knife to his gut. "What about after tonight?"

Her chin trembled and she looked away. "Nope. Not going there. If I think about that, I'll lose it. We get through Christmas Eve like everything is right as rain. Channel your inner Chevy Chase. We're going to be the 'jolliest bunch of—well, you know—this side of the nuthouse.'"

She walked away on those parting words and Dylan watched her car disappear out of the parking lot, wondering how his life had gone to hell so quickly.

It was like ten years ago all over again. Maybe he'd done it on purpose. Or on purpose without realizing that was what was happening. He'd never believed he deserved the kind of happiness he'd found with Carrie, and now he'd proven it to both of them.

CHAPTER TWENTY-ONE

CARRIE IGNORED THE doorbell as it rang insistently on Christmas Day.

She glanced at the clock. Two in the afternoon. Which meant she only had ten more hours to get through and this infernal holiday would be officially over.

The cheery decorations she'd put out around her house seemed to mock her. A trio of snowmen stared at her from their place on the bookshelf, tiny button eyes silently judging her for her pathetic broken heart.

The doorbell rang again, followed by a loud banging.

"Open up," Avery called from the other side. "Or I'll make Gray come over here and do his fireman routine to bust in."

"Go away," Carrie shouted from the sofa, where she'd been sprawled since early that morning binge-watching any show that was holiday themed. "Go have a Merry stinkin' Christmas somewhere else."

"We're not leaving," Meredith shouted back. "And I don't need Gray. I can bust down this door all on my own."

As if to prove her point, the door rattled on its hinges.

"Are you crazy?" Carrie yelled but got up off the couch and headed for the door.

"Not as crazy as you've been acting since yesterday," Avery said when Carrie opened it. "We know about Dylan and his development partner." Both women pushed past Carrie into the house.

"He wasn't supposed to tell anyone."

"Sam messaged Shae after he got home last night," Meredith explained. "She called me this morning. It all makes sense now—the vibe from last night was faker than a pro wrestling match."

"I thought dinner was fine," Carrie lied. She'd done her best to get through the evening, buoyed by the festive moods of everyone other than Dylan, Sam and herself. But it had been a struggle and she realized she'd been a fool to think her sisters wouldn't notice.

Avery wrapped her arms around Carrie's shoulders. "You should have told us."

"It would have ruined the day for everyone. I didn't want that." She stayed stiff in her sister's embrace, afraid if she let herself do anything but buffer the heartache, she might never recover.

"You're not alone," Avery said gently. "You don't have to take on everything by yourself."

"There's nothing to take on," she insisted as she pulled away. "Dylan won. He's doing the thing I'd tried to stop. Magnolia is going to become a haven for the wealthy. It's not what any of us wanted, but we can't stop him. We'll make sure it's not the end of the world as we know it."

"Sam told Shae that Dylan isn't going to officially sign until after the New Year. We can try to convince the companies interested in Magnolia to sweeten their offer for a lease or outright purchase of the factory and adjacent land from Dylan. We'll ask residents to protest his plans and make sure the town council is ready to deny permits or approval of whatever he submits. We don't have to give up without a fight."

"I don't want to fight," Carrie said, her shoulders slouching under the weight of her disappointment. "Dylan told me I'm holding on to some sort of antiquated vision of the town. Perhaps I'm more like Niall than I want to admit?"

Meredith snorted. "You're nothing like Niall and everyone knows it. That was a low blow, even for Dylan."

"I'm going to give him a piece of my mind the next time I see him." Avery's eyes narrowed. "If he thinks he can get away with—"

"Stop." Carrie shook her head. "I don't want this—any of it. I'm going to New York City."

Both Avery and Meredith stilled. They exchanged looks with each other before their gazes landed back on Carrie.

"For good?" Meredith asked after a moment.

Carrie swallowed around the ball of anxiety that had risen in her throat when she'd made the declaration. She hadn't, in fact, been planning to go to the city. Not until she'd said the words out loud.

"I'm not sure." She glanced down at the fuzzy pink robe she wore, brushed a piece of dried cereal off the front. "Another gallery owner called a few days after the festival. Someone who was here took photos of my work and texted him. He wants to meet and talk about representation and he sounds even more serious than the woman who reached out after the newspaper article. That felt like she wanted the notoriety I bring with me. This man seems interested in me."

"Why won't he come to Magnolia?" Avery asked. "Your studio and paintings are here."

"He offered that," Carrie admitted. The truth was the man had offered to represent her without even meeting her. He said he thought she had a bright future just from the pictures of her work. "But I want to go to the city. He has ideas for a show at his location in Tribeca. I'd like to see them. I'd like to feel the energy of New York. Dad always talked so negatively about the art scene there, but I realize that's because of how the critics viewed his work. I want to see it for myself. I'm tired of letting other people determine how I live my life."

"We'll support you in whatever path you take." Avery's smile was gentle. "But remember this will always be your home."

She knew that, of course, but the words were still a balm on her heart.

"And we can take out Dylan Scott if you want," Meredith offered, making a show of cracking her knuckles. "That guy deserves a good throttling."

"No." Carrie shook her head. "He's doing what he thinks is right. For the town and for Sam. I wish he could see a different way, but maybe he's right."

Meredith frowned. "Don't say that. He's a lowlife, lying slime ball. Don't give him an out."

"I'm not trying to," she protested weakly. "But I don't want to live with my head in the sand any longer. I have to face life, even the difficult parts of it."

"No matter what happens, today is Christmas and you shouldn't be alone." Avery glanced at the television. "Get dressed and come to the house. Violet is so excited to show off her presents, and even Gray's mother is coming over. I still think she likes you better than me."

"She doesn't like me at all," Meredith said with a laugh. "I'm going to have a great time with that."

The two of them turned for the door, arguing over how to handle Avery's soon-to-be mother-in-law. It took almost a full minute for them to notice that Carrie hadn't moved.

"I'm serious," Avery said, turning again. "You can't

spend Christmas alone. I see where this is going. You'll tell us everything is okay and then end up sitting in the dark on the wrong side of a bottle of wine with Joni Mitchell's *River* playing on repeat."

"Such a good song," Meredith murmured. "But sad as all get out."

Carrie shook her head. "I'm not planning on drinking," she promised. "But I'm staying here."

"Carrie, come on." Avery's mouth thinned. "We're worried about you. This is your first Christmas without Niall. Things have changed and—"

"I've changed," Carrie whispered. "It hurts right now, but I'm going to be fine."

"Are you sure?" her sisters asked in unison. Neither of them looked convinced.

That made three of them, but she took a deep breath and nodded. She might not know how she'd survive, but there was no doubt she'd find a way to figure it out.

"What about Dylan?" Meredith held up a clenched fist. "I could still throw down if you want me to. I'm pretty sure I could take him."

"I don't want to think about Dylan."

"You fell for him again," Avery commented. "And he hurt you *again*. How can we ignore that?"

"He never really promised me anything." Carrie tried not to flinch from the pain of that truth. "I thought his views on the town had changed. I thought he wanted to be with me. Obviously, I read more into great sex than I should have."

Meredith sniffed. "Or maybe he used his ninja bedroom skills to ensure you."

The last thing Carrie wanted to think about was Dylan's ninja bedroom skills. The idea that he'd purposely worn down her defenses made the pain of her heartbreak spike hot and bright in her chest. Perhaps wine and a Joni Mitchell marathon weren't such a bad idea after all.

"I need to get ready for the trip," she told her sisters, hoping she sounded more convincing than she felt. "It will be good for me to have a change of scenery."

"If you change your mind about Christmas dinner," Avery said, her gaze filled with a quiet concern, "come over. Don't call. Don't hesitate. Just come over. You aren't alone."

Tears pricked at the backs of Carrie's eyes.

It felt strange but right to let them out of her house and return to the quiet. Instead of resuming her position on the sofa, she padded to the kitchen table and flipped open her laptop.

Her inclination might be to close herself off, but she wasn't that person anymore. She used to think fear and doubt made her weak. Now she realized that those two emotions could only control her if she let them.

The only way to overcome fear was to keep moving forward. That was what she intended to do.

She found a flight leaving Raleigh the following morning and booked a seat on it. Then she grabbed her phone and punched in her mother's number.

Vanessa answered on the third ring. "Merry Christmas, Carrie. I only have a few minutes to talk. A local choir is about to begin performing in the lobby."

Her mom had called earlier for their traditional holiday conversation, undoubtedly when she'd had a break in her schedule, but Carrie hadn't answered and understood she'd missed the window of her mother's attention. She admired Vanessa's dedication. She worked every major holiday, showing a devotion to the guests at the hotel that she had never displayed with her family.

In a way, both of her parents had wanted to control their own lives. They'd just gone about it very differently. Carrie let out a long breath. She was a grown woman, and it was long past time she claimed control of *her* life.

"Hi, Mom. Merry Christmas. I need your help."

She heard the soft gasp on the other end of the line. She couldn't remember the last time she'd asked her mother for anything. It clearly felt as strange to Vanessa as it did for Carrie.

"What can I do?" her mom asked without hesitation.

"I'm going to New York City to meet with a gallery owner. I've looked at a couple of hotels online, but everything seems to be booked for the holidays. I don't know if you have any contacts but—"

"I can get you a room. That's easy." There was a long pause. "Is this about your father's work?"

"The gallery is interested in me," Carrie said, feeling pride swell inside her despite the ache in her heart. "I've been painting again, Mom. Different than what I used to do."

"You have talent, Carrie. You always have." Vanessa laughed softly. "When you were little, your father used to brag to anyone who'd listen about what a chip off the old block you were. Don't think he didn't recognize it. I'm sorry he sabotaged your confidence once he realized your gifts would eclipse his, although I suppose it's not a surprise. Another reason for me to feel horrible about leaving you with him."

"That's not what I want, Mom." Carrie's chest heaved with her attempt to reconcile the way her father had derided her teenage efforts with her mother's assertion that he'd once been proud of her.

"I'll call the hotel in New York right away," her mother

promised. "In fact…" Her mother paused, drew in a breath. "I could come up to the city and meet you."

Carrie's immediate reaction was to say no. She assumed, because that was her way, that her mother was making the offer out of guilt or some sense of duty.

"I mean it," Vanessa continued when Carrie didn't answer. "It would be fun for the two of us to spend some time together."

"Would it?" Carrie murmured. The tea she'd shared with her mom at the start of the holiday season had been strained at best.

"For me it would."

"You tell me every year how busy you are during the holidays. The hotel is packed, and you have returning guests to take care of. Isn't that why you could never have Christmas with me?"

Vanessa gave a soft laugh. "Let me ask you a question, Carrie. Would you have ever left your father alone for the holidays?"

Embarrassment stabbed at Carrie's gut. "I didn't mean to cut you out of my life."

"I know," her mother said, her tone soothing. "And I should have fought harder to keep you in mine. Yes, the hotel is busy at this time of year. But I haven't taken a vacation in years. They'll live without me for a few days. If you're willing, I'd like to come to New York with you. I'd like to meet this potential agent and take you around to my favorite places in the city. I know I haven't been much of a mother, and for that I'm sorry. I'm not even sure if I know how to change at this point. I'd like the chance to try."

Carrie lifted her fingers to her cheeks to find them moist with tears she hadn't even realized were falling. These weren't the sad kind she'd shed over Dylan late last night.

This crying felt cathartic, like a part of her evolution into the woman she wanted to be.

"That would be nice."

"I'll text you the details once I confirm the reservation. Let me get a pen and I'll write down your flight information. I can book the same one."

"Thanks, Mom," Carrie said. Maybe she'd gotten a different kind of Christmas miracle than she expected.

DYLAN KEPT HIS EYE on Daisy as she sniffed a lamppost on the corner outside the row of buildings he owned in downtown.

The street was surprisingly crowded given that it was a few days after Christmas. He would have expected the crowds to disappear now that the holiday rush was over, but it seemed that visitors were still drawn to Magnolia and the town's festive atmosphere.

He forced himself not to look across the street to The Reed Gallery. He hadn't spoken to Carrie since he and Sam had left her house after a painfully awkward Christmas Eve dinner.

But damn he missed her.

Christmas had been almost the easiest day to get through. He'd focused all of his attention on Sam and, once again, the kid had blown him away with his insight.

He'd been thrilled—if overwhelmed—with the wealth of gifts Dylan had wrapped and shoved under the Christmas tree. Dylan hadn't expected anything in return, but Sam had handed him a box clumsily wrapped in red paper.

He'd opened it to find an oil color painting of a place that held more memories than he could count. "It's the dock off your grandpa's cabin at the lake."

Sam gave a jerky nod. "I copied it from a picture I found

on the internet. It was the last time we were all together and I thought it would be good to…you know…remember something happy."

"Yeah," Dylan whispered around the emotion clogging his throat. He'd knocked himself out buying all kinds of fancy presents to take Sam's mind off the family he'd lost only to receive the most precious gift in a reminder that memories could comfort as well as cause pain.

It had seemed safer to ignore the difficult emotions. That was what he'd learned to do in his family—distract and buffer against anything that made him feel. Because feelings made him vulnerable, which meant they were dangerous.

"Is this day especially hard?" he'd asked the kid, holding his breath as he watched varying degrees of sorrow play across Sam's features.

Then the boy began to talk about his parents, and that sadness morphed into something different, shades of emotions ranging from upset over the loss and trauma to joy at the memories he had of them. All of the money Dylan spent couldn't hold a candle to the significance of everything Sam shared. They'd continued to talk through breakfast and then as they drove out to the beach for a walk along the shore.

It truly felt like some kind of Christmas miracle. When they'd returned home, both of them had been exhausted, and they'd spent the rest of the afternoon watching movies, playing video games and laughing at Daisy and Barnaby's shenanigans.

By the time Sam said good-night, Dylan's heart felt so full he thought it might explode out of his chest. Except for the gaping hole in it where thoughts of Carrie continued to consume him.

Like clockwork, Steven Ross's attorney had called the

day after Christmas. Clearly, Dylan's instructions to wait until the New Year had been roundly ignored.

It made him wonder how much else Steven might ignore as part of this partnership. There was a reason Wiley had always dealt with their investors. Dylan didn't want to compromise when it came to his vision. But by taking another firm's money, he would have to give up some control.

He looked up as a group of people walked out of Il Rigatone. The smell of garlic and sweet tomatoes filled the air and a sudden vision of an updated version of the restaurant flashed across his mind.

As Carrie had predicted, he and Sam had one of the best meals Dylan could remember when they'd ordered carry-out based on her suggestion. Thick cuts of chicken with a savory marsala sauce for him and a slice of lasagna that probably weighed close to five pounds for Sam. The quality of food had never been in question, but the image of a down-home mom and pop diner simply didn't fit with what he wanted for the town.

What if his vision was wrong?

Ever since he'd left Magnolia, Dylan had been moving forward. Always fast and with unwavering faith that momentum would keep him going. The same thing had kept him going even upon returning to Magnolia.

He hadn't listened—hadn't wanted to hear anything Carrie was saying about the town and what might be best for it. He knew what was best. He always had.

He'd made a promise to his cousin. For Dylan, taking care of Sam meant ensuring the boy's financial future. Giving him a legacy. Something that would belong to him. The one thing Dylan had always craved.

Listening to Sam discuss his memories of his parents—both good and bad—Dylan realized that keeping Wiley and

Kay's memories alive and helping Sam understand that both his parents loved him would be far more beneficial than anything material he could give the kid.

"You should go in."

He turned as Mary Ellen Winkler approached from across the street.

"Nah. I've got the dog and, besides, it smells greasy from here. I'm just imagining the upscale steak restaurant that's going to replace it."

He'd wanted to punch himself in the face even as the words spewed from his mouth. What was it about this place—the town he'd chosen to return to—that made him act like such a jerk?

At least he could take comfort that he knew who he was in Magnolia. No one expected anything more. Except for Carrie.

Instead of huffing away or giving him a well-deserved lecture, Mary Ellen laughed. "Il Rigatone is the best Italian food you'll find in either of the Carolinas. You're just grumpy because Vinnie Guilardi hasn't been willing to beg and plead for you to keep the restaurant open. He's a proud man."

Dylan narrowed his eyes. "I don't need anyone to beg or plead. In addition to the steak house, I might hire someone to open a bakery. I'm friends with the guy who's been voted best pastry chef in Boston for three years in a row." Even though it was a low blow, the mention of some potential competition should stop her from having a laugh at his expense. Dylan hated being laughed at.

To his surprise, Mary Ellen's smile broadened. "I remember that about you," she said, dabbing at the corner of her eye with one chubby finger. "Your pride trumped everything. I think back to when you vandalized Sunnyside.

You would have gladly worked unpaid for another month if it meant you didn't have to say you were sorry for the damage to my shop. The apology cost you dearly."

Guilt zipped through him, and he had trouble meeting her gaze. He'd thought he'd worked through the issues from his past but clearly he hadn't. He was still copping an attitude. "I owed you a sincere apology more than anything," he admitted ruefully. "I was a punk kid with too much attitude back in the day."

"I imagine you developed that attitude in order to survive," she said gently.

Irritation bristled across Dylan's shoulders and he tugged on Daisy's leash. He didn't like discussing his childhood with anyone. Or his parents. Especially his father. Dylan would rather people see him as the bad guy than pity him for the way he was raised.

He wouldn't tolerate pity.

"We all do what we can to survive," he answered through clenched teeth. "I'm no different than anyone else in that respect."

"This is for you." Mary Ellen handed him the bag she'd been holding. "I saw you from the window of the bakery and thought Sam might enjoy a couple of donuts for tomorrow's breakfast." She smiled. "I know how much he likes them."

Dylan nodded. "Um, thank you." He didn't quite know how to respond to the random act of kindness. It didn't matter that she hadn't done it for him directly. The gesture meant more because it was for Sam. This was why Dylan had brought him here in the first place—so that the kid could see what it was like to be in a community that cared. He knew Magnolia could be that place for Sam, even if it hadn't for Dylan.

"I included a couple of sticky buns. You aren't fooling me sending Sam in to buy your favorite."

Daisy whined softly as she settled next to Dylan.

"There's a biscuit for you, too, girl," Mary Ellen told her, earning a tail thump like the dog understood the words.

"Well, I'm banned so what choice did I have?" Dylan peeked in the bag, inhaling the scent of all that warm, sugary dough. "Like I said, we all do what we can to survive."

"Surviving isn't good enough," Mary Ellen told him with a motherly tsk. "We should aim to thrive. I'm lifting your ban. Dylan Scott, you're welcome in the bakery anytime."

"Even though I'm the guy who's going to ruin Magnolia's future?"

"Even if you import every highfalutin celebrity baker you can find. You aren't the same troubled teenager you used to be. I may not agree with what you're planning for the town, but we've survived worse than you." She leaned in closer. "And we continue to thrive."

Somehow, the words didn't make him feel any better.

"You might change your mind once you talk to Carrie," he said, flicking a glance toward the gallery.

"I already have." Mary Ellen's smile was sad. "She wouldn't say exactly what had happened between the two of you, but I know you both look equally miserable. I gave her an extra chocolate croissant for the flight and—"

"What flight?" he interrupted, his fingers curling harder around the edge of the bag.

"She took off for New York City," Mary Ellen told him. "Going to meet some big-wig art gallery owner who saw photos of her work. It's gonna be a sad day for this town if Carrie moves away, but that girl deserves her shot at success."

"Yeah," Dylan muttered even as his mind tried to process the news. Carrie in New York. His chest clenched as he thought of her discovering the city and its energy for the first time.

Damn, he wished he could be there with her.

Would she love it? Would she decide to stay?

He hadn't even come to terms with not having her a part of his life. The thought of her leaving Magnolia at the same time was almost too much to stand.

"Honey, are you okay?" Mary Ellen placed a hand on his arm. "You look like you've just seen a ghost."

"It could be the ghost of Christmas future," he said numbly.

"Sometimes you don't know what you've got until it's gone," she said. "So maybe you want to rethink paving paradise?"

His brow furrowed. "That's a Joni Mitchell reference. Carrie used to listen to her songs all the time."

The older woman smiled. "Good taste, that girl."

"I might be the exception." Dylan shook his head. "Is it possible to lose something I never had?"

"You know she loves you."

"Past tense. I screwed it up." He massaged a hand over his face. "Again."

As if sensing his darkening mood, Daisy pressed nearer to him. Ever since Christmas Eve night, the dog had been sticking close to Dylan's side as if she were trying to offer some bit of canine comfort. She still startled at loud noises and remained wary of strangers and indifferent toward the kibble they poured into her bowl at night. But the dog had become part of their motley family. The animal's attention one more reminder that most of the things Dylan had tried to do for Sam had ended up just as much a benefit for him.

Like the move from Boston.

Like embracing the spirit of Christmas.

Like opening his heart to Carrie.

"Do you know what you need?" Mary Ellen glanced down the main street.

"Tell me." Dylan held his breath. At this point it felt as though he needed—

"A miracle," the woman whispered.

He laughed without humor. Right. A miracle. Like something out of a perfect holiday movie.

"Too bad I'm fresh out of miracles," he murmured.

Her gaze sharpened. "That's where you're mistaken, Dylan. Miracles are always waiting for you. You just have to recognize them."

He thought about the unspeakable tragedy that had changed everything in his life and all the tiny miracles that had led him to this point. Out of so much sorrow, he'd found a happiness he hadn't expected. One that had scared him so badly that he'd sabotaged it instead of risking his heart to claim a future he hadn't even realized he wanted.

He cleared his throat. "Will you help me?" The words felt strange on his tongue, but he forced himself to meet Mary Ellen's too-knowing gaze. If he was going to produce a post-Christmas miracle, he understood he couldn't do it alone.

CHAPTER TWENTY-TWO

"YOU DIDN'T NEED to pick me up." Carrie settled against the soft leather of Avery's Lexus sedan. "I could have hired Jack and his shuttle service again. I think he liked making the money." Capitalizing on the influx of visitors to town, one of the local mechanics, Jack Grage, had started a car service between Magnolia and the Raleigh airport as well as around the town to popular tourist spots. Nothing as formal as Uber, but it worked for Magnolia.

"Don't be ridiculous." Avery reached across the console and patted Carrie's jeans-clad knee. "We want to hear all about New York."

"And spending time with your mom," Meredith said with a small laugh from the backseat. "She's all kinds of intimidating."

Carrie shook her head. She and her mom had flown back from the city together after three amazing days touring Manhattan. "What you saw in the airport was her trying to be extra friendly," she reported.

Avery threw her a look. "That's terrifying."

"We actually had a lovely time." Carrie felt a smile curve her lips. "She led the way because she knows the city, and it was good to be with her in a neutral location. Magnolia has too many memories and I feel weird when I'm at her hotel, like everyone knows I don't belong there. Don't get me wrong. There were plenty of awkward moments. I'm not sure either of us knows how our mother-daughter dynamic is supposed to go when we've had so little interaction since the divorce. But we're figuring it out. I'm figuring out a lot of things lately."

"What did you think of the gallery owner?" Avery asked.

"He was intimidating, larger-than-life and asked questions about my paintings and the process I use to create them that made me think he really understood me." She bit down on her lip then added, "He respected my talent."

"As well he should," Meredith said with a sniff. "Did the subject of Niall come up?"

"Yes," Carrie answered. "I expected it. The art world might have eviscerated him critically, but no one could deny that he was a force. Max, the gallery owner, is around the same age and had actually met him years ago. Said he was a pompous ass."

Both her sisters laughed. "I like Max already," Meredith said.

"He took my mom and me to a reception for one of his long-time clients. Even I could tell it was a who's who of important people in the New York art community. Niall certainly didn't have the market cornered on being pompous."

"Or an ass, I'd imagine," Avery added.

"True, but I met people who were quite lovely, as well. It's a vibrant community and an amazing city. I can understand why so many artists are drawn there."

Carrie pressed her fingers against the car's cool window, watching condensation spread around her fingertips from the warmth of her touch. The day was gray and blustery, as if a storm might blow in at any moment. The turbulent weather was a direct contrast to her mood. Her trip to New York City had grounded her in some way, given her a glimpse into the life she thought she'd wanted and could still claim if she chose.

Only being there made her realize that dream belonged to the girl who'd felt trapped by her overbearing father and the expectations he placed on her.

The woman she'd become understood that Magnolia was her home and no matter what direction the town took for the future, she wanted to be part of it. Her life here with her sisters and the friends she was finally allowing herself to let in made her feel complete, despite her broken heart.

Silence stretched out in the sedan's interior, as if her sisters were waiting for her to say more.

"I'm staying in Magnolia," she told them, the four simple words a sliver of sound in the quiet. But they felt monumental as she spoke them.

Avery and Meredith let out cheers and squeals of delight, startling Carrie and making her heart thrum in her chest. Or maybe that was the relief from the sense of claiming her life. Truly claiming what she wanted. Most of it anyway.

As they continued to talk, Avery and Meredith avoided the topic of Dylan and his plans to develop the properties he owned in town. Carrie didn't bring up the subject, either. The trip had given her a different perspective on her hometown. A small dot on the map along the coast of North Carolina didn't have much in common with a big city, but the diversity of people and neighborhoods she'd seen on her trip had impressed her and given her hope for Magnolia. An influx of luxury properties and upscale businesses wouldn't wipe out the quiet charm she loved.

Dylan could do whatever he felt like he needed to for his cousin's legacy or for Sam or whatever he wanted to call it. She wouldn't let that stop her from making it her home, as well.

As if he knew she'd been thinking about him, a text from him came through at that moment.

"Everything okay?" Avery asked as she pulled off the highway and onto the two-lane road toward Carrie's house.

"Can you drop me off at the gallery?" Carrie typed in a quick response and hit Send before she lost her nerve.

"You bet," Avery answered. "What's going on at the gallery?"

"I'm not sure." Carrie bit down on her lower lip then said, "Dylan asked me to meet him there." She waited for the protests from both her sisters, but neither of them said a word.

She turned in her seat to eye Meredith, who was suddenly busy staring out the window at the houses she'd probably passed hundreds of times over the years like they were the eighth wonder of the world.

"You have nothing to say to that?"

Meredith shrugged. "What do you think he wants?"

"Did you talk to him while you were in New York?" Avery asked, flicking a curious glance toward Carrie.

"I don't know what he wants," she said to Meredith then studied Avery. "I haven't spoken to Dylan since Christmas Eve dinner."

Avery lifted a brow. "But you're willing to meet him now?"

"I'm staying in Magnolia and unless something changes, so is he. I'm not exactly the gunslinger 'this town ain't big enough for the two of us' type," she admitted. "I tried that when he first returned, and it got me nothing but a ticket to a broken heart."

"You don't sound angry anymore," Meredith said. "Have you forgiven him?"

"No," Carrie answered then shook her head. "Maybe. I don't even know if he needs my forgiveness. He didn't do what I wanted…" She darted a glance between the two of them. "What all of us wanted. But I'm not sure it was fair of me to expect him to. He gets to do whatever he wants with the real estate he owns. I still think we can turn Magnolia around and into a town that attracts younger residents and visitors from all over."

"We're already talking about a Valentine's Day campaign," Avery told her. "Plans haven't gone too far without you and your amazing ability to organize everything but—"

"You should go forward without me," Carrie told her sister on a rush of breath. "I want to focus on the gallery and my art. Being in New York inspired me, and not just to paint more. I want to bring other artists from around the state and show their work at The Reed Gallery. We could host an art co-op in the space and make it a hub for artists in the region."

"Okay," Avery said slowly. "What about the paint-and-sip parties?"

Carrie shook her head even as nerves made her flush with heat. "I'll finish the bookings, but that's it. I know we need immediate money to pay off Niall's debts, but I don't want to teach those classes. When the estate gets through probate, I'd like to buy the gallery."

"It's already yours," Avery told her.

"That place has always belonged to you," Meredith added, leaning forward to pat Carrie's shoulder.

"I appreciate that, but it's not true yet. I need to make it true. And we need to put Dad's house on the market as soon as we can. It's our best chance to get the money to ensure both the properties downtown and Last Acre are secure."

Avery parked the car across the street from the gallery and turned in her seat to face Carrie. "Are you sure? We thought you might eventually want to move back there."

As she glanced between Avery and Meredith, Carrie understood her sisters hadn't brought up the issue of Niall's house because they didn't want to upset her.

"I'm positive," she assured them. "That house is part of the past. I'm looking toward my future."

Meredith hitched a shoulder toward the gallery. "Could Dylan still be a part of that?"

"We don't want the same things." Carrie ran a hand through her hair, feeling suddenly exhausted from her trip. "But I don't want to be his enemy, either."

"I guess you should go see what he wants," Avery told her with an odd smile. "Who knows with that man."

"He did adopt a dog and a kitten this month." Meredith sighed. "I suppose he can't be totally evil."

Carrie raised an eyebrow at her younger sister. "That's high praise coming from you."

"Just make sure you take care of yourself," Meredith answered cryptically. "And know we have your back no matter what."

It felt like there was some deeper meaning in her sister's words, but for the life of her Carrie couldn't decipher what it could be.

"I'll drop your suitcase at your house on my way home," Avery promised then did a little shooing motion with her fingers. "Stop dawdling."

"I'm not dawdling." Carrie sniffed but dug around her purse for a tube of lip gloss. Of course she was delaying seeing Dylan. Just the thought of it made her stomach hurt. She could tell herself all day long that she simply wanted to make peace with him, but that wasn't the truth. What she wanted was to throw herself into his arms and share every detail about her trip.

She should hate him, but her heart hadn't quite gotten that memo. Despite being on different sides with regard to the town's future, she truly believed he was on her side as far as supporting her personal goals.

"Here goes everything," she whispered and exited the car.

She winced when Avery honked as she pulled away from the curb and watched the taillights disappear around the next corner.

For a moment she looked around the town where she'd spent her entire life, trying to see the old buildings with new eyes.

She and her sisters really had done a lot to transform things in Magnolia over the past few months. Main Street was quiet, as she'd expected for a Wednesday afternoon, but the shops and businesses looked welcoming and cheerful in a way she couldn't have dreamt of last year at this time.

Glancing behind her, she could see a few tables filled within Il Rigatone. Vinnie Guilardi stood next to one booth, his arms outstretched and his face animated. She could imagine the stories he was telling the family who waited for their food. The man had never met a stranger.

Carrie drew in a deep breath and considered the ideas that had bloomed in her mind as she toured New York City with her mother. There was still a vacant storefront on the far corner of the block in one of the buildings her father had owned. If her paintings actually sold in the way Max anticipated, she might be able to qualify for a loan and help the Guilardis relocate their restaurant.

That would put her back into direct competition with Dylan, a thought she didn't relish. But she remained determined to focus on the positive. She'd find a way to muddle along with him in town, even if he wasn't a part of her life in the way her heart craved.

A movement from across the street caught her attention and she started forward as Dylan appeared in the doorway of the gallery.

She liked seeing him there, more than she should, and reminded herself that this wasn't a reconciliation. At best, she hoped for a truce. A way to move past what came before.

"Thanks for meeting me," he said as she approached, looking annoyingly handsome as ever in a navy fleece and faded jeans, stubble shadowing his jaw. "How was New York?"

"Good." She swallowed, her mouth suddenly dry. Okay, this might have been a mistake. When she'd thought about seeing him again, she hadn't counted on her heart's reaction or feeling the heat that always seemed to radiate from him or the way he smelled like a mix of mint and spice and how she'd want to throw herself into his arms.

She definitely couldn't throw herself into his arms. Instead, she clenched her fists and kept a firm grip on her purse, like he was a potential mugger.

His mouth tugged up one side, but it wasn't a smile of happiness.

Did he feel the loss of her in anywhere near the same way she missed him?

"Is Sam here, too?" she asked, hoping for some kind of a buffer in this moment.

Dylan shook his head. "He went with a friend to the trampoline place in Raleigh for the day."

"Fun," she said, wondering if the word sounded as lame to his ears at it did to hers.

"Actually, it sounds like torture, but he was excited," Dylan said with a forced laugh.

"Why are we here?" she blurted. She gestured to the gallery window. "And why are the lights out inside? Lindy should have—"

"I sent Lindy home," Dylan told her, running a nervous hand through his hair. "I needed to talk to you in private."

"You don't own the gallery," she reminded him, her temper simmering. "You don't get to give instructions to our employee."

"Avery and Meredith actually approved it."

"Excuse me?" Carrie took a step back. Her sisters had known about this? She couldn't understand what was going on right now.

"I'm sorry," Dylan said on a rush of breath. "For a lot of things. Right now I'm sorry that I'm messing up this moment. Will you come into the gallery with me?" He took a step toward the door, regret and something that looked like fear flashing in his gaze when she didn't follow. "Please, Carrie."

Oh, she would have words with her sisters about this.

She followed him into the space, somehow feeling like she was entering it for the first time. Then he flipped on the light to the main room, and her breath caught in her throat.

"What is this?" she asked, turning in a circle to take in the sheets of paper and poster board that covered all four walls.

"The future, I hope." Dylan gently took her hand and led her forward. Carrie registered the warmth of his touch and the awareness pricked along her skin. But her heart was beating so hard in her chest she could hardly form a coherent thought.

"They're drawings of the town," she murmured, still trying to make sense of what she was viewing.

"What Magnolia could be," Dylan clarified. "Or will be. I'm not going forward with my original plan, Carrie. You were right. This place is special already. I don't need to create something new here." He reached out and plucked one of the sheets of paper from the wall. "The community will decide what's best for Magnolia and how to make its future a success." He handed the paper to her. "Mayor Malcolm got the word out and asked for ideas about what people want to see as part of a revitalization."

"Is this a water park?" she asked with a smile as she studied the drawing in her hand, done in colorful markers.

"That's from Violet." He indicated another, larger drawing that hung on the wall. "We also have suggestions for a performing art center, a new workout facility, an outdoor mall and affordable housing. And this is what's come in over the past forty-eight hours."

"Really?" Her heart was hammering so loud now she could barely form a thought around the pounding in her head. "People are that interested? I mean, I knew the business owners cared about making money and..." She shrugged. "I sometimes wondered if it meant more to me because of what my dad had let happen to the town."

"It means a lot to the people around here," he confirmed. "You mean a lot. You've gotten people thinking with hope about the future. All of your work has made them understand that Magnolia has a lot more potential than anyone gave it credit for."

He tipped up her chin with one finger. "It's made *me* understand that and so much more."

"Oh, yeah?" She tried to sound casual, but the question came out on a squeak of breath. "Like what?"

"Like the fact that I love you more than I thought possible." His voice caught on the last word and he cleared his throat, like he felt as nervous as she did. "I'm not sure I ever stopped loving you, Carrie. That first night when I saw you on the street, it was as if no time had passed between us. My heart understood why I'd returned to Magnolia even if it took my brain a little while to catch up."

"You came back here because of Sam," she reminded him, wanting to believe it could be more but afraid to let herself hope. Afraid that if she opened herself up again she might not recover.

"He's part of it," he agreed. "A big part of it. I didn't think I was capable of giving him the life he deserved just like I didn't believe I had it in me to love you the way you deserve to be loved. But Christmas in Magnolia…" He cupped her face in his hands and the look in his eyes melted her defenses like they were nothing more than candle wax. "These past few weeks with you have shown me that I have to move beyond my past. I want to become the man you and Sam need me to be. The man you both deserve."

She blinked away the tears that filled her eyes. "You already are that man. I shouldn't have made you the bad guy. You were never the villain for me. Always my hero."

His sigh reverberated through her, and then he leaned in and brushed his lips across hers. A gentle touch filled with hope and promise and all the love she could imagine.

"Give me another chance," he said against her mouth. "I want a future with you, Carrie. I want to build a home and decorate for Christmas and Halloween and string lights across the porch to celebrate every full moon if it will make you happy. I'll go to every small-town parade and coach little league and volunteer at bingo and—"

She pressed her hand to his mouth to silence him as joy rushed through her like a tidal wave. "Bingo might be laying it on a little thick," she said with a laugh. "But I'll take everything else. All of it, Dylan. I love you and I'll give you—us—as many chances as we need."

He kissed her again and as Carrie wrapped her arms around him, her heart settled like it had finally found its place. In the arms of the man she'd love for the rest of her life.

* * * * *

THE ROAD TO MAGNOLIA

CHAPTER ONE

"REMEMBER TO BREATHE," Lily Wainright muttered to herself as she grabbed two plates from the pass-through window in front of the restaurant's kitchen. It felt like a boa constrictor had wound its way around her lungs, squeezing tight. "Remember to breathe," she repeated.

She turned and then narrowed her eyes at the man who watched her from his usual seat at the counter. "What?" she demanded.

"Breathing is an involuntary function." Garrett Dawes shrugged, one big shoulder lifting and lowering as his dark gaze flicked from her to the bowl of oatmeal in front of him. "You don't need to remind yourself."

"So helpful, Garrett," she said through clenched teeth and moved to deliver the order to a booth near the front of the restaurant.

She forced a smile as she scooted between crowded tables at MJ's Cafe, the popular diner in the Silver Lake neighborhood of Los Angeles, where she'd worked for the past year. Quite possibly the only bright spot in the worst twelve months of her life.

And her breath caught in her throat. Involuntary, indeed. What did that gruff, unfriendly, unfeeling robot of a man know, anyway?

Her inability to pull off even automatic bodily functions

was just one more thing to add to his unspoken but still obvious list of judgments against her.

At least her animosity toward the diner's most consistent customer gave her a few seconds of relief from the anxiety pounding through her due to the most recent implosion of her life.

The relief lasted a few seconds, until the child at the table she was passing suddenly pushed back his chair, directly into her path. Her foot caught on one leg and she stumbled, the two plates sliding out of her hands and crashing to the tile floor. Eggs, bacon and toast splattered while the porcelain splintered, right along with Lily's self-control.

As the diner went immediately silent, her eyes filled with tears, big sloppy ones that couldn't be blinked away. They rolled down her cheeks, and she swiped at them as she drew a shuddery breath, then bent to pick up the mess.

"Was that ours?" one of the businessmen at the booth where she was headed asked. "I'm so hungry."

"We'll get another order right up and it's on the house." Lily heard Mary Jo Marsh, the diner's owner, answer the customer, her tone both conciliatory and commanding. "Come on, sweetie," she said to Lily, a gentle hand on her back. "You go take a break in my office. We'll deal with things out here."

Lily should have argued. This was her mess, after all. But she could feel the weight of a dozen eyes upon her, a restaurant full of strangers and people she considered friends bearing witness to her breakdown.

With a sniff, she nodded and straightened. "I'm so sorry," she said to the man who'd spoken. She must have looked even more pathetic than she realized because he appeared embarrassed that he'd voiced a complaint.

"It's fine," he muttered.

She ruffled the hair of the boy who'd caused her to trip. His head was down as his mother chided him in hushed tones for not being able to sit still. "That was on me, buddy," she told him. "You didn't do anything wrong."

He stole a glance in her direction and then nodded and picked up his fork.

Lily managed a smile for the kid's mother, then hurried through the tables and past the counter, doing her best not to make eye contact with anyone. From her peripheral vision, she saw Garrett Dawes watching her.

Insult to injury. That seemed to be her current lot in life.

Lily pulled her cell phone out of the front pocket of her apron as she entered Mary Jo's cramped office. File cabinets and boxes of paper napkins and plastic straws—no saving the turtles in this rundown corner of LA—lined the walls.

In the span of an hour, since she'd taken that first call from her sister Helena, Lily had received six texts. Four from her oldest sister and two additional from Meg, the middle Wainright sister.

She didn't know how to respond to their increasingly insistent messages. She wanted to delete the messages, pretend that she wasn't about to come face-to-face with all of the ways she'd failed in her life, especially compared to her successful, upwardly mobile siblings.

But there was no choice. No use making excuses or wishing things could be different. With jerky movements, she typed in a response to the two of them.

I'll be in Magnolia by the weekend.

Anxiety rolled through her gut as she hit Send, and she flipped the phone onto the desk and sank down in the worn leather office chair. She pressed the heels of her palms into her eyes, hoping that would make the pounding in her head subside.

As if anything could make this moment better.

Lily Wainright was going home.

CHAPTER TWO

"What's going on, hon?"

Mary Jo walked into the office a few minutes later and shut the door. Luckily, Mary Jo Marsh was as tiny as she was strong-willed, so there was room for both of them in the cluttered space.

"I'm leaving," Lily said quietly, even as a scream tried to rise up inside her. She swallowed then swallowed again, determined to hold herself together. Of all the challenges she'd faced since moving to California, why did returning to her hometown near the North Carolina coast feel like the most insurmountable?

"Okay," Mary Jo answered with a frown. She grabbed a Diet Dr Pepper from the tiny fridge in the corner and offered a can to Lily, who declined. "Take the rest of the day and even tomorrow if you need it. Life has pelted you with a lot of lemons, and you've been downing so much lemonade it's a wonder your eyeballs aren't floating. I'll find someone to cover your shifts so—"

"For good," Lily clarified. "I'm going back to my hometown."

Mary Jo paused with the can of soda halfway to her mouth. "Is that so?" she asked, her tone carefully measured.

Lily tried and failed to offer a smile, tucking a loose curl behind her ear. "My sister called this morning. Dad fell and broke his hip. He's scheduled for surgery and needs someone there to help with his recovery."

The older woman shook her head. "Don't they have healthcare workers in Magpie?"

"Magnolia," Lily corrected her. "My father still lives in the house where he grew up. He and my mom bought it from my grandparents when they got married. He's run the family's hardware business for almost forty years now. He's proud and stubborn and I can't imagine him letting someone outside of the family help him."

"Your sisters—"

"Have lives of their own." Lily rolled her shoulders against the shame that coursed through her when she thought of how little she'd accomplished in her own life. "They have jobs and husbands and kids and neither of them live in Magnolia anymore. I'm the logical choice to help him."

Mary Jo scoffed. "Because you live on the opposite side of the country and haven't once gone back since you drove away from that town? I don't see the logic there, sweetie."

"I'm a waitress with no family and really no friends other than my coworkers." Lily gave a humorless laugh. "I have a string of loser ex-boyfriends, a crappy furnished apartment and tons of debt thanks to the last loser ex. I've given up the dream of becoming an actress." She sighed. "I've given up dreaming. There's nothing keeping me here."

"You sure don't paint a rosy picture," Mary Jo admitted. "But I believe in you, Lil. I believe you'll get back on your feet. You've been knocked around a bit—"

"Literally, thanks to the one prior to the last loser," Lily added, anger and embarrassment rushing through her in equal measure.

"You've got a big heart and so much potential."

"I love you for saying that." Lily choked back another round of tears. "I owe you so much, MJ. But he's my dad. I have to go home."

"You can always come back," her boss said gently.

Lily nodded. "Maybe. I've told my sisters I'll be there by the weekend. I don't even know how I'm going to make that happen with no money and no car."

"I knew Kenny was bad news when I met him. He had shifty eyes."

Lily wished she'd listened to her boss's advice about her last boyfriend. She'd met Kenny at a TV pilot audition, a final effort to make something happen in the acting career Lily's mother had wanted so badly for her. Seven years in California and Lily had been in exactly two commercials, one miserable play that closed after opening weekend and a blink-and-you-miss-it role as a serial killer victim in a network crime show.

She felt bad about her failure but never quite mustered up the sadness over not becoming a star that her mother might have expected.

"I can buy you a plane ticket," Mary Jo offered without hesitation.

Truly, the best thing about Lily's time in LA was working at MJ's.

"I can't take Chloe on a plane," Lily said, biting her lip.

"You could leave her—"

"No. She's coming with me. I'm all she has. I might try social media or an online classified site. Maybe I could find someone who wants a copilot for a cross-country trek."

"Absolutely not." Mary Jo plunked down the soda can on the desk and wagged a sparkly polished finger in Lily's direction. "Ted Bundy wasn't an urban myth back in my day."

"I'd be careful," Lily promised. "My other option is trying to rent some cheap car and drive alone."

Mary Jo closed her eyes for a long moment and when she opened them again, they gleamed with a light that made Lily more than a little nervous. "I've got an idea. Stay here."

"Mary Jo." Lily stood and wrapped the older woman in a tight hug. "You don't have to solve this for me. I'm your employee, and you've been generous and kind and all those things."

"You deserve that in your life, sweetheart." MJ pulled back and patted a soft hand against Lily's cheek. "We both know the dream you've been chasing out here belonged to your mother. I'm sad to see you go and would love for you to come back, but mostly I want you to be happy. When was the last time you felt happy, Lil?"

Lily shook her head. "I can't cry again. Tears get me nowhere."

"Stay here," Mary Jo repeated and left the office, closing the door behind her.

Lily's mind raced as she considered the logistics of packing up her life to get from one coast to the other in less than a week. With no money and her ex-boyfriend's Great Dane riding shotgun.

The dog had been the final straw that ended their relationship. Kenny had purchased the year-old purebred on a whim from an expensive breeder that he couldn't afford.

Little did Lily know that the jerk didn't need to be able to afford the dog. He'd taken out several credit cards in Lily's name, so almost all of the debt he'd incurred during their six months together legally belonged to her. She hadn't even admitted how much she owed to Mary Jo.

Then Kenny had gotten in a car accident, totaling Lily's old Nissan. Chloe, who'd been riding in the back seat, had broken her leg. He'd been ready to dump the dog at the humane society but instead Lily had dumped him.

Her standards for men might be embarrassingly low, but she drew the line at animal cruelty.

"I'll figure it out," she told herself, then glanced around the empty office. Another reason she liked having Chloe was that the dog made Lily feel better about her tendency to have out-loud conversations with herself.

Maybe the Great Dane couldn't answer with words, but she was still a sympathetic listener.

Guilt plucked at her nerves as the distant sounds of the kitchen drifted through the thin walls. She should go out there and at least finish her shift. She'd miss not only Mary Jo, but Darcy and Kristin, the two other waitresses, as well as the trio of older men who worked in the kitchen.

She might not have the life her mom had dreamed of for her, but Lily had survived. At some point in the past year, though, that no longer felt like enough.

The office door opened as she took a step forward, then froze when Garrett entered.

"The bathroom is on the other side of the hall," she told him, smoothing a suddenly trembling hand over the front of her apron.

Garrett Dawes was—or had been—some kind of hotshot movie producer or writer or another type of Hollywood executive. Not wanting to compare his success to her failure, she'd done her best to ignore him.

It wasn't hard. Garrett might be the diner's best customer, but he rarely spoke to anyone. He showed up at the counter five days a week for either breakfast or lunch, ate in silence while reading a book and then left. Kristin, who took care of the counter, loved the man because he was no trouble and an excellent tipper, but he'd always made Lily feel self-conscious.

He was tall with a lean frame, angled features and thick chestnut-hued hair the same color as his eyes. She didn't know what he did when he wasn't at the diner, but his skin was bronzed like he spent time outdoors. He had the kind of long lashes that tons of women in Hollywood would pay good money for.

"My aunt sent me in here to talk to you," he said, massaging a hand across the back of his neck. Sinewy muscles bunched in his forearm and—drat—Lily did not want to notice Garrett's muscles.

Or the fact that this close he smelled like laundry detergent and cloves.

Focus, she commanded herself.

"Who is your aunt and why does she want you to talk to me?"

He inclined his head as he stared at her. "Mary Jo," he answered slowly like he was talking to a toddler.

Lily felt her mouth drop open. A year working at the diner and countless lunch hours of seeing Garrett order a turkey club—always a turkey club—and she'd never realized he and her beloved boss were related.

"Um…" Garrett took a deep breath as he suddenly focused on a spot somewhere over her shoulder. "According to Aunt MJ, I'm driving you to North Carolina in the morning."

CHAPTER THREE

GARRETT WASN'T SURE what reaction he'd expected from Lily Wainright, but a cackle of hysterical laughter wasn't it.

Maybe it should have been. Ever since she'd started waitressing at his aunt's popular down-home diner, the chipper waitress had been an enigma to him.

Garrett was a loner by nature, at least since he'd gotten sober almost five years ago. The booze and the drugs had made him the life of the party, living the dream in Hollywood with a blockbuster movie made from the script he'd written based on his debut novel. The success of that thriller had taken him from the total obscurity of a high school teacher in Oklahoma to the next big thing in the City of Angels.

Too bad there had been hell to pay for his moment of stardom—in the form of his relationship with his family, a broken heart and almost two years of his life down the rabbit hole of parties and fake friendships in a place where, to him, nothing felt real or true or decent.

His aunt was real, a salt-of-the-earth Sooner who never compromised her morals or values to get ahead by California standards. Plenty of Hollywood bigwigs and A-listers frequented her diner, but there was no preferential treatment. Garrett wondered if that was part of her long-term appeal. Aunt MJ was the most decent person he knew, and she employed damn good people, which is what kept him tethered to her.

Plus he knew if he didn't show his face at her cafe at least a few times a week, she'd come looking for him, as she had when he'd hit rock bottom.

Then there was Lily Wainright, not the first disenchanted wannabe starlet his aunt had hired, but the only one who Garrett felt pulled toward. Because of his past, he made a point of not acting on his attraction. Lily made him feel out of control, and Garrett valued control above all else.

With her heart-shaped face, pale skin, rosebud lips and those huge iridescent green eyes, she looked like some kind of animated princess come to life. Her tendency to hold conversations with herself and burst into song at any vague reference to lyrics she recognized only completed the picture.

She'd suffered plenty of disappointments and setbacks, even in the short time he'd known her. But every time he saw her, she had a smile on her face and a kind word for the diner's customers, new and long-standing. Not for him, of course. As if she could sense the emptiness inside him, Lily steered clear of Garrett. It was for the best.

"Why would you want to drive cross-country with me?" she asked.

"I don't," he answered honestly. "I owe my aunt a favor. A big one." He released a small laugh. "Huge. It's been long enough that I wasn't sure she'd ever collect on the debt. Now I understand she was waiting for it to really count."

"A charity case your conscience won't let you refuse," Lily murmured with so much resignation it made Garrett's heart clench.

He rubbed at his chest, bewildered that she could so easily breach the walls he'd built.

A few sentences spoken between them, and Garrett understood his instincts about Lily had been spot-on. If upbeat princess Lily was dangerous, this sad, defeated version made her truly deadly.

"You're doing me a favor," he lied. "I've been having lunch here on the regular for years, holding out hope that one day I'd be given the opportunity to settle my debt. You're my chance."

Her eyes narrowed as she thought about this. Would he convince her? It wasn't exactly a lie. Garrett owed his aunt so much, he could drive a dozen down-on-their-luck waitresses halfway around the world and wouldn't scratch the surface of repaying how Mary Jo had rescued him once upon a time.

Lily didn't need to know that.

"I've never been someone's chance at redemption."

"Let's not go full rom-com here," he said, crossing his arms over his chest. "I have an SUV so your giant horse of a dog will fit. I'm a good driver and not some potential creep you found on the internet." He leaned in slightly. "That was a horrible idea, by the way. Aunt MJ was practically apoplectic when she came barreling out of here."

"I didn't mean to upset her." Lily bit down on her bottom lip, and desire hit him like a freight train.

How fast could he make this trip?

"Just say yes," he prompted. He'd been trying to write more lately—anything so he could feel like he was making progress toward a comeback. But he continued to struggle and an excuse to take off a few days wouldn't be the worst thing. "My aunt takes care of the people who work for her, whether they deserve it or not. She has a real soft spot for you. She's not going to rest until she knows you have safe passage home. With your dog in tow, I'm the best bet."

She laughed again, then covered her mouth.

"What part of that was funny?"

"I didn't know you could string together so many words at once." Her smile faded. "Wait. By your standards, am I someone who deserves Mary Jo's kindness or not?"

She tried to look sassy as she asked the question, as if she were daring him to take issue with her. But he could see the vulnerability in her eyes she tried to hide, and it just about slayed him. "You do."

"Oh." She let out a breath, then gave him a shy smile. "I guess I should say thank you in advance. We're going on a road trip."

"Yes, we are," Garrett agreed, wondering what he'd gotten himself into. He handed her his phone. "Put your address and phone number in there. I'll pick you up tomorrow morning at eight."

He watched as her slender fingers went to work punching in her contact information. "I'll help pay for gas and hotels," she told him.

He shook his head. "That's part of the deal. I've got it covered."

"Snacks, then," she amended. "Do you like red or black licorice?"

He shook his head. "Neither."

"Gummy worms? Chocolate?" She handed the phone back to him, her smile widening. "You don't strike me as a Skittles type of guy, but maybe—"

He took the phone from her, careful not to let their fingers brush, and shoved it into his back pocket. "Lily, stop. We're not Thelma and Louise here. This isn't a great adventure where we do sing-alongs and play the license plate game. I owe my aunt a favor, and you're the way I'm repaying it."

"It's a big favor."

"You have no idea." He took a step toward the door. "But we're not going to be friends. I don't want to be your friend. We have four days together in a car. Then it's over. Got it?"

"I've got it," she answered, shoulders slumping just a bit. "No fun. No friends. You're my ride home."

"Yeah." No, his mind screamed. He wanted more, a glimmer of something he'd given up years ago. But he wouldn't tell her that. He'd set the boundaries, and they both needed to adhere to them. "I'll see you tomorrow," he said, then turned and walked away.

CHAPTER FOUR

LILY WAITED ON the sidewalk in front of her crappy apartment building the following morning, trying to enjoy the beautiful September day. She was exhausted from lack of sleep and the realization that all she had to show for the past seven years was a dozen sad boxes of clothes and trinkets.

Chloe nudged her big head against Lily's leg, a reminder of the best thing she'd gained during her time in Los Angeles. The dog was almost two years old now, a shedding, drooling, gentle giant of an animal.

They were an unlikely pair. Lily stood only a few inches over five feet and had never been especially strong. Often it felt like Chloe was walking her rather than the other way around. The dog suffered from separation anxiety and had a penchant for chewing leather shoes. The one decent pair of boots Lily owned had been an early casualty, and she'd learned to put anything of value out of reach. But she loved the furry beast with her whole heart.

A shiny late-model Toyota 4Runner turned the corner, out of place against the shabby buildings and older cars that lined the street. Lily breathed a sigh of relief.

He might be nothing like most men she knew, but Garrett Dawes was her knight in a shining SUV at the moment. She still couldn't believe he'd agreed to drive her all the way to North Carolina. She'd tried to ask Mary Jo about him, curious as to their relationship and what kind of favor he owed that would take him so far out of his obvious comfort zone.

But the older woman had simply patted her cheek and given a vague response about Garrett being one of the good ones.

Lily had been shocked at how simple it was to say goodbye to her friends at the diner and pack her meager belongings. She'd never examined why she'd been unable to really put down roots in California. Maybe part of her had known this life was never meant to be.

She hated that her mother would have been disappointed at Lily giving up the dream of stardom. Even more, shame filled her knowing she'd half-heartedly pursued a future because she'd never actually wanted it in the first place.

Her father had called from the hospital last night, and she'd assured him that coming home was her choice. He'd sounded tired but grateful. Even if she didn't stay in Magnolia once he recovered, Lily had no doubt she was doing the right thing now.

Garrett parked at the curb and climbed out of the vehicle. He wore a heather gray T-shirt, faded jeans and mirrored aviator sunglasses that prevented her from seeing his dark eyes.

Probably for the best as she could imagine the condemnation in them as he took in the boxes that made up the sum total of her life.

She had enough judgment for them both.

"Good morning," she said, offering a cheerful smile. "It's great weather for a drive."

He humphed an inarticulate response, and Chloe barked in greeting.

"The dog is enormous," he muttered. "Even for an SUV."

"But she loves riding in cars," Lily told him, keeping

her tone light. "The motion puts her right to sleep so she won't be any trouble." She smoothed a hand along Chloe's strong back. The dog was fawn-colored with a black mask over her snout, around her eyes and on the tips of her ears.

"Does she shed?"

"Not too much." Lily ignored the cloud of dog fur that rose into the air like dandelion fluff as she patted Chloe's rump. "I mean, not normally. She's nervous now. I was up most of the night packing and she didn't understand what was going on."

Garrett took a step forward and held out a hand for the dog to sniff. "I'm surprised you didn't explain it to her."

"As a matter of fact, I did." Lily nodded. "She'll understand more once we're all together in the car."

"You know she's a dog," he said, and Lily felt color bloom in her cheeks.

He'd been making a joke at her expense. Plenty of people did given her typical sunny personality and the fact that she talked to herself. In this world of constant snark and going viral from being a hater, Lily sometimes felt like society saw her optimism as a threat.

Garrett rarely spoke to her—or anyone, for that matter—but she could imagine what he thought.

"Chloe is still my best friend," Lily told him, refusing to be embarrassed. She'd managed to hold on to her positive outlook on life through way worse struggles than a few days in the car with Garrett Dawes. "Let's get going."

"Is this all you have?" he asked as he opened the cargo area, then bent to retrieve one of the boxes.

"Yep." She gave him an even wider grin, ignoring the way her cheeks ached. "I'm only bringing home my most important possessions."

He lifted a SpongeBob bobblehead doll out of the top of one lidless box. "I can see that."

"My dad gave that to me when I was in third grade. I got mono right before Christmas and missed a week of school. He watched a ton of cartoons with me so I wouldn't be alone all the time. SpongeBob was our favorite."

"Aunt MJ told me you're going home to take care of him."

"He fell off a ladder at the hardware store my family owns. He broke his hip, so he'll be having replacement surgery."

"I hope it goes well," Garrett said quietly.

"Thank you." Lily sniffed and swallowed back the emotion that rose up in her throat. It was difficult to imagine her ox-strong father incapacitated in any way.

They finished loading the car in silence other than an occasional whine from Chloe. The dog's long tail wagged when Garrett opened the door to the back seat and motioned her forward. She glanced at Lily for confirmation then jumped in, trying to fold her oversized frame into the SUV.

"Good girl," Lily said. In the seconds it took her to climb into the passenger side, Chloe had already shoved her block head between the seats, clearly interested in starting the journey on Lily's lap.

"She doesn't realize her size." Lily grunted as she shoved the dog back.

Garrett's knuckles went white as he clenched the steering wheel while she continued to struggle with Chloe. Eventually the dog settled into the back seat with an overdramatic sigh.

"This is going to be a long few days," Garrett muttered as he pulled onto the street.

"We'll make it fu—"

Lily clamped shut her mouth at the look he gave her.

"No fun," she amended. "We'll make it quiet and easy. You'll barely know we're here."

"Promise?" he said, sarcasm dripping from his voice.

She nodded and did her best to look convincing. She might not have had much success in her career aspirations, but Lily didn't think she was the worst actress in the world.

"I promise," she answered at the same time Chloe let out an ear-splitting howl.

CHAPTER FIVE

Five hours into the trip, Garrett plucked a piece of licorice from the bag Lily had placed in the cup holder between the two seats.

He'd forgotten how much he liked red licorice.

He bit off half of the string, then handed the other piece back to Chloe, who swallowed it down without appearing to chew, then placed her head onto his shoulder over the seat.

The dog's round eyes shifted to Lily, who'd been asleep for most of the morning. He patted the dog's head when she started to whine.

"You'll wake her," he admonished. "Clearly she needs to catch up on sleep."

Once they'd gotten out of the congestion on the interstate around Los Angeles, he'd started enjoying the drive on the open road. It had been a long time since he'd traveled outside the normal routine of his daily life. His aunt's restaurant, the gym, the grocery and…hell…he needed to get out more.

Lily snored softly and shifted lower in her seat. The seat belt cut across her neck in a way that looked like it might leave a mark on her creamy skin.

He reached out a hand and adjusted it, his fingers brushing against her collarbone. Even accidental, the touch burned through him like a brush fire, and he yanked back his hand.

How could anyone have such soft skin?

Her hair had been pulled back in a low ponytail this morning but now many of the thick, dark strands had escaped, falling over her shoulders in loose waves. She wore a yellow sundress with a pattern of wildflowers splashed across it.

He'd gotten so used to seeing her in the blue button-down, denim skirt and green apron that was the uniform at the diner. The dress made her look more ethereal, like some kind of elfin forest sprite come to life.

"Forest sprite," he muttered. "I'm losing it."

The dog's tongue laved his ear, and Garrett suppressed a shudder.

"You've made friends."

Lily's sleep-roughened voice filled the SUV's interior. Garrett could just imagine what it would be like to wake up next to her and have that voice whisper in his ear.

The dog lumbered to its feet and immediately tried to climb over the console to get to Lily.

"I was a poor substitute for you," he said, keeping his eyes on the highway in front of them.

"Sorry I haven't been better company," she said as she turned to give Chloe a kiss, then pushed the dog into the back seat again. "I might be getting too old to pull an all-nighter."

He laughed at that. "What are you? All of twenty-three?"

"Twenty-five," she corrected him. "What about you?"

"Thirty."

"How long have you lived in California?"

He gave her his best side-eye. "What makes you think I'm not a native?"

She redid her ponytail as she laughed. "You have 'boy from the heartland' written all over you."

"I do not." He made a show of examining his arms.

"Nebraska? Kansas?"

"Oklahoma."

She pumped her fist. "I knew it. I also knew you'd like the licorice." She leaned closer and the scent of vanilla washed over him. "Are you sure I can't convince you to play the license plate game?"

"Not a chance."

Her pert nose wrinkled. "So how long in LA and what brought you to the West Coast?"

"My first book got made into a movie."

"Wow. Anything I would have heard of?"

"A thriller called *Point of No Return*."

"Shut the front door!"

Chloe let out a series of sharp barks that made Garrett wince, clearly riled up by her owner's outburst. Lily took a moment to quiet the animal, then turned to him. "Brad starred in that movie. It was huge. That's so cool."

"I thought so, too, but things didn't quite turn out the way I'd planned."

"Did you meet Brad Pitt?"

He nodded. "Decent guy."

"Did you get to know any other famous people?"

"Tons of them," he said, thinking back to that first heady year when he'd come to Hollywood, certain it was the start of an illustrious career.

"Are you famous?" she asked, inclining her head.

"For a hot second in certain circles." He didn't like to talk about that time. It brought back too many dark memories of the mistakes he'd made and the way his ego and pride had led him to a place where his life circled the drain. "I was what you might call a one-hit wonder or a flash in the pan. I went from being the next big thing in the world of Hollywood writers to nothing. Now I'm less than nothing."

"Don't say that." She reached out and placed her hand on his arm. The gentle touch reverberated through him. "The industry doesn't define you."

"It does in LA."

"But you wrote the book before you moved to California?"

She pulled her hand away and it took every ounce of willpower he possessed not to ask her to keep it there.

"I was a high school English teacher. It feels like that life was a million years ago."

"I know what you mean."

"How long have you been chasing the dream?" he asked.

She sighed. "Seven years. Not much chasing recently. Turns out the chase isn't all that fun when it's someone else's dream."

He raised one brow when she didn't elaborate.

"My mom wanted to be an actress when she was younger," she explained. "But she got pregnant with my oldest sister and married my dad. They stayed in Magnolia, but she always talked about what could have been if she hadn't been trapped in a small town."

"Ouch," he murmured.

"She didn't exactly make my sister or my dad feel special. But she saw something in me." Lily gave a soft laugh. "I guess it was because I looked like her. Both of my sisters took after my dad. They're really smart. I was...you know...ordinary other than being pretty."

"I don't think that's true."

"You don't know me," she countered immediately.

Garrett shrugged. "I've watched you interact with customers over the past year. You're always kind and remember details. You don't mess up orders, and you give Mrs. Garinski water with no ice every time."

"She has sensitive teeth."

"My point is you're a good person. That's not ordinary, at least in LA."

She studied him for several moments. "Since when did you become a nice guy?"

"What made you think I wasn't?"

"You're always scowling or frowning or giving me stink eye."

"I don't give stink eye."

"Total stink eye."

"Kristin likes me," he offered, not quite sure why he felt the need to prove some strange point.

"She thinks you're a good tipper."

Chloe put her snout through the two seats and shoved her wet nose into Garrett's armpit. "Gross, dog." He pushed his elbow into the animal's face—gently but enough to get his point across.

"I believe in tipping," he said, "but she and I are friends. We go to the Brentwood farmer's market once a month."

"Seriously?" Lily looked genuinely confused. "I didn't think you spoke to anyone in the diner, let alone made friends. Maybe it's just me?"

Garrett opened his mouth to answer, then snapped it shut again. Of course it had been her. No one else affected him the way Lily did.

"Oh, my gosh." Lily let out a delicate snort. "It *is* just me. You don't like me."

"I never said that."

"Everyone likes me." She shook her head. "Even the casting directors who reject me tell me how nice I am."

"A comfort, I imagine."

"Are you making fun of me?"

"No."

She didn't look convinced. "I'm going back to sleep. Wake me when we stop for gas."

He watched as she reclined the seat, then turned so she was facing the window, seat belt still fastened.

He liked this Lily Wainright—the spunk and sass—just as much as he did the chipper, amiable waitress he knew from the diner. He had a feeling he'd like every aspect of Lily he discovered.

Which was why he had to get across country and drop her off without delay.

CHAPTER SIX

"HAWAII."

Lily looked up from the book she'd been reading. They were almost through the ten-hour drive of day two on the road that would keep them on schedule to arrive in Magnolia late Friday night.

She felt sore and sticky despite the cool air blowing from the vents on the dash. The Oklahoma sky was in the midst of turning from pink to gray, but thanks to the late summer days, it still wouldn't be full dark when they reached their destination.

She threw a questioning glance at Garrett, who managed to look unrumpled and strangely attractive with the shadow of stubble across his jaw and his hair curling around his ears.

He pointed to the sedan in front of them. "A Hawaii license plate."

"Seriously?" She straightened in her seat. "That's amazing. I would have totally missed it." She checked her list. "Now we only need Maine, Alaska, Vermont and South Dakota."

"You need them," he clarified. "I'm not playing."

She laughed softly. "Whatever you say as long as you keep looking."

He rolled his eyes and adjusted the radio to a country station with decent reception.

Lily hummed along with the old Luke Bryan song while she glanced behind her. Chloe's big body was stretched across the back seat, tongue lolling out of her mouth as she slept. The dog didn't seem to mind the hours of driving, sleeping through most of them and perching her chin on Garrett's shoulder to look out the front window when she was awake.

To be honest, Lily didn't mind the long hours either. Something inside her had loosened as they got farther away from Los Angeles, and she realized how unhappy she'd been.

Why had she gone through the motions for so many years with no regard for what she'd truly wanted?

Because it would have made her mom happy? Tears had clogged her throat when she'd explained to Garrett that her mother's dying wish—as the pancreatic cancer had decimated her body—was for Lily to pursue the dream of stardom. To succeed where her mother had failed.

That had been Lily's senior year of high school and, despite her father's protests, she'd done it. She'd moved to Hollywood and tried to find work as an actress, hoping that her mom would be watching over her and guiding her on a path to success.

A path that Lily now wished she would have gotten off of sooner.

"I think a hotel for tonight is a better idea," Garrett said as Luke's crooning voice faded and a song Lily didn't recognize came on. She hadn't listened to country music since she'd left Magnolia and had forgotten how much she liked it. Another tiny piece of herself she'd stripped away trying to become a person she was never meant to be.

"No way." Lily shook her head. "I heard your mom when

you talked to her earlier. She's so excited to see you, even if it's just for one night."

"I can stop on my way back."

"Garrett." She waited until he glanced her way and then squeezed his arm. It was odd that she kept finding excuses to touch him in the confined space of the SUV. Or when they stopped for gas or food. Potty breaks for Chloe. No wonder she'd kept her distance at the restaurant. Some part of her obviously knew that she wouldn't be able to ignore her attraction to him.

Just as she understood that he wasn't the type of guy who'd be interested in her. Garrett was an English teacher who'd written a rabidly popular debut novel that had been turned into a blockbuster movie. He might not have had much follow-up success, but he was intelligent. Book smart like her sisters. Not like Lily, who'd struggled with school most of her childhood.

She'd learned to make the best of her strengths, and having super-smart friends or boyfriends wasn't part of that.

Unlike her older sisters, Garrett didn't make her feel stupid. As the miles rolled by, he'd become less guarded, and they'd talked about everything from their families to favorite books, movies and flavors of ice cream.

She'd been the one to suggest he call his mom after realizing their journey would include a night near his home.

"Trust me," she said gently, "I get how hard it is to return to where you came from. At least you'll be just passing through. You can visit your mom and then drive away tomorrow morning. I won't have that luxury." She laughed, trying to sound flippant even though it came out more like a squawk. "Not that anyone other than my mom believed I'd make it big. My return proves them right."

He drummed his fingers against the steering wheel in time with the beat. "Do you care what they think?"

Lily sucked in a breath, his question hitting her like a punch to the gut. She turned and pressed her palm to the window, watching the plains zoom by between her outstretched fingers. When she finally had control of her emotions, she shook her head. "I feel so much relief at leaving California it makes me regret not going back sooner. But my mom would have been disappointed, and I hate that."

"You can't know how she would have felt after all these years. Maybe if she'd lived, she would have missed you. Maybe she would have realized that your happiness was more important than her unrealized dream."

How could she have ever thought this man was a cold-hearted jerk? In a few simple sentences, he managed to give her the comfort she'd never been able to find on her own.

"I want to believe that," she told him.

"Then do." He rolled his shoulders. "On the other hand, I had the dream in my hot hands and messed it all up. Hollywood welcomed me with open arms, and I wasted my chance."

Last night, as they'd had dinner in an authentic Mexican restaurant outside of Albuquerque, Garrett had shared the downward trajectory of his career once his book had become a bestseller. He'd gotten involved with drugs and alcohol, partying hard with his so-called friends. His girlfriend had left him for one of the stuntmen on his movie, and after his second book tanked, he'd spiraled out of control.

"Do you believe in second chances?" she asked. "You know Hollywood loves a good redemption story."

"I'm not sure there's anything worth redeeming."

"Don't say that. Your aunt believes in you, and from what you've told me, your mom does, too."

"She didn't care about the money or the fame. I could have been a high school teacher by day and obscure novelist at night for my entire life. If it made me happy, she'd be happy for me."

"Were you happy then?"

One side of his mouth turned up in a sad smile. "Yeah," he whispered.

"Have you thought about moving back to Oklahoma permanently?"

He shook his head. "I don't think I belong there anymore, and I definitely don't belong in Hollywood." He glanced at her and the emotion in his gaze made her heart beat faster. "Have you noticed how much easier it is to breathe away from LA?"

Lily nodded, shocked that he felt the same way she did. "At first I thought it was the lack of pollution but..."

"It's more than that."

"You'll find your home," she told him, hoping the words were true for herself as well as Garrett. "We both will."

CHAPTER SEVEN

"How DID YOU put all this together in eight hours?"

Garrett looked around the fenced-in backyard of his childhood home, hoping he remembered the names of all the people his mother had invited for this homecoming s'mores party, as she called it.

"The neighbors understand how happy I am to have you here," Alice Dawes explained with a watery smile. "Even if it's just for one night."

"I promise I'll stay longer on the return trip." Garrett wrapped an arm around his mother's shoulders. As a single mom, Alice had done her best and always made Garrett feel loved and wanted, even if his deadbeat father hadn't given a damn about either of them. When he'd left for Hollywood, he promised her that he was going to make it big for both of them. She deserved to be taken care of after working so hard to support him.

He'd sent her and his aunt on a Caribbean cruise, Alice's bucket list vacation. But the black hole of partying and excessive spending drained the money he made from the book and movie before he could truly set her up for life. He still received royalties, but when his second book failed, so did his dreams for a long literary and showbiz career.

"You have a beautiful home, Mrs. Dawes." Lily's sweet smile eased the ache in Garrett's chest. Did she realize her effect on him? Could she tell he was on the verge of losing his composure? He mentally kicked himself in the teeth for the list of mistakes he'd made that had destroyed the life he thought he wanted.

"Call me Alice," his mother said, reaching out to pat Lily's cheek. "I'm so glad you needed a ride and my son was available to give you one."

"Me, too." The blush that stained Lily's cheeks pink made awareness dance across his skin.

"I'm going to get another bag of marshmallows for s'mores." His mom gestured to the kids surrounding the fire pit on the back patio.

Garrett rocked back on his heels as she walked away and tried to be subtle about checking out everyone who'd come to welcome him home.

"This is not what you had in mind," Lily said, taking a step closer to him.

He sighed. "It's making me rethink my commitment to sobriety."

"Garrett, no. You can't—"

"Sorry," he said, placing a gentle hand on her shoulder. "That was a bad joke. I'm using inappropriate humor to defuse my anxiety."

She tipped her chin, her knowing gaze assessing him. Her eyes were the color of the deep moss that grew on the trees in the forest behind the house. She'd taken a shower when they got to his mom's, and her hair was still damp on the ends. He wanted to run his fingers through it.

"I'm four years sober, Lily. Trust me. If I could stay clean in LA, I'll be fine at a backyard picnic."

"Your mom is so proud of you," she murmured, her smile wistful.

He nodded. "Despite all the ways I've screwed up. I don't deserve that kind of love from her or from my aunt."

"Of course you do." Lily's eyes flashed. "Everyone deserves love."

His mouth went dry. He'd never experienced anything quite like the way Lily Wainright made him feel.

"Can I show you something?" he asked.

"Sure."

Without overthinking it, he took her hand, lacing their fingers together, shocked but elated when she didn't pull away.

He whistled sharply and Chloe, who'd been sniffing around the buffet table most of the night, trotted over.

"Will it upset your mom if you leave the party?" Lily asked as he led her through the gate that led to the woods.

"Her friends saw me. They know I'm alive and not a drug-addicted bum in southern California. Mom will be thrilled."

"That's a problem with small towns," she said with a sigh. "People latch onto something and don't like to let go. I'm sorry if the attention bothers you."

He squeezed her fingers. "I didn't expect all of this, but I'm glad for it. With one fell swoop, we got all of the business of people seeing me again out of the way. It made my mother happy, and that makes me happy."

Chloe yowled and galloped after a squirrel running into the forest.

"That dog makes me happy," Lily said with a laugh.

The animal barked and lifted her paws onto the trunk of the tree where the squirrel had retreated. The small woodland creature squawked from a branch, making Chloe bark even more frantically. "Not exactly the world's greatest hunter," Garrett observed.

Lily laughed harder and the sound flowed over him like warm honey.

"Here we are," he murmured as they moved into the canopy of elm trees. The temperature had dropped a few degrees, making it a perfect late summer evening.

"It's a fort." Lily let go of his hand and moved toward the structure that had meant so much to him through most of his childhood.

"I wasn't sure it would still be here. Max Campbell and I built it the summer between fourth and fifth grade. We hooked up wagons to the backs of our bikes so we could transport the lumber."

"Did you have a club name or secret handshake?"

He shook his head as he opened the door and peered in at the dusty interior. As a kid, the woods and this clubhouse had been his sanctuary. It was empty of the books and trinkets that had filled it back then, but he remembered every detail of the hours he'd spent there. Revisiting it now was an unexpected gift, especially with Lily at his side. "No, but I have an idea for a new series built around a clubhouse in the woods. Think *Stranger Things* meets *WarGames*."

"I like that mash-up."

"I'd like it if I could meet a deadline, even if it's self-imposed at this point."

"You can do it."

"How is that those four words sound so convincing coming from you?"

She looked up at him through her long lashes. "Because I believe in you."

Emotion rippled through him, a seismic shift that seemed to make the walls he'd built around his heart crumble. He cupped her face and touched his lips to hers. She tasted like sugar and felt like heaven.

When he would have pulled back, trying to rein in his desire, she wound her arms around his neck and deepened the kiss. Their tongues met and melded, and he drew her closer until their bodies pressed together.

Suddenly he was knocked off balance as Chloe ran headlong into his legs. The dog barked and circled, rearing up on her back paws like they were playing some game that she wanted in on.

Lily lifted two fingers to her mouth, as if she couldn't believe what had just happened between them. Garrett's brain scrambled for purchase as he tried to stave off the rising tide of feelings rolling through him. He wasn't great with emotion and had no idea how to handle himself in this moment.

Two days from now, he'd drop Lily in her small North Carolina town and head back to his hollow, lonely life in California. Getting involved now would only complicate things. Part of his recovery and subsequent sobriety hinged on keeping his world simple and straightforward.

The woman standing before him was neither of those things.

"Sorry," he said automatically. "That was a mistake."

Her mouth formed a small O as hurt flickered in her eyes. She lowered a hand to scratch Chloe's ears, and Garrett tried not to notice the way her fingers trembled.

Then she gave him a flippant grin that was so different from one of her real smiles. "Don't let it happen again, buddy," she said with a tinkling laugh. Even that sounded phony, but he didn't call her on it.

Let them both pretend the kiss hadn't meant anything. It would make saying goodbye easier. At least that's what he told himself.

CHAPTER EIGHT

A STRANGE MIX of excitement and panic filled Lily's heart as they drove down the familiar streets of Magnolia two days later.

Her body ached after so many hours in the car and her heart hadn't been the same since the kiss she'd shared with Garrett in the woods.

It would be easy to blame her feelings for him on the situation. She was nervous about starting over in her hometown, and a quick embrace shouldn't be a big deal. They were two adults, after all. It didn't have to mean anything.

But she couldn't deny that it did.

Obviously he felt the change in her. The past two days in the car together had been awkward at best, with neither of them speaking about the kiss or anything beyond casual observations about the scenery or comments on Chloe's silly behavior.

The distance between them bothered Lily. Even though she'd only really known Garrett for a few days, their time together had been a revelation. A lesson in not judging a person before she got to know them. He was one of the good ones, and she couldn't ignore the way her heart hammered when he smiled at her or how she craved more time with him.

"That's my house," she said, pointing to a two-story colonial on the tree-lined street. "My dad's house, actually."

"The house where you grew up," Garrett said with a nod. "It will always feel like home."

She sighed and nodded. Little comments like that made her feel as though he understood her and really cared.

Half of the reason she was so unlucky in love stemmed from the fact that she led with her heart and always wanted to see the best in a person. She might want to believe a special connection had developed between them during the past four days, but that was silly. People didn't fall in love over the course of a cross-country road trip.

Pressing her knuckles against the sharp ache in her chest, Lily opened the car door when he pulled into the driveway.

She hooked Chloe to the leash then led the dog to the back of the SUV to begin unloading boxes.

"I'm happy to give you a ride to the hospital after we unpack your stuff," Garrett said, his quiet tone making goose bumps erupt across her skin.

"My sister left me the keys to my dad's truck. I'm sure you want to get back on the road anyway." She forced a smile. "You have a new book to start and all that."

"All that," he repeated, giving her a look she couldn't quite decipher. "Sure."

They each grabbed a box, and he followed her up the walk. Helena had texted that she'd left the front door unlocked. Magnolia was that kind of town.

Lily hadn't realized how much she missed home until she arrived. Yes, the town had seen better days, largely funded by famed artist Niall Reed, Magnolia's most famous resident. But even now, in need of a facelift, Magnolia looked beautiful to her. She realized she didn't care that she'd failed as an actress because it wasn't her dream.

She wanted a place to call home, to care for people and be a part of a community. Magnolia would give all of those things to her. Her father's house was the same as she remembered, cozy and cluttered. It still smelled of linseed oil from the woodworking her dad did in his spare time. She could hardly wait to visit the hardware store. As a child, she'd loved the neat rows of tools and supplies, the potential in the items her family sold.

If only things hadn't gone bad between her and Garrett, Lily would love to show him around the town and introduce him to her dad. She wanted a chance to get to know him better and see if the tender spot he'd so quickly occupied in her heart was more than just infatuation.

But as she met his gaze over the pine dining room table that her great-grandfather had built for her great-grandmother's first Thanksgiving as a wife, he looked away, and all her hopes that their ending might be a happy one faded into nothing.

Chloe whined and tugged at her leash.

"Great house," he said, taking in the framed photos on the wall. "I'll grab the rest of the boxes if you want to take care of her."

"Okay." Biting down on the inside of her cheek, Lily led the dog through the kitchen and out into the backyard with the town's namesake tree blooming in one corner. She unfastened the leash and Chloe trotted away to investigate her new surroundings.

The privacy fence that surrounded the property would keep the dog contained, but Lily didn't move for several minutes. She watched Chloe and tried to smile at the animal's usual antics. Tried not to acknowledge that she'd been foolish enough to open her heart to Garrett, and now she'd have to deal with that pain on top of everything else.

True to his word, he'd gotten the rest of her belongings unloaded by the time she returned to the front of the house.

"Thank you," she told him but couldn't quite force the muscles of her face into a smile.

"No problem."

Lily wrapped her arms around her chest. "You've paid your debt."

"Aunt MJ will be thrilled."

They stood with a heavy silence between them for a few long moments.

"I'm going to head out." Garrett scrubbed a hand over his jaw. "You probably want to get to the hospital anyway."

"I do," she confirmed. "Thank you," she repeated, unable to come up with anything better. "For everything."

"Good luck, Lily." He leaned in for a hug, but she shoved her hand out instead. He took it, and even that small bit of contact was almost too much in her current state.

"Have a nice life, Garrett," she managed as he turned away.

CHAPTER NINE

L<small>ILY WALKED OUT</small> of the hospital later that night, physically and emotionally drained but with a peaceful heart. Her father would be transferred to a rehab facility tomorrow and then be released to come home a few days after that.

She'd spent the past four hours at his bedside, visiting with her dad and her two sisters, who'd both head back to their own lives the following morning.

The homecoming should have been awkward or laced with the familiar tension of their fraught sibling bond, but all of the difficulties of the past seemed to fade away in the joy of their reunion. Even sharing the stories of dozens of failed auditions hadn't carried its usual weight. No one in her family was disappointed in her. On the contrary, they seemed happy to have her home.

That could be just the initial reaction, but it was enough for now. Helena and Meg had left an hour earlier with instructions for feeding Chloe her evening meal.

Alone in the room, Lily and her dad had watched sitcoms and eaten pudding cups, and a sense of contentment had covered her like a warm blanket.

As she crossed into the hospital parking lot, her fingers itched to pull out her phone and call Garrett. He was the person she most wanted to share this moment with. In their hours together, she'd confided so many of her hopes and fears about returning to Magnolia, and he'd made her feel like everything would turn out for the best.

Now it had. Everything except him driving away.

A familiar bark broke the silence of the evening, and she turned to see Chloe standing under one of the parking lot lights with Garrett Dawes holding on to her leash.

Lily's breath caught, and she remembered that morning in the diner when he'd explained the involuntary function of breathing to her.

"Are you kidnapping my dog?" she asked as she approached, heart pounding so hard she could almost feel it banging against her ribs.

"Just borrowing her," he clarified. "I met your sisters."

"Oh."

"You seem just as smart as they are, in my opinion."

Lily let out a small laugh as she reached out to love on her giant dog. Chloe whined and licked Lily's hand. "I'm not sure you know them well enough to judge."

"I know you," he said, the rough timbre of his voice sending shivers along her skin. "I'd like to know you more, Lily."

"I'm not exactly a long-distance relationship type of girl," she forced herself to say. As quickly as her feelings for Garrett had developed, living on different coasts wouldn't work given how wholly he'd captured her heart.

"Me neither." He made face. "Not the girl part," he clarified. "But the rest. I don't want distance between us. This sounds completely strange, but I think I fell in love with you somewhere between Amarillo and Memphis."

"Wow." Lily inclined her head as joy zipped through her. "It took you a whole two days? I was long gone for you by the time we hit the New Mexico border."

"Thank God," he breathed and reached for her, drawing her close and wrapping her in his arms like he never wanted to let her go. His mouth fused to hers in a kiss that set her soul on fire.

"I had no idea if I'd ever find a place to belong," he said when he finally pulled back. His dark eyes were intense on her, filled with so much promise and love. "But you're my home, Lily Wainright. My north star. I tried to drive away, but I didn't get any farther than the town water tower. I want to be with you. I want to make you happy and hold you when you're sad. I love you."

She grinned and blinked back the tears of happiness that clouded her vision. "I love you, too. And I better be the first person who gets to read the next great novel from Garrett Dawes. I will always be your biggest fan."

"Always," he promised and kissed her again.

In that moment, Lily knew she'd truly come home.

* * * * *

Scott's heart rate kicked up a tad as he tightened his hold on the cord. He leaped off the beam and swung down. As he soared through the air, his senses heightened and his vision tunneled on the threshold of the open barn doors. But instead of a clear path in front of him, a woman carrying a tray was walking past.

As she glanced his way and froze, shock came over her face and her mouth formed an "O."

Decisions synced in his mind. He dropped short of his mark on the shock-absorbing pad, executed a tighter roll than planned and sprang to his feet.

As he wrapped an arm around the flabbergasted woman's slender waist, she released a sound between a scream and a squeak. He braced his other hand under the tray with hers, catching it before it slipped to the ground.

Her eyes, a spectrum of hues from deep gold to sepia, met his. She breathed unsteadily and a glow tinged her smooth dark brown cheeks. "Are you out of your mind?" Taking hold of the tray, she slipped from his grasp. "What are you doing?"

He didn't mean to chuckle, but her exasperated expression looked more cute than threatening. Scott tipped his hat and gave his best charming fake Western drawl. "My job, ma'am."

"So you get paid to crash into people?"

"On occasion, but I just performed some of my greatest work."

She gave him a puzzled look. "What?"

"I saved two out of two. You and these." He glanced down to the sheet pan clutched in her hands. The lid was halfway off… and what looked to be two pies were smooshed against the side of it.

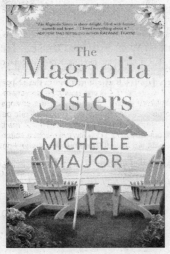

Get 4 FREE REWARDS!

We'll send you 2 FREE Books plus 2 FREE Mystery Gifts.

FREE
Value Over
$20

Both the **Romance** and **Suspense** collections feature compelling novels written by many of today's bestselling authors.